Stephen Booth is the internationally bestselling, CWA Dagger-winning author of eleven acclaimed thrillers featuring Cooper and Fry. The series is in development as a TV programme. Booth lives in Nottingham.

DEAD AND BURIED

STEPHEN BOOTH

sphere

SPHERE

First published in Great Britain in 2012 by Sphere

A CIP catalogue record for this book
is available from the British Library.

ISBN 978-184744-481-3

Papers used by Sphere are from well-managed forests
and other responsible sources.

 MIX
Paper from
responsible sources
FSC® C104740

Typeset in Meridien by Palimpsest Book Production Limited,
Falkirk, Stirlingshire
Printed and bound in Great Britain by Clays Lts, St Ives plc

Sphere
An imprint of
Little, Brown Book Group
100 Victoria Embankment
London EC4Y 0DY

An Hachette UK Company
www.hachette.co.uk

www.littlebrown.co.uk

To the most important people of all –
the readers

Acknowledgements

Thanks go to all the police officers, crime scene examiners, fire investigators and Peak Park rangers who have willingly talked to me about moorland fires and many other subjects. Special thanks to everyone at Chesterfield Police Station for their hospitality, and to (now retired) Chief Superintendent Roger Flint for giving so generously of his time, knowledge and experience. Always appreciated!

1

From a distance, it looked solid – a black wall lying across his path, dense and impenetrable. But as Aidan Merritt drew closer, he could look into its depths. He was able to watch it coil and seethe as the wind drove it across the heather. It was like a vast sooty snake crawling relentlessly over the moor. But he didn't need to watch it for long to realise it was an illusion. This thing didn't crawl. Its speed was frightening.

Further up the hill, Merritt saw more dark spirals, drifting low to the ground. Two, three or maybe more of them, disappearing over the moor. He could smell their acrid stink, feel their heat on his skin, taste the millions of burnt fragments choking the air as they passed.

Smoke. Acres and acres of smoke. The world was full of it.

A sudden awareness of danger made him pause. That smoke was poisonous, lethal. It could kill him if he let too much of it get into his lungs. And the blaze behind it would scorch his flesh in a second. Yet today this smoke might actually be his friend. That fire could save his life.

But still Merritt hesitated before he left the path. A strange foreboding froze his limbs. He felt as though he was about to step into a great inferno. He would be a solitary human figure walking out on to a fire-ravaged wasteland.

'My God, what am I doing?' he said aloud to himself. 'Who in his right mind would be out here?'

Within the space of twenty-four hours, this part of Derbyshire that he'd known so well had turned into a landscape resembling one of the nine circles of hell. Merritt imagined there ought to be a guide to take his arm and point out the glimpses of tormented souls writhing in the flames.

It was something he'd read in the sixth form at school. The guide was some Roman poet, surely. Virgil, was it? Yes, Dante's *Inferno* from *The Divine Comedy*. It wasn't taught any more. Not in his school, anyway. The kids he dealt with would think he'd gone mad if he even mentioned it. But years ago he'd used it himself in an essay on the use of allegory in European literature. The *Inferno* was all about the symbolism of poetic justice. Fortune-tellers walking with their heads on backwards, violent criminals trapped in a river of boiling blood. Each circle reserved for a specific sin, until the ninth circle centred on Satan himself.

Merritt recalled that the narrator of the *Inferno* had fallen into a deep place where the sun was silent, and found himself on the edge of hell. He'd never had any use for the knowledge until now. Yet it had stuck in some corner of his mind. And now he was thinking only of the ninth circle. The devil was in that detail.

Merritt looked up. He supposed the sun was still up there somewhere, hanging over the Peak District moors. But it was clogged and blackened with smoke, as silent as it would ever be.

He pulled out his phone, and saw that for once he had a signal. There were only a few places on Oxlow Moor where you were out of the dead spots. He dialled his wife's number, and got her recorded message, her voice sounding much too jaunty and cheerful.

'Sam, it's me,' he said.

Then he stopped, his mind suddenly empty. He couldn't think of anything meaningful to say. Instead, he told her about the ninth circle of hell, trying to explain what was in his thoughts. But he knew he was becoming incoherent, and he ended the call abruptly.

'That was stupid,' he said. 'Stupid.'

Merritt wiped the sweat from his forehead, took a deep breath and coughed at the dryness in his throat. Poetic justice? Yes – and that meant not just divine revenge, but a destiny chosen freely by a soul during life, and fulfilled in death. The inevitability was the most terrifying thing of all. It was what had struck him deeply as a seventeen-year-old, just starting to think about the future and what life might hold. The idea that he might already have chosen his own destiny weighed on his mind like a millstone. His place in the inferno was pretty much guaranteed. Well, that was the way it had seemed back then.

And now here was the physical manifestation of hell, almost exactly as Dante had described it. Those indistinct figures flailing in the smoke could only be the demons of his imagination – inhuman forms with the heads of beasts, their bodies glittering and suffused with bright artificial colours, their movements lumbering, their hands filled with strange instruments of torment. God, yes – they were there. All the creatures from his nightmares. He could see them in the smoke. See them, hear them, smell them. They were so close that he could practically touch them.

Yes, that was one other thing that Merritt remembered. According to Dante, the nine circles of hell weren't located in some mythical universe, detached from the real world. All that torture and suffering was taking place among us now. This minute, this second. Hell was right here on earth.

'Damn it, man – get a grip.'

3

He found that the sound of his own voice reassured him a little. There was a job to finish, and he didn't have much time. Focus. He must focus.

Merritt looked to his left. No, not that way. The angry red of flames flickered deep in the banks of smoke. The fire was burning at ground level, consuming the heather, surging across the miles of dry peat. With the wind behind it, a wildfire could advance faster than any human being could run. He mustn't get himself trapped where the flames could cut him off. That would be suicide.

To the right, then. That way he could just see a stretch of post-and-rail fence, a dry-stone wall. Beyond it, scrubby grass and patches of bare soil. A field. The wall marked the point where the moor ended and rough grazing began. That was the direction he wanted.

'Hey!'

A voice calling out of the smoke. Not a demon after all, but a human being, living and angry. One of the firefighters, he guessed. Small teams of them were scattered across the burning moor, thrashing at the flames with their beaters or spraying mists of water from backpacks. They'd been on duty fighting the moorland fire for hours already, and would be weary and irritable.

Merritt kept moving, trying to get up speed over the rough ground, regretting that he'd never tried to stay fit the way some of the others had. Now that he'd reached his mid-forties, it was really starting to tell on his body. His breath was soon rasping and his lungs began to burn.

'Hey, you there! Stop!'

Well, they were too far away to see him clearly, and he was sure they wouldn't bother trying to chase him. They had enough on their hands already.

Oh, but wait. There'd be a police presence somewhere, though. As he jogged over the heather, Merritt imagined a couple of bored coppers not too far away, given the job of closing the road and stopping traffic. He needed to be more careful. It was important not to draw attention to himself. No more than necessary, anyway. Let them think he was just some rambler who'd strayed too near the fire, and had turned back to leave the area the way he came.

Yes, this was the right direction. The line of the roof was visible now. He recognised those high chimneys, cowled against the moorland gales. He could picture them the way they once were, trickling smoke in the winter, with log fires roaring in the rooms below. The scent of woodsmoke was in his nostrils for a moment. He thought it was just another memory, until he realised his eyes were stinging and the back of his throat was sore with the acid taste of charred vegetation.

The smoke had caught up with him. It billowed around his legs and swirled into his face. It rapidly became thicker and thicker.

Frightened now, Merritt began to run, stumbling as the woody stems of heather and bracken caught at his feet. His boots felt heavy, and his corduroy trousers were sticky with insects and clinging burrs. The fabric of his shirt grew damp with sweat under the armpits of his jacket. He was wearing the wrong clothes for running. That was so typical. He was always doing the wrong thing. Always making the worst decisions. Always, always, always. Was there time to put it right? At least to put *something* right?

Startled, Detective Sergeant Ben Cooper hit the brakes of his Toyota. For a moment the wheels skidded on loose dirt before the car came to stop halfway on to the grass verge.

'What the devil . . .?'

Cooper winced as a muscle strain from a game of squash

earlier in the week sent spasms of pain through his lower back. Sitting alongside him in the passenger seat, Detective Constable Carol Villiers had been busy reading a file. She was thrown against her seat belt, scattering papers on the floor. They both stared ahead through the windscreen.

'Well, that looks bad,' she said.

Automatically, Cooper glanced in his rear-view mirror to check there was no traffic behind him. But the road was quiet at this time of day. That was lucky, because there was hardly enough room for two cars to pass, and those dry-stone walls on either side were pretty unyielding. That was normal for minor roads in this part of the Peak District, as the scrapes on his bodywork often testified.

Cooper shook his head. 'Another one. That's the fourth this month. The sixth so far this year.'

'And it's a big one, too.'

The sight of wildfires sweeping across the moors was always worrying. Once those fires got out of control, they threatened every type of wildlife, as well as the homes of people who lived in the national park. In serious incidents, human lives could be put at risk.

But for Cooper, there was an extra stab of personal distress. He knew these hills so well. He'd been born in this part of the Peaks, had grown up on a farm surrounded by moorland in every direction. Those vast expanses of rock and heather had been his playground. They still were, when he had time. The sense of peace, the closeness to nature, the sheer exhilaration of feeling the wind and breathing pure air – they were part of his own being. He could hardly bear to watch these fires destroying everything he loved.

His move away from Bridge End Farm to his flat in Edendale had partly broken that connection. The town had become his new home, and the police service his life. Yet it had also made the landscape more precious to him. Ben feared that one day he would no longer see the Peak District in the same way – not as he once had, with every bend in the road providing a glimpse of an enchanted land. In a few years, the countryside around him might seem like an endless series of crime scenes – some of them fresh in his memory, others still waiting to happen.

'I can't imagine the amount of devastation up there,' he said. 'It'll take years for the moors to recover.'

'It was the same last year,' said Villiers. 'Do you remember?'

'Which means that some areas haven't even had time to grow back properly. If it goes on like this every year, Carol, Derbyshire will never look the same again.'

Villiers had been brought up in this area too. In fact, they'd known each other at school. She was the only member of the CID team at Derbyshire Constabulary's E Division who came close to sharing his background. Her arrival after a spell of service with the RAF Police had been like a breath of fresh air. Cooper couldn't imagine speaking like this to anyone else – like, say, Diane Fry, who had been his boss when he was still a DC. Well, not without being sneered at as a country bumpkin, anyway.

A sudden gust of wind dispersed the smoke for a moment. Then it thickened again, scudding across the hillside in dark, roiling masses. Cooper and Villiers peered fruitlessly up the road, trying to make out any details beyond the barrier fifty yards ahead.

'It doesn't look as though this route is closed,' said Villiers.

'It should be. It's getting dangerous.'

'Maybe it's just deteriorated in the last few minutes.'

'Perhaps.'

Cooper coughed and pressed the button to raise the windows. The day was unseasonably warm for April, and the air conditioning in the Toyota wasn't brilliant. But one breath of that smoke rolling towards the car was enough to make him want to withdraw from the area as soon as possible.

'I'll turn round,' he said. 'Did you notice a gateway?'

'The nearest one is back round the bend there.'

'Okay. Let's just pray nothing comes round too fast.'

When he twisted round to look over his shoulder, Cooper felt another stab of pain. He hated twinges like that. Not for the discomfort itself, but because they made him feel that middle age might not be too far away. He was only in his thirties, for heaven's sake. But the job could take a disproportionate toll on your body sometimes. His wedding was coming up in a few months' time, and he ought to be fit for that. Liz certainly would, judging by the amount of dieting and exercising she was doing, the number of health and beauty treatments she was booking. At this rate, he'd look like the bride's elderly uncle instead of the groom.

Villiers got out to direct him back to the gateway. By the time Cooper had turned the Toyota round, a Traffic car was coming up the road towards them. The officer driving lowered his window when he recognised Cooper.

'Yes, it's bad,' he said. 'But the wind is shifting so much we can't keep track of which routes are being affected. I keep expecting to come across an RTC, but so far we've been lucky.'

Cooper could see the likelihood of a road accident in these conditions. It only needed one unsuspecting motorist to come round a corner too fast. It happened often enough anyway, without the additional hazard of reduced visibility.

'We'll leave you to it then,' he said. 'Good luck.'

'Oh, thanks.'

When he and Villiers got to the higher ground on the main road, Cooper had a clear view across the valley to the burning moorland. Only then did he realise that the ribbons of smoke they'd run into stretched for miles. Black clouds rose against the sky on the high plateau, swirling and breaking to reveal banks of flame scattered across the moor. Within a few yards of the fire the smoke dipped suddenly where it was caught by the wind. From there it slithered down the hillside, forming long trails like black fingers reaching towards the houses in the valley below.

'We're going to run into that smoke again in a minute,' said Villiers.

'You're right.'

'And it's even worse there, Ben. It's thicker and blacker.'

'We can't avoid it,' said Cooper. 'It's directly above the road.'

'Take it steady, then.'

'Of course. You know me. I always do.'

They began to descend the steep hill towards the town of Edendale. And a few moments later, the sun went out.

By the time his hands touched the wooden boards, Aidan Merritt was nearly blinded by the tears streaming from his eyes. He banged on the boards with his fists, fumbled along the edges of the wall where the door frame should have been, but found no crack to get a grip on.

Desperately, he felt further along the stone facade. There had been windows here at one time, but they too had been boarded over. He tugged at a corner of a board, but couldn't shift it. He realised the building itself had been blinded. No door, and no windows. It was an eyeless dinosaur abandoned in the burning landscape.

Finally he found a side door left open a crack, and slid inside. It was so good to be out of the smoke. But the interior was even darker – pitch black as a cave, thanks to the boarded-up windows. No doubt the electricity was off too. He could smell the mustiness that always invaded empty buildings, though the pub hadn't been closed for all that long. Decades of stale beer and cigarette smoke were coming into their own now, oozing from the corners and seeping out of the floorboards.

And there was something else too, lurking beneath the mustiness. A thick, rank smell that seemed to stick to the mucus in his nose and throat. On top of the smoke, it made him feel nauseous. He struggled to control the instinct to gag. It was a stink like the smell of fear.

'Hello!' he called. 'Anyone here?'

The sound of his own voice echoed back to him. He wasn't certain what part of the building he was in. He had never used this side door when the pub was open. He might be somewhere near the kitchens, he couldn't be sure. He would have to wait a few minutes for his eyesight to adjust to the darkness.

Merritt took a step forward, hands outstretched to feel for the presence of a wall or doorway. His boots crunched on broken glass. The noise sounded unnaturally loud, as if the glass had been left there deliberately as a warning of intruders.

'Hello? Hello?'

There was no answer. Or was there? Did he detect a faint rustle in the darkness, the sound of breathing that wasn't his own?

He turned quickly, overwhelmed by a sudden fear that there was someone behind him in the blackness. The broken glass squealed under his boots like a small creature crushed to death against the concrete.

'Is that : . .? Is . . .?'

But the blow on his skull came out of nowhere. Merritt cried out in pain, saw flashes of blinding light in the darkness, felt his legs begin to crumple. Then a second impact drove consciousness from his brain, and he hit the floor, stunned and bleeding, with fragments of glass pressing into his skin, his eyelids twitching as his nerve endings spasmed in agony.

As he lay face down in the dust, Aidan Merritt never felt the third blow – even though it was the one that killed him.

2

The E Division headquarters building in Edendale was starting to look a bit grubby these days – in some parts as grimy as if it had been in the middle of a fire itself. Outside, the woodwork hadn't been painted for a while, and the stone facing was becoming dark and mottled. Even the brackets for the lights near the security cameras looked as though they were being slowly eaten by acid rain.

As Cooper drove up West Street towards the police station, it seemed that only the rails to the disabled ramp stood out, bright yellow and gleaming in the sun.

But no, he was wrong. There was one other patch of yellow noticeable on the front of the building – the public phone used to contact officers at times when the station was closed. And the times it was closed were becoming increasingly frequent.

When they'd gone through the security barrier and parked among the marked vehicles and CID cars at the back of the building, Cooper locked the Toyota and stood for a moment looking up at the hills above the town.

Edendale sat in a kind of shallow bowl. In every direction you looked, you saw hills. Any road you took out of town went uphill. In the streets down by the river, the climate could be totally different from what was happening up there on the moors of the Dark Peak. A bit of drizzle falling on shoppers on Clappergate could have turned into a snow-storm by the time you reached the Snake Pass on your way to Glossop.

Today, though the sun was shining on Edendale, Cooper could see that the moors to the north and west of the town were black with smoke. It had been another dry spring, with little rain falling on Derbyshire for months. Despite heavy falls of snow in the winter, the high expanses of peat moor soon dried out. And it didn't even need to be warm – this spring certainly hadn't been. The plateaux were constantly scoured by wind, which evaporated the moisture and left the peat and banks of heather parched and vulnerable to the threat of wildfires. One January a fire had ignited at minus five degrees Celsius, burning dry winter vegetation above soil that was still frozen solid.

Summer could be a bad time too, when the sun was hot and more visitors crowded on to the moors. But at least there was new growth of foliage then. In the spring, there was only the old vegetation, woody and desiccated. Firefighters called it the fuel load. This spring, the moors were like a vast tinderbox, just waiting for a spark to create these catastrophic fires.

With so much flammable material, and ideal conditions, the fires could burn for days, or for weeks. To the north, near Sheffield, a moorland fire had been smouldering continuously since 1978, after it burned down through the peat into under-lying strata of coal. Once that happened, there was no way to put it out.

'I remember fires like these when I was growing up,' said Villiers, coming to stand at his shoulder. 'I thought the whole world was coming to an end. It was like Armageddon. I can't recall what year it was, but I was quite young.'

'The worst year was 1976,' said Cooper.

'What? I'm not that old.'

13

'Nineteen eighty, then. And 1995, 2003 – they were all bad years. All showed spikes in the number of moorland fires.'

For weeks now, national park rangers had been warning people not to light barbecues or camp fires, because of the higher than normal risk of fires. There had already been six moorland fires in the national park in the past two months.

Moorland fires could have a particularly devastating effect at this time of year, wiping out ground-nesting birds and even small mammals such as lambs, which couldn't escape the advance of the flames. Wildfires not only harmed wildlife but destroyed rare plants and caused erosion. They undid years of hard work in managing those rare environments.

In the past few weeks alone, fires had broken out at Stanton Moor, at Ramshaw Rocks near Warslow, and on Moscar Moor near Ladybower Reservoir. Much of the land was owned by the water companies like United Utilities. In a way, that was an advantage: the companies couldn't tolerate the resulting run-off into the water supply, so they were willing to cough up the money needed to hire helicopters at two thousand pounds an hour.

Over the Easter period in 2003, landowners had spent around sixty thousand pounds in five days on helicopters to help extinguish three simultaneous fires on Kinder and Bleaklow. There was no contribution to the cost from the state, and lobbying government to fund the use of helicopters had proved fruitless.

Ironically, one of the problems was developing sustainable water supplies out on the moors. The most difficult and severe fires were in remote, inaccessible locations. Water was usually some distance away – and the key to putting fires out was to get water on them. One of the biggest challenges was a logistical one. For years, the authorities had been talking about developing a network of ponds and

14

pipelines across the moors to increase the speed of delivering water to a fire site. It hadn't happened yet.

They walked towards the door of the station, and Villiers keyed in the security code. A prisoner transport vehicle had drawn up outside the custody suite, and a prisoner was being unloaded from the cage at the back.

Cooper had worked in this division for fifteen years, some of that time in section stations like Bakewell and Matlock, but most of it here at divisional headquarters in Edendale. He was becoming almost as well known as his father had been before him, that old-fashioned copper people in the town still talked about, both for the way he had spent his life and the way he'd died.

In the CID room, the atmosphere felt strained. Cooper detected it as soon as he walked through the door. He looked round the room. The two youngest DCs, Becky Hurst and Luke Irvine, were busy, their heads down, desks piled with paperwork, keyboards clattering, phones ringing intermittently. As usual, they were trying to deal with several things at once.

Meanwhile, the most experienced member of the team, DC Gavin Murfin, was amusing himself by filling in application forms for jobs he could never hope to get, and would never actually apply for. Today he was completing Form 518, the Specialist Post Application form for a Surveillance Operative at the East Midlands Counter Terrorism Intelligence Unit. He'd said yesterday that he liked the fact that the form was designated *Restricted when complete.*

Murfin looked up when he saw Cooper arrive. His pen was poised dramatically in mid-air.

'Ah, boss,' he called. 'Would you say I "create processes that make sure stakeholders' and customers' views and needs are clearly identified and responded to"?'

15

'No,' said Cooper.

'Would you agree that "this officer's performance in their current position is satisfactory"?'

'No.'

'Or that "the officer meets the person specification/promotion criteria"?'

'No.'

'Ben, I have to tell you – my line supervisor's comments are a very important part of the application process.'

'It's still no.'

Murfin sighed. 'Well, that's buggered this one, then.'

Keyboards had fallen silent, and the rustle of paperwork had stopped. Even the phones seemed to have taken a break. Cooper could feel the rest of the team watching him carefully.

'For heaven's sake,' he said. 'Give me that, Gavin.'

'It's restricted,' protested Murfin.

'Only when complete.'

'Well, all right.'

Cooper glanced over the form, feeling slightly uneasy about what Murfin might have been writing. When he was in this mood, anything could happen. And as Gavin had pointed out, Cooper was his line supervisor and therefore responsible for his activities.

He ran his finger down the first page, which asked for personal details. For the question 'Which of the following best describes your religious affiliation?', Murfin had crossed out all the options and written 'Jedi knight'. The next question was: 'How do you identify your sexual orientation?'

'I'll put "backwards" for that one,' said Cooper.

'But I'm not—'

'Yes you are. And now I'm going to file your application in the usual manner.'

Cooper ripped the form slowly in half, and dropped the

two pieces into the nearest waste-paper bin. As he did it, he could almost hear the tension in the room ease, like a quiet sigh of relief. Even Murfin smiled, as if it was just the result he'd been hoping for.

'Gavin, why are you even bothering with all that?' asked Villiers in the subsequent silence. 'You're due to retire next month anyway.'

'Well, exactly,' said Murfin. 'I wouldn't have dared do it before. Blimey, I would have got myself into so much trouble. But now I'm retiring, it doesn't matter, see. I can put what I like on the forms, and no one will take any notice.'

'Has this been some lifelong ambition, then?'

'It's been Jean's ambition. You know how I hate to disappoint her.'

'She's been disappointed in you all her life, Gavin.'

Murfin shook his head. 'No, that's not true. It's only since she married me. She was perfectly happy until then.'

Cooper bit his lip, trying not to laugh. Though Gavin seemed to be joking, it felt as though laughing would be the wrong thing to do right now.

Murfin was becoming such a contrast to Hurst and Irvine, who were still young in service. A couple of weeks ago, Cooper had overheard Irvine referring to his colleague as a 'flub', and had to caution him about his attitude. The ironic thing was that Irvine could only have picked up the expression from Gavin Murfin himself, since no one else used it these days.

In the last few months, Murfin had reverted to the language he'd learned on the job as a young PC thirty years ago, in less politically correct times.

'I seem to have mislaid my acronym book,' said Murfin. 'What's NIM?'

'The National Intelligence Model. You ought to know that

if you're applying for a job as . . . what is it? A Surveillance Operative with the Counter Terrorism Unit.'

'Right. I'm an ideal candidate as a SOCTU with a specialised knowledge of NIM and, er . . . give me another one.'

'BONGO,' said Irvine.

Murfin frowned, and ran his tongue round the inside of his teeth as if searching for a last crumb. Then he seemed to take the decision to ignore the jibe. The relaxed attitude of his shoulders seemed to say, 'All water off a duck's back, mate.' BONGO was the old-timer's slang for a lazy police officer. It stood for 'Books On, Never Goes Out'.

'Maybe we should get some work done,' said Villiers.

Carol Villiers had been back in Derbyshire for only a few months. She'd been lucky with a successful application when her period of service in the RAF Police came to an end. There certainly hadn't been many successful applications since then. Derbyshire Constabulary, like every other regional police force, had been finding ways of saving money for a couple of years now. That meant reducing staff numbers wherever possible. Specialist functions were being shared with neighbouring forces, and officers who left were rarely replaced. Retirement was more than encouraged; it was being made compulsory for those who had already served their thirty years.

'Did anything come of that last tip-off, Gavin?' asked Cooper.

'No, it was a LOB.'

'A load of . . .?'

'Yeah. That. There's been another theft, though. One more down for Postman Pat.'

'Where?' asked Cooper.

'Luke has the details.'

Murfin aside, one of the reasons for the tension was that Cooper's team had been working on an inquiry into the

18

theft of postboxes. All over Britain, the famous red Victorian boxes were being stolen by criminals who sold them for thousands of pounds on internet auction sites. In rural areas, they were ripped from lamp posts and telegraph poles, or chiselled out of walls. In some cases, entire pillar boxes had been uprooted from the ground, with vehicles used to drag them from their foundations. Many antique boxes were being sold as souvenirs to collectors abroad, especially in the USA. It wasn't an opportunist thing people did on the way home from the pub. You needed heavy cutting equipment to take some of those boxes away.

Postbox prices had risen since the Royal Mail stopped auctioning off old stock nearly ten years ago. It was said that boxes dating back to Queen Victoria's reign and bearing the VR mark could fetch up to five thousand pounds in America. George V boxes were worth around a thousand quid, while even the more modern ones could go for hundreds.

Originally the theory had been that thieves wanted the scrap metal, but any legitimate scrapyard wasn't going to want those postboxes – they were far too distinctive. One of the difficulties, though, was distinguishing them from genuinely sourced items and Chinese replicas.

So it was the boxes themselves that appeared to be the target, rather than the mail they contained. The number of thefts had been accelerating, with around thirteen boxes removed in the last two months alone. In one incident in a village near Edendale, thieves had posed as workmen to be inconspicuous, and waited until the mail had been collected.

It forced Cooper to picture a gang of thieves lurking behind a wall with a JCB until the postman had left. But more bizarre things than that happened in the Peak District every week.

Irvine waved across the room, while taking a phone call at the same time.

'I'll bring you up to date in a minute,' he said.

'Okay. Other than that, anything happening?'

'There's been a cow rampage,' said Murfin. 'But uniforms are dealing with that.'

'Could you try to communicate a bit more clearly, Gavin?' said Cooper.

Murfin eyed him cautiously.

'Oh yeah. Walker with a dog, chased by cows when he tried to cross their field. Walker escaped with a scare, but dog got badly knocked about by cows. It happens every year.'

'With relentless regularity.'

And so it did. People thought it was only bulls that were dangerous, but cows were more likely to attack you, especially if you had a dog, and particularly in the spring. It was the animal they were going for, of course. They associated dogs with the loss of their calves.

Some things came round every year, as regularly as Christmas. Other types of crime, like the postbox thefts, were steadily increasing – and therefore figuring more prominently in Cooper's preoccupations. The number of farms being targeted had gone up by sixty per cent in the last twelve months, as his brother Matt would readily testify from his recent experiences at Bridge End.

Poaching was a good example, too. It wasn't unexpected, when jobs were being lost and everyone was feeling the effects of the downturn and financial cutbacks.

At least there had been no riots and outbreaks of looting in Edendale. That was a phenomenon that was generally confined to the cities and larger towns. Derbyshire Constabulary had sent officers to help out in London at the height of the troubles the previous summer.

'Oh yes,' said Murfin. 'And the control room took a call

from one of the fire crews up on the moors. The white-hat guy, you know.'

'The incident commander.'

'Yeah. Well he's called in to report a break-in at an old pub. His firefighters passed it on their way to the fires. They saw a white pickup driving away, and they say some boards have been pulled off one of the doors at the back.'

'He must mean the Light House. It's been empty for months, ever since the last owners went bust.'

'Oh, I know that place,' said Murfin. 'And you're right – it was all boarded up last time I went past. Would they have left anything inside worth nicking?'

'Maybe.'

'I think it's due to come up for auction in a few weeks' time,' said Hurst. 'They must be hoping someone will take it on as a going concern.'

'Rather them than me,' put in Irvine. 'Only a fool would pay out good money to start running a pub these days. Especially when the last owners couldn't make a go of it. It's madness.'

'There might be equipment inside,' said Cooper. 'Scrap metal is still going up in value.'

'I bet there's no beer, anyway. Some of the lads went up there to help drink it dry on the day it closed.'

'So what action have we taken?'

'None yet.'

'Inform the owners, and suggest they make the place secure.'

'If we can find out who the owners are exactly. Right now, it might be the bank.'

'I don't suppose they'll be in much of a hurry. I can't imagine anything will be done today anyway.'

From the first-floor windows of the CID room, there was an even clearer view of the drifting smoke.

'Has anyone been reported in connection with the fires?' asked Cooper, knowing that he was being unduly optimistic.

'No. We've only had vague sightings of quad bikes coming down from the moors. You know what it's like, Ben.'

'Only too well.'

Cooper thought of all the fires there had been over the years. He'd seen in a report that 345 moorland fires had been recorded in the national park since that disastrous year in 1976, affecting sixteen square miles of moor. In the Dark Peak, more than two square miles of peat still lay bare, having never recovered from the devastation.

And all of those fires had been caused by people – there were no recorded natural fires in the Peak District. The damage had often been caused by carelessness, with people dropping cigarettes or building camp fires, or as a result of controlled burns by landowners that got out of hand. But many of these fires were undoubtedly deliberate. They were the result of arson.

The sight of the moors being destroyed day by day was breaking his heart. The loss of habitats, the blackened wreckage of the hills, they tore at his heart in a way that he couldn't fully explain. Those hills had always been his home, and he'd never wanted to live anywhere else. He recalled the lines of a song by the folk singer Ewan MacColl, written about the Peak District after the celebrated Kinder Trespass back in 1932.

> *Sooner than part from the mountains,*
> *I think I would rather be dead.*

Watching the fires from a distance was making him feel helpless, and the necessity of being in the office was even more irksome than usual. He had to admit that he was itchy and restless, bothered by the nagging sensation that his past was being obliterated, even as his future was being planned out, fixed down and tied up in a neat bow with a bit of wedding ribbon.

'They've asked for a police investigation, though,' said Murfin. 'The cost of the damage is rising astronomically. There's a request in for attendance by scenes of crime, too.'

Cooper nodded.

'You know what?' he said. 'I think I'll go myself.'

3

St Luke's Hospice had been built in a quiet location just behind Edendale General Hospital. Patio doors from the ground-floor rooms opened on to the hospice gardens, where patients could look out at a fish pond and mature trees alive with birds and squirrels.

The room occupied by Maurice Wharton had an electrically operated positional bed, air conditioning, a flat-screen TV and en suite toilet facilities. Wharton would have felt he was staying in a nice three-star hotel, if it wasn't for the fact that he was dying.

During his stay in the hospice, he had received the constant attentions of the palliative care nurse, the health care support workers and the occupational therapist. At intervals he was given aromatherapy massage with essential plant oils. He was becoming familiar with their powerful scents, which clung to his body. Camomile, lavender, rosemary, eucalyptus. So very different from what he'd been used to all his life – beer and cigarette smoke, the smells of cooking. He was starting to believe that death would smell of lavender.

It was two weeks since he'd moved from palliative care on a day basis, and taken up permanent occupation in St Luke's. It was progress of a kind, he supposed – another step on the road towards his inevitable destination. And 'permanent' was a word that didn't mean quite what it used to do.

Terminal care. They said the aim was to make the last few months of life relatively peaceful and pain-free. Some patients escaped the pain, he'd been told. But intractable pain was experienced in more than seventy per cent of cases with inoperable pancreatic cancer. Ninety-five per cent of patients died within five years. He'd lived most of his life being considered out of the ordinary. Now, in his last few weeks, he'd become part of the majority.

The pain in his abdomen, the loss of appetite, the yellowing in his skin and eyes, the fatigue and nausea, the insomnia. Why was the list so long? Doctors had initially related his symptoms to depression. So the pancreatic cancer had already been well advanced when the diagnosis was confirmed by CT scans of his abdomen, and surgery had become impossible. The only available treatment by then had been chemotherapy, a drug called Gemcitabine. It was ironic that the side effects of the drug were nausea and vomiting, skin rashes – and the fluid retention that swelled his body again.

Maurice Wharton had never really believed in God, or heaven. But occasionally he had a chat with the hospice chaplain, while he waited for his personal visitors at three o'clock in the afternoon. Should he be afraid of hell? Was there some endless ordeal waiting for him when this tempo-rary suffering was over? If so, the chaplain had never mentioned it. Eternal torment only came to him in his dreams.

Wharton wondered whether he should stop trying to keep up with the news from the outside world. But sometimes, when his family visited, he couldn't avoid it. There were things they wanted to talk about. There were the moorland fires, which had been burning for weeks and were now destroying Oxlow Moor. There was the campaign against the building of a new Tesco store in town. Nancy and the children knew how irrelevant those topics were to him, yet it was important to talk about them, as if everything was normal.

But nothing was normal now. His four-hourly doses of oral morphine were vital to get him through the day, though they made him prone to vomiting, constipation and dry mouth. The cancer had also affected his liver. The doctors told him that worsening renal function altered the metabolisation of the morphine and caused toxicity. The explanation meant nothing to him. But he knew what the results were. Agitation, confusion, hallucinations, involuntary jerking of his limbs and vivid dreams.

Yes, those vivid dreams. Sometimes he couldn't sleep at all. At other times he was afraid to sleep, because his dreams woke him in a panic, sweating in the face of unnameable fears.

Were those nightmares caused by morphine toxicity, or by something else entirely?

The road from Edendale climbed steeply over the edge of Abney Moor and passed through the Hazlebadge parish. From here, the Light House was already visible. Cooper glimpsed it now and then from the highest points of the road as a distinctive feature on the horizon.

The pub had always seemed to draw his eye, as if it was trying to lure him, to tempt him to call in for a visit. It was a famous landmark in this part of the Peak District. Famous when it was open, at least. The Light House had shut its doors six month ago.

Well, it was just one of thousands of rural pubs that had closed during the last few years. But this one was such a shame. The pub stood on the highest point of Oxlow Moor and was known as a landmark for miles around. The roof line and the shape of the chimneys were recognisable from a great distance, unmistakably the Light House. When it was open, the illuminated facade of the pub had been visible at night in all directions, from the B6061 above Winnats Pass to the main road running south-west out of Edendale towards Peak Forest.

The Light House might still be visible now, once the smoke of the wildfires had cleared. But it was no longer the landmark Cooper had known. The roof line was still there, and the shape of the chimneys. But the pub itself was a blank, windowless and dead.

Finding the place was the difficulty, though. Its presence on the skyline gave no clue how you were supposed to reach it. And within minutes it had vanished again as the road descended past the abandoned open-cast mine workings at Shuttle Rake and Moss Rake.

From one short stretch of road, he could see part of the vast quarry that served the Castleton cement works. Its walls were blasted into deep ledges like an enormous Roman amphitheatre glowing white in the sunlight. A stack of white silage bags formed a startling feature of the landscape, an unexpected contrast to the usual black silage stores. Many of the road signs directed quarry lorries towards the best routes to reach the sites that were still operating. Without them, large vehicles would constantly be attempting to negotiate the narrowest of lanes, getting stuck and bringing traffic to a complete halt.

Cooper turned on to a short stretch of Batham Gate, the old Roman road, where he glimpsed a herd of piebald horses grazing in the field. Then he turned again towards Bradwell Moor, where the Light House soon came back into view.

The dark expanses of Oxlow Moor stretched away west and south, increasing the pub's impression of isolation. Since the only approach was up the hill from the east, you used to be able to step out of the pub and feel as though you were in the middle of nowhere. Well, you *were* in the middle of nowhere. There was almost nothing in sight to remind you of civilisation, except the occasional farmstead nestled into the landscape on the more distant hills.

To the north he could see Rushup Edge and Mam Tor, with the plateau of Kinder Scout a ghostly grey presence behind them. Away to the east, he was looking across the Hope Valley to Winhill Pike, the distinctive conical tor on Win Hill. To the south-west, the view was over Jewelknoll Plantation to Ox Low, and a glimpse of farmland near Peak Forest. He knew Edendale was somewhere to the south-east, beyond Bradwell Moor, but the town was lost from view now.

He stopped for a moment, wound down the window and looked up the hill at the pub. A large auctioneer's sign had been fixed high on the wall. *Historic landmark inn for sale by public auction.*

Below his position, a track snaked away towards the remains of some disused lead mines, crossing the Limestone Way about a mile down. There were walkers on the trail now. He could hear the clang of gates being closed as they passed from one part of route to the next, sprung stainless-steel latches crashing into place. The sound was perfectly clear, though the trail was a long way below him.

All around the edges of the moor were irregular clusters of bumps and hollow – the traces of those long-abandoned mine workings, their mounds of spoil thrown up like giant ant heaps. At another time, sheep would have been dozing on those mounds, using the extra height for vantage points, or places of safety. Beneath a tumble of stones in the bottom of each hollow would be the entrance to a disused mine shaft. Not so safe at all.

Many of the shafts had been filled in completely over the years. But some of them hadn't. These workings were centuries old, and a few had been lost and forgotten – lost, that was, until someone stumbled on a loose stone and broke a leg, or slipped through a corroded capping plate and disappeared into the ground for ever.

Cooper put the Toyota back into gear and drove on over the moor, heading inexorably towards the clouds of black smoke on the skyline.

On Oxlow Moor, some of the firefighters were dousing smouldering hotspots with water from backpacks like garden sprayers. Others were stamping and kicking out the smaller fires, or flailing them with beaters.

Cooper found the incident commander by his white helmet and white tabard. He turned out to be the watch manager from Edendale fire station. This was a major incident, so somewhere there would be a Level Two commander in overall charge.

'How dense is the smoke up there?' asked Cooper.

'How dense? You can't see your hand in front of your face,' said the fire chief, pushing back the visor of his helmet.

'What's the current Fire Severity Index?'

'The FSI has been at five for the past two days. It can't get any higher.'

Several square miles of moorland were burning now, with dense smoke trailing across the sky. At least barriers were out at strategic points along the adjacent roads to stop traffic. Some areas where earlier fires had started had been dampened down after a huge operation, but the ground was still smouldering.

Cooper could see a silver-grey ranger's Land Rover Defender towing a water bowser on to the moor, and one of the national park's eight-wheel-drive Argo Centaurs operating alongside the fire service's Unimog all-terrain tender.

Derbyshire Fire and Rescue Service were only part of the operation when it came to a moorland fire like this one. National park rangers, National Trust wardens, water companies and other major landowners all became involved. They'd come together to form the Fire Operations Group more than fifteen years ago, after a serious moorland blaze. They drew up joint plans, shared specialist equipment and worked side by side to tackle major fires.

The fire chief shook his head at the scene on the moor. 'I'd be a lot happier if you could get hold of the people who caused these fires.'

'They aren't accidental?'

He laughed. 'Accidental? I'm not convinced you could even *do* this accidentally. It isn't so easy to start a moorland fire just by dropping a match or something. When you drop a spent match or a cigarette end, it's almost always on a path anyway. Bare earth or rock. Nothing that burns easily. These fires began way out in the middle of the dry heather, where they had the best chance of catching. If we'd found the remains of any Chinese lanterns, I might accept it as accidental.'

'Chinese lanterns? Really?'

'Absolutely. There's been a complete craze for them recently. It's mad. I mean, what is a Chinese lantern? You're basically lighting a candle inside a paper bag and letting it drift off wherever the wind takes it. People send off whole swarms of them at once. Then they land on someone's crop, or on a baking-dry moor like this, and the result is no surprise to anyone. Certainly not to me. And yet they call that an accident. Well, not in my book – it's sheer recklessness with someone else's property. They're talking about banning the things in some places, and it's none too soon in my opinion. It's already the case in other countries, even in China.'

Cooper remembered his brother complaining about Chinese lanterns too. Of course, Matt complained about a lot of things. But the National Farmers' Union had said the lanterns were not only a fire hazard, but could also wreck farm machinery, or be chopped up and get into animal feed, with potentially fatal results for livestock.

'But no signs of Chinese lanterns in this case? No one been holding a party and letting them off?'

'Not so far as we can see,' said the fireman. 'There'd be wire frames left, even after they'd burned up.'

'Arson, then?'

The watch manager shrugged. 'Without a confession, there's no way anyone can actually prove the fires were started deliberately.'

'But that's your gut instinct?'

'Yes. But my gut instinct isn't proof of anything.'

'Fair enough.'

'Our own fire investigator is on his way, but we've narrowed down the location where we think the fire started. Or was started. Whichever. We believe there are traces of accelerant use.'

'Petrol? Lighter fluid?'

'Something of that nature. The burn pattern is distinctive. A higher rate of combustion, a greater degree of heat. In that one patch, the fire has just left ashes.'

'Can we have a look?'

'Sure. Just take care.'

As they walked, the fireman pointed up the slope, where the heather and bracken had been burnt off completely, leaving a blackened stretch of ground devoid of vegetation of any kind.

'Next thing, we're going to have the archaeologists poking about up here,' he said.

'Why?'

'Remains of some old stone buildings are showing through where the fire has caused most damage to the ground cover.'

'Really?'

Cooper took a few steps up the slope to see more closely. Bare peat was visible in many places, and he could just see a line of muddy masonry protruding from the eroded surface. From this angle, it did look like the remains of a wall, or the foundations of a vanished structure.

'How old?' he asked.

'No idea, Sergeant. But I'm sure there'll be no shortage of people wanting to come out here and tell us. It could just be some old shepherd's hut. On the other hand . . .'

'Yes, it could be anything. There's supposed to be an abandoned medieval village around here somewhere. There are always Roman sites turning up. We're only a stone's throw from Batham Gate, the old Roman road. There could have been a small fort here, for all we know. It's an ideal position. Look at the vantage point they would have had.'

The fireman shrugged. 'I wouldn't know. I just hope we don't start getting the blame for any damage that's been done to it.'

Cooper knew that Oxlow Moor had a lot of history. Some of it, though, was more recent, and less harmless than a few passing Roman legionaries.

He turned and looked across the moor. The Light House wasn't visible from here, because of the shape of the land. It must be over a mile away from his position.

'I passed the old pub on the way here,' he said. 'There was a report of a break-in.'

'That's right. We used the place as a rendezvous point earlier, but the fires have been moving this way pretty fast, as you can see. The prevailing wind is moving to the east.'

There was no mistaking the path of the fire. A huge tract of charred heather and bracken had been left in its wake as the flames advanced across a wide front. It looked as though an invading army had passed through, leaving nothing but scorched earth behind them.

'Well I can check the pub on my way back,' said Cooper. 'I pass fairly close to it.'

There was a disturbance among the firefighters and rangers further up the hill. Someone called down and waved a hand in an urgent gesture.

'What's going on now?' asked Cooper.

'Oh Lord. It looks like they've found something else.'

'More archaeological remains?'

'Chief,' shouted one of the firemen, 'you might want to take a look at this.'

Out of curiosity, Cooper followed the watch manager up the hill through the remains of the burnt heather to where the firefighters had gathered. And within minutes he'd forgotten all about the break-in at the Light House.

A couple of hours later, the scene of the find on Oxlow Moor had been taped off, but only by driving plastic stakes into the burned peat around it. The taping seemed a bit unnecessary in view of the nature of the surroundings, but at least procedure was being followed. E Division's crime-scene manager Wayne Abbott was present, which indicated the seriousness with which someone had responded to the finds. Cooper had been joined by Carol Villiers, dispatched from West Street on his call.

'What have we got, then?' he asked.

Abbott had been crouching in his white scene suit, but

33

stood up and greeted Cooper. The knees of the paper suit were stained with brown from the churned-up peat.

'The main item is a small rucksack,' he said. 'Nylon manufacture mostly, so it's survived being buried. I couldn't say how long it's been here, but a few years certainly.'

'You're saying "buried". It wasn't just dropped and lost?'

'No way. It was dug into the peat and covered over. It was only a few inches down, but a layer of peat and then the heather or whatever growing on top of it would have concealed it pretty well. In fact, by the shape of it and the position it was lying in, I'd say it had been deliberately flattened, possibly by somebody jumping up and down on it.'

'They were hoping it wouldn't be found, then?'

'Not for a long while. In fact they might have been hoping it would rot down eventually, but, like I say, it's nylon.'

'Non-biodegradable.'

'Yes.' Abbott lifted off a fragment of charred bracken that had fallen into the hole. 'If we're really lucky, we might get a partial footwear impression,' he said. 'That looks like a boot print to me, near the shoulder strap there. Out here, the soles of anyone's boots would be covered in muddy peat, just like ours. You couldn't stamp on a clean surface like this without leaving a mark.'

'Could the rucksack have been damaged in some way?'

'What do you mean?'

'Is there a hole torn in the bottom? Are the shoulder straps intact? I'm thinking that someone might have decided it was too badly damaged to be useful any more, and they couldn't be bothered taking it home with them, or even carrying it off the moor to dispose of.'

Abbott narrowed his eyes as he looked into the hole. 'I understand what you're getting at. It looks perfectly sound to me, but we won't know for certain until we get it back and examine it properly.'

Cooper straightened up. 'There's more than the rucksack, though. It isn't just some hiker who decided to dump a bit of old kit in the heather.'

'No, certainly not. There are other items coming to light. We have a couple of anoraks – quite expensive garments from the labels, and stains on them that could be blood at first glance. We'll need to confirm that. There's a mobile phone. Dead as a dodo, of course. And look at this.'

He was holding a partially decomposed lump in an evidence bag. On closer inspection, it turned out to be a leather wallet, probably also quite an expensive one when it was bought.

'The peat has preserved this pretty well,' said Abbott. 'I can even make out a name on one of the credit cards.'

'What? There are still credit cards in there?'

'Yes. And some cash too, by the looks of it.'

'We assumed the stuff must have been thrown away by some thief when they'd emptied out the valuables.'

Abbott was silent for a moment. He gave Cooper a meaningful glance. 'No, that's not the situation we have here. It's something quite different.'

Cooper caught his breath. He knew only too well what Abbott meant. This discovery had been coming for the past two years. It had been inevitable ever since an incident one snowy night in December.

'What's the name on the card?' he asked finally.

'You could guess, I think. The name is David James Pearson.'

A light dawned on Villiers' face too, then. It wasn't just E Division who remembered the case. Carol had been serving in the RAF Police at the time. She might even have been stationed overseas – it wouldn't have made any difference. Cooper could see that the name rang a bell. The story had been in the news continuously for months.

35

'And did you say there was blood on the clothing?' he asked.

'We think so. I'm about to do a presumptive test, but my instincts are bristling like an angry hedgehog.'

An instinct wasn't proof of anything, as Cooper had been reminded a few minutes ago. But this was different. In this instance, he trusted Abbott's instinct. Because his own gut was telling him exactly the same thing.

'You know what this means, Ben?' asked Abbott.

'Yes,' said Cooper, with a deep sigh. 'It means the Major Crime Unit.'

4

Detective Sergeant Diane Fry was in the outside lane of the M1 motorway when she got the call. Her black Audi was travelling at just over seventy miles an hour, passing a convoy of French lorries occupying the inside lanes. Her CD player was blasting out one of her favourite albums, *Songs of Mass Destruction*. She loved Annie Lennox's voice, always full of soul, even when rocking on 'Ghosts in My Machine'.

Her fingers tapped on the steering wheel in a rare moment of relaxation. Her car was almost her only personal space, the last refuge where she could escape from the tension that ruled the rest of her life.

Fry turned the CD off to take the call. While she listened to the message, she looked ahead, saw the overhead gantry signs for Junction 26, the Nottingham exit. She was pretty sure there was a link on to the A610, which would take her back into Derbyshire.

'Yes, give me an hour or so.'

'Understood.'

She indicated to move into the inside lane and slowed for the exit. At the same time she began to reset the route on her sat nav.

'Can you send me an outline of the original inquiry?' she asked.

There was a pause. 'We'll ask the locals to give you a copy.'

'That'll do.'

She hit the roundabout and found herself stuck behind a car transporter as she filtered left towards the A610 for Ripley and Ilkeston.

'Well, maybe a bit more than an hour,' she muttered.

Fry had been with the East Midlands Special Operations Unit – Major Crime for six months now, part of the Derbyshire contingent allocated to the new unit when the county's own Major Crime Unit was wound up.

The joint initiative was headed up by the former divisional commander from D Division in Derby. He was the man who'd expanded the city's burglary and robbery squads and introduced Operation Diamond to deal with serious sexual and violent assaults. He was also behind Operation Redshank, set up to target gun and gang crime after a spate of shootings in Derby that had culminated in the death of fifteen-year-old Kadeem Blackwood in 2008.

Just as importantly from Fry's point of view, this chief superintendent had joined Derbyshire from the West Midlands, just as she had herself.

It was funny to think now how frustrated she'd felt at being co-opted into discussions about inter-force cooperation last year. At the time it had seemed to have no relevance to her own career. She'd felt as though she was just waiting for an opportunity to move back to Birmingham, something that was beginning to look less and likely among all the cuts and restructuring.

But then the regional Major Crime Unit had become a reality, as all five forces in the East Midlands disbanded their own units in an effort to save cash. Its remit was to investigate all murders and other major crimes in the region, including kidnappings.

Though murders were still few in number, they caused massive disruption to local forces, especially in the first week of an inquiry. The regional unit meant that officers from Derbyshire had to support their colleagues in neighbouring areas, even those as far away as Lincolnshire or Northamptonshire. She now had the chance to operate in towns and cities well away from the rural wastelands of the Peak District.

The Northern Command of EMSOU – MC was based in the city of Nottingham, barely more than a forty-mile drive from Edendale, yet it might as well be a world away.

Fry called her office back.

'This turn-out. Who's on the ground at the moment?'

'Local CID officers. I don't know exactly who. Do you want me to get a name to make contact with?'

'No, it won't make any difference,' said Fry. 'I'll find out soon enough when I arrive.'

Local CID. Oh well. At one time not too long ago, that could have meant her. But she knew it was always important to have local officers on scene, especially in the first days of a murder. Her new boss was very keen on the benefits of local knowledge. She'd read a newspaper interview in which he'd talked about his earlier career. He'd said that during one murder investigation he'd been approached at a crime scene by two burglars whose sentences he'd applied to have extended, but who wanted to give him information about the suspect. They'd done that just because they knew him. Personal contact created a strange kind of bond. It earned trust, even from someone you'd helped to put away for a spell.

Fry knew there were plenty of officers in the northern part of Derbyshire who had that kind of local knowledge and experience, particularly the personal contacts that might prove invaluable.

She was on the dual carriageway now, passing the old brewing town of Kimberley and the IKEA retail park.

'Control?' she said. 'Is Oxlow Moor located in B or E Division?'

'E, I think.'

'Okay, thank you.'

Fry sighed. Well, it would only be temporary. In the subsequent weeks of an inquiry, when more detailed forensic investigations were taking place, it wasn't so vital to have local officers involved. Everyone was trained to the same standard and used identical systems, so it wasn't necessary. A central capability resulted in a more sensible use of available resources.

Of course, it was disloyal of her to think like this, in a way. She remained employed by Derbyshire Constabulary, though she had a new base away from the area she lived in. Her chief had said publicly that, despite his change of role, he would not be leaving Derby, which had been his family home for years.

But that was where she parted company with him. She didn't feel quite the same about Edendale.

'One last thing . . .' she said.

'Yes, Sergeant?'

'Have you got a postcode for this place I'm going to?' she said. 'My sat nav doesn't seem to recognise it.'

While he waited on Oxlow Moor, Cooper walked a few yards away from the smoke still drifting off the hill, and found himself looking down at the long drop into the valley.

Below him the road was crossed by the Limestone Way, one of Derbyshire's most popular trails, which ended a few miles to the north in Castleton. Its name was pretty accurate. From Mayfield, in the south of the county, the route passed through the rugged greyish-white limestone landscape of the White Peak.

For centuries this had been the heart of England's lead-mining industry, a rich ore field that had been mined continuously since Roman times. From the pigs of lead found with the official stamp and the abbreviation 'Lut', it was believed that Lutudarum, the Roman centre of lead mining, had been located somewhere in this area. Some sections of the Limestone Way used miners' tracks, and even older pathways, a few of them dating back to the Bronze Age, when they'd linked prehistoric henges, hill forts and burial sites.

The Romans had built their own roads across this area, of course. And even in the Peaks they were straight as an arrow, irrespective of the hills. The route he'd crossed, known as Batham Gate, ran from the town of Buxton to the Roman fort of Navio, near Brough. Much of it was no longer used, but a Roman road could always be recognised on the map – their artificial straightness was such a contrast to the winding lanes that had grown up organically over hundreds of years of human activity, following the natural inclination to take the least demanding route.

The present Batham Gate was an oddity, though. Long stretches of it twisted and turned in a very un-Roman fashion, diverting to avoid the quarries and fluorspar workings that had sprung up alongside it. Curiously, the modern electricity pylons seemed to follow the route of the old Roman road, marching dead straight across the countryside in a way the road itself no longer did.

'Parts of this area are quite dangerous,' said the fire chief. 'And I don't mean because of the fires.'

'Dangerous?'

'The old mines. You have to be careful where you walk if you stray off the path.'

41

'You're right, of course.'

Because of its history, the area was riddled with old mine workings, capped-off shafts and thousands of small grassy hillocks covered in wild flowers, most of them spoil heaps, which formed the only visible legacy of the lead-mining glory days of the eighteenth century. And then there were the limestone and fluorspar quarries – great white gashes blasted from the hillsides, many of them now abandoned in their turn, grown over or gradually filling up with water.

With one hand Cooper swiped his mouth, realising that he could still taste smoke in his saliva when he swallowed. Unless the rain came in the next few days, this whole landscape could soon be reduced to ashes.

Cooper recognised the black Audi has as soon as it turned on to the track approaching Oxlow Moor. There was something about the tinted strip across the windscreen blocking out the sun, and the way the car was driven, slowly and skittishly, as if it was only used to travelling on dual carriageways and expected those stone walls to move in from either side and crush it.

Diane Fry looked thinner than ever, which hardly seemed possible. But he'd noticed something strange about her over the years. She'd always looked much more fragile outdoors, when she was out of her natural environment. Inside, in the office, she was quite a different person. She seemed to grow and become stronger. Her fair hair was longer than it used to be, which did at least soften her features.

'Is there mud?' called Fry when she got out of her car at the bottom of the track.

'Not here.'

Fry walked across the verge, but halted the moment she

stepped off on to the moor in the direction of the crime-scene tent.

'Damn. I thought you said there wasn't any mud?'

'It isn't mud, Sergeant. It's burned heather and ashes. It's wet because the fire service have just finished extinguishing a fire.'

'In my book that makes it mud,' said Fry.

She covered her mouth with her hand against the wisps of smoke still rising here and there from among the burnt heather.

'We'll have to get a supply of masks if we're going to be out here any length of time,' she said.

Cooper nodded. 'I'll organise it.'

So far she hadn't greeted him, let alone acknowledged that she'd known him for years, had served with him, been his immediate supervisor before his promotion to detective sergeant. More than that, they'd been through a lot together, and no one could argue that they owed each other something. At least that was how Cooper felt.

He was used to this taciturn way, of course. Most of his own family were like that. But in their case they didn't need to speak because they understood each other's thoughts without words. It was a silence born of ease and familiarity. With Fry, there was no question of either. He felt neither easy nor familiar in her presence. If she didn't speak, he had no idea what she was thinking.

A few minutes later they stood together at the partially excavated site. Fry looked down at what Abbott had uncovered.

'David Pearson,' she said.

'Yes.'

'Any indication of, er . . .?'

'Trisha. Yes, evidence of her too.'

'There's quite a story to the Pearson inquiry,' said Fry.

43

'It's all in the file,' said Cooper. 'Not our greatest success.'

'It was more than two years ago. But there were theories . . .'

Abbott shook his head. 'I've done a presumptive test for blood on the rucksack. It's positive.'

'Could it be animal blood? If there's one thing I've learned from my time in the Peak District, it's that these sheep are suicidal. They all have a death wish.'

'They might be suicidal,' said Cooper, 'but they don't dig shallow graves for themselves. When they die, they generally just lie about on the surface until the scavengers get to them.'

'Grave?' said Fry.

'Well, it seems to be where the possessions of David and Trisha Pearson were buried. Whether the Pearsons are also dead and buried . . . I guess that's what you're here to find out.'

'No bodies, then.'

'No,' said Cooper. 'No bodies. Not yet.'

Fry turned and pointed.

'The building I passed a mile or two back,' she said. 'A pub, is it?'

'It was.'

The auctioneer's sign on the wall of the Light House was legible from half a mile away, and visible from much further. *Historic landmark inn*. Cooper wondered how many more questions he would have to give obvious answers to.

'It's been empty for about six months,' he said.

'Looks a grim place.'

'It wasn't so grim when it was open.'

'I'll take your word for it.'

'You don't remember it, do you?'

Fry frowned. On her face a frown looked more like a

scowl, as if being forced to remember something made her really angry.

'Have I been there?' she said.

'Yes, with me,' said Cooper.

'No, I don't recall the occasion, then.'

'Never mind.'

Cooper remembered it, though. He recalled sitting in the conservatory after driving up here from Fry's flat in Edendale one summer evening, when it stayed light long enough for them to enjoy the spectacular views for an hour or two. It had been busy at the Light House that night, but they'd managed to get a table in the conservatory, just as the first drops of rain began to fall on the glass roof. He remembered being surprised when he offered to buy the drinks and Fry asked for a vodka. When he thought back, he could still recall the clatter of those raindrops on the roof, sounding much too loud in the awkward pauses in their conversation. The memory was so firmly lodged in his brain that the sound of rain had become a sort of musical accompaniment to the history of their relationship.

And Fry said she didn't remember it. Well, he wasn't surprised. She was capable of erasing him from her life as easily as she might wipe away a splash of rain.

It was amazing to think now that he'd once considered . . . well, it was probably best not think about it at all. He was marrying Liz Petty in a few months' time. That was what he was put on this earth for. Diane Fry had just been an irritant, sent to make him appreciate better things. He ought to be thankful that she'd existed. If only he could bring himself to be thankful that she had gone.

Fry seemed to be gazing at something, but not the nearby scene. She was staring into the distance, where the smoke was still billowing towards them across the moor. The wind must have changed again.

'We might have to move,' said Cooper.

'Possibly.'

But then he realised that she was gazing in the direction of the Light House, even though it wasn't visible from here. He wondered what it was that fascinated her. Had she perhaps dredged up a fragment of memory? But if he knew Diane Fry, she would have pushed any memories she didn't want right to the back of her mind, where they would never be found.

'Why did it close?' she said.

'The pub? Lots of reasons.'

Cooper knew there were several factors contributing to the closures of rural pubs. The traditional lunchtime trade had been dying on its feet. The crackdown on drinking and driving, the ban on smoking in public places, the availability of cheap alcohol in supermarkets – they'd all played their part in the slow erosion of pub business. For many licensees, the increase in VAT to twenty per cent had been the last straw, a sudden hike in their quarterly bills too much to cope with at the wrong time.

In addition, the Light House had always been one of the places worst affected by spells of bad weather in the winter. Prolonged periods of snow meant no one could reach the pub for weeks. Over Christmas and New Year, that was a disaster. The holiday period was the one time of the year when a pub could expect to make a profit. Cancelled bookings and an empty bar turned a bad situation into a catastrophe beyond recovery.

He started to tell Fry this, but soon ground to a halt. Not for the first time, he had the distinct impression that she wasn't listening to him, that she was just letting him talk as a form of noise to fill the void, the way you might play familiar music on a long car journey. It allowed your thoughts to be elsewhere.

'Is there . . . anything I can do, Diane?' he said instead.

She looked at him then, as if he'd just appeared at her side.

'No. You've done well.'

'Oh, thanks.'

Cooper turned aside, hoping to get more sense out of Wayne Abbott. At least he wouldn't be so patronising.

'Who was that?' said Fry suddenly.

Cooper stopped and turned back in surprise. 'Where?'

'Didn't you see them? Running across the moor.'

'Towards the fire?'

'Into the smoke, anyway. It was only a second, then I lost sight of him again.'

'Him?'

'Well . . . I can't be sure. It was so quick it could have been anybody, I suppose.'

Cooper had automatically taken a step towards the hill, but she grabbed his arm and held him back.

'There's no point, Ben. Let's warn the firefighters to keep an eye out for them.'

He stopped, accepting her decision without question, and surprised at himself for it. He looked at her hand on his arm, wondered why he was so struck by her use of his first name. It sounded odd after all these months.

Fry dropped her hand.

'You're getting married soon,' she said.

'Yes.'

Small talk now? Surely not.

'Good.'

Gavin Murfin appeared, trudging up the track in his green anorak with an armful of files. He wheezed, dropped the files on the ground and threw a mock salute.

'Messenger boy reporting, ma'am. They said you wanted these.'

47

'Thanks,' said Fry. 'But I don't know why they sent you. Any uniform would have done. A PCSO could have managed the job.'

Murfin smiled cheerfully. 'In view of my vast experience as a detective, they thought I might be of some use to you.'

'I doubt it.' Fry picked up the files and began to turn away.

'So how's life at the East Midlands Special Operations Unit?'

'Interesting,' said Fry sharply.

'Have you got an acronym for yourselves yet? EMSOU – MC doesn't have much of a ring to it, does it?'

Fry turned to him with a sour expression on her face. At one stage in their relationship, a look like that from her would have quelled Murfin without a word being spoken. It didn't seem to have any effect now.

'Don't you have work to do?' she said. 'I heard you had an urgent inquiry involving stolen postboxes to deal with. Or has that proved beyond your capabilities?'

Murfin chewed thoughtfully.

'You know they're giving me a medal, don't you?' he asked.

'They ought to give you a brain scan,' said Fry over her shoulder.

'Why?'

'Well, someone needs to carry out a proper examination of your pathological behaviour.'

'Hold on,' called Murfin as she walked away. 'Are you calling me a pathologist?'

Fry gritted her teeth, told herself to hang on. Her own DCI would be here in the morning to take charge as senior investigating officer. Until then, it was a question of holding

48

the fort. Grin and bear it. Except she didn't feel much like grinning.

It would actually be a whole lot better if she could just get rid of some of these people cluttering up the scene. Almost all of them, in fact.

She looked at the firefighting operation still continuing on the moor, the road closure below. There was only one road in, and one road out. That was good. The crime scene was protected, and the evidence collected. Nothing was going anywhere until morning. She knew DCI Mackenzie would back her up.

Alistair Mackenzie was also on a transfer from Derbyshire's D Division. He was the reason she'd landed the job with EMSOU – MC. She'd worked with him on a case last year – a case she probably shouldn't mention to Ben Cooper. Well, not unless he started to annoy her, anyway. It had involved Cooper's brother, and they were all lucky that the outcome hadn't been much worse.

She looked at the people around her at the scene. Dusk was starting to fall. That was good, too.

'Okay, I think we can call it a day,' she said. 'We'll pick it up again tomorrow morning. Full daylight, a complete team, a proper scene examination.'

'All right.'

She could see Cooper was reluctant, but he didn't argue. In fact he didn't say anything as the others began to drift slowly away. Perversely, Fry felt the need to provoke some kind of response from him, even if it was a negative one.

'Can I leave you to organise a scene guard for tonight?' she said.

Cooper met her eye calmly. 'Yes, of course. Whatever you want.'

And for some reason, when Fry gazed at him, the thought that came into her head was: *And that was your first mistake.*

5

An hour or so later, Ben Cooper was standing uncomfortably in the middle of a room. He was used to entering people's homes, studying their furniture and bookshelves, getting an idea of the way they lived from an observation of small details. But this was different. He was being asked to examine things he wasn't really interested in, and which seemed to have no significance. The size of the windows, the height of the ceilings, the decorative stonework on the exposed lintels. It was making him feel uneasy – especially when he was aware that he was being closely observed himself.

'And look at this. We installed this ourselves.'

He found he'd been ushered into a bathroom. There was something very odd about four people crowding into a bathroom all at once, the whole lot of them gazing at a free-standing claw-footed bath with whirlpool effect, as if it was the prime exhibit at a crime scene.

The thought sent Cooper's imagination spinning out of control. He began to picture a dead body lying in that bath, a head sprawled against the taps, blood pooling around a claw foot on the laminate flooring as it dripped from a slashed wrist. The wrist would be his if he didn't escape soon. This house was making him feel suicidal.

'Lovely, isn't it?'

'Oh . . . yes.'

Actually, it wasn't this house, but all the other houses that had come before it. Number fifteen Meadow Drive was just the latest in a long series of properties he'd looked at this week, not to mention all the others last week and the week before. If he'd been asked, he would have suggested there were far too many homes for sale in the Edendale area right now. If it was a difficult time for the housing market, then surely some of these vendors should be holding off putting their properties on the market for a while. That would make the list shorter, at least.

Not that anybody was likely to ask him, of course. But he'd obediently turned up for the viewing appointment. He'd even taken the opportunity presented to him by Diane Fry to escape from the scene on Oxlow Moor. Normally he'd never have done that. Deep down, Cooper felt as though he'd abandoned a job half done. He hoped Liz appreciated the compromises he made for her.

'Perhaps you'd like to talk about it.'

That was the estate agent. She was one of a long line of anonymous salespeople with a folder full of glossy brochures and a mouthful of misleading terminology. He'd learned that 'easy to manage' meant 'not enough room to swing a cat' and 'full of period features' meant 'needs knocking down and completely rebuilding'.

Cooper nodded, and stepped outside. As soon as they were out of earshot, Liz leaned closer.

'What do you think, Ben? I love it.'

'We can't afford it.'

'But look at the size of the kitchen, and those fireplaces. Look at the garden, and the view. We won't find anything better than this.'

'But we can't afford it.'

The estate agent looked round the edge of the door with a bright, artificial smile.

'How are you getting on?' she asked.

Liz smiled at her. 'We need to talk about it a bit more.'

But as they walked back through Edendale town centre towards his flat in Welbeck Street, the one thing they didn't do was talk about it.

Liz was good at this. She could detect his mood with great accuracy, and know exactly how to respond to it. She instinctively saw that it wasn't the right time to discuss the subject most on her mind. He supposed this was how couples were when they knew each other very well. It had been a new experience for him over the last year or two, one which he would gladly get used to.

Instead, they chatted away about inconsequential things – the weather, their families, the gossip in the office, and of course the wedding arrangements. Well, perhaps not all so inconsequential.

'This new evidence in the Pearson case,' said Liz. 'I suppose DS Fry is hoping to make it into a murder inquiry.'

'Why?'

'Well, it helps to justify her existence, doesn't it? There's no point in having a Major Crime Unit without major crime.'

'You're so cynical sometimes,' said Cooper.

'Come on, Ben. We all have to justify our existence these days.'

He had to admit that was true. They were all looking over their shoulders, wondering whether their job would be the next to be declared surplus to requirements in this time of austerity. When police stations were being closed and the most experienced officers forced into retirement, the concept of front-line policing was becoming less and less clear. No role or department was really safe from the cuts. There was no such thing as job security, not any more. If you couldn't make a good case for the importance of your role, then you shouldn't expect anybody else to be doing it on your behalf during all those meetings going on at headquarters in Ripley. Even for Liz, there was no immunity from cuts in her job as a civilian crime scene examiner.

They passed the little baker's shop in Clappergate, which during the day had wicker baskets standing outside on the pavement and an ancient delivery boy's bicycle strung with onions. A few doors down, the New Age shop was still there, though it wasn't so new any more. Its rich smells of aromatherapy oils and scented candles and the glint of crystals in its window were strangely redolent of the 1970s.

On the corner of Hulley Road, near the market square, they stopped automatically in front of one of the estate agents and gazed at its darkened display of properties.

Most of their searching for a home was done online, just like everyone else. Liz had set up email alerts on all the main property sites. Rightmove, Primelocation, Findaproperty. Her search parameters were way out, in Cooper's opinion. She'd set the maximum price too high, the minimum number of bedrooms too many, the requirements for a garden and double garage too ambitious. But it meant that suggestions were flooding in, without any effort on their part. Everything was found on the internet now. And yet there was something irresistible about an estate agent's window when you were house-hunting.

Properties in the more desirable parts of old Edendale were well out of their league. The picturesque lanes of Catch Wind and Pysenny Banks, where the River Eden ran past front gardens filled with lobelias and lichen-covered mill-stones. Those were just a dream. The properties they were looking at were smaller, newer, less full of period features. But still too expensive.

'Why would anyone visit an estate agent's at night?' said Liz. 'Who would do that?'

'We would,' said Cooper.

She squeezed his arm. 'So we would. We must be mad.'

'I don't think so. It's nice to dream sometimes.'

'That's one of the things I like about you.'

In fact they'd looked at this estate agent's window before, in daylight. It was very upmarket, handled high-end properties for equestrian interests and buyers with plenty of spare cash. If he looked, he knew he would see plenty of nice properties displayed on those boards. Old farmhouses full of character, with stable blocks and pony paddocks. But he wasn't looking too closely, and he never would. The prices made his eyes water. They rose to seven figures and just kept on going.

'We ought to have a list of estate agents,' said Liz. 'There might be some we've missed.'

'Oh, of course. Why not?'

There was a list for everything. So many choices to be made before the day. Which photographer, what sort of music, whether to have a video made. If it wasn't on a list, it didn't exist.

Liz squeezed his arm.

'Everything's going to be perfect,' she said.

'Of course it is. Perfect.'

And he so wanted it to be perfect. For himself, he would be happy just to be married to Liz, no matter whether the ceremony was in the local register office or Westminster Abbey. To be married and planning the rest of their lives – that would be enough.

But he knew how important the wedding was for her. The bride's big day and all that. And he aimed to make it absolutely perfect.

She was a little tired now, he could tell by her voice. It

was such a warm voice, soft and caressing. He loved to hear that familiar sound, the intimate touch on his arm.

Cooper remembered standing right here once before, and catching their reflections in the glass of the estate agent's window. It didn't surprise him any more how well matched they looked. Being with Liz felt comfortable, as if it was what he'd always been destined for.

'What are you looking at, Ben?' she said.

'Oh, nothing.'

'Not that very, very expensive house, then?'

'Er, no.'

'Shame. I thought you might be having the same dream that I do when I see a property like that.'

Liz always looked small at his side, her dark hair shining in the street lights, her face lit up with a simple, uncomplicated pleasure. It delighted him that she could respond this way whenever they spent time together. Who wouldn't love to have that effect on someone?

'Kiss?' she said, as if remembering the same moment that he was reliving.

He kissed her. And it was only then that he remembered it was her way of making him agree to anything.

Later, after he'd parted from Liz, Cooper entered his ground-floor flat at number eight Welbeck Street, just by the river near Edendale town centre.

He was only a tenant here, but it had been home for some time now. The flat carried its own significance in his life. It marked his break away from the family, the first place he'd lived in apart from Bridge End Farm, where he'd grown up. The day he moved into Welbeck Street had been the first real step towards independence. It was only after he left the farm that he realised quite how stifling the constant proximity of your family could be. He loved them all, of course. But it was such a relief not to have them around all the time.

But the flat would have to go soon. His landlady, Mrs Shelley, who lived next door at number six, was aware of his approaching marriage and the fact that he and Liz were house-hunting. She'd expressed her regrets about losing him, twisting her ancient cashmere sweater about her shoulders with hands that were becoming increasingly arthritic. The old lady found a lot of advantages in having him living right next door. She'd considered him available to call on in an emergency, even if it was nothing more urgent than changing a light bulb she couldn't reach herself. And she appreciated the reassurance, she said. Young Ben was in the police, after all.

But when it came right down to it, he didn't think she was sorry that he'd be giving her notice soon. She was ageing now, and becoming quite frail. The pain of the arthritis was etched more deeply into her face day by day. Cooper could see in her eyes when she talked to him that giving up the responsibility of having tenants would be a relief. In the first-floor flat there was a student called Matilda, from Lund in Sweden, gaining experience with a local placement before she completed her training. She would be gone at the end of the year, too.

And he had no doubt that number eight Welbeck Street would be put up for sale then, another property added to the housing market. This one would sell quickly, though. It was a small stone-built semi, and would make an ideal first home for a young family. The conversion into two flats hadn't been perfect, and the stud walls were a bit shoddy, if the truth were told. But it had always felt comfortable to Cooper. Cosy, even. It would never suit Liz.

He took off his jacket and walked through the flat into

the decrepit conservatory at the back, overlooking the garden. And there was another problem.

The cat came running towards him, tail up, purr like a motorbike engine. Cooper bent to stroke the tabby fur and look into the bright green eyes.

'And I really don't know what's going to happen to you,' he said quietly.

When everyone had finally left the scene on Oxlow Moor, Diane Fry reversed her Audi down the track, turned and drove back over the moor towards the deserted pub.

She'd measured the distance at about a mile and a half from the scene on Oxlow Moor. Not an easy walking distance. But Fry was sure she'd seen it. A figure, running through the smoke. Impossible to tell whether it was male or female.

The building was dark and silent, in a way no pub should ever be. Fry walked round the outside in the gathering dusk, examining the windows. Even the first floor had been boarded up. High above her, just a single dormer window set into the roof had been left uncovered. A determined vandal had managed to reach it with a stone, and the glass had shattered outwards from a small hole, as if it had been hit by a gunshot.

She did a complete circuit, and ended up standing outside the back door, which had clearly been forced open.

Fry pulled her jacket closer around her shoulders as she stepped through the broken door frame. She took two paces into the darkened pub, and stopped, all her senses twitching. Something was wrong, and it was right here. Her instincts had drawn her to it unerringly.

Slowly, she backed up. She fetched her Maglite from the Audi, and went back into the pub. The electricity supply was turned off, of course, and she had no hope of finding the consumer unit to switch it back on.

Bit by bit she swept the light around the room she'd entered. Not a room exactly, but a passage that seemed to widen out to her left into a storage area where empty cardboard boxes had been stacked.

The light of her torch showed that the dust on the floor had been disturbed close to the doorway. Not just footprints, but distinct signs of a disturbance. Two sets of feet at least, she guessed. Two or three people involved in a recent scuffle.

And what was that? Dark spatters on the floor, a spray of droplets spreading towards her, stopping just short of her feet. She smelled a familiar metallic tang. Not overwhelming, but definitely fresh. The odour was so distinctive that she felt the hairs stirring on the nape of her neck.

Fry took a step back towards the door, made another sweep of the interior, focused her beam on a darker patch in the shadows across the other side of the room. A huddle of clothes and awkwardly sprawled limbs.

She sucked in a sharp breath, all her suspicions confirmed.

'My God,' she said. 'How did anyone miss this?'

6

Cooper had a message waiting for him next morning. He had to see Detective Superintendent Hazel Branagh, the head of E Division's CID. That never boded well. But it was even worse when he had no idea what he was being summoned about.

Before he went up to the management floor, he took a couple of minutes to bring himself up to date on what had been happening overnight. His heart sank when he read about the discovery at the Light House. The incident report read like his worst nightmare. Especially when it began: *Call received from DS Fry of East Midlands Major Crime Unit . . .*

Damn, he said to himself when he'd digested the details. Better get it over with then.

The top floor at West Street was marginally more comfortable. A bit of carpet here and there, a recent paint job on the office doors. There was less of an air of desperation: no piles of evidence lying around waiting to be processed, no signs of the public intruding, let alone sweating suspects and drunks detained for a night in the cells.

Superintendent Branagh's office was near the end of the corridor, where the quietness was itself intimidating. He knocked and was called straight in.

Whenever he looked at Branagh, Cooper couldn't help

remembering Gavin Murfin's comment when he'd first set eyes on her: *She'd look good in the front row of a scrum.* It was the shoulders that did it.

'Ah, DS Cooper,' she said.

He knew it was serious then, just by the tone of her voice, the underlying hint of disapproval or disappointment. The super had always liked him, or so he thought. But things could change.

'So. How did we miss a body in the pub?' asked Branagh.

'It was just bad luck.'

'Worse luck that Detective Sergeant Fry made the discovery instead. One up for the Major Crime Unit. It makes us look incapable.'

'I know,' said Cooper. 'Believe me, I know.'

He could have wished it was anyone else except Diane Fry. Even Gavin Murfin would have been acceptable, stumbling across the body while looking for a cup of tea. Murfin would have gloated, but it might have been bearable.

He knew Diane Fry. He anticipated that she would say nothing about it. But she would definitely look smug. Boy, would she look smug.

Branagh spread her hands on her desk, and looked at Cooper thoughtfully. They were strong hands, probably the strongest he'd ever seen on a woman. They inspired confidence in him, a feeling that he could rely on her leadership.

'The death of the man found in the abandoned pub should be our first priority,' she said. 'It's a fresh case, and we're still in the first twenty-four hours. We're far more likely to get a result.'

'We haven't even identified him yet, ma'am.'

'Well, get on to it.'

'There's a briefing in half an hour,' said Cooper. 'DCI Mackenzie from the EMSOU.'

'I know him,' said Branagh. 'Alistair Mackenzie will do a good job. But . . .'

'Yes, ma'am?'

'If you do have problems, talk to your DI, who will keep me in the loop. EMSOU need our help at the moment. We won't let ourselves be pushed around by them.'

'I understand.'

'It would be nice,' said Branagh, 'if we could tie up the Pearson inquiry as well as the new case. David and Trisha Pearson are names that have been haunting this division for years. And not only E Division. The subject comes up regularly at meetings of the Senior Command Team. It's never been forgotten. We hear about it often from the family.'

Cooper nodded. 'I'll make sure I get up to speed on the Pearson situation before the briefing starts.'

'That's an excellent idea.'

'I wasn't on duty myself at the time it happened,' he said. 'But I think I know someone who was.'

It was more than two years since David and Trisha Pearson had gone missing. Two visitors from Dorking in Surrey, they had been known to no one in the area until they disappeared. Now everyone had heard their names.

The Pearsons had vanished one night in December, when a snowstorm closed in suddenly as they walked back to their rented cottage. Their winter break in the Peak District had ended that night. They had been in their thirties, fit and active. But they had never been seen since.

It had been just before Christmas, too. Cooper knew what that would have been like. All over Derbyshire people would be winding down for a long break at home with their families, snatching up those last-minute presents, gathering for seasonal parties with their friends or office colleagues, going out and getting drunk on any old excuse. Well, who needed an excuse? It was nearly Christmas, after all.

That was how it had been for most people. But not for those who were obliged to work over the holiday period. There were always a few who drew the short straw. And they tended to let you know how they felt about it.

'Yes, I was duty DC,' said Gavin Murfin, when Cooper sat him down in a chair in the CID room. 'Funny how I always seem to pull the Christmas rota. Anyone would think there was a conspiracy to land all the worst jobs on the local sucker. I must have a big neon sign on my head or something. *Dump your unwanted shit here.*'

Cooper signalled to the rest of the team, and they gathered round Murfin like a family listening to their ageing grandfather tell a favourite story. Becky Hurst sat upright with her arms folded and a sceptical expression on her face. Luke Irvine slouched casually in a swivel chair, eyes moving constantly from his computer screen to Murfin and back. Carol Villiers leaned against the wall, the light from the window behind her. Cooper perched on a desk and studied Murfin as closely as if he'd been a suspect in an interview room.

'Did you go up to Oxlow Moor, Gavin?' he asked.

'Well, not at first. I was called out to the cottage where the Pearsons were staying. They were reported missing by the farmer's wife, who'd gone to see if they needed anything after the snow stopped. That was quite late the next day, you understand.'

'The day after they disappeared?'

'Right.' Murfin shivered at the memory. 'It was damn cold up there. Snow on the ground, a wind that cut right through you like a knife. You should have heard me moaning about being dragged out of a nice warm office on a false alarm. We were having a bit of fun here, those of

62

us who were in over Christmas. There were mince pies and everything.'

'But it wasn't a false alarm, was it, Gavin? Did the incident escalate quickly?'

'I wouldn't say it was quick. People are reported missing all the time – everyone knows that. And they were adults, after all. It wasn't as if they were kids who'd run away from home. But given the weather conditions . . . well, there was a bit of concern about their welfare, like.'

Cooper could understand why Murfin sounded defensive. Decisions could seem mistaken with the benefit of hindsight. But no one wanted to call it wrong in the early stages and end up looking like a fool.

Murfin gazed round the circle of faces. 'Well, the owners of the property had keys, so there was no problem getting inside the cottage. But we could already see the Pearsons hadn't slept there the night before. In fact, no one had been there since before the snow started. There was a drift up against the door, and no footprints in the snow outside, except the owner's. The cottage was cold, too.'

'The Pearsons' car was still there, wasn't it?'

'Yes. A Range Rover, as I recall. Smart motor. It was covered over in snow, so it hadn't been driven for a good twenty-four hours.'

'That must have set alarm bells ringing.'

'Right. People die of exposure in those conditions. But we had no idea at first where they might have been, what they'd been doing – what they were wearing, even. They might have gone to stay with friends, been picked up by a taxi. We just didn't know. No one was keen to start making big decisions that would tie up a massive amount of resources over Christmas.'

'What was the deciding factor in the end?'

'We got hold of a mobile number. Either from the

property owner or the agency who handled their holiday lettings. It must have been on their booking details, I think. That was David Pearson's phone. We kept trying it and trying it, but there was no answer. It was dead.'

'That must have been the phone we found in the peat.'

'I guess so. Well, we started to get properly worried then. The incident went up the chain of command. And suddenly I was just an extra body in a crowd. And I've got to tell you, no one liked being called out at Christmas time. But they all did their bit.'

Murfin looked up suddenly. Cooper sensed a presence at his shoulder and turned, just as a new voice broke in. A voice he recognised instantly. Diane Fry.

'And meanwhile,' she said, 'they were all hoping they could knock off work and get home, or to the pub, as soon as possible. Because no one wanted to start making big decisions, did they? God forbid. Especially not you, I suppose.'

One thing Cooper had never got accustomed to was the way Fry could appear unexpectedly. She was able to move almost silently when she wanted to. Most disturbing was the fact that you didn't know how long she'd been standing there, listening.

Murfin's face changed as he looked at her. 'Wouldn't *you* want to get home? Oh, but you don't have a family, I forgot. Nothing for you to go home for.'

Fry's lips tightened, but Cooper stepped in before she could respond.

'This sort of thing doesn't help. Diane, you're welcome to sit in, but we need to listen. Go on, Gavin.'

Murfin waited to see if Fry took a chair. But instead she paced restlessly between the desks, her thin shoulders hunched like a prowling cat.

'Well, it was a while before we managed to trace their movements. The Pearsons hadn't told anyone where they were going, and of course the people at the pub where they'd been for dinner earlier that evening had no idea the couple were missing. It was a double whammy, if you like. That's what caused the delay. Well, mostly.'

'It could have been what caused their deaths, too,' said Fry.

She had remained standing in the middle of the room. Of course, she no longer had a desk in this department, but Cooper felt sure she did it deliberately, to make everyone else feel uncomfortable.

'*If* they died,' replied Murfin stubbornly.

Fry raised her eyebrow. 'You're on the "deliberate disappearance" side of the argument then, are you?'

'Yes, they legged it, without a doubt,' said Murfin. 'It's obvious. They were about to get pulled by the fraud squad in Surrey, so they did a bunk with the cash. I reckon David Pearson planned the best time to make a break for it, when they were away from home anyway. And they set up that delay for themselves so they had time to put some distance in before anyone noticed they were gone. They played us all for idiots, as if they knew exactly what we do.'

'And . . . what? David Pearson deliberately left his wallet and phone behind?'

'Of course he did. It makes no difference.' Murfin leaned forward, directing his comments at Fry. 'It's what I would do myself, if I was going to change my identity. I wouldn't carry proof of who I really was. The Pearsons wouldn't care if their stuff was found, not once they'd got clear. In fact, you know what? I reckon they've been laughing at us all this time for not finding those things sooner.'

When the impromptu meeting broke up in preparation for the full briefing, Cooper took Fry to one side.

'Gavin could be right, you know,' he said.

'When did that ever happen?'

'He has experience,' said Cooper. 'More experience than you or me. Doesn't that count for anything, Diane?'

'The actions taken in the initial stages of the inquiry were flawed,' said Fry impatiently. 'And the first mistake was sending DC Gavin Murfin.'

Exasperated, Cooper watched her go, walking down the corridor to greet her DCI from the Major Crime Unit. He shook his head in despair. He seemed to have spent a huge part of his life watching Diane Fry walk away.

'But hey,' he called. 'Diane – what about the victim you found at the Light House?'

Fry paused just for a moment, barely breaking her stride.

'Oh,' she said. 'Don't you worry about that, DS Cooper. The investigation is in good hands this time.'

Cooper nodded, reluctantly forced to accept her answer, and even the tone it had been delivered in.

But it was true what he'd said. There were very few murder cases that dragged on for months, let alone years. Usually the story was an obvious one. A body turned up, and a suspect presented himself on a plate. Charges were brought and the crime went down in the files as detected.

So there was a powerful temptation to use the logic in reverse. If a case like the Pearson inquiry had gone on for years, with no sign of a body, the chances were high that it wasn't a murder. Experience alone suggested that conclusion, and statistics backed it up.

So Gavin Murfin was far from alone in the opinion he'd formed. He might just be the only one prepared to voice it so openly right now.

DCI Alistair Mackenzie had arrived to take charge as senior investigating officer. He was a big man, over six feet tall and wide across the shoulders. A bit top-heavy perhaps, carrying too much weight above the belt to be fast on his feet. He had a shrewd stare, and a habit of tilting his head on one side when he looked at you.

Fry had begun to get used to him. She liked to know who she was dealing with, particularly if they could be influential in her career. She'd weighed him up when they'd worked together briefly after he was drafted into E Division for the Bridge End Farm inquiry. She didn't think he'd be difficult to handle, even though he'd once accused her of being a farm girl. That impression she could dispel pretty quickly.

'Everything all right, Diane?' asked Mackenzie.

'Yes, sir. Fine.'

'It's a bit strange to be back among your old colleagues so soon, I suppose?'

'It's not a problem.'

'That's what I like to hear.'

Fry knew he liked to hear that. She'd heard him say it before. The DCI wanted to think his officers could cope with anything. Finding yourself back among your former colleagues, the ones you'd tried so hard to escape from, was definitely nothing to worry about. It was no problem. No problem at all.

In a back street in the north of Edendale, a white Mitsubishi L200 pickup was parked at the kerb outside a semi-detached council house. People on the street passed it without comment – barely noticing it, in fact, seeing just another workmen's vehicle. Repairs were being carried out on some of the homes on the Devonshire Estate. Vans, pickups and builder's skips had been a common sight in the street for months.

The paintwork of the Mitsubishi was spattered with tarry black specks, as if it had been parked under a sycamore tree. But that wasn't unusual either. The clouds of smoke drifting over the moors had been depositing sooty debris far and wide, ever since the first moorland fire had started in the Peak District six weeks ago.

So when two men appeared from one of the houses, no one took any notice of them. After they'd driven away, not a single passer-by in the street could have said what the men looked like. No one could have had a guess at the make or registration number of the pickup. A few wouldn't even have been sure that it was white.

But that was always the way with memories. There was almost nothing you could rely on as being completely accurate.

7

When Cooper entered the conference room, he found that his immediate boss, Detective Inspector Paul Hitchens, had been drafted in for the briefing to represent E Division. Hitchens had the unenviable task of summing up the efforts made in the original Pearson inquiry, and the sparseness of the ultimate results.

As he listened with the other officers in the room, Cooper became aware for the first time of the complications of the inquiry. He'd been a DC on the division then, but too lowly in the hierarchy to grasp the overall picture. He recalled taking witness statements that had provided nothing of any value to the investigation, talking for hours to people who had no useful information to give. He'd been sent back to ask more and more questions, until he felt he was scraping the barrel and not producing a thing for his efforts.

So much was known about David and Trisha Pearson after all those months of careful investigation. Yet so little of it had proved to be of any use in finding them.

David Pearson, aged thirty-six, a senior adviser with Diamond Hybrid Securities, based in London. His wife Patricia Pearson, known as Trisha, aged thirty-three and working in public relations. A couple with no children, but a nice home in the Deepdene Wood area of Dorking, Surrey. They had spent a summer holiday in the Seychelles that year, but had chosen to take their Christmas break in the Peak District.

On the night they disappeared, the Pearsons had been to the George in Castleton for dinner. Mushrooms in peppercorn sauce, Bantry Bay mussels, honey-glazed ham shank. At least they'd eaten well on their last night, not to mention the two bottles of wine they'd drunk.

At the end of the meal they had set off to walk back to their holiday cottage on Brecks Farm, near the village of Peak Forest, a distance of about three miles from the George. And that was the last anyone saw or heard of them. Not a phone call, not a single confirmed sighting, not a shred of paper trail to follow.

Hitchens tried to summarise the main facts of the case as best he could. The DI had been putting on weight recently, and there were traces of grey in his hair. His manner suggested this was one inquiry that had contributed to his premature ageing.

'The Pearsons stayed late over their meal at the George, finishing the extra bottle of wine,' he said. 'They stayed much too late. By the time they left the restaurant, the snow had started. They were foolish to attempt to walk back to the cottage across the moor in those conditions. It wasn't surprising that they never made it. The mystery was what happened to their bodies. They were never found.'

'So what were the theories?' asked someone.

'There were several. But they boil down to two basic scenarios.'

Hitchens turned to use the whiteboard, perhaps hoping that it would draw the attention of all those eyes away from him for a few minutes. He wasn't a natural public speaker, which was a drawback in anyone with aspirations to become a senior officer. The TV crews would be arriving before long, and the DI wasn't the sort of man to make a good show in front of the cameras.

'Scenario number one,' he said, scrawling the phrase as he spoke. 'The Pearsons lost their way in the snowstorm and died somewhere on the moors before they reached their destination. In that case, we would normally have expected to find their bodies, which we didn't. So, what then? Well, they might have strayed so far off their route that they hit the flooded open-cast workings at Wolfstones Quarry, which were partly frozen over. Or they could have taken shelter in a cave, or the entrance to one of the old lead mines, and gone in too deep. They wouldn't be the first to go in and never come out. Some say that a party of cavers will turn up their bones one day.'

'Did we send divers into the quarry?'

'No, it wasn't feasible. The edges of the water were searched, but there was no indication at what point they might have gone in. It isn't a small body of water, you know. Without a reference point to start from, it was futile. You could tie up a team of divers for months without anything to show for it.'

DCI Mackenzie looked up at the pause. He was reading from a file, as if following the explanation by Hitchens and comparing it to the written record.

'There was another theory too, though,' he put in.

Hitchens sighed. 'Yes, this was the one that seemed to find most favour at the time. It was the easiest option, of course. Not that I'm saying it influenced the outcome of the inquiry exactly, but, you know . . . it might have been a factor.'

'And this theory was . . .?' prompted Mackenzie.

'Okay. Scenario number two.' Hitchens wrote it on the board. 'The theory that the Pearsons disappeared deliber-ately, did a bunk and changed their identities. The suggestion

71

was that they wanted people to assume they'd died an accidental death.'

'Why would they do that, sir?'

The voice came from the back of the room, and Hitchens scanned the faces, looking for the speaker. Cooper recognised it as Luke Irvine. He turned and saw Irvine sitting with Gavin Murfin on the back row. That could be an unholy alliance.

'When the police in Surrey looked into their backgrounds, they found evidence that David Pearson had been defrauding his employers, and their clients,' said Hitchens. 'It seems he'd been sifting funds out of client accounts for years, bit by bit. Some of it was in various savings accounts under his and Trisha's names, but the suspicion was that far more money had been taken that wasn't accounted for. It might only have existed in the form of cash.'

'So they staged their own disappearance and vanished with the cash to make a new life for themselves somewhere?' asked Irvine. 'Anywhere in particular?'

Hitchens shrugged uncomfortably. 'Spain, South America. Who knows?'

'There was the Canoe Man case a couple of years before.'

Becky Hurst. That was a voice Cooper didn't expect. He swivelled and caught Hurst's eye. She gave him a small smile, perhaps intended to be reassuring.

'Yes, I'm sure we remember that,' said Hitchens.

'In that case, he almost got away with it,' pointed out Hurst. 'If he hadn't let the estate agent take his photograph when he bought the apartment in Panama, he might still be there. He didn't realise they were going to use it in their advertising on the internet. But the Pearsons . . . they would have learned from what he did wrong.'

'If that's what they were planning.'

'How did they get away from the area, then?' asked Hurst.

72

'Was there any evidence they actually did go back to the cottage that night? Or did they have another vehicle kept handy somewhere?'

'We don't know.'

'I suppose they were smart enough to cover their tracks pretty well.'

Hitchens hesitated, and glanced at Mackenzie, who didn't react.

'This was only a theory,' he said. 'It was never established as a fact. The reality is, we don't know what happened. We need that information first.'

'Before we do what? Write them off as accidental deaths? Just another misadventure?'

'That would be up to the coroner.'

Diane Fry hadn't yet spoken. Cooper could see her sitting to one side, near the wall. Like Mackenzie, she had been slowly turning pages of the file. He knew Fry well enough to be aware that she had a terrific memory for details. The significant facts of the case would already be logged in her mind.

When she did speak, Fry chose her timing perfectly – not raising her voice, but inserting her question precisely into the momentary silence.

'Two people went missing in bad weather, and there was no proper search?'

Hitchens looked surprised.

'I wouldn't say that. It just wasn't feasible to mount a full search operation straight away, given the conditions. The helicopter couldn't fly, and it was pointless trying to get boots on the ground. We would only have been putting more lives at risk.'

'According to the incident log, it was five days before the search of the moor was completed.'

'We did our best. Buxton Mountain Rescue went up there.

They did a sweep of the immediate area as soon as the snow stopped and they had daylight hours to work in. Cave rescue checked out the disused mine shafts. No signs of the missing people. There was nothing. But, yes – it was five days before we were satisfied that we'd done a thorough search.'

Cooper thought of the expanse of Oxlow Moor, and the neighbouring areas. Old Moor, Bradwell Moor. That was a lot of ground to cover.

'Did they check *all* the shafts?' he said.

Hitchens held out his hands in a half-apologetic gesture. 'Who even knows how many shafts exist out there? How can we say it was all?'

'And why didn't they get dogs in?'

'Oh, the wrong kind of snow on the roads. The wrong kind of wheels on the snow. You know how it goes.'

'Would you say the inquiry was ongoing?' asked Fry.

'Theoretically. It was never officially closed, but . . .'

'But nobody has been putting any work into it, I suppose.'

'Not for a long time. There have been no new leads. What do you expect?'

DCI Mackenzie stood up as a set of photographs was handed out. A head shot of Trisha Pearson, cropped from a group picture. She was dressed up, perhaps for a wedding, with her hair pulled tightly back. In the photo, it looked to be a deep chestnut red, but it could be misleading. He wouldn't have said she was beautiful, but she was quite a striking woman, her face radiating health and confidence. She was laughing, and her eyes glittered as if life was just a bit of fun.

And then there was her husband, David Pearson. Clear blue eyes, and fair hair that was a bit longer than was fashionable these days. He reminded Cooper of a young Robert Redford from the 1970s. About the time of *The Way We Were*, perhaps.

'As we all know, time is of the essence at the beginning of any investigation,' said Mackenzie. 'We have the golden hour, when there's the best opportunity to make progress in an inquiry. Okay, we might push it further to the first twenty-four hours, or then the first forty-eight. But once you give up a crime scene, you start to lose things. Evidence becomes lost or tainted, and then it's worthless. In this case, we lost control of the crime scene more than two years ago.'

He allowed a moment for that fact to sink in. Officers in the room shuffled their feet uncomfortably, as if they were already being told that this inquiry had failed.

'So,' said Mackenzie, 'it looks as though our only hope of progress is to concentrate on the victims.'

'Didn't we do that last time?' asked someone.

Mackenzie hesitated for a second. 'Yes. But now we're going to do it again.'

Cooper glanced across at Fry, but she wasn't meeting anyone's eye. Not on this side of the room, anyway. He knew she would be feeling in her element now. Forensics aside, it was the piecing together of the final minutes, hours and days of the victims that was the foundation of a modern murder investigation. Fry would already be working through in her mind the procedures to be followed, the files to be reopened, the potential leads to be analysed and followed up. Murder investigations these days were a world away from the TV stereotype of two detectives rolling up to the crime scene.

Many lessons had been learned from botched inquiries like the Stephen Lawrence fiasco. These days, the tactic was to flood a crime scene with officers to maximise the chance of uncovering vital early clues.

The original inquiry had tasked more than thirty officers to cover all the possible angles. Some had been assigned to the family, others were involved with the forensic examination. Uniformed officers had conducted house-to-house inquiries, while detectives spoke to witnesses. The Senior Investigating Officer had logged all his decisions – and after twenty-eight days, because there was no breakthrough, a review team had been called in to provide a fresh pair of eyes. Every decision had been recorded and was open to review.

It was known as victimology – the picture that a murder inquiry tried to build up of the relationship between the deceased, the location and the suspects who came into the picture.

As a result of the strategies and protocols put in place, the clear-up rates for murder in England and Wales were very high – more than ninety per cent of suspicious deaths were detected, meaning someone was either convicted, or charged and later cleared.

Yes, there were a few unsolved murders. Derbyshire Constabulary had ten of them on the books. No one wanted another one to add to the tally, and especially not two. The initial inquiry had failed to produce a result, but now they had another chance.

The trouble was, within a few days Divisional CID would get sidelined, and they'd all be back on burglaries and stolen postboxes.

'If local officers could help us by reviewing the original inquiry into the disappearance of the Pearsons, going over the ground to see what might have been missed, it would be greatly appreciated,' said Mackenze. 'I think we could also use another physical search, but over an expanded area. I realise this will tie up some resources at an operational level.'

Branagh nodded her agreement, and Cooper knew his workload for the next few days had just been doubled.

'Of course, our big piece of luck,' continued Mackenzie, 'is the find on Oxlow Moor. These are believed to be the Pearsons' belongings.'

Now there was a stir of interest in the room. They were no longer going over old territory that had already proved fruitless. This was something new. Police officers were only human. They were motivated by the prospect of making genuine progress and achieving results. It was what gave them that frisson of excitement.

Mackenzie indicated large photos fixed to the whiteboard behind him.

'So – first we have a couple of matching Levi's anoraks in bright orange, with chambray linings. Not my style, but nice and visible in bad conditions, I'm told. As you can see, the larger of the two garments has staining on the left shoulder and left arm, here and here. Confirmed as human blood.'

The stains were clearly visible in the scenes-of-crime photos, dark against the orange fabric of the anorak, which had been laid out on a table under powerful lights. Some forensic expert would even now be trying to analyse the direction of the spatter, the force of the spray, calculating angles and the position of the wearer.

'Then there's a small Italian leather rucksack. This purple doesn't seem to go with the anoraks, but what do I know? All three of these are items the Pearsons were seen with during their visit to Castleton on that last evening, and have been confirmed as their possessions. And even if we didn't have those . . .' The DCI gestured at two more photos. 'This is David Pearson's wallet, containing a little over two hundred and fifty pounds in cash, three credit cards, his own business cards and several membership cards – gym, AA, frequent flyer points and so on. Obviously this leaves us in no doubt. All of these items, ladies and gentlemen, were deliberately buried in peat on Oxlow Moor, about a mile from the cottage where the Pearsons were staying.'

Cooper studied the photographs carefully. The items might leave no doubt about identification, but they certainly left room for speculation about motive. If David and Trisha Pearson were attacked and killed, why weren't they robbed too? In particular, why would anyone leave that amount of cash?

'Fingerprints?' someone was asking.

'Working on it.'

That was a given. No expense spared, probably. After all this time, there would be an all-out effort to get forensic results. But it could take time.

'Luckily,' said Mackenzie, ' a complete forensic sweep of the cottage was done at the time. No sign of a break-in, or of any violence taking place there. But after some work by the lab, they did manage to obtain enough DNA from tooth-brushes, used clothing, follicles on hairbrushes and so on to build DNA profiles for the victims. I mean, for David and Trisha Pearson, of course.'

'If they are victims.'

'Absolutely. Meanwhile,' Mackenzie looked towards Fry, 'we'll also be concentrating on making some early progress on the fresh incident. Let's see if we can confirm a connec-tion between the two.'

There was a hesitant murmur of agreement.

Mackenzie cast his eye round the room. 'Everyone up to speed? Good. Form your teams. There's a lot of work to do.'

Cooper looked round in amazement as the meeting broke up. He caught DI Hitchens by the arm as he passed on his way to the door.

'Wait a minute,' said Cooper. 'The body at the pub?'

Hitchens nodded towards the front of the room, where Fry had her head down talking to DCI Mackenzie.

'Sorry, Ben,' he said. 'EMSOU – MC are keeping that to themselves.'

A few minutes later, Villiers turned to Cooper with a puzzled expression.

'What did he mean about the wrong kind of wheels on the snow?' she said.

'Oh, that?' Cooper smiled. 'The dog handlers in Derbyshire are equipped with adapted Vauxhall Zafiras, which are underpowered anyway. They're also front-wheel drive, and with all the weight of equipment and dogs at the back, they don't go anywhere in snow.'

'So what happens?'

'Well, for four or five weeks in the average winter, our handlers are reduced to operating on foot, or begging a lift from a traffic officer in a four-wheel drive. Not many of the traffic boys like the idea of having a salivating long-haired German Shepherd sitting behind them on the back seat of the car, though.'

'I can't blame them really,' said Villiers.

'You don't like dogs?' asked Cooper in surprise. He wasn't sure why, but he'd got an idea in his mind that Carol was a dog person. Horses, dogs, anything related to the outdoors.

'Not when they remind me too much of a wolf,' said Villiers.

Hitchens took Cooper aside for a moment.

'Ben, Mr Mackenzie has asked us for a DC to work with DS Fry. Short term, of course.'

'One of ours?' said Cooper.

'Yes. Who would you suggest?'

Cooper ran quickly through his team in his mind, dismissing Gavin Murfin immediately, following him closely with Luke Irvine. Fry would eat Irvine alive. Carol Villiers, or Becky Hurst? Both could cope with the assignment, and one of them would benefit from it tremendously.

'DC Hurst,' he said. 'Shall I tell her?'

Hitchens nodded. 'Yes, Ben. Good choice. And someone needs to liaise with the firefighters. Find out exactly what they saw.'

Cooper looked round. 'Gavin, can you do that?'

'I dare say it's within my capabilities.'

Cooper turned as the DI left, and saw Fry scooping up the photos of the Pearsons. Murfin gave her a mock bow as he moved out of her way.

Fry nodded at him brusquely. 'Gavin.'

'Don't mind me,' he said. 'I won't be in the way. I'm off to talk to Trumpton.'

Fry turned to Cooper with a raised eyebrow.

'Trumpton?' she said. 'Do police officers still talk like that in the middle of the twenty-first century?'

'I didn't hear it,' said Cooper.

'I see.'

In fact, it was the first time he'd ever heard Murfin use that expression, though it had been common at one time as a derogatory reference to the fire service. The children's TV series had, after all, finished decades ago. He hoped Murfin wouldn't address the Edendale crew as Captain Flack, or Cuthbert, Dibble and Grub.

Murfin was proving difficult enough these days, but Cooper had never been able to figure out Diane Fry. Never. And he didn't think that was ever going to change now.

When she'd gone back to Birmingham to resolve the issues that had been haunting her for years, he'd imagined there might be some kind of closure for her, that she would be able to put the past behind her and start living a more normal life. Yet still he sensed a dark shadow in her life, one whose cause he couldn't even guess at. She was far too complex for him to comprehend, and he was past the point where he wanted to keep trying. It was like grasping at smoke and expecting it to stay in one place. No matter what you did, or how hard you tried, it always slipped through your fingers and left you holding nothing.

'Wait,' said Cooper. 'Diane, could you let me see those photographs again?'

Fry looked at him curiously for a moment, but flipped open the file. Cooper could sense her watching him closely. She had never known quite what to expect of him, but he couldn't blame her. Right now, he didn't know what to expect of himself.

The man in the photo was about thirty. He was leaning on a sports car, smiling at the camera with the sort of intimate smile that suggested he knew the photographer very well. He wore faded jeans and a white T-shirt with a slogan that had been made illegible by the angle of his arms stretching and folding the fabric. Cooper thought he could see a 'the'. Perhaps it was the name of a band.

In the background, familiar hills and the glint of water. One of the major reservoirs in the Upper Derwent. Howden, he guessed. The picture could have been taken at one of the pull-ins along the single-track road that skirted the edge of the reservoir.

'Do they look like hikers to you?' asked Cooper.

'I think Trisha was the outdoors type. She had a couple of horses back in Surrey, member of the RSPB, donated to animal charities.'

'A bit of an odd couple, do you think?'

'Not necessarily.'

'Had they been to the Peak District before?'

'Yes. They'd even stayed in the same cottage, but during the summer of the previous year.'

'I see.'

'And?' said Fry impatiently.

But Cooper ignored her. There was something familiar not only about the background, but about the stance of the man, the intimate expression. But most familiar of all was the face – blue eyes, a shock of fair hair. Yes, a young Robert Redford, with a hint of Brad Pitt.

'Do you fancy him, or what?' said Fry.

'No,' said Cooper. 'But I remember him.'

'So when did you see David Pearson?'

'I'm not sure.'

She glanced at him suspiciously. 'You never were a good liar, Ben.'

He shrugged. 'It might just be that I've seen the photographs before. In connection with the missing persons inquiry. I don't know.'

Fry was silent, forced to accept it as a possible explanation. But he could tell that she still wanted to ask more questions.

'He's distinctive,' she said at last. 'Looks like a film star. I can't quite remember which one . . .'

'Robert Redford.'

'Oh?' She seemed to think about it for a moment. 'Before my time, I think.'

'*Butch Cassidy and the Sundance Kid*? *All the President's Men*?'

'I can't quite picture—'

'Think of Brad Pitt, then.'

'I suppose so. I prefer Johnny Depp myself.'

Cooper shook his head. 'Wrong type altogether.'

'So – you'll be going over the ground again in the Pearson inquiry. Where are you heading first?'

He looked at her vaguely.

'Back into the past, I think,' he said.

'I suppose I shouldn't say it . . .'

'What?'

'Best place for you,' said Fry.

'No, you shouldn't.'

Murfin was beaming at them from his desk, his phone poised in mid-air. He seemed reluctant to let Fry leave the office without a parting jibe.

'Happy to be back among the sheep again, Diane? I bet you've been missing the little woolly darlings.'

Fry spun on her heel, an angry glower on her face.

'Once I drive away from Edendale for the last time, I'm never going to leave civilisation again. Trust me, I'll be happy if I don't have to see another damn sheep ever in my life.'

As an exit line, it wasn't bad. It was certainly one Cooper would remember.

8

It really was such a shame about the Light House. For generations, people had known where they were when they saw the pub. They had chosen it as a meeting place, as a halfway point on a journey, as a perfect spot to stop for a breather and admire the view.

The trouble was, not enough of them had actually been going inside, except to use the toilets. No one had recommended eating a meal there for years. No one even chose the Light House for a drinking session. It was impossible to include in a stag-night pub crawl because it was so far out of town. In its last few years it didn't even have real ale on tap to attract the aficionados, and that meant even morris dancers stayed away. Reputation was everything in the pub business. The Light House had possessed a good reputation once. But that had long since trickled away – and with it the majority of its customers.

Cooper walked up from the car park on to the front terrace, which looked out over the valley. It had been a favourite spot to sit in the summer, when the weather was good. He'd sat there many times himself, gazing towards the horizon where the hills disappeared in a warm haze.

But his eye was still drawn towards the pub itself – blank, windowless and dead. The facade had looked Georgian in style, with big sash windows placed in perfect symmetry.

Now, those windows had vanished underneath the boarding. He wondered if they would ever re-emerge and light up the way they once had, re-creating that familiar landmark. He didn't feel optimistic about the prospect. Once things had gone, they tended to stay that way. The past didn't come back.

'I thought they would be here already,' said Villiers, leaning against the bonnet of Cooper's car. 'I wonder where they are.'

'I don't know,' said Cooper. 'They don't intend to share everything they do with us, that's obvious.'

'Is that the way it is these days?'

'I think we just got unlucky,' said Cooper.

'DS Fry is a good officer, I think.'

Cooper glanced at Villiers, wondering why she felt the need to defend Diane Fry.

'Yes, of course she is.'

He couldn't make his mind up about Carol Villiers any more. He'd thought he knew her well, but the woman who'd transferred into Derbyshire Constabulary wasn't the same person who'd left the area for service with the RAF Police.

He recalled the day not long after Villiers had arrived when he'd see her driving away from the car park at E Division headquarters with Diane Fry. He'd thought about the moment many times in the weeks afterwards, trying to imagine what they might have in common, what they might have had to talk about. But he'd never come to any logical conclusion, not one that made any sense to him anyway. Not one that he wanted to think about too deeply.

And it was a sign of how his trust in Villiers had begun to ebb away that he'd never felt able to ask her the question. It was too late now, of course.

Villiers looked at her watch. 'Maybe we should get on.'

'We'll be okay for a few minutes.'

'If you say so.'

Cooper had wanted to get a look at the pub one way or another. It wasn't right that he'd let Fry find a body when he should have been here himself. This building seemed to stand like a rebuke, a symbol of his failure. He needed to find out what its secret was, if it had one.

Close up, the story of the Light House was even sadder. Weeds sprouted in the tarmac of the car park, along the edges of the walls and even in the guttering. Green stains ran down the stone where the gutters were blocked. Bird droppings streaked every surface. Foxes had left their spraints in the long grass growing rank and untidy where the beer garden had once been. From the looks of it, the only visitors to the pub in recent months had been a string of vandals, who'd scrawled casual graffiti on the boards over the windows.

It was disturbing how quickly a building began to deteriorate when it was left unoccupied. The pub was like a grand old lady down on her luck, left alone and unloved, with her elegant clothes frayed at the edges, her hair unwashed and her fingernails dirty. She looked lost and ashamed, with her eyes closed against the light.

At the rear stood a range of outbuildings that had been used for storage, including two garages. Rubbish had been burned in an open space. A huge pile of old furniture was stacked against the back wall of the pub. Heavy tables with metal bases, wrought-iron chairs, a heap of torn parasols on steel posts.

On the south side, even the conservatory had been boarded over. Since it consisted mostly of glass, the result was a monstrosity of hardboard, like some giant armoured beetle or an above-ground nuclear bunker. In its time it had been a pleasant place to sit, even on a cold day, its bright and airy space a contrast to the dark interior of the pub.

This was the place where he'd once sat with Diane Fry. But that was in a whole different universe.

He turned and looked up the hill. The smoke was drifting closer again. Cooper screwed his eyes up against the light, unsure of what he was seeing. Shadows. Yes, shadows in the smoke. Dark and insubstantial, moving in and out of the murk, their movements flickering and unnatural. He tried to follow their direction, but quickly lost them. It was as if they had simply slipped out of the world around them and stepped into another dimension.

He strained his eyes to probe the billowing clouds, and thought he saw something once again. But it resolved into the corner of a stone wall, which dropped teasingly into sight for a moment, then vanished again. Perhaps they had been just shadows after all, an effect of the sun still shining down through the smoke. Or maybe it had been a couple of stray sheep, lost and bewildered on the moor.

'Really,' said Villiers. 'We should probably get moving.'

'Don't worry.'

Although Fry and Mackenzie weren't here, the pub was far from deserted. It was a suspected murder scene, and that changed everything. The scenes-of-crime team were at full stretch now, with scene examiners drafted in from other divisions. He couldn't see Liz, but he knew she was on duty, so she'd be working somewhere. They tried not to see too much of each other on duty, in case there was talk.

The forced door and loose panel had been examined for tool marks and dusted for fingerprints, and the position of the suspect white pickup had been established from evidence of flattened weeds in the car park. It was lucky that the road had been closed for the fire on the moors. It meant that no one had been here between the departure of the pickup and the arrival of Fry's Audi, which she'd left in the entrance.

Inside the pub, lights had been set up and a series of stepping plates and yellow evidence markers surrounded the position of the body, as well as the route the victim and his assailants had taken from the door. Two SOCOs in scene suits were still combing the adjacent floor and walls for traces, tracking the direction of blood spatter and photographing shoe marks in the dust.

'DS Cooper, isn't it? You're on my crime scene.'

Cooper backed away from the door and found DCI Mackenzie behind him, with Fry at his elbow. Mackenzie's voice was mild, but there was a cool undertone to his words, and a penetrating gaze in the eyes below the quizzically raised eyebrows.

'I thought DC Villiers ought just to see the location,' Cooper said.

He gestured towards Carol Villiers, who was waiting at a safe distance. Trust Carol – she had more sense than he did at a crime scene.

Mackenzie nodded. 'Okay. Well while you're here, Cooper, you might see if you can deal with the natives for us.'

'Who'

Cooper looked towards the road, and saw a silver Volvo estate that had been stopped at the outer cordon. An elderly man in a suit was standing talking to a uniformed officer just outside the tape.

'Fine,' said Cooper. 'I know who that is.'

Thomas Pilkington was the old man of the auctioneers Pilkington and Son. He'd been around the Eden Valley for years – a member of the Rotary Club, a former town councillor, a drinking companion of the golf club captain and

88

the editor of the *Eden Valley Times*. The son of the firm was Jeremy Pilkington, quite a different proposition, more often to be seen in a red MG on his way to the sailing club at Carsington. Cooper felt sure Jeremy must now be the driving force behind the company.

Old Thomas had been the auctioneer at the cattle market in Edendale for decades. His voice was familiar to generations of farmers and livestock dealers. In fact it had been hard to escape for anyone passing within two hundred yards of the sale ring near the town's railway station. Cooper remembered the sound as an integral feature of shopping trips to Edendale on cattle market days. Thomas Pilkington's voice still played as part of the soundtrack to his childhood memories, along with the pop music he'd grown up listening to during all those long, hot summers.

But Edendale cattle market had closed years ago, losing the battle against movement restrictions and competition from the new agricultural business centre fifteen miles away at Bakewell, part of a twelve-million-pound regeneration project. With the loss of the mainstay of their business, Pilkington and Son must have been close to the edge. No doubt it had been Jeremy who pushed for the move towards property auctions. That was still a thriving sector. Booming these days, in fact. But it was ironic that the firm should find itself auctioning off other businesses that could no longer compete.

Pilkington must be well into his seventies now. He was a red-faced man with an expanding belly almost bursting the buttons of his suit jacket. His complexion was just right to allow him to blend in with the farmers and livestock dealers who'd been his customers for all those years. He could have passed for a butcher or gamekeeper. But as a property agent, he was projecting the wrong image.

Cooper escorted him from the cordon via the safe route that had been marked out, and Fry cut across to intercept them, as if she didn't trust Cooper within fifty yards of the crime scene.

'My son is dealing with this property actually,' Pilkington said, confirming Cooper's suspicion. 'I don't know all that much about it. But he's out of the country at the moment and it seems I'm responsible for it, so I'm the one who was called out by your people.'

'Can't you tell us anything, Mr Pilkington?'

'Well, this is a free house and can be sold with all fixtures and fittings, should someone wish to continue with the current use. Alternatively it can be sold as a development opportunity and could feasibly be turned into residential accommodation, or a bed and breakfast business. Ample parking, et cetera.'

'The pub was owned by the licensee himself? Not by a brewery or a pub company?'

'No, Mr Wharton owned the pub outright. Or rather . . .'

Fry looked at him. 'What?'

'Let me consult the file.'

'Please do.'

After a moment, Pilkington seemed to find the form he was looking for.

'Yes, here we are. There's quite a substantial charge against the property. Mmm. Yes, quite substantial. Mr and Mrs Wharton committed themselves to a large refinancing package, with the property as security. It seems they defaulted on payments to the financial institution involved. That's very unfortunate. It should never have been allowed to get to that stage. I suspect Mr Wharton must have received some bad advice.'

'So it belongs to the bank?'

'Well . . . mostly to the creditors, yes. It seems the Whartons were obliged to sell when the incomings no longer matched the outgoings.'

'They went bust.'

'It's rather a crude term. More of a tabloid journalist's expression.'

'But still . . .?'

'That's the gist of it, yes,' admitted Pilkington.

'And now it's a dead duck. Who would buy a failed pub?'

'It's an opportunity to regenerate an underperforming business,' said Pilkington stiffly. 'An adjustment of the food and drink split, a shift to a more dry-led trading model. The potential incomings—'

'Save it,' said Fry.

'It could be a unique destination food house. We expect to get a good price at auction.'

Fry looked at Pilkington as if she was going to hit him. Cooper was more reluctant to upset anyone in the property business. You never knew how word might get around in a place like Edendale. But Fry didn't care, clearly. She had no intention of ever buying property in this area. She'd never made any secret of it. Property ownership meant roots. It certainly involved financial ties. All the things Diane Fry didn't want.

'This is a landmark property, freehold and free of tie, with function room and guest accommodation. It ought to be an easy sell.' Pilkington looked faintly apologetic at his use of the phrase. 'Well, that's what my son says. A full commercial kitchen, with glass wash and preparation room. Three-bedroom self-contained owner's accommodation, with four en suite guest bedrooms. Goodwill, plus stock at valuation.'

Cooper recalled reading in the local newspaper that the freehold for another famous landmark inn in the Peak District had sold recently for one and a half million pounds. Who would have that kind of money available to rescue the Light House from its fate?

Pilkington eyed Fry nervously as she walked away. Then he turned to Cooper as if to share a confidence.

'To be honest, the turnover doesn't look too good on paper,' he said. 'We're advised by our clients that business was more than acceptable a few years ago, but it began to decline. Potential buyers don't like to see a downturn on gross profits when they examine the financial records.'

'No, of course.'

'There were particular problems here, though.'

'Oh, were there?'

'Well, for example – a lot of businesses in the hospitality sector rely on making a profit over the holiday period. It can compensate for flat trading during the rest of the year. But the Light House had developed the practice of closing over Christmas. You can understand it on a personal level, I suppose. We all like to spend time with our families. But from a business point of view, it didn't help the bottom line at all.'

A scatter of soot on the wind and the acrid smell of burning heather reminded them that a wildfire was burning on the moor not too far away.

'They need to put that fire out,' said Pilkington nervously.

'They're doing their best, sir.'

'They need to put it out. It mustn't be allowed to get any closer to the property.'

'I'm sure the firefighters will have it under control in a day or two.'

'A day or two? Are you serious?'

'These moorland fires can burn for weeks. The fire gets right down into the peat, you see, and then there's no way of putting it out. It just keeps smouldering away down there, and burning back up to the surface again. That could go on all summer. Or until we get some decent rain, anyway.'

'That can't be possible surely.'

'I'm afraid so, sir. But the firefighting teams will make it a priority to prevent the blaze spreading this way so as to protect your property.'

He turned and looked at the derelict inn as he spoke, the shuttered windows and boarded-up door, the grass growing on the car park, the weeds sprouting from the roof. And he wondered what there was to protect, really.

'They should have had protection by occupation,' said Pilkington. 'My son advised it, but they didn't take up the option.'

'A live-in guardian, you mean?'

'Exactly. Someone who lives on site temporarily for a small rent. It would have worked here, I'm sure. There's separate owner's accommodation already in place. A guardian could have looked after the property a bit better, and prevented it from becoming such an eyesore. Not that the right buyer won't see the potential . . .'

'Yes, of course.'

'There have been a lot of rumours about problems with the pub since it closed. Reports of squatters and drug users, but they turned out not to be true. And word has been going round Edendale that there were major subsidence issues, due to the old mine workings.'

'Yes, I heard that rumour myself.'

'Well that isn't true either,' said Pilkington. 'It's all very unhelpful. That type of story tends to put off a lot of buyers.'

Cooper thought about where the Light House stood. He supposed its original builders hadn't chosen its position for the views. Until the arrival of the Romantic movement, this landscape would have been considered wild and barbaric, so lacking in civilisation as to be devoid of interest. After all, the eighteenth-century novelist Daniel Defoe had called the Peak District 'a houling wilderness'. The heather itself had been despised as a symbol of rural poverty.

No, this had been a practical choice of location. Travellers passing over the moors needed somewhere to stop for the night, a place to change or rest their horses. The inn's lights appearing in the dusk must have been a welcome sight to many thousands of people over the years. It was only much later that they came here for the view.

Thomas Pilkington left after handing over the keys to the pub. As his Volvo estate drove away, another vehicle was pulling up to the outer cordon. An unmarked Vauxhall Corsa CID pool car. And surely that was Gavin Murfin at the wheel? Not many officers drove with one hand while eating a sausage roll from the other.

Cooper shook his head. Murfin was probably just curious about what was going on. He couldn't blame him for that. It was why he was here himself. But Gavin's presence at the Light House was the last thing he needed right now. It was like tossing a burning rag into a pool of oil.

He tried making gestures at the Corsa. *Go away, Gavin.* But Murfin had wound the driver's window down and was having a chat with the uniformed officer on duty. Everyone knew DC Murfin. He'd been in E Division for ever. Within a few minutes, he would know far more about the crime scene than Cooper did himself.

Cooper wasn't the only person who'd noticed the pool car arrive, either. Fry was stomping about like an angry wasp.

'Shouldn't you and your team be somewhere?' she said, approaching Cooper. 'Going over the Pearsons' movements, perhaps? Wasn't that what we all agreed at the briefing this morning?'

'I'm just on my way,' said Cooper, but he didn't move.

'So . . .?'

'Well the thing is – I'm not sure about the route,' he said.

'The route?'

'The one the Pearsons took on their way back to the cottage from Castleton. It seems to have been assumed that they just followed the Limestone Way.'

'Yes.'

'But according to the statements in the case file, some customers waiting outside the fish and chip shop reported seeing them on The Stones.'

'That was when the Pearsons were on their way down *in* to Castleton earlier in the evening.'

Cooper knew he shouldn't have been surprised that she had the smallest details of the couple's movements off by heart. It was one of Fry's skills, along with the knack of making him feel useless. Well, superfluous at least.

'Yes, but . . .?' he said.

'Ben, all that sighting does is confirm that David and Trisha Pearson went into Castleton for the evening. And we know that already from the staff at the George.'

'But don't you see . . .?'

'Just go over the ground,' she said slowly, as if to an idiot. 'Check everything from the original inquiry. And we'll take it from there. Okay?'

Cooper swallowed his words in frustration. There were none so blind as those who refused to see, and Diane Fry was one of the most stubborn.

When he'd looked at the reports and witness statements from the night David and Trisha Pearson disappeared, an idea had occurred to him. He needed to explain it to someone, but Diane Fry had been the wrong person.

9

Fry supposed this was what would have been called an old-fashioned pub. She pictured an open hearth and log fires in the winter, a place where dogs were welcome – sometimes more welcome than human patrons. What had the old man from the auctioneer's called it? A unique destination food house? It wasn't her idea of a destination. She wouldn't waste petrol coming up here if she didn't have to.

The pub had a stone slate roof, with a satellite dish high on the wall, and spotlights that must once have lit the facade of the pub and made it visible for miles. A sign was faintly chalked on an A-board left lying on the ground outside: *We serve REAL chips.*

A smokers' shelter had been built against one wall. Ironically, there were plenty of butt bins provided, so it was probably the one place where cigarette ends could be disposed of safely anywhere on Oxlow Moor, where she could see the wildfires burning.

Sometimes Fry liked to see a fire. For her, flames could be cleansing, a means of getting rid of the old and clearing the way for something better. But she supposed Cooper and those like him wouldn't see it that way. No doubt they would be panicking right now about the damage to their precious landscape, as if was a fossil that ought to be preserved in aspic and never altered.

It was nonsense, of course. Everyone knew that places like the Peak District looked the way they did because of centuries of human interference. Moorland landscapes had been shaped by deforestation and changes in farming methods. Yes, the credit for maintaining the moors went to all those damn sheep.

Fry stepped over the low boundary wall on to the terrace of the pub. The wall was lined with terracotta pots full of dead plants. Someone had made an attempt at decorating the main entrance with hanging baskets. They might have been full of petunias and trailing lobelias once. Now they hung from their rusting brackets, bare of flowers, spilling torn shreds of coconut-fibre liner.

She couldn't see into the bar because of the boarding over the windows. But she didn't really need to. The interior of a place like this was too predictable. She pictured flag-stones, oak settles and low doorways. She imagined an aged local sitting with a pint of Old Moorland Original in front of him on a wobbly table, a bored landlord reading a copy of the *Daily Mail* at the bar, a deathly silence broken only by a clock ticking away the seconds until closing time.

'Sergeant, I think we need Gavin Murfin here,' said Hurst tentatively.

'Why?'

'Local knowledge. Gavin has it.'

'Oh God. See if he's still outside, then.'

'Will do.'

The interior of the Light House was a strange dichotomy. Part of it was a major crime scene, brightly illuminated and tightly controlled, busy with SOCOs in scene suits, rich with the familiar smells of a forensic examination. But the rest was exactly as it had been left when it closed for business six months ago.

The main rooms on the ground floor had been securely

locked, so were available to Fry with the help of the set of keys handed over by Thomas Pilkington.

Here in the bar, the atmosphere was stale and dusty. Although scenes of crime had found the main switch for the electricity supply and turned on the lights, the boarding over the windows kept the room as gloomy as if it was permanently night.

A few tables stood around, chairs stacked haphazardly, empty shelves and optics behind the long counter. Brass fittings that might once have gleamed with polish were now dull with accumulated grime. The big fireplace where the log fire would have burned during the winter was filled with scraps of old newspaper, fragments of a bird's nest and the remains of a soot fall.

Fry watched Becky Hurst walk back into the bar. She was pleased that she'd been given Hurst. Of all the members of the CID team in Edendale, this was the officer she might have hopes for. Hurst was smart and tenacious, and Fry had seen how she dealt with Murfin, and even with Luke Irvine, who had about the same length of service.

'It's a pity,' said Hurst. 'This place would make a good youth hostel or something.'

Gavin Murfin was standing behind her in the doorway.

'It'd make a better pub,' he said grumpily. 'Oh, I forgot – that's exactly what it was, until the bean counters put the boot in.'

'Didn't you used to drink here, Gavin?' asked Hurst.

'Drink here? I was practically brought up in this pub. My old man used to leave me outside in the car with a packet of cheese and onion crisps, while he played snooker in the public.'

'A packet of crisps?' said Hurst. 'And a bottle of dandelion and burdock, surely?'

'Coke. We were quite a trendy family, for plebs.'

'It's haunted, I suppose?'

Fry snorted. 'Aren't they all? I thought it was an essential feature to get a listing in the tourist guides, like having toilets and satellite TV.'

'No, this one is genuinely haunted,' said Murfin. 'They say it's the ghost of some servant girl who burned to death in a kitchen accident. Set her clothes alight when she was cooking or something. Now and then she still walks the corridors, giving off a horrible fiery glow.'

'Yeah, right. They tell those stories because they think it'll bring gullible American tourists in.'

'No,' said Murfin solemnly. 'I saw her once.'

'Come off it.'

'I did. I was about to leave here one night, and had to go to the gents. They're down a corridor round the back of the bar there, you know. And that was when I saw her, all glowing. Gave me the shock of my life, it did.'

'Glowing?'

'Yeah, glowing. Like she was on fire.

'You were drunk, Gavin.'

'Believe what you want, I don't care.'

Fry looked at Murfin closely, sure that he must be joking. She'd known him for a long time, and he wasn't the kind to believe in ghosts and all that stuff. But his face never slipped. He appeared to be serious.

She looked out across the moor, where the smoke and flames seemed to be getting ever nearer to the pub.

'If that wind changes direction,' she said, 'your flaming kitchen maid could be in danger of burning to death all over again.'

The pub was accessed directly from the car park, and was essentially a one-room open-plan layout, although in visually distinct sections. A games room featured a pool table, darts board and plasma-screen TV. At one end, a dark-panelled snug with pew benches had been left as a reminder of days gone by. It had been heated by a small wood-burning stove.

In this part of the pub, some of the old pictures had been left on the walls. A few portraits, hunting groups, dukes and squires posing with their dogs and horses. In the dim light, there were too many eyes in the room for Fry's comfort, squinting at her beneath their layers of dust.

And what was that smell? She made her way along a short passage and found herself in a galley-style catering kitchen with tiled walls and overhead stainless-steel extractor hoods. Yes, this was where the smell was coming from. The odour of scampi and chips seemed to have been absorbed into the walls and ventilation ducts, and was now being released back into the air.

Fry was reminded of the theory that ghosts were the lingering echoes of people whose lives and deaths were imprinted indelibly in the stone. This smell seemed to bring a sense of life back to the stale air, peopling the abandoned kitchens with the shadowy spirits of those who'd worked there over the years.

But that was Gavin Murfin who'd put the idea of ghosts into her head. She ought to know better than to listen to him, even for a moment.

'Owner's accommodation?' she said.

Murfin jerked his head. 'Upstairs.'

She found the access to the stairs just past a series of doors marked as ladies, gents and disabled toilet facilities, and another door giving access to the rear yard area.

Upstairs, a room had been turned into a small function suite, with its own corner bar for private parties. It was the brightest room in the pub, thanks to four large sash and case windows looking out over the moor. It was laid with a dark blue carpet, leaving a tiny wooden dance floor area in the middle. It would never have hosted any major events. Thirty or forty people would have filled it to capacity. A small wedding, perhaps. An office party. Groups of laughing workers deposited by minibus. No chance of walking home from here.

The guest rooms were also on the first floor. Just three of them. According to the name plaques on their doors, they were called the Bakewell, Buxton and Bradwell rooms.

There was another, narrower set of stairs leading to the top floor, where the pub's owner had lived. But the owner's accommodation was completely bare. In every room, the furniture had been removed, the carpets stripped from the floor, the curtains pulled down from the windows. There were clear marks against the walls where a picture had hung or a chest of drawers had stood. The former occupants had removed themselves completely.

A few minutes later, Fry found herself looking down two flights of stairs into the rear corridor, the gloom in the doorways barely relieved by the light from the huge sash window on the landing. For a moment she was puzzled and disturbed by the way the shadows seemed to move below her, as if the darkness was writhing around itself, invisible snakes stirring the dust on the floor.

It was only when her eyes adjusted to the light that she realised what she was seeing. Smoke and flames from the hillside, casting their distant outlines through the window, thrusting their ominous presence right into the heart of the building.

'If you want to know about the pub, you could start with Mad Maurice, I suppose,' said Murfin.

'Who?' asked Fry.

'Maurice Wharton, the last landlord. He ran the pub right up until the day it closed.'

'He lived on the premises too, of course?'

'Yes, with his wife and children. I can't remember their names, but we can soon find that out.'

'No live-in staff?'

'Not that I remember. The bar staff usually came up from town for their shift. A lot of them were students earning a bit of money during the evenings or at weekends.'

Fry sniffed the air, detecting again that faint whiff of chips.

'Who did the cooking here? There must have been some kitchen staff.'

Murfin didn't answer, and Fry glanced at him, ready to ask the question again.

'I don't know,' he said.

Fry turned to Hurst, softening her instinctive response a little.

'Find out, will you?'

'Sure.'

She looked at Murfin again. 'Gavin, did I hear that you were liaising with the firefighters?'

'Yes,' said Murfin. 'Trumpton reported seeing a white pickup. They can't be specific about the make or model, or how many people were in it. Or how long it was here before it left. They were a bit vague about the colour, come to think of it – white being so easily confused with blue or red, like. I suppose it's true what they say in the song. Smoke does get in your eyes.'

'Trumpton?' said Fry again.

Murfin ignored her with a complacent smile.

'So two people were here, at least,' he said.

'Well that didn't take much figuring out, Sherlock, since one of them got left behind, and he happens to be dead.'

'And someone drove the pickup away,' added Murfin helpfully.

'Thanks, Gavin.'

'Just saying.'

'What were they doing here? It doesn't make sense.'

Hurst shrugged. 'People break into empty buildings all the time. They could have been looking for somewhere to smoke dope, have sex, find a squat for a few weeks.'

'In the middle of burning moorland? They'd have to be particularly desperate, or stupid.'

'Fair point.'

Fry looked around the empty rooms. 'I'd say they might have taken the opportunity to find something worth stealing, but it seems a bit unlikely.'

'I don't know,' said Hurst. 'That could be the most likely explanation. Okay, there's no cash here, or the sort of small electrical items that opportunist thieves usually go for. But scrap metal is worth a fair bit these days. Ask the vicars whose church roofs keep getting stripped of lead.'

Fry shook her head. 'I still can't see any signs that anything has been taken.'

'There was definitely a vehicle here, though. The fire crews saw it. A white pickup. Just the sort of vehicle you'd use for scrap.'

'*Probably* a white pickup.'

'There were too many people up here. Too many for it to be just a coincidence. Too many for there to be a logical explanation. Not an *innocent* logical explanation anyway.'

From Fry's research when she first transferred here from the West Midlands, she knew about the ten unsolved murders in Derbyshire Constabulary's history. The oldest went back to 1966, the case of a Chesterfield teenager found beaten to death in a disused factory. It was senseless killings like that that tended to be the most difficult to detect and the most unlikely to result in a successful prosecution.

But whatever had happened inside this pub, it wasn't senseless. At least two people had come together here, if only for a short while. There had been a reason for the killing.

Murder, or the idea of murder, wasn't all that unfamiliar a concept to a lot of people, most of them ordinary, law-abiding citizens. It had been a part of human experience since Cain killed Abel. Normally it all went wrong with the disposal of the body. The killing itself was easy. It didn't take much thought – a red mist in front of the eyes, a violent swing of the arm, and it was done. But a corpse on the floor was a different matter. There were bloodstains on the walls, one of your hairs on their clothes, a fragment of your skin caught under their fingernails. And perhaps a witness who had seen both of you arrive but only one of you leave. From that point, it took a lot of thought. And who was thinking straight in those circumstances? Most people just panicked and ran.

They'd interviewed some of the firefighters, and a couple of rangers who'd been in the vicinity. But the interviews had produced little of any use. Understandably, their attention had been on the fires, not on the pub. And that was a shame. Given the location, they were the only potential witnesses available.

'The last landlord, you said?'

'Mad Maurice,' repeated Murfin. 'Moved back down into Edendale with his family when the pub closed. Name of Wharton.'

'Why do they call him Mad Maurice?' asked Fry.

'Because he used to get mad a lot,' said Murfin. 'There were loads of things he couldn't stand. Mobile phones, children, people who just came into the pub to use the loo or ask directions. Anything like that, he'd get mad about. Maurice became a tourist attraction in his own right.'

'How do you mean?'

'Well, folk used to come in the pub just in the hopes of seeing him get mad. They thought it was funny. "Let's go and see Mad Maurice," they'd say. Where other landlords called the traditional "Time gentlemen, please", Maurice's shout was "Come on, you buggers, clear off. Haven't you got homes to go to?"'

'Charming.'

'It was just his way.'

'If he shouted that at me, I'd never go back there again.'

'Well that's the point. If you couldn't put up with a bit of abuse, he didn't want you in his pub anyway. It meant you were the wrong sort of customer.'

'Good grief. It's no wonder the place went bust, if he chased away all his custom like that.'

'On the contrary, it was one of the pub's unique selling points. People used to go there because of Maurice. It's a bit like customers going to Gordon Ramsay's restaurant hoping to hear him say the F-word. You know what I mean.'

'Gordon Ramsay is a celebrity chef who's always on the telly. He's famous.'

'Well so was Mad Maurice, in his own way. He was a *local* celebrity. For every customer he banned from the pub for a using a mobile phone or talking too loud, he'd get ten more coming in to see him do it.'

'A clever marketing ploy on his part, then.'

'No,' said Murfin. 'He just got mad a lot.'

Hurst took a call, and turned immediately to Fry.

'We got an ID,' she said. 'Name of Aidan Merritt, a thirty-five-year-old teacher from Edendale.'

'A teacher? What was he up to at the Light House?'

'Dunno. But here's the interesting thing. His name came up in HOLMES in connection with the Pearson inquiry.'

10

Ben Cooper parked his Toyota by the little green in the centre of Castleton and opened his Ordnance Survey map. It was a well-used, heavily creased copy of Outdoor Leisure 1, the Dark Peak.

As usual, the area he wanted went off the edge of the map and crossed into the White Peak. That was just to make things more difficult.

Above the town, a team of officers were attempting to follow the route that the Pearsons might have taken from Castleton on the night they disappeared. It had been done before, but DCI Mackenzie had insisted on it being done again. The scope of the search had been widened, taking in a broad sweep of the moor right over to Speedwell Cavern and Winnats Pass on one side, and including the Limestone Way itself on the other.

In most parts of the country it would be impossible to imagine how two people could simply disappear in open countryside like this. But Cooper was aware of what lay underneath his feet. The whole of this landscape was hollow. It was one huge lump of porous limestone, scooped out over millennia by running water to form endless caves and tunnels and passages.

The Peak Cavern system alone ran for more than ten miles before it emerged at Speedwell, and it included the deepest shaft in the UK, twice the size of St Paul's Cathedral. Rain falling on the surface in Cavedale found its way through to the show caverns below and fell as lime-stained waterfalls on the heads of tourists.

Even Sir Arthur Conan Doyle had once said: 'All this county is hollow. Could you strike it with some gigantic hammer it would boom like a drum.' In that wider context, it was far too easy to imagine anything disappearing.

Cooper glanced out of the car window. Up Castle Street, he could see the sign outside the George, directly opposite the parish church. He dialled Carol Villiers' mobile number, and she answered after three or four rings.

'Where are you, Carol?'

'Still at the George.'

'Anything?'

'No. The story stays the same, right down to the details. Except the details are becoming a bit vague by now. I've been going through the names of the other people who were eating here that night. I know it's been done before . . .'

'Hasn't it all?' said Cooper.

'Well . . . anyway, they're all in the clear. No connection with the Pearsons, so far as I can tell. One couple were from Sussex, which I suppose is not a million miles from where the Pearsons lived.'

'Did they speak to each other?'

'Not that we know of. Not that anyone saw.'

'A washout, then.'

'Of course, we don't have all the names,' said Villiers. 'Some of the customers are unaccounted for. So there are gaps.'

Cooper sighed. 'I know. Thanks, Carol.'

'I'm leaving the George in a few minutes. I'm going to go past the Green.'

'Fine.'

Details of the Pearsons' movements towards the end of that night were sketchy, and had to be partly speculation. What was known for certain was that they'd arrived at the George, where they'd booked a table for dinner at seven thirty. Since their Range Rover III was still standing outside The Old Dairy next day, the presumption was that they'd walked to Castleton. The owner of the cottage confirmed they were keen walkers – that was why they came to the Peak District, they'd said. At the George, staff who'd served them remembered that they'd come in wearing outdoor clothes and walking shoes. It wasn't at all unusual; Castleton was a centre for walkers at any time of the year.

Cooper thought about the photographs of the Pearsons again. You couldn't always tell the outdoor types, of course. And the Peak District had enough variety to attract anyone. But personally, he wouldn't have pegged David Pearson as the kind of man to be hiking over the moors in the middle of winter. The activity had its attractions, without a doubt, but it was minority appeal. Most people would have jumped into the car and driven to Castleton. Almost everyone, in fact, even if they hadn't bothered to check the local weather forecasts. It was one of the factors that had fuelled theories that the Pearsons had set the whole thing up. If you looked at it that way, it was the unlikeliest element of the scenario. Yet from the evidence, that seemed undoubtedly to be what had happened.

Okay, so the meal had gone off uneventfully. The mushrooms in peppercorn sauce, the Bantry Bay mussels, the honey-glazed ham shank. The Pearsons' table hadn't been close to the windows, so they might not have noticed the weather deteriorating. It was only a bit of sporadic sleet anyway. A few wintry showers. What was that to a couple of determined, experienced walkers with the right gear?

But wait a minute. Exactly how experienced were the

108

Pearsons? Cooper made a note to find out. The original inquiry had traced their movements the day before their visit to Castleton, but those had all been by car, surely? They'd filled up the Range Rover at Sickleholme service station, so they must have been using fuel. A trip into Buxton for the Christmas market, maybe. Afternoon tea at the Old Hall Hotel. The Twelve Days of Christmas at Chatsworth House. That would have been David and Trisha's style, if he wasn't mistaken.

But still, they seemed to have decided to walk to Castleton – a distance of about three miles from the cottage. He estimated an hour at a brisk pace. No one could say exactly when they'd set off, so the couple might have taken their time, a leisurely stroll over the moor to work up an appetite, with a nice meal awaiting them at the end of it.

Well, not quite the end of it. There had been the hike back to The Old Dairy to take into consideration.

So what about when the meal was over? When they left the George, the Pearsons were believed to have walked in this direction, past the green and into Bargate, where they could turn directly on to the start of the Limestone Way as they headed back to their cottage.

He watched Villiers do it now, walking up Castle Street, passing his car and stopping at the gift shop by the green.

And that was what bothered Cooper. From the statements taken at the time, there was really no confirmation of it – only a passing reference to the Limestone Way in the course of conversation with staff at the George.

What if the Pearsons had instead turned the corner of Castle Street by the youth hostel on to the narrow lane called The Stones? Extensive interviews and appeals to the public had resulted in an identification earlier in the evening by customers who had been waiting at the little fish and chip shop a few yards up. The couple had been seen to

109

cross the bridge over the Peak Water. According to the statements, they'd seemed very relaxed, and had stopped, as everyone did, to listen to the water rushing under the parapet as it tumbled from the mouth of Peak Cavern.

But, as Fry had pointed out, that was when the Pearsons were on their way *in* to Castleton, not out of it. It was merely confirmation that they'd arrived on foot. It gave no indication how they'd left. They had talked about the Limestone Way, and that was the safest route back to their cottage in bad conditions, wasn't it?

Yet it was perfectly possible that the Pearsons had taken the other route. If they'd left Castleton the same way they'd come in, they would have gone over the slopes of Hurd Low and found themselves on the edge of Oxlow Moor. Their route should have connected them to the Limestone Way to the east, and a straight run back to the cottage at Brecks Farm. But what if they'd strayed to the west? With no landmarks or reference points to guide them, it would have been all too easy. Once you'd lost your way in those conditions, you could walk round in circles for hours and be none the wiser.

There was a track to the west, too. He pictured the Pearsons struggling across the snow-covered heather, stumbling over rough ground and finally feeling a path under their feet. They would have followed it, surely. If they were desperate enough by then, they would have grasped at it like a drowning man sighting an oasis.

He shook his head in dismay. But all that did was widen the search area dramatically. His suggestion would not be welcomed.

Yes, the Pearsons would probably have found it easier to follow the track to Hurd Low, but it would have meant leaving the lights of the town behind sooner, as the trail started in Cavedale, deep below the ruined walls of Peveril

Castle. If they'd walked over Hurd Low on their way to the George, it would have seemed logical to go back the same way.

Logical, but possibly fatal.

He'd lost sight of Villiers now, so he redialled her number. 'Carol?'

'I'm going through the gate into the dale,' she said.

'Cave Dale?'

'Yes. It's pretty gloomy in here, you know. Lots of dark corners among the rocks. Caves, even.'

'Well, that's why it's called Cave Dale.'

'Right. I was just thinking it would be an ideal location for an ambush.'

'Ambush? Is that your military training coming out again?'

'I suppose so.'

'Who would want to ambush the Pearsons?'

'I have no idea,' admitted Villiers. 'I'm just using my imagination. Isn't that what you do, Ben?'

'I wouldn't always recommend it,' said Cooper.

'The start of the Limestone Way is straight ahead. There's no missing it once you're in the dale.'

'You can come back now, Carol.'

A few minutes later, Villiers opened the door and slipped into the passenger seat of the Toyota. Cooper showed her the map and told her his theory.

'It's not really a theory,' she said. 'It's speculation.'

'You're right. I know.'

'But I suppose speculation is what we need right now.'

'We don't have anything else.'

They both sat in silence for a moment. Cooper guessed that Villiers was thinking what he was – how disappointing it would be if they went over all the old ground and came up with nothing but the same old facts and the same worn-out theories.

Cooper had never known a case where the events they were investigating were so ambiguous. He could see why the inquiry had eventually run out of steam. There was no firm evidence that the Pearsons had died. Nor was there definite proof that they were still alive and living under new identities somewhere.

'The Pearsons both had mobile phones, didn't they?' said Villiers. 'Why didn't they make an emergency call?'

'Yes, that was looked into, of course. David had an iPhone.'

'Oh yes. At the George, they said he was using it constantly to access the internet, to read emails and even to look at maps of the area with its GPS feature. The staff overheard Trisha telling him that he would run the battery down.'

'Well if he was using GPS when they walked across the moor, it would have drained pretty quickly,' said Cooper.

'That would be the phone found buried in the peat.'

'Yes, that was David's. As for Trisha, she had a smartphone too, but she was on a different network. According to the phone company's records, her handset wasn't logged on during the relevant time. It seems likely that she couldn't get a signal. It isn't unusual in that area. Heck, it isn't unusual anywhere in this part of the county.'

'So where is Trisha's phone?' asked Villiers.

'We don't know, do we?'

'No.'

Villiers looked thoughtful. Cooper waited, watching her expression, trusting her to put her finger on some significant point. Or at least hoping that she would.

'The conversation in the restaurant sounds a bit staged, doesn't it?' she said finally.

'What do you mean?'

'It seems to me it could have been acted out by the

112

Pearsons specifically so that the staff or other diners would hear it, and be able to report later that David's battery was running low. It's far too convenient.'

Cooper nodded, feeling slightly disappointed, though he didn't know why.

Villiers opened the door of the car again.

'I'll do The Stones, then, shall I?' she said.

'We'll both go,' said Cooper.

She watched him lock the car and pull on his jacket, folding the OS map and shoving it into his pocket.

'You want to go all the way up to Hurd Low and check out your theory, don't you?' said Villiers. 'Your speculation?'

Cooper smiled. 'You know me too well.'

They turned the corner by the youth hostel, past the entrance to Peveril Castle, which loomed above them on the hill. They entered The Stones by an outdoor clothing shop and found themselves in a narrow space between buildings, their footsteps echoing against the walls as they passed the tables outside the fish and chip shop. The river and the Peakshole Water bridge were just a few yards further on, where The Stones met Goose Hill.

Cooper tried to imagine that he and Villiers were David and Trisha Pearson leaving the George after their meal. With a bit of effort he could see the whole thing in his mind's eye – the Pearsons looking at the falling sleet as they walked out of the door of the George, pulling up the collars of their coats and setting out to walk in the direction of their holiday cottage.

It had been dark for hours by then, of course. But if the Pearsons had chosen this route via The Stones and Hurd Low, they wouldn't have left the street lamps of the town behind until they were on Goose Hill, just passing the last house and the back gates of Goose Hill Hall. He realised they were climbing quite steeply already, as they made their way up the slope of the hill overlooking Cavedale and the gorge of Peak Cavern itself.

He could picture the Pearsons reaching the top and coming out on to this gentler slope near Hurd Low, which had fine views in daylight towards Winnats Pass and Mam Tor. They must have had torches with them, because they would have been beyond any lights by that time, and the sky was heavily overcast. They would surely have been aiming to follow the path that linked up with the Limestone Way, just over the moor.

But the weather had changed in that time. The light flurries of sleet that had already been falling while they lingered in the George must have become more frequent as they walked up Goose Hill, turning to snow by the time they left the shelter of the town.

Cooper shook his head again. People so often didn't realise how different the weather conditions could be when you gained a few hundred feet in height. Within minutes, the Pearsons could have been struggling through a blizzard blown across the moor by the wind. Their torches would have been almost useless, the track disappearing rapidly under drifting snow.

Was that what they'd done? He wondered if there was a point where they'd considered turning round and going back to Castleton. Or had they simply pressed on, perhaps misjudging the distance to their cottage, which had been such an easy walk in daylight and fine weather? He imagined them laughing and thinking what fun it was to walk through the snow in the darkness, with the mountains of the Dark Peak lurking in the low clouds and the sounds of civilisation deadened by the snowfall. He could see even David Pearson running ahead, kicking up the snow, calling to his wife, perhaps making a snowball to throw at her. All a big joke. Just a bit of a laugh.

114

The amount of alcohol they'd consumed might well have impaired their judgement. Those two bottles of wine could have led them astray from the path. It only needed one rash decision, and they were lost. It was so easy to get disorientated on the moor, to follow a dry-stone wall for reassurance, then cross a stile in the wrong direction. He supposed the Pearsons didn't have a map with them, let alone a compass. Far too many walkers went on to the hills without any of the proper equipment.

Cooper looked at the OS map again. Those last few hundred yards, where the path south from Goose Hill ran alongside the Limestone Way, were scattered with the ominous symbols indicating disused mine workings.

Villiers had stopped, and he turned to see what she was doing.

'I'm starting to get the idea,' she said, with a hint of surprise in her voice.

'You are?'

'It felt really safe when we walking up past the houses. You're so closed in there, it's as though you're protected. It evens feels a bit claustrophobic, because the buildings are packed so close together.'

'I've often thought that about Castleton,' said Cooper.

'But it's misleading, isn't it? It gives you a false sense of security. Because once you're up here . . .'

She gestured towards Mam Tor, the sweep of her arm expressing the sudden wildness of the landscape. It was quite unexpected after the intimacy of Castleton's narrow lanes, even for someone who knew the area well.

Cooper followed her gaze. So when the Pearsons got up on to the moor, what would they do? Were they looking for a light in the distance to guide them? Had they been searching so hard that they hadn't seen the headlights of a car sitting on Goose Hill, where someone had been waiting for them? Were they surrounded by that eerie silence created by snow, the world around them white and dead and hushed? Or had the snow been driving horizontally across the moor, the wind moaning and whining like an animal?

It was funny how in winter everyone found it difficult to remember what summer was like, and in summer it was just as hard to imagine the cold of winter.

Yesterday, surrounded by acres of blackened heather, with smoke still drifting across the slopes, Cooper would have found it almost impossible to picture Oxlow Moor deep in snow. After months of dry, unseasonably warm weather, it took quite a leap of the imagination to visualise the freezing-cold conditions the Pearsons would have been struggling through that night. They must have gone over that same hill he could see now in the distance, but in the teeth of an icy wind and zero visibility.

Cooper recalled driving back from the Light House to Bridge End Farm one winter night many years ago, with horizontal sheets of snow streaming through the headlights of Matt's Land Rover and sweeping across the road. No one lost on the moors in those conditions would have stood a chance, unless they found shelter.

To the north of Oxlow Moor, Winnats Pass was hardly an easy road to negotiate at the best of times. But once a bit of snow began to settle, and drivers found their wheels failing to get traction on the first incline, they soon turned back and looked for another way out of Castleton. Well, there wasn't another route – not in this direction. The old A625 had been swept away by the landslides off Mam Tor years ago.

So, even if they had any visibility in the snowstorm, the Pearsons would have seen little or no traffic passing to the north. No headlights to reassure them that there were other people around that night.

Where was it the family came from again? Surrey, somewhere just south of London. Dorking, that was it. In their day-to-day lives, they were probably never out of sight or earshot of a major trunk road. They were within spitting distance of the permanently congested M25, almost under the flight paths of two of the busiest airports in the world.

The Peak District wasn't exactly the remote, inaccessible wastes of the Antarctic. But that night, for the Pearsons, it might as well have been.

When Villiers had gone, Cooper looked at his watch. It would be a good time to catch his brother at Bridge End Farm. Matt didn't like being disturbed during milking or when he was out on the tractor. But right now, he'd probably be tinkering in the workshop or the equipment shed.

'Ben? How's it going?' said Matt when he answered. 'Nothing wrong, is there?'

'No, no. Everything's fine.'

'We've not seen you and Liz for a while. We thought you might have called round.'

'Oh, why?'

'Well, aren't there things to discuss? I mean . . .'

'Oh, you mean the wedding.'

'Well, yeah.'

'We've been a bit busy, Matt. House-hunting, looking at cakes . . . You know the sort of thing.'

Matt sighed. 'Yes, I remember.'

'But you're right, we do need to talk some time.'

'Kate says I can't make any rude jokes during my speech,' said Matt. 'Is that right? I thought it was traditional for the best man.'

'You can say what you like, as far as I'm concerned,' said Ben.

'Good. I'm working on it. There are one or two incidents I remember . . .'

'Yes, well . . . don't forget how faulty your memory is sometimes.'

'We'll see.'

Ben hesitated, listening to the clang of a spanner in the workshop, picturing Matt carrying on working with one hand while holding his phone with the other.

'How's everything on the farm?' he asked. 'Are things picking up?'

'Well, I'm hoping we might make a bit of money from the wool this year,' said Matt. 'At least a fleece will be worth more than the cost of shearing it, for once.'

'That's good.'

There was a brief silence.

'Well,' said Matt, with a laugh. 'You didn't phone me to talk about the wedding arrangements, and I don't think you're really all that interested in the price of wool. So . . .?'

'You're right. It's do to with an inquiry that's come up again.'

'Ah, let me think. According to the news, they're reopening the case of that couple from down south who went missing.'

'That's right. The Pearsons. That's what I wanted to ask you about.'

Matt stopped clanging the spanner. 'Me? What would I know about it? I read the papers and listen to the local news like everyone else, but that's it.'

'That Christmas, around the time the Pearsons disappeared. Do you know when I mean?'

'Yes?'

'There was a party of some kind at the Light House, wasn't there?'

'The Eden Valley Young Farmers Club. It was their Christmas piss-up. I mean, celebration.'

'What night would that have been, Matt?'

'Monday, I think. I haven't been a member of the YFC for a good few years now, Ben. I'm too old. They don't want you when you're past twenty-six. We were only there that Christmas as guests. I judged the handling classes at the show for them earlier in the year.'

'Yes, I remember,' said Ben uncertainly.

In his mind were fragmentary flashbacks to the evening. A lot of sweating, laughing faces. Music, shouting, perhaps a bit of dancing. Christmas lights had been strung over the doors; a decorated tree stood in one of the windows.

'It was always a good do at the Light House,' said Matt. 'It was held just before they closed the pub for Christmas. There wasn't as much pressure to leave when eleven o'clock came round, if you know what I mean. The YFC lads took it as a challenge to drink the place dry.'

'Yes, of course. I'd forgotten the Light House used to close for Christmas until old Thomas Pilkington mentioned it.'

'The Whartons, who ran it, liked to have Christmas on their own, as a family. I can't fault them for that.'

'No.'

Ben was trying to picture the main bar area. Who had been there? He saw three middle-aged men sitting on a bench discussing the quality of the beer, two young couples laughing at a table full of vodka bottles, an elderly woman on her own in the corner with a glass of Guinness and a plastic carrier bag. Oh, and a noisy group standing at the bar. Not locals, surely.

'I wonder what happened to the Whartons when they had to leave the pub,' said Matt. 'I never heard.'

'I've no idea,' said Ben. 'I'll have to find out.'

'Anyway, you were quite a hit that night in the Light House.'

'Was I? I usually try to keep a low profile. So many people know that I'm a police officer.'

'Nobody would have taken too much notice of that, once you started singing.'

'You're kidding.' Ben shook his head. 'I don't remember that.'

'It's no wonder you don't remember.' Matt laughed again. 'You never could hold your drink that well, Ben. You were as pissed as a newt that night.'

11

Samantha Merritt would be in shock later. But Diane Fry knew the early stages could provide valuable information from bereaved relatives, details she might otherwise have to wait days for.

To some, her approach might seem cold and insensitive. Exploitative, even. She could practically hear it being said about her now, though behind her back, of course. But the family of a murder victim wanted the killer found, didn't they? And for that to happen, she needed information about the victim – as much of it as possible

'The funny thing is, Aidan called me and left a message,' said Samantha. 'He said he was on the moor near the fire. It can't have been very long before he, you know . . .'

'He was on Oxlow Moor? Near the pub where he was found?'

'Yes, up there somewhere. I just thought he'd gone to watch the fires. A lot of people do that, don't they?'

'Yes, I'm afraid so.'

'It's a funny kind of spectator sport. But Aidan was interested in things like that. He wanted to be at any big event he thought was likely to be in the news. I suppose it made him feel he was seeing history take place.'

Fry studied the room as Mrs Merritt spoke. The house was neat and clean, but otherwise unremarkable. The furniture and decor ranged through beige to off-white. Everything she saw seemed bland, much like the victim's widow herself. Samantha was a plain woman, with straight brown hair that seemed to have become instantly damp with her tears and hung raggedly round her face. She nervously tore tissues in half from a box at her elbow on the sofa.

'What did he say to you when he called you?' asked Fry.

'Well, he was rambling, not making any sense at all. Something about the ninth circle of hell.'

'The what?'

'The ninth circle of hell.'

'He must have been referring to the fires, I suppose.'

'He could have been,' said Samantha doubtfully. 'It feels so strange, the fact that those were his last words to me. And yet I couldn't understand what he was talking about. I wish he'd left me a different message.'

'I'm sorry.'

Fry was silent for a moment, allowing Samantha Merritt the surge of emotion. It mustn't overwhelm her, though. Not at this stage. Fry still needed her to focus.

'We found your husband's car, Mrs Merritt,' she said. 'A blue Ford Focus?'

'Oh, yes. I didn't think about the car. Where was it?'

'It had been parked at the side of a road near Oxlow Moor. It seems Mr Merritt left it there and walked the rest of the way to the Light House across the moor. It's possible he intended to get nearer, but was prevented by a road closure.'

'Road closure?'

'The fires.'

'Of course.'

Fry could see that the woman was having difficulty. In these circumstances, the mind tended to go round in circles, unable to cope with the facts it was being presented with. Unless she was guided, Samantha would keep coming back over and over to the ninth circle of hell, which wasn't helpful at all.

To concentrate Mrs Merritt's attention, Fry leaned forward and clasped her hands tightly together until the knuckles turned white, forming a focus point they could both see. She waited for the woman's eyes to settle on her hands.

'Mrs Merritt, have you any idea why your husband would have gone to that pub? It had been closed for six months.'

'The Light House, you mean? Aidan went there a lot.'

'Yes, but there could have been no point this time. It was closed,' insisted Fry, spelling out the words slowly and clearly. 'He must have known that.'

'Of course. Well . . . yes, I'm sure he did.' Samantha stared vaguely at Fry. 'I can't imagine. I don't know what he was thinking of.'

'Didn't he talk to you about it?'

'Not about where he was going. He must have gone up there right after school. He sometimes had to stay behind for a meeting or to do some marking or something like that, so I didn't expect him home straight away. He didn't drink heavily, but now and then he went for a drink with a few of the other teachers. They like to get together and have a good moan, you know.'

She laughed. It was that short laugh with the slightly hysterical overtones that Fry had heard from relatives before. It could mark the beginnings of denial, an insistence that nothing as ludicrous as the story she'd just been told could possibly have happened. *But I only spoke to him that afternoon,* they'd say, as if the whole world had taken an unbelievable turn of events in the meantime.

'He was a teacher at Edendale Community School,' said Fry. 'Is that right?'

123

'Yes. Aidan is . . . was an English teacher. He was good at his job. Oh, does the school know? I'll need to tell them. They'll be wondering where he is. Aidan isn't the type to call in sick, you see.'

'We'll deal with all that,' said Fry. 'There's no need for you to worry.'

There was a family liaison officer sitting in the room, a young female PC who'd made the tea now standing on a table in front of Mrs Merritt. Fry could see that it was untouched and going rapidly cold, a scum forming on the surface.

'The Light House,' repeated Fry. 'Why would Aidan have gone there? Please try to think what his reason might have been. Did he mention the pub at all recently?'

'Aidan never mentioned the Light House, once it had shut,' said Samantha. 'He started going somewhere else. Actually, he's been going to several different places. He never settled on a regular pub after the Light House.'

'Did he talk about meeting anyone?'

'No. Not that I can remember.'

'Didn't you go to the pub with him sometimes?'

She shook her head. 'I don't like pubs. I do take a drink now and then, but I prefer to stay at home with a nice bottle of wine and watch a DVD.'

'Perhaps you can give me the names of the other teachers,' said Fry.

'Who?'

'The ones he used to drink with sometimes after school.'

'Oh, certainly. I can give you one or two.'

Fry offered her a notebook. 'Please write them down while you're thinking about it.'

Mrs Merritt did as she was asked, scrawling two or three names with a shaky hand and passing the pad back to Fry.

'I need to ask you . . .' she said.

'Yes?'

'How did he die exactly?'

Fry had a copy of the post-mortem report right in front of her. When Mrs Merritt asked the question, she instinctively covered the file with her hand, in case any details were visible.

'Blunt-force trauma,' she said, repeating the Home Office pathologist's practised phrase.

Most murders in the UK were the result of blunt force or a bladed weapon. Bashing or stabbing – the two methods favoured by the British for doing each other in.

Samantha nodded, balling a tissue in her fist.

'Do you know what he was hit with?'

'Not exactly. Something heavy, made of wood. We're doing more tests, of course. We're hopeful of getting some forensic evidence that will help us catch the person who did it.'

'You haven't found the . . . weapon, then?'

'No.'

Fry knew that Mrs Merritt had identified the body of her husband earlier. Although Merritt had been cleaned up in the morgue, it would have been obvious what his fatal wounds were. It was impossible to conceal head injuries in the way the mortuary staff could sometimes keep damage to other parts of the body from the family.

The report in front of Fry talked about the results of the blows on Aidan Merritt's skull. There had been brain injuries both at the site of impact, and on the opposite side of the skull due to the contrecoup effect of the brain ricocheting within the skull.

In fact there had been three blows, the pathologist said. The first two had not been immediately fatal, but they had cracked the skull and certainly concussed the victim. They had also caused the leaking of cerebrospinal fluid, cerebral contusions, lacerations to the scalp and haemorrhaging of the skin. If Merritt had survived those two injuries, he might well have been left in a coma and suffered permanent brain damage. The bruising from the floor, the glass cuts to his face and hands – they seemed almost irrelevant.

But the third blow, the one that had struck Aidan Merritt when he was already on the ground, was the one that had pulverised the right side of his brain.

'Mrs Merritt, did your husband ever talk about David and Trisha Pearson?' asked Fry.

She shook her head in confusion. 'Who? Do they work at his school?'

'No. They were two visitors to the area who went missing a couple of years ago.'

'I don't understand.'

'Mr Merritt was interviewed at the time. The Pearsons visited the Light House shortly before they disappeared.'

'I think I remember that,' said Samantha, with a great effort. 'I didn't like him being interviewed by the police just because he was there at the pub that night. But he told me it was only routine. Isn't that right?'

'Yes, it is,' said Fry.

'Well then. I don't understand. I don't seem to understand anything.'

Fry watched her, judging that the moment had come when she wouldn't get any more information. She hadn't got very much at all from the visit. But she hoped that some day Mrs Merritt would be able to understand a little bit better.

Ben Cooper examined the buildings critically. On the night they disappeared, the Pearsons had been setting off from Castleton to walk here, to their holiday cottage, which turned out to be a two-bedroom conversion from some ancient outbuildings on Brecks Farm.

The Old Dairy, it was called. Looking at it, Cooper suspected it had been used for some less picturesque purpose than a dairy, but he supposed the name sounded better in the tourist brochures. The cottage stood well away from the farmhouse and the more modern agricultural buildings that had been erected much closer to the tarmac roadway running south towards the back road out of Peak Forest.

Whatever their purpose, the buildings that had become the Old Dairy would quickly have become awkward and inconvenient for modern farming practices. A rough track running back from the present farmyard had been maintained for the benefit of paying guests, but otherwise the situation of the cottage was quiet and undisturbed. Ideal for a peaceful holiday. Perfect if you wanted to drop out of sight for a while.

Cooper turned until his back was to the door of the cottage. The view was pretty peaceful too. It encompassed several acres of rough grazing dotted with sheep, and a backdrop of moorland, with a few other farmsteads nestled here and there in the landscape, all of them a good walk away from The Old Dairy.

And there, prominent on a rise to the north-west, was the Light House. Unlike the distant farms, its position made it seem surprisingly close. If he was a visitor to the area staying at this cottage, he would certainly have been tempted to walk to the pub in the evening. Probably every evening. Although it was uphill, the slope wasn't too steep and didn't look difficult to manage. No problem for anyone reasonably active, and eager for a pint or a bar meal. And there was always the reassurance that it would be mostly downhill coming back.

The Pearsons would have been familiar with the Limestone

Way. They'd used it earlier in the week, according to the statements. Coming back in the dark, in the snow, they would have looked for the little circular signs with their yellow arrows identifying the route. For most of its length here, the trail ran between dry-stone walls, which would have offered some protection from drifting snow for a while. In his own mind, there was no question. That was the way he would have come.

Well, as long as he was in his senses and not too befuddled by drink. Then, there was no saying what he might have done. The Pearsons might have taken the most familiar route, but not necessarily the safest.

David Pearson had that look in the eyes. Confident, but unpredictable – the sort of man who would get an idea in his head, and then move heaven and earth to follow it through, against all the best advice and in the teeth of good sense. Trisha must have seen that in him. It was probably what had appealed to her, that aura of danger and unpredictability.

Cooper consulted the OS map again, and scanned the countryside around Brecks Farm.

'Where does that track go to, I wonder?' he said.

'Shall we see?' asked Villiers.

'Fine.'

They bumped up the track, kicking up dust from their wheels, until they turned a bend and were stopped by a steel barrier.

It was an abandoned quarry. Some sites in the Peak District had been cleared up and machinery removed, then either converted to a different use, such as landfill, or restored to agriculture. This one was too recently abandoned, perhaps. The entrance gate was blocked by large chunks of calcite, left as if for display as geological samples.

Just inside the site, a series of blue shipping containers

stood at one side of the roadway, with their doors left gaping open. One of them had been used as a store for equipment spares such as conveyors, pumps and screens. The sides of the interior still carried labels with faintly mysterious names: *Transfer Conveyor*, *Crusher*, *Cobbles Belt*, *Pearls One*. The door had been wedged open with a wooden pallet, and there was little left inside it now.

Outside, though, the ground was littered with long strips and rolls of black conveyor belt. They were heaped and scattered everywhere, as if the departing workers had simply thrown everything out of the containers before they left the site. Among the debris were broken bits of machinery, part of a drive shaft from a quarry vehicle. Two smaller containers were perched precariously on a pile of corrugated-iron roofing sections.

Further into the quarry was an abandoned lorry, digging equipment, a caravan that might once have been used as a site office. The signs warned of blasting and cautioned Cooper to observe a ten miles per hour speed limit. The barriers would not stop anyone who wanted to enter the site, but the machinery was too big to steal, so it had been left.

Now, only the sound of birds disturbed the site, where once there would have been a deafening cacophony of machinery, crushed stone and blasting.

'This must have been searched at the time,' said Cooper. 'Oh, surely.'

He wished he could feel as confident as he was trying to sound. Something had gone wrong in the original investigation of the Pearsons' disappearance, and he wasn't yet sure what it was. In fact, he had no firm idea at all.

Back at the office, Luke Irvine had been landed with the job of ploughing through all the old witness statements, search reports and case files. It was a thankless task, but someone had to do it, just in case a fresh pair of eyes spotted something new.

'I'll get Luke to check,' said Cooper. 'It might make him feel a bit more involved.'

Returning to the entrance, Cooper found himself standing in a gateway looking at a little circular sign with its yellow arrow identifying the Limestone Way. He'd noticed that right below it was another sign, with no words on it, only a simple graphic. It showed a small human figure falling head first into a hole in the ground.

Its message ought to be clear. But how many people set off to walk across the moors without any realisation of the dangers under their feet?

Cooper tried to imagine the Pearsons thinking they could follow the Limestone Way in the dark, and in a snowstorm too. If that was what they'd done, it could only be called foolhardy in the extreme. He supposed they weren't the first ill-prepared travellers to have lost their lives on these moors. But it shouldn't happen in the twenty-first century.

12

When they arrived back at West Street, Cooper soon heard that the body at the Light House had been identified, and the dead man's wife already interviewed. That was Diane Fry, working fast as usual. If he wasn't careful, she'd have this whole thing tied up in a neat bow within a few days, and all his vague doubts would count for nothing.

Cooper made a point of asking Fry to bring the team up to date. He suspected it wouldn't happen otherwise. She would be reporting to her own DCI, and local CID would get bypassed. He couldn't bear the thought that he'd continue to be left out in the cold, wondering what was happening, until he heard about some development on the office grapevine.

Fry had been allocated an old office that had recently been vacated by some centralised civilian staff member. It was little more than a cubbyhole, with frosted glass in the windows. It meant that she couldn't be seen when she closed the door, except as a blurred movement inside.

Rather reluctantly, she emerged from her little office and joined everyone else in the CID room. Watching her enter, Cooper could see her already in the role of a detective inspector, shutting herself off from the troops because she had more important things to do than the same old donkey work. He wondered when her promotion would come. It was long overdue now, surely? He bet Fry herself secretly thought so. It might even be eating away at her inside, making her even more grouchy than usual.

'Aidan Merritt was never a suspect,' Fry explained, when she had everyone's attention. 'He was interviewed when officers in the original inquiry were trying to trace the Pearsons' movements over the last couple of days before their disappearance.'

'What was his connection?'

'The Pearsons were at the Light House the night before their visit to Castleton. So far, that seems to be the only connection with Aidan Merritt, who was a regular there. It's a rather tenuous link, admittedly. But the fact is that Merritt's name was in the system from the original inquiry. An officer spoke to him when they were trying to plot the Pearsons' movements. And once you're in the system, the computer is likely to keep coughing your name up whenever there's a hint of a match.'

'I went through the statements taken from Merritt and some of the other regulars,' said Irvine. 'It seems there was another group of visitors in the pub that night. Two men and two women. Several witnesses mentioned seeing them talking to the Pearsons. They were thought to be staying in a holiday cottage nearby too.'

Cooper looked out of the window at the distant edges of the moor. 'Do we know which one exactly?'

'No.'

'The Pearsons were definitely alone at the George, weren't they? They didn't meet up with this other group?'

'It doesn't seem so.'

'We'll never know what was said between them, anyway. Not unless we can trace the unknown group, and that looks like a very tall order.'

'Yes, I agree.'

For a start, they would have to identify all the holiday cottages within walking distance of the Light House. Some of them might have been sold in the last two years and converted into permanent homes. More likely, though, the trend would be the other way round. He expected to find a greater number of holiday cottages in the area now than there were when the Pearsons visited.

'Another rented cottage, I suppose?' he said. 'Not one they owned themselves.'

'Oh, I think so. If they owned it, they would probably have visited the area regularly, wouldn't they? Someone would have known them.'

Cooper nodded. In that case, he'd be relying on a property owner with good records, or a lucky entry in a guest book.

'Needle in a haystack come to mind?'

'I don't suppose it was followed up all that well,' said Fry. 'Another lead that was just recorded and written off, I imagine.'

This was what Cooper had been worried about. The Pearsons had been in the Light House the night before they disappeared. That had been picked up by the original inquiry, with all those unproductive witness statements taken from the likes of Aidan Merritt and the other regulars and staff at the pub.

But he was pretty sure the couple had been there the previous evening too, the night of the YFC party. Why had no one ever mentioned that?

Well, it seemed the investigation had only examined the final two days before David and Trisha Pearson went missing, at least in any detail. The SIO might have made a decision not to expend resources needlessly on trying to trace the Pearsons' movements earlier in the week. There was a law of diminishing returns in these things. You could spend more and more time on a particular line of enquiry, allocating

133

more and more resources, but find that you got fewer and fewer returns on the effort. Someone had to make a decision where the cut-off point came.

Still, it was a little bit odd, if the Pearsons had also been present at the Light House the night before, that no mention was made of it anywhere in the statements. Was that actually the case? He hadn't been through the statements himself, so he couldn't be certain. He'd better tell someone now, before things went any further.

'Diane,' he said, 'have you got a minute?'

She raised an eyebrow, but led him back into the little office she'd been allocated.

'What is it?'

Cooper explained to her about the evening at the Light House, the Young Farmers Club, and his recognition of David Pearson.

'A Young Farmers' event?' said Fry. 'You mean prehistoric mating rituals, with extra straw?'

'Something like that,' said Cooper, feeling a flush rising.

'And I suppose a vast amount of alcohol was consumed?'

'I'm afraid so.'

Fry studied him for a moment, a smile playing at the corners of her lips. Cooper rarely saw her break into a smile, and he didn't care for this one. He knew he was the object of her amusement, and he found it infuriating.

'From experience, I'm guessing that you weren't entirely sober either, DS Cooper,' she said.

'It was a Christmas party.'

As he said it, he could hear Matt's voice in the back of his mind. *You were as pissed as a newt that night.* If Matt thought he was drunk, then it was certainly true. Fry's 'not entirely sober' was an understatement, for once.

'I just thought it would be surprising if no one mentioned it in the statements taken from the Light House.'

'Due to a communal alcoholic haze perhaps?'

'Possibly. I'll get Luke Irvine to double-check, shall I? He's been going through the files. What do you think?'

Fry had stopped smiling now, which was a relief. He could see her brain working, weighing up the advantages.

'Yes, good idea.'

'I'll get on to it.'

Cooper felt a bit more bounce in his step as he went back into the CID room. He had a slightly different view to Fry's, though that was perfectly normal. He wasn't thinking of a communal alcoholic haze on the part of the Light House staff and customers – more of a rather curious bit of collective amnesia.

In fact, the original inquiry had done a surprisingly thorough job of examining accounts of the Pearsons' visit to the Light House. There was an entire file containing statements from staff and customers, and even a sketch plan showing where all the people spoken to had sat or stood in the bar, in relation to the Pearsons. Someone had worked quite hard on that. It must have taken a considerable amount of time to put together. Above and beyond the call of duty, really.

Then Cooper noticed the date on the plan, and realised it had been drawn up some months after the disappearance. He wondered if the date would correspond with some particularly high-profile bit of media coverage, or additional pressure from the Pearson family.

'If only we could understand why Aidan Merritt had to die.'

'Well, it's simple. He must have had incriminating information. Someone needed to shut him up.'

'But why leave it all this time? If he knew something

135

about the fate of David and Trisha Pearson, the chances are he'd known it for the past couple of years. So why wait until now? Did they think he was about to start talking?'

His last question sounded rhetorical, even to himself. No one bothered answering it. Instead, Villiers moved quickly on to the next question.

'And what made him agree to meet the person who killed him? Because that's what must have happened, isn't it? Merritt went to the Light House voluntarily. There could have been no other reason, except to meet someone. The pub had been closed for months. And in view of the fires spreading across the moors, it was a location you'd want to avoid unless you had a very pressing reason to be there.'

'You wouldn't meet a person you were about to incriminate, though, would you?' said Fry. 'That doesn't make any sense. Aidan Merritt wasn't stupid, after all. Do you think he'd agree to a meeting with the one individual who had a reason to get him out of the way? And on his own, in an isolated spot? No.'

'He could have been lured to the pub by someone else,' suggested Hurst. 'Someone he trusted.'

'Conspiracy now?'

'Well, what else?'

'Are we suggesting that Merritt was somehow implicated in the Pearson inquiry himself?'

'Yes, I think so.'

'We've found nothing in his circumstances to suggest that.'

'The fact that you haven't found anything doesn't mean he was innocent. You can't prove a negative. Not like that, anyway.'

'He was there at the pub on the night before the Pearsons disappeared. We've established that much at least.'

'But we don't have a single witness to suggest he had any contact with them.'

'Where does our chart put him?'

'Down at the far end of the bar, at a table near the games room,' said Irvine.

'He was on his own, though?'

'Sort of.'

'Sort of? What does that mean?'

'Well, he was a regular at the Light House. He knew a lot of people. You know what it's like when you're in your local.'

Irvine looked at Diane Fry, seemed to decide that she might not know what it was like at all.

'Look, we interviewed a number of customers who spoke to Merritt during the evening. He chatted for a while to some old biddy called Betty Wheatcroft. She remembered discussing how badly behaved young people were these days.'

'Old biddy?'

'Yes. Every pub has one.'

'All right.'

'So . . . he chatted to Mrs Wheatcroft. At one point Merritt was asked to make up a foursome for a game of pool. They might not have called him a friend, and he certainly seems to have gone there by himself. But he had a lot of acquaintances. He was among people he knew. Some of them he'd known since childhood. That's not the same as being on your own.'

The expression on Fry's face suggested that it might be possible to be alone among any number of acquaintances, but she let it pass.

'It still seems odd,' she said. 'I mean, no matter how many casual acquaintances he had, it's a bit odd for a man to go the pub on his own just before Christmas and sit at a table by himself, surrounded by crowds of people celebrating, having parties, getting drunk.'

She glanced at Cooper briefly as she made the last remark. It was a very quick gesture, but everyone noticed it, he was sure. Fry didn't always need to say anything to make her point.

'We talked to his wife,' pointed out Hurst. 'She doesn't like going to pubs. She does drink, but says she prefers to stay at home and get a bottle of wine, watch a DVD or something. But she accepted that Aidan liked the company in the bar. He didn't drink heavily, she says. So it was perfectly normal, for him.'

'He didn't drink heavily?'

'No.'

'So he must have been relatively sober on that night. And from his seat near the games room, he would have had a clear view down the bar. Correct me if I'm wrong, but surely he would have been able to watch David and Trisha Pearson from there all evening, without any trouble.'

'You're wrong,' said Irvine.

Fry raised a cool eyebrow at him. 'Oh?'

'Well, you're forgetting something.'

'What?'

'The bar was absolutely packed. It was heaving. There must have been dozens of people between Merritt and the Pearsons, and most of them standing up too. He would have had trouble fighting his way to the bar to get served, let alone continually observing someone at the other end of the room, especially if he was sitting down. It's just not feasible.'

'That's not to say . . .'

'All right,' admitted Irvine. 'That's not to say he didn't see something. Like you said, we can't prove a negative.

138

'Not in that way,' said Fry. 'Not at all.'

'The only thing we can do is make a start on interviewing everyone we know to have been in the bar, and try to cross-match from their accounts.'

'There must have been people coming and going all night. It's hopeless.'

'We need to cover all the ground again,' said Fry. 'But we should also be looking for things that weren't done at the time. If Aidan Merritt had some connection with the Pearsons, we need to find out what it was.'

'How do we do that?'

'Talk to people who knew him. There must have been some at the Light House.'

'We've got the name of a full-time barman, Josh Lane,' said Irvine. 'And a few of the kitchen staff. Then there are the customers Merritt spent time with. It's a short list, though. Vince Naylor, Ian Gullick . . . and that's about it. The person Mr Merritt seems to have talked to most is Betty Wheatcroft.'

'The old biddy?'

'That's the one. From her statement, she sounds to be as odd as Merritt. But I suspect as well educated.'

'Kindred spirits, then.'

Cooper surveyed his mental image of the bar at the Light House, managed to locate someone like Betty Wheatcroft sitting in a corner with a glass of Guinness and a plastic carrier bag. As Irvine had said, every pub had one. He might just be filling in the details from a hundred other old biddies sitting in the corner of a bar, but the image seemed real enough.

'What are you thinking?' asked Villiers.

'I'm thinking that I can see her already.'

'Ben, there's no need to start imagining things. Just stick

to the facts. That was always your weakness, you know – you're much too imaginative for a police officer.'

'Thanks for the advice, DC Villiers. I'll bear it in mind.'

Fry pulled on her jacket and turned to leave. Cooper caught up with her and stopped her with a touch on her arm.

'Diane . . .'

'Yes?'

'Our tasks are overlapping now,' pointed out Cooper. 'There's no way round it.'

'I suppose so.'

'I realise your DCI has other irons in the fire on the Merritt inquiry – forensic evidence must be producing some leads?'

'Yes.'

'But we could be turning up some equally useful information from our end.'

'Just keep feeding it into the inquiry through me,' said Fry. 'And we'll assess its value.'

Cooper knew he'd have to accept that. He'd tried his best to get further into the inquiry, but he'd failed. Fry was a brick wall. He'd have to find another way, that was all.

'There's one more thing,' he said.

'Spit it out, then. I've got plenty of things to do.'

'I think you're coming down too hard on Luke and Becky. They're my team. You don't have any right to talk to them the way you do.'

Fry gritted her teeth before she spoke.

'Have you any idea how frustrating this is for me?'

'What is?'

'To think that I've finally got away from this place – and then to find I have to come back, and it's full of all these irritating little Ben Cooper clones that I'm supposed to work with.'

Cooper found himself breathing too quickly, the surge of anger coming so fast that it frightened him.

'Luke and Becky? They're good kids. I can't believe you said that.'

'Try taking a look at yourselves from the outside, that's all.'

She began to turn away, which angered him even more.

'You can't—'

'Yes I can,' she said over her shoulder. 'I can do anything I like now. And there's no way you can hold me back any more.'

DI Hitchens had his office door open, and called Cooper in when he saw him passing in the corridor. The DI still looked tired. Perhaps even more than ever. He had the air of a man battling a long, slow war of attrition. And a man who also knew he was losing.

'We have a visitor arriving in Edendale tomorrow,' said Hitchens.

'Who?'

'Mr Henry Pearson. That's David Pearson's father.'

'Oh, I see.'

'He's been campaigning for years to find out the truth about what happened to his son and daughter-in-law.'

'Yes, I know,' said Cooper. 'He was in the papers every week for quite some time.'

'And on TV, making appeals to the public. Until the media eventually lost interest.'

'As they always do.'

'It was worse than that, though,' said Hitchens.

'What do you mean?'

141

'There was that theory about what had happened to the Pearsons. The deliberate disappearance, you know?'

'That was total conjecture, wasn't it?'

'Yes, but it was picked up by the media with unholy enthusiasm. They don't like stories where the outcome is just left hanging. Their readers get frustrated. So the suggestion that David and Trisha Pearson had planned their own disappearing act and were living abroad somewhere under false names was perfect fodder for them. They took it and ran with it for months. Even now, if you do an online search for their names, you'll come up with page after page of stuff on the internet supporting that theory. Countries where they're living have been suggested. People say they've seen evidence that they're still alive – photos, emails, credit card purchases. You know the sort of thing.'

'We must have pursued those leads at the time.'

Hitchens laughed. 'Of course. Well, the ones that seemed to have any merit, anyway. You can't just sit on your hands, no matter how much you think they're rubbish. You've got to be seen to be doing something, especially these days. Otherwise you get bombarded with complaints about police inactivity and incompetence. turning a blind eye or looking the other way. Corruption even. So, yes – a lot of those reports were followed up, and none of them turned out to have any merit. It was all conspiracy theory stuff. People love it, don't they?'

'And Henry Pearson?'

'He became a victim of the conspiracy theorists. Because he was so high profile, because he was so vociferous in his efforts to argue that David and Trisha had met some tragic end, he turned himself into a target. The accusations were that he was the cover-up man, that he was making as much fuss as possible to distract attention from what had actually happened. People said that all his emotional hand-wringing was just an act designed to influence the direction of the inquiry, to ensure that all our attention was focused on conducting a futile search for bodies.'

'Did he do a lot of emotional hand-wringing?' asked Cooper.

'Actually, no,' admitted Hitchens. 'I always thought he was very calm and controlled. I was impressed with him. It seemed to me that he always put his points across powerfully, but very reasonably. There was a logic to his arguments. If you've had much experience of bereaved family members, you'll appreciate how rare that is, Ben.'

'Naturally. Very few people can keep emotion out of their reactions in a situation like that.'

Hitchens nodded. 'Mind you, I'm not saying Mr Pearson was never emotional. He and his wife came up here when David and Trisha were first reported missing. They both went through the emotional stage. But Henry was the stronger of the two. He got himself under control pretty quickly. We found that very useful in the early days. He was able to give us all kinds of information that we asked for. In the end, though, that was one of the problems.'

'Problems?'

'In a sense. You see, the information Mr Pearson gave us actually supported the theory about a deliberate disappearance. Without Henry Pearson's assistance, it would have taken us a lot longer to find out what his son had been up to.'

13

At the house in Manvers Street, on Edendale's Devonshire Estate, the door was answered by a woman in her mid-forties, with hair in blonde streaks and a hint of hardness in her eyes. A lifetime spent in the pub business could leave some individuals jaundiced about humanity. In fact, any job where you dealt with the public all the time could do that to you, as Diane Fry knew only too well herself.

'We're looking for Maurice Wharton,' said Fry.

The woman looked at him oddly, a stare with no perceivable emotion.

'Well you're too late,' she said.

'Why? Where has he gone?'

'He'll be up there in the cemetery soon.'

She jerked her head towards the slope that led up to Edendale's new burial ground. Fry studied her more closely, seeking a clue to her emotional state. Grief was difficult to interpret sometimes. She might just have caught this woman at an early stage, before the shock had worn off and the barriers came down.

'I'm very sorry. And you *are* Mrs Wharton?'

'I suppose so. I still carry the name, don't I?'

Fry glanced at Hurst, but she was too good at maintaining a neutral expression on her face to give anything away.

'I apologise if it's a bad time, Mrs Wharton,' said Fry. 'But we do need to speak to you. It's about the Light House.'

Mrs Wharton shook her head wearily. 'Oh, the Light House. I thought we'd buried that, too.'

She ushered Fry and Hurst into the house. A teenage girl stood in the hall, a thinner version of Nancy Wharton.

'Are you the police?' she said.

'Yes.'

'I'm Kirsten Wharton, this is my mother.'

'We're sorry to hear about your father.'

Kirsten shook her head. 'He's not actually dead.'

'What? But I thought your mother just . . .?'

'Mum gets like that sometimes. I think she's trying to get used to the idea that Dad will be gone soon.'

'I don't understand.'

'He has pancreatic cancer. Terminal. That's what they call it, isn't it? When they're trying to tell you someone is going to die, without actually spelling it out.'

'I'm sorry,' said Fry again.

The teenager shrugged. 'It's no skin off your nose, I suppose.'

They entered a cramped sitting room. The room wasn't just small, it was stuffed with too much furniture. Fry had to squeeze past the arm of a large black leather sofa and a couple of armchairs to reach a cream rug laid in front of the fireplace. The rug covered the whole of the available floor space, except for a few glimpses of carpet in the gaps between display cabinets, standard lamps and occasional tables lining the walls. The mantelpiece and the shelves of the cabinets were packed with china and brass ornaments.

She turned and looked at the fireplace, but a large gas fire stood on the hearth in front of it. A real coal fire wouldn't be possible here – its heat would scorch the furniture and roast the feet of anyone sitting so close to it.

Fry would have liked the chance to study the ornaments more closely, and to examine the bookshelves, if there were any. Those details could tell you a lot about the owner, more than any number of personal questions.

But that wasn't possible here. Even if Mrs Wharton wasn't standing looking at her expectantly, she couldn't have reached a single display cabinet without moving the rest of the furniture out of the room first.

She recalled the deserted owner's accommodation at the Light House. There had been far more space for the Whartons when they were living there. Two adults with two children? They could have spread themselves out as much as they wanted. Some of this furniture might even have been in the bar, or the dining area. But there was no way they could have brought everything with them to this council house in Edendale. Other items might be in storage somewhere, but a lot must have been left behind as fixtures and fittings, all part of the package for a potential buyer at the forthcoming auction.

'About the Light House?' said Mrs Wharton. 'Go on, then.'

'There's been an incident.'

She looked unperturbed. 'Yes, I heard there'd been a break-in.'

'More than a break-in. One of your old regulars got himself killed there.'

Nancy looked up then, her face creased in puzzlement.

'Killed?'

'Haven't you been following the news? Didn't you know someone had been killed?'

'No, I suppose I must have missed it.'

'Mum has more than enough on her mind,' put in Kirsten. 'She doesn't have time for worrying about what's going on in the news.'

Fry turned to her. 'Not even when it's at the Light

146

House? I thought someone would have mentioned it to you.'

'We've lost touch since we moved into town. We never see anyone. Do we, Mum?'

Nancy was still looking at Fry intensely.

'Who was it?'

'Aidan Merritt. Do you remember him?'

'Yes, I remember him. He drank at the pub a lot when it was open. But what was he doing there . . .?'

'We don't know. I was hoping you or Mr Wharton might be able to help.'

'You were wrong there, then.'

'But you must recall the Pearsons? David and Trisha?'

'Oh, the tourists who went missing.' Nancy sounded weary to the core now. 'We know nothing about them. We knew nothing then, and we know nothing now. What's the point of going over it?'

'Is your husband well enough for us to speak to?' asked Fry.

'I told you, he's dying.'

In fact she'd said that he was already dead, but Fry let it pass. She looked at Kirsten instead. She was what? Fifteen or sixteen? But she seemed very mature for her age, the way some teenagers were these days.

'Dad is in the hospice,' said Kirsten. 'St Luke's, here in Edendale. He won't be coming out again now.'

'I'm sorry.'

'Yes, you said. We didn't believe you the first time.'

Nancy stood up. 'There's no way I would let you talk to Maurice, even if he was well enough. I'll phone the hospice right now and tell them not to let you through the door. If you try to harass him, I'll make your life hell. Give the man a bit of peace in his final days.'

It was clearly a waste of time. On her way out, Fry looked

147

at Nancy Wharton again, noting that hint of hardness in her eyes. The result of a lifetime in the pub trade? Perhaps.

But Fry reminded herself that Nancy had gone through particular troubles of her own in the last couple of years. She'd lost the Light House after a fruitless struggle against financial difficulties, and now she had to deal with the husband's terminal illness, which was likely to be another long, futile battle.

Betty Wheatcroft lived in an old cottage right on the outskirts of Edendale. It must have been in a village once, but the town had swallowed it up decades ago. Now the cottage, and a few others like it, was sandwiched between the clubhouse of Edendale Golf Club and a small industrial estate whose units housed an MOT test centre and a signmaker's.

When he got out of the car, Cooper inhaled the air, detecting an all too familiar smell. Even on the edge of Edendale, a hint of acrid smoke was on the wind. He looked at the roof of a car parked outside the nearest house. Black flecks speckled the surface like the first spots of a dark, soot-filled rain.

As soon as he knocked, a woman's face appeared round the edge of the door and scrutinised his ID.

'Detective Sergeant Cooper, Edendale CID,' he said. 'Are you Mrs Wheatcroft?'

'Come in, come in,' said the woman. 'Don't stand outside. Our neighbours are like the CIA – they'll have the binoculars and microphones trained on you already.'

Cooper thought she was joking, but she took hold of his sleeve and almost dragged him into the hall.

Betty Wheatcroft had wild grey hair, and her eyes showed a faintly manic gleam. If there had been any weapons in the room, a kitchen knife lying on the table maybe, he wouldn't have felt entirely safe. As it was, he found himself checking his route to the door, in case he needed to make a hasty retreat. Strange, how that fixed stare could be so unsettling. He supposed it was an instinctive fear of insanity, a primal distrust of the unpredictable.

'It's very distressing,' she said. 'I haven't been able to eat since I heard. I haven't been out of the house.'

'There's no need to be afraid, Mrs Wheatcroft,' said Cooper.

'Are you sure?'

She looked towards the window, as if fearing a murderer stalking her street. But what threat could there be to her from the golf club or the MOT test centre?

'Aidan,' she said. 'Yes, I knew poor Aidan. Shocking business. Shocking. But that's the sort of thing that happens these days, isn't it? It goes on all over the place. None of us is safe. We're not safe even in this street. That's why the so-called Neighbourhood Watch knock on my door all the time.'

'Aidan Merritt,' said Cooper, realising straight away that his main task would be to keep Mrs Wheatcroft on track. He was very accustomed to these visits to old people living on their own. They were often lonely, and didn't get many visitors. The result was that they seized eagerly on any human company and the chance of a bit of conversation. It was one of the things that made them so vulnerable to distraction thefts, and attractive as prey for the smooth-talking conmen who pretended to be from the electricity company. Many elderly people had lost hundreds of pounds just because they wanted someone to talk to.

But this was his last job of the day, and he hoped the visit wouldn't stretch out too long. Liz had plans for the evening. She'd lined up a viewing of her preferred wedding venue, and his presence there was essential.

'I felt sorry for him, trying to teach children these days,' said Mrs Wheatcroft. 'It must be a thankless task. Schools are all about targets and test results. You don't really get a chance to *teach* them anything. Well, that's what I told him. And he seemed to agree with me.'

Cooper smiled as he looked round the interior of the cottage. Plenty of books and papers in haphazard piles, framed photographs of a younger Mrs Wheatcroft with groups of small children, a home-made farewell card covered in scrawled signatures.

'Were you a teacher yourself, Mrs Wheatcroft?' he asked.

'Yes, how did you know?'

'It was just a guess.'

'I worked in local schools for thirty-five years,' she said. 'I've seen some changes, I can tell you.'

'Aidan Merritt,' said Cooper. 'Who else did he talk to at the Light House?'

'Oh, well . . . I suppose there was that Ian Gullick. Horrible man.'

'Gullick?'

'He's a van driver, delivers motor parts to garages or something.' She chuckled. 'At least he does when he's got his driving licence.'

'Meaning?'

'He got banned from driving.'

Mrs Wheatcroft's look of satisfaction was unsettling. The smile was a little too smug – the contentment of a trick or spell that had worked successfully.

'What happened?' asked Cooper.

'He had too much to drink at the Light House one night. Not that that was unusual. But he'd made himself particularly obnoxious that evening. Someone called the police and reported him for drink-driving. But he'd never actually tried to drive away. He was arrested while he was sleeping in his van in the pub car park. The police found the keys in his pocket, and charged him with being drunk in charge of a vehicle. Banned for twelve months.'

'So who reported him? Who made the call?'

'How should I know?'

Cooper was starting to get a bit irritated by the way people answered his questions with another question. Especially that one. *How should I know?* It was always employed to sound like a denial, but it was actually just another evasion.

'There were a few others,' said Mrs Wheatcroft. 'Vince Naylor. Mmm . . . not many, though. Aidan was a bit of a loner, actually. You might say he was quite odd, in a way.'

Interesting. Those names had already been mentioned earlier, in the office. Ian Gullick, yes. And Vince Naylor. Cooper made a discreet note.

'The night before the Pearsons disappeared,' he said, 'there was another group of visitors in the pub. They were seen talking to the Pearsons.'

'Not local?'

'No. Visitors.'

She ran a hand through her hair, disarranging it even more.

'I think I remember. They were from down south somewhere.'

'They were staying in a holiday cottage nearby too, were they?'

'Rented, yes. Most visitors are only around for a week or two.'

Cooper gazed out of the window, and saw that the edge of the moor was just visible beyond the green at the ninth hole of the golf club.

'If you can remember the name of those people, or where they came from in the south, that would be a big help,' he said.

Mrs Wheatcroft looked at him with a sudden flash of inspiration. 'Watford,' she said. 'They came from Watford. I can see them now, sitting in that corner near the window. I can see their matching cagoules and woollen sweaters. And I can hear him talking about the football club. They came from Watford.'

'You went to the Light House often, didn't you?'

'Not that often,' she said cautiously. 'Not on my pension. Besides, I don't have a car. I needed a lift to get up there. Either that or a taxi, which is too expensive for a pensioner like me.'

'And that night?'

'I went with my daughter. She's divorced.'

'And was Aidan Merritt there?'

'Yes, of course.' She leaned closer, with a conspiratorial half-wink. 'But there was one night the previous week when his wife was there on her own.'

'Mrs Merritt?' said Cooper in surprise.

'Samantha, that's her name. Plain-looking girl. She ought to put in a bit more effort. But I had a bit of a joke with her.'

'Did you, Mrs Wheatcroft?'

'I told her that if she sat on her own in that place, she'd be pestered by men all night. But she didn't seem to care.'

Cooper frowned. 'Do you think Samantha might actually have been there with the intention of picking up a man?'

Mrs Wheatcroft gave a short laugh, then shook her head again. 'No, that's wrong. I shouldn't laugh. We don't know anything about other people's lives, do we? She might have been doing that, for all I know.'

'Did you see her talking to anyone?'

'No, I don't think so. There were people around her, at other tables. But she didn't seem to be speaking to anyone.'

'You're sure?'

'Yes. Well . . . pretty sure.'

Mmm. Perhaps a hint of a memory there that might surface later?

'If you do remember anything later, Mrs Wheatcroft, please give me a call. It could be important.'

'Yes, I see that.'

'And it was definitely Watford, was it?' asked Cooper. 'The town those visitors came from?'

She looked surprised. 'Watford? No, no. Coventry – that was the place.'

Mrs Wheatcroft beamed at him, her face lighting up with a smile that suggested pride in an achievement. Cooper recognised that look. He'd seen it often in his own mother as she grew older – that delight in plucking a name from the air that had almost managed to elude her. After a while, every accurate recollection became a minor triumph.

Then she frowned.

'Or it might have been Northampton,' she said.

Cooper sighed. When he looked at Mrs Wheatcroft again, he realised that she was just like his mental image of the typical madwoman in the attic – the first Mrs Rochester perhaps, prone to alcoholism and fits of violence.

The impression was so strong that Cooper found himself expecting an insane laugh to follow him as he left her cottage and walked back towards the gate.

14

Cooper's life was becoming dominated by lists. Their headings ran through his mind like a well-practised litany. Organists, choirs, cakes, cars, bells, banns, veils, vows, videos, rings, dresses, flowers, music, DJs and seating plans for the reception. Bridesmaids, bouquets, ushers, pageboys, speeches, guest lists, gift lists, hen nights and centrepieces for the tables at the wedding breakfast. Even honeymoon outfits, for heaven's sake. If they ever made it that far.

He'd bought Liz a Kindle for Christmas. The first books she'd downloaded were *The Complete Wedding Planner* and *The Step by Step Guide to Planning Your Wedding*, closely followed by *Get into Shape for your Wedding Day*. Well at least she'd stopped looking at brochures for destination weddings in the Seychelles.

There was a list of potential wedding venues too, of course. The venue currently top of the list was deep in one of the wooded dales on the banks of the River Wye, not far from Bakewell. It was a former mill owner's house, quite a fanciful piece of gothic architecture in itself, but standing in a wonderful position, with twenty acres of woodland and the most fantastic views over the river.

Liz had her eye on the floral arcade for an outdoor ceremony. It was bit optimistic, given the vagaries of the weather in this part of the world. But no bride ever expected her wedding day to be spoiled by rain. Everything was going to be perfect, including the weather.

There was always the orangery, where the reception would take place. Cooper measured the distance by eye. It wasn't too far to run if the rain started. Well, unless you were wearing a wedding dress with a train as long as the Monsal Viaduct. He wondered if it was one of the groom's duties to carry the bride indoors to escape a thunderstorm, as well carrying her over the threshold of their new home. That wasn't mentioned in any of the wedding planning guides.

Nor was the fact that their new home might only be a pipe dream, its threshold purely notional as well as symbolic.

'The orangery can seat up to ninety, if we use the room that opens into it as well,' said Liz.

'Ninety?'

'Up to.'

'Do we even know ninety people to speak to?'

'I've got a big family, especially on my dad's side. There'll be cousins coming from all over the place.'

'Oh yes. The Scottish Pettys. Half of Dundee will be coming down on a coach trip, I suppose.'

'And they can stay right here, Ben. It's perfect. There are cottages in the grounds. They can accommodate up to fifty people at a time. No one will have to drive back home afterwards if they don't want to.'

'So they can all get well oiled on the Glenlivet.'

'It *is* a celebration,' she said accusingly.

Immediately he began to regret sounding flippant.

'Yes, of course it is. The Dundee Pettys can drink as much Glenlivet as they want, as far as I'm concerned. I might even check to see if the bar has any Laphroaig.'

She squeezed his arm. 'It's going to be wonderful, you'll see.'

155

'Just perfect. Everything will be perfect.'

'A lovely traditional wedding.'

'Absolutely.'

Was an outdoor ceremony in a floral arcade particularly traditional? Cooper wasn't sure. His brother had married his sister-in-law Kate at All Saints, the parish church in Edendale, followed by a buffet and disco at a local pub. That was what he thought of as tradition, though he supposed traditions changed over time, like everything else.

Well, he knew the wedding cake would be traditional. Liz had shown him a photograph of a four-tier confection from Love Cakes of Derby, covered in little iced flowers. At least it wasn't a cupcake tower, which was what he'd been afraid of.

'We can do photos in the grounds, and they say we can use the main staircase too, if we want,' said Liz.

'The staircase? Use it for what?'

'You know, Ben – for the photos with the dress and the train spread out over the steps, and the bridesmaids behind me. It'll look fantastic.'

'Oh, okay. Am I in these photos, by the way?'

'Only if you behave yourself.'

The orangery was nice, he had to admit. It had been restored about ten years ago to its early nineteenth-century elegance. According to the brochure, the restoration had received a commendation for its design from the Council for the Preservation of Rural England.

'Okay, the staircase. Well, that's a selling point.'

'And look at the views.'

'Yes, I can't fault the views.'

Liz looked at her list. 'So how many stars shall I give it? Four or five?'

'Out of how many?'

'I don't know.'

Sometimes he thought it would be better if he just let Liz and her family get on with organising the wedding without him. But he always hastily put the thought aside, in case it popped out of his mouth in an unguarded moment. That would definitely land him in big, big trouble.

'What's the matter?' she asked.

'Nothing.'

Cooper knew she wouldn't believe him, but she accepted his answer for the moment. If she pressed him, he would find it very difficult to tell her what actually was the matter. The fact was, he was feeling guilty. He was bothered by a persistent, nagging certainty that he'd made a mess of the job last night, that he ought to have been the one to find the body of Aidan Merritt, instead of leaving it to Diane Fry. All right, it might not have made a huge amount of difference. An hour or two perhaps. But those first few hours were crucial, as everyone knew.

Besides, there was a question of pride. He would never live down the fact that a body had been lying a few hundred yards away, without him being aware of it. A murder victim, no less. It would haunt him for the rest of his career.

And the reason it had happened was simple. He'd grasped the opportunity to leave the scene on Oxlow Moor early because he had an appointment to view a property that he couldn't afford to buy. He'd compromised his professional integrity to please Liz.

And the worst of it was something he could hardly explain to himself. When he looked at Liz now, and saw how happy she was, he even felt guilty about feeling guilty.

At Bridge End Farm, Ben Cooper stopped by the stable to say hello to his two nieces. The elder, Amy, was really growing up now. She was a proper teenager, a bit gawky,

157

yet obsessive about her appearance. Josie wasn't far behind either – there were only a couple of years between them. Matt would really have his hands full soon.

A few weeks previously, the girls had got the horse they'd always wanted. The eight-year-old chestnut gelding belonged to Amy really, a present on her last birthday. But the two girls were very close, and it was good to see them sharing the pleasure, as well as the hard work grooming and mucking out. The arrival of the horse had been a joint project anyway. They had been nagging their father about it for the past two years.

Ben suspected that emotional blackmail had played a large part in their strategy. Crucially, their mother had been on their side too. Kate's opinion would have been a clincher.

Matt Cooper was coming back from the hill behind the farmhouse with the old sheepdog at his heels. They had been moving the sheep between fields. Ben could smell the lanolin from their fleeces, which had impregnated Matt's clothes and the skin of his hands where he'd been handling the ewes to check them for foot rot.

Ben was reminded of Gavin Murfin's jibe at Diane Fry, and her response: *Trust me, I'll be happy if I don't have to see another damn sheep ever in my life*. Not much chance of that in the Peak District. They were everywhere.

Matt watched his daughters busy with their grooming equipment.

'That blasted horse costs a fortune,' he grumbled. 'It eats its own weight in hay and oats every day, and doesn't produce a thing. And hay isn't cheap this year, as you know.'

Matt looked tired. It was a busy time of year for farmers. Not that any time of year *wasn't* busy. That was what Matt would have told him, if he'd been silly enough to ask.

But Ben didn't need telling – his childhood at Bridge End

had been ruled by the seasons. Not the usual seasons known as spring, summer, autumn and winter, but lambing, shearing, harvest, ploughing and all the other jobs in the endless round of activities that a farm demanded.

'Well, I spoke to a few of the blokes who were in the Young Farmers back then,' said Matt. 'They're not quite so young as they were, of course. But then none of us are. And some of them aren't even in farming any more.'

'What did they say?'

'I told them you were asking about the Pearsons. They were aware of the couple in the bar, because they were strangers. I think we were all aware of them.'

'Who did you talk to?'

'I'm not giving you names.'

'This isn't a game, Matt. I'm trying to find out what happened to two tourists who went missing near the Light House and have never been found. They might be dead. The smallest bit of information could be useful to us right now.'

'I know, I know. I've heard all that before. But there's a question of loyalty, you see. I think you've forgotten that.'

Ben stared at him, feeling suddenly frightened by the huge gulf that had opened up between them. It had been widening for years, but now its extent was terrifying. It was as if he'd just looked up from his feet and found that the earth had opened in front of him. A yawning chasm was staring him in the face, a gulf far too wide to cross.

Sometimes it felt as though everything had changed since the death of their mother. In the years of her illness, Isabel Cooper had been the glue holding the family together. Without her, they had fragmented and gone their different ways. Now they hardly even knew how to communicate.

'Who did you turn to when there was that incident last year?' said Ben coldly.

'Me? No one. It was Kate who rang you. And it was your friend Diane Fry who got me out of a cell.'

Of course the problem was that they had never really talked about that night. Now its memory lay between them, shocking and impossible to ignore, like a pool of blood on the carpet.

'You know they wouldn't let me get involved,' said Ben.

Matt nodded abruptly. 'Yes, because they thought there would be a conflict of loyalties. Isn't that right? Don't they give that as the reason? You don't really understand it, though, do you? To you, it's just procedure, a form of words, all written down in the rule book. To me, loyalty is very real.'

'Okay.'

'So you see, you're going to have to trust me. If you can't do that, Ben, it's just tough.'

'Matt, it's not a problem.'

'Good.'

'So what did you notice about the Pearsons?'

Matt reacted with a clumsy jerk, as if he'd been expecting the question and had tried to rehearse his response. He'd never been a good actor. Ben remembered him being cast as one of the Three Wise Men in their school nativity play, presenting his myrrh to the Baby Jesus like a robot handling a suspicious package. Wooden didn't quite express it.

'What sort of people were they?' asked Ben. 'Do you remember?'

'Well, they weren't noisy or anything. They kept themselves to themselves mostly. Though there did seem to be . . .'

Ben looked up at the hesitation, saw from his brother's face that Matt was trying to assemble unfamiliar thoughts and fit them to appropriate words.

'There seemed to be what, Matt?'

160

'I was going to say, there seemed to be a bit of an atmosphere between them. That's it.'

'An atmosphere.'

'Yes.'

Ben frowned. 'Between David and Trisha? You mean they'd had an argument?'

'They weren't speaking to each other much. Just like when you've had a row. You know what I mean?'

'Yes, I know.'

'That's what caused the atmosphere.'

'So you think they'd been arguing. Just from the atmosphere.'

'Yes.'

'The atmosphere,' repeated Ben.

'Why do you keep saying it?'

'Oh, just trying to take it in.'

'Like I say, they'd been arguing. You could tell from the way they spoke to each other, their expressions when they looked at each other, the way they sat. Their body language, if you want.'

'Their body language? Really?'

Matt began to look sullen. 'Well that's what you asked me for, my impressions. I can't say any more. If you don't like it, it's tough.'

'Oh no,' said Ben. 'That's great. I love it.'

Cooper turned the Toyota carefully in the farmyard, and bumped his way back up the track towards the road.

Now that he thought about it, he seemed to remember that the Light House had served Robinson's, one of his favourite beers. He could practically taste it now. They did a strong ale that tasted of ripe malt and peppery hops, with a colour like cherry brandy. Old Tom, it was called.

Some beers were seasonal and only came out for Christmas, but Old Tom had been going for ever. It wasn't a Derbyshire ale, though. It came from just over there to the west, from what used to be Cheshire.

Cooper wondered how many pints of Old Tom he'd sunk that night in the Light House. It made him cringe to think how much he used to drink back then, especially if he was in company like the Young Farmers or the rugby club. Matt could put a few away too.

And that made him wonder. If he'd been a little too drunk himself to remember what had gone off, how capable was everyone else? How sober had his brother been? Not sober at all, surely. Matt wasn't the most observant of people at the best of times. Particularly not in a social situation. He might be able to tell from half a mile off which of the ewes in his field were ready to lamb, but he didn't notice much about people. If a friend hadn't introduced them in the most blatant manner possible, Matt would never have been aware that he'd clicked with Kate. In emotional matters, he was like a slow old bull who had to be prodded into action.

So why would he have come to any conclusions at all about the relationship between David and Trisha Pearson? Matt wasn't the type who sat in a pub watching the other customers for his own entertainment. He kept his eyes on his beer glass, and talked only to people he knew. If he found himself on his own, he'd study a copy of *Farmers' Weekly*, even if he'd read it before. In fact it would be fair to say that Matt Cooper went out of his way to avoid contact with strangers. If they appeared to be tourists, he was likely to look the other way. Sometimes Ben thought his brother must be afraid that any passing stranger might curse him with the evil eye.

'No, that's wrong,' said Ben out loud. 'That wasn't Matt speaking. He's been coached.'

Later, when he was looking for a reason to explain what happened next, he decided that must have been it. He had been too absorbed with his thoughts about Matt.

At least that was the reason he gave himself – the reason why he didn't notice he was being followed.

Diane Fry still had her old flat in Grosvenor Road, deep in student bedsit land. It was a place that had never felt like home. It never would do, no matter how long she stayed in Edendale. But she wouldn't be here much longer. As soon as she was settled with EMSOU – MC, she'd be moving out. Somewhere much nearer to Nottingham. That, she promised herself.

In fact her lease on the flat would run out in a few months, so the decision might be forced on her, she supposed. It would hardly be a wrench. She had taken the flat furnished, so her entire possessions could be packed in a suitcase and a few cardboard boxes.

Her old colleagues in E Division had often asked her why she didn't find somewhere better. She could have afforded it on a detective sergeant's salary, of course. She might have put down a deposit on a small house somewhere and tied herself to a mortgage. But tying herself down didn't feature in her planning for the future, not in any way. Yes, there was money in the bank – but she had other purposes in mind for that.

Fry switched on the TV and left a quiz show babbling to itself while she found a frozen pizza and slid it into the microwave. She never had much appetite when she was in the middle of a case. Her biggest problem was turning off her mind, which tended to keep ticking away, turning over and over the events of the day.

She knew she wouldn't get much rest tonight, not even

163

with the help of her sleeping aids. A promethazine hydro-chloride tablet would only give her a few minutes of disturbing dreams before she woke up feeling dry-mouthed and groggy. She suspected she'd been taking the tablets for much too long now for them to have any effect.

She'd always thought of her older sister Angie as the addictive personality of the family. But at least Angie had cleaned herself up and escaped the heroin. Now she was back in Birmingham, working in a vintage clothes shop, still refusing to talk about some of the things she'd been doing in these past few years.

Fry felt envious of her sister sometimes. She would love to be able to disappear for a while, then come back, start a whole new life and never feel she had to talk about her time in Derbyshire.

It was funny, though, how things worked out. No matter what she did, certain aspects of Derbyshire seemed determined to keep coming back to haunt her. Deep down, Fry knew that she would never be allowed to escape completely.

15

'Well, it arrived,' said Gavin Murfin next morning. He had his feet up on his desk, ready to soak up any attention like a basking seal.

Cooper stopped halfway into the CID room, with his leather jacket still hung over one shoulder. He really wasn't in the mood for Murfin this morning.

'What arrived, Gavin?'

Murfin held up a box. 'My OBE. Special delivery by a bad-tempered bloke on a pushbike. He was disguised as our usual postman, but I reckon he must have been a royal equerry at least. I'm sure there was a corgi peeking out of his bag when he rode away.'

'Oh, it's your DJ medal. Damn, I haven't got mine yet.'

That made Murfin beam. 'Priorities, mate. Someone has to get it first. So Maj chose those of us with the longest and most distinguished service, like.'

'That could be it, I suppose.'

'I'll let you have a look, though.'

'Cheers.'

Cooper cradled the box carefully. The medal bore an image of Queen Elizabeth II on one side, looking a bit severe, with the inscription *Elizabeth II Dei Gratia Regina Fid Def*. On the reverse was a diamond symbol with the royal crest. It resembled a ten-pence piece in size, and carried the dates 1952–2012.

They were all due to get their medals to celebrate the Queen's Diamond Jubilee. They were being presented to the armed forces, emergency services and prison service staff, as well as community support officers who had completed five full years of service in February.

With that thought, Cooper's eyes were drawn across the room to where Becky Hurst sat. Not everyone in the office would receive the medal. Hurst hadn't quite completed five years. She'd moved rapidly into CID from a spell as a response officer in C Division, which was a testament to her ability. But she missed out on the qualifying date for the Diamond Jubilee medal by a week or two. He knew that it bugged her, especially when medals were being handed out to PCSOs and even to Specials, the unpaid volunteers who turned out at weekends to help at major events.

'Nice,' said Cooper. 'Take it home with you, Gavin.'

'But I thought—'

'No. Take it home.'

Murfin looked at him, and for once he didn't object or make a sarcastic comment.

'Okay, boss.'

It was going to be hard to avoid the subject altogether during the next few weeks, as other officers received their medals. Murfin was the first, but all the medals were due to be awarded in the first half of the year. The Diamond Jubilee celebrations themselves would take place at the beginning of June. They had even moved the Spring Bank Holiday from the last Monday in May to coincide with the anniversary.

Cooper took off his jacket and sat down at his desk, feeling that he was always skating on thin ice in some way, whatever he did. Here in the office, when he was at Bridge End

Farm, when he was with Liz . . . Was this what life was going to be like from now on?

'So tell us, Gavin,' said Cooper, 'what did Diane Fry do yesterday?'

'She talked to the family of the old landlord from the Light House,' said Murfin, seeming equally ready to change the subject.

'Mad Maurice Wharton?'

'Not him, but the wife and daughter. And she made a right mess of it, too, by all accounts.'

'Oh?'

There could only have been one source for that account, since Becky Hurst had been allocated to work with Fry. Cooper couldn't resist a small smile of satisfaction at this evidence of how little loyalty Fry had earned for herself. Then he let the smile drop. It was an ungracious thought. He had no real reason to be jealous of Fry, did he? No, of course not.

'The wife and daughter?' he said. 'What about Maurice Wharton himself?'

Murfin shook his head sadly. 'He's in a bad way, apparently. Cancer of the pancreas.'

'Ouch.'

'Ouch is right.'

'You know, on the way here I was trying to recall what he looks like,' said Cooper.

'Are you kidding?' said Murfin. 'Did you never actually *see* that bloke? Once seen, never forgotten. If you wanted to describe him to someone, you'd have to invent a whole new word for ugly.'

'I think I do recall him now, though. A big guy, long hair growing over his collar at the back, and a fine set of jowls?'

'Two fine sets of jowls,' said Murfin. 'I always found him a bit scary, in fact. But in a good way, if you know what I mean. Like watching a horror film to give yourself a fright when the monster appears.'

Cooper looked at the files and found a photograph of Wharton. 'Well I'm not sure he's that bad.'

'No, no – that doesn't do him justice,' said Murfin. 'Trust me. You've got to see him in the flesh to get the full effect.'

Villiers and Irvine entered the office. Cooper reminded himself that Luke had been spending all his time ploughing through the case files, reading reports, going over old witness statements. He was starting to look a bit jaded already.

'Are you okay, Luke?' he asked.

'Sure.'

Cooper looked around his team. Such as it was, they were all here.

'So what do we really make of this theory that the Pearsons skipped the country?'

'We?' asked Irvine, as if surprised to be asked.

'Well, give me an overview. What has everyone been saying over these past couple of years?'

'Oh, pretty much everything you can imagine has been said at some time,' said Irvine, warming up as he got the chance to share what he'd learned from all those reports. 'In the early days, there were lots of crackpot rumours springing up, as always. People reported seeing the Pearsons in New Zealand, in Guatemala, in Florida. Someone started a Facebook page called "I've seen David Pearson", with faked pictures using the shots of them issued for the press appeals. Basically, they treated David like some latter-day Lord Lucan, with Trisha as a female sidekick. Stories went round that the Pearsons had bought a villa in the Algarve, an apartment in Moscow, a council house in Inverness. David was even spotted busking on the London Underground. He'd apparently learned to play the guitar, grown a beard and gained three inches in height while he'd been missing.'

168

Hurst laughed, but Irvine's face didn't change. His expression said it was only what he would expect from some people, who were pathetic.

'Did that go on for long?' asked Villiers.

Irvine shook his head. 'It was a one-month wonder. People soon got tired of it and moved on to the next craze. None of it helped us, of course. We didn't have a hope of sifting through everything, so we just concentrated on a few of the more likely sightings. And I'm using "likely" in a very relative sense, to mean the least bizarre.'

'There was nothing else? No credit card transactions, no cash withdrawals, no record of the Pearsons passing through customs or buying air tickets?'

'No, none of those.'

'Well, either that was a particularly good disappearing act,' said Villiers. 'Or they've been dead all this time.'

Irvine shrugged. 'We all know it's possible to drop off the grid completely, if you have enough money. And the Pearsons had the money. They could have bought forged passports, new identity documents, opened bank accounts in new names. It only needs one contact to fix the whole thing.'

Cooper flicked through the file for financial details. 'They both left money in their bank accounts. Quite substantial amounts, too.'

'The inquiry team were aware of that. They watched those accounts closely for any signs of activity, but there were no transactions other than a few standing orders and direct debits, which kept going out until the bank put a stop on them.'

'So they didn't have any money?'

'On the contrary. From the evidence of fraud and embezzlement that we and HMRC uncovered in David Pearson's business activities, there's a large of cash unaccounted for somewhere.'

'How much?'

'The best part of two million pounds.'

Villiers gave the low whistle required whenever a large amount of money was mentioned.

'Wow.'

'Actually, it isn't all that much,' said Irvine.

'A cool two mil? Not all that much? What do you mean? Your salary must be a lot higher than I thought, Luke.'

'No, he's right,' said Cooper. 'It's not enough. Once you've paid out for all the forged documents and your new identity, bought your villa in the Algarve or wherever and met all the expenses of setting up a different life from scratch . . . not to mention lying low for however long is needed.'

'Yes, the money would have run out by now.'

'I think so. They would have had to raise their heads above the parapet in some way by this time. And they would have been located.'

'Unless . . .?'

'Well, as Carol said – unless they're dead.'

In the little office she'd been allocated across the corridor, Fry was looking at the photographs of the Pearsons again. Cooper wondered what she was thinking, why she had that faintly puzzled look. He'd studied the photographs long enough himself, and he hadn't noticed whatever it was that Fry was seeing, the factor that she found so mystifying.

She looked up when she became aware of him standing near her.

'Diane, would you agree to me speaking to Nancy Wharton?' he said.

Fry considered it for a moment, and he thought at first that she was going to say no. It certainly wouldn't have surprised him. As far as she was concerned, most of his ideas were set up to be rejected out of hand.

'I suppose it can't do any harm,' she said.

'Thank you.'

'Why do you think all the public attention focused on David Pearson?' she asked. 'Trisha is quite attractive, isn't she? The press normally go for shots of a photogenic young woman. It draws more sympathy, or something.'

Cooper had to agree. Usually that was the case.

'But look at David again,' he said. 'Remember what I said about the film star?'

'Oh. Robert Redford, was it?'

'Yes. He has that look about him. Handsome, dashing, a bit of a rogue. He was tailor-made for the story, especially when his skill as a conman started to come out. The media loved the fact that he was on the run. He was Robert Redford in *Butch Cassidy*, or Steve McQueen in *The Great Escape*.'

Seeing Fry's expression remain blank, he searched desperately for something she could relate to.

'Oh, I don't know . . . Leonardo DiCaprio in *Catch Me if You Can*.'

'I've seen that,' she said.

'Good.'

Fry screwed up her eyes. 'He doesn't look anything like Leonardo DiCaprio. Wrong hair colouring altogether.'

'That's not the point . . .' began Cooper, then gave up. 'Oh, never mind. Some of the locals are pointing their fingers at this other group of visitors. We have descriptions of them, but no names.'

'Is there a suggestion that they knew the Pearsons?' asked Fry.

'We have no indication what their conversation was about. It might just have been a bit of casual chat, if they realised they were from the same part of the country. Or fellow feeling between outsiders. We can't say. And there's no chance of tracing them unless we trawl through the records of every holiday cottage and guest house within twenty miles.'

'Well, that's something that wasn't done at the time,' said Fry. 'And now it's probably too late.'

'Yes.'

Cooper shut the door a little too hard, just as a gesture, and strode back into the CID room, where his team looked reassuring, and less difficult to deal with.

'Luke,' he said, 'can you dig out everything we have on Ian Gullick, please?'

'A regular at the Light House?' said Irvine. 'I recall the name.'

'Yes.' Cooper consulted his notebook. 'And an associate of his.'

'Vince Naylor?'

'Right.'

'Was that from the old biddy?' asked Irvine.

'Surprisingly, yes.'

'I was wondering,' said Villiers, 'why the Pearsons didn't go to the Light House for an evening meal on that last night. It was closer to their holiday cottage than the George.'

'The food wasn't up to much at the Light House,' said Murfin. 'It had been rubbish for years. If the Pearsons were bothered about getting a decent meal, they would have gone anywhere else but.'

'That's true,' said Cooper.

'And in any case, the Light House always closed for a few days over Christmas. They would already have stopped serving food by then, and they never took any bookings for accommodation.'

Cooper knew that its position was what the Light House was most famous for. It vied with the Barrel Inn at Bretton to be known as the highest pub in Derbyshire. On a clear day you could see across five counties, they said. But its location was also a drawback. To find it the first time you had to programme it into your sat nav. It wasn't a place you passed by accident.

And Murfin was right – for the last few years the food menu hadn't competed with anywhere. It hadn't even tried. No seasonal locally sourced produce here like the pheasant, venison and wild boar you might find at the Barrel. From a culinary point of view, the Light House had been stuck in the 1980s. And there had been nothing available at lunchtime except a packet of pork scratchings.

'By the way,' said Murfin. 'Speaking of food, I've got a line on Maclennan, the chef. He's working at a French restaurant in Chapel-en-le-Frith now.'

On the way to Chapel-en-le-Frith, Cooper drove through Sparrowpit, and turned up a lane by the Wanted Inn that would take him towards the A6, where it bypassed the town. He saw a board by the roadside advertising 'Livery vacancies'. Now, that was a sign of hard times.

He crossed the national park boundary just before he reached the A6, and followed the road that ran through Chapel. He passed the turning for the high school and the railway station on Long Lane. Since he was early and had time to spare, he decided to call at the local police station.

Chapel police station was a little way out of the old part of town, on Manchester Road. It had originally been a couple of old police houses, and was also the base for a traffic policing unit for the north of the county. There was a dog unit parked in the yard outside, and a mobile police office. It had one of the best views of any police station in

Derbyshire, with an outlook at the back over rolling farm-land towards the National Trust site at Eccles Pike.

Half an hour later, Cooper met Niall Maclennan in the little cobbled marketplace in the oldest part of Chapel-en-le-Frith. Maclennan was sitting on a bench between the corner of the NatWest Bank and the old market cross, under a horse chestnut tree, watching the world going by on the high street below.

Although it was tiny, like all the best marketplaces it seemed to be surrounded by pubs. One of them, he noticed, had a sign outside. *Pub for let*. Near the traditional stocks was the Stocks Café, advertising itself as *Great British Breakfast Winner 2010*. Lucky Gavin Murfin wasn't here.

Niall Maclennan had dark eyes, prominent cheekbones and designer stubble. He was trying very hard to ooze the impression of a TV celebrity chef. At one time his image might have been spoiled by the fact that he was working in Chapel-en-le-Frith, this old market town on the edge of the High Peak. But these days Chapel was claiming to be the gourmet centre of the Peak, thanks to the number of restaurants, cafés and pubs, and a reputation for locally sourced produce.

Less was said about the fifteen hundred Scottish soldiers who had been imprisoned in St Thomas Becket church and starved to death during the Civil War. That ought to be worthy of some kind of commemoration.

'There are good jobs here,' said Maclennan. 'And in Buxton, too. I was just marking time at the Light House, getting a bit of experience.'

'So you left the Whartons for a better job?'

Maclennan hesitated. 'Not exactly. It took me a few weeks to find another position.'

'What made you leave, then?'

Thoughtfully, Maclennan took a long drag on his cigarette.

'The atmosphere, I suppose. Things were getting bad. Everyone knew that.'

'Bad financially?'

'Yes, business was down. It's heartbreaking to put all your effort and creativity into producing an exciting menu, and then have no one turn up to get the benefit. Everybody was tetchy, especially Nancy and Maurice. I could see it would only get worse. Once you're on that slippery slope, it takes new management to turn it round.'

'Reputation being so important.'

'Exactly.'

'But it wasn't just that, was it?' asked Cooper.

'What do you mean?'

'Well, you mentioned Nancy and Maurice getting tetchy. Running a kitchen can be quite stressful anyway. If the Whartons became difficult to work with, I can see why you might have walked out on them.'

Maclennan laughed. 'I'm not some kind of prima donna, you know. I don't storm out in a hissy fit every five minutes. It was a fully thought-out decision, made in the best interests of my own career.'

'So who took over the kitchen when you left?'

'Nancy, so far as I know. She had a couple of staff to help her, but they weren't exactly qualified chefs, if you know what I mean. It's hardly a surprise that the quality of the menu nosedived. I tried to be a bit adventurous, and produce quality. They went for pub grub. What a phrase. Pub grub.'

He said it with such venom and contempt that Cooper could imagine the conflicts there might have been at the Light House while Maclennan was working there. Maurice Wharton was famously irascible – in fact, he'd made it his trademark. And Nancy was no soft touch, either.

'Do you remember the time the couple from Surrey went missing?'

'Sure,' said Maclennan. 'It was on all the news programmes.'

'You were still working at the Light House then, weren't you?'

'Yes – but you appreciate I was in the kitchens all the time? I didn't see any of the customers. At least, not until we'd finished serving and cleaning down, then I might go out into the bar for a drink to wind down.'

'Just staff in the bar by then?'

'Well, unless Maurice had let a few regulars stay for a bit of a lock-in. You know it happens.'

'Yes, everyone knows it happens,' said Cooper.

'But then it was just a few of the same old faces. I never stayed long on those nights. Not my idea of congenial company.'

The hostility in his voice sounded genuine. It was more than just the resentment of an ungrateful public that was common among people working in the hospitality and service industries. Maclennan's tone suggested that he knew too much about these particular customers personally.

But a moment later he seemed to have second thoughts. He straightened up, took a look round, stubbed out his cigarette.

'Well, it was a shame when they had to close the pub,' said Maclennan. 'I suppose they'd seen it coming for quite a while, though.'

'The Whartons, you mean?' asked Cooper.

'Yes. Well, Maurice in particular. You could see him getting more and more depressed. I reckon it was weighing on his mind for years before they eventually had to pull the plug. I mean, a man wants to believe that he can support his family and run a business properly. Maurice was a proud sort of bloke. I'm not surprised it hit him so hard.'

'You say he was getting depressed?'

'Oh, aye. Morose, he was. He'd always been such a

character. Cantankerous, you'd say. Crabby and bad-tempered maybe. But a lot of it was show. He liked to live up to his reputation.'

'His image as Mad Maurice,' said Cooper.

'That's it. He loved all that. It gave him a bit of fame. He played up to it something rotten at times, winding up the tourists and so on. Regulars who knew him thought it was hilarious. "That's Mad Maurice for you," they'd say. But, well . . . when the pub started to get into trouble, you could see it was more than that. Maurice lost heart all of a sudden. One day we all realised that he wasn't joking any more. He really was moody. He began to drink, too. Well, when a landlord starts to drink his own booze, it's the beginning of the end, in my view. A very slippery slope. Poor old Maurice.'

'I dare say you know Mr Wharton's health is very poor?' said Cooper.

'That's on account of the booze, though, isn't it? The booze and the stress. I couldn't say which caused which. Probably a bit of both. Like a vicious cycle.'

'Circle,' said Cooper.

'What?'

'It's a vicious circle.'

'That's what I said.'

Cooper found himself distracted by the sight of a couple of estate agents he wasn't familiar with. They didn't have offices in Edendale, so their properties were probably more on the western borders of the county.

He realised Maclennan was looking at him strangely.

'Sorry, what were you saying?" asked Cooper.

'I was saying that you might want to talk to Josh Lane, Sergeant. He was their regular barman. The Whartons had quite a few casual staff while I was there, but Josh was full time, right up to the end. He became almost like one of the family.'

177

'Thank you.'

Cooper took a last look round Chapel-en-le-Frith. The men's hairdresser's was doing good business. Two women were chatting outside the post office, near a recruitment poster for Hope Valley Rugby Club. At a beauty parlour in the high street they were offering a fish foot spa treatment. Ten pounds for a fifteen-minute session.

'I can't tell you anything else,' said Maclennan. 'As you can see, I got out before it was too late. You might call me a rat deserting a sinking ship, I suppose. That would be fair. But if you ask me, Maurice Wharton was sinking in a sea of his own alcohol.'

16

At the council house on the Devonshire Estate, Nancy Wharton was on her own. She examined Cooper critically for a moment on the doorstep. He knew she would be weighing him up, placing him for what he was, but hopefully remembering him too.

She glanced then at Gavin Murfin. It had been a difficult decision whether to bring Murfin along. In many ways, Carol Villiers would have been a better choice. But Gavin had been well known at the Light House. Mrs Wharton should recognise him, even if she didn't know Cooper himself.

'Old faces,' she said. 'I suppose you want to come in.'

'Please, Mrs Wharton.'

Every house had a unique smell. Cooper never got tired of walking into someone else's home and trying to identify the aromas. Sometimes it was a mix of artificial scents – air fresheners, perfumes, furniture polish. At other times it could only be called a stench. Substances too noxious to mention oozed out of the furniture, and the carpet stuck to his feet as he crossed a room.

Here, the Whartons seemed to have brought subtle hints of the Light House with them on to the Devonshire Estate. He couldn't quite put a name to the smells, but they were creating those momentary flashes of memory, the way scents sometimes could, being so much more evocative than the other senses.

It might be the type of furniture polish used, or the mingling of old beer and smoke that you might get used to if you'd lived with it for years. But if he closed his eyes, he could almost imagine himself sitting in the snug at the Light House. He could practically taste the beer, hear the buzz of conversation around him.

One smell in particular was teasing him. When he caught a fleeting whiff of it, Matt's face loomed up in his mind, red and sweating, with the suggestion of a snatch of conversation that he couldn't quite grasp. It was like the elusive memory of a dream that he knew was still there in his mind when he'd woken up, but which slipped away whenever he thought about it.

As a result of the sensations Cooper was experiencing in the Whartons' sitting room, Murfin was the first to speak.

'You might remember us, Nancy. We both knew Mad . . . er, Mr Wharton. Sorry.'

Nancy noticed Murfin's moment of embarrassment, and her face slipped into a bitter smile.

'Oh don't worry,' she said. 'I've heard it all before. Don't you think I know what people used to call him? Imagine what it was like being "Mrs Mad Maurice" for all those years.'

'I'm sorry,' said Murfin again, though it wasn't necessary and was obviously too late.

Cooper gave him a warning glance. If Gavin was going to mess up with the public, it was a different thing altogether from what went on in the office. That couldn't be tolerated.

He knew he had to tread carefully with the Whartons if he was going to get any more out of them than Diane Fry had. Questions about Maurice's tendency to alcoholism were probably out, then.

'It was such a shame about the pub closing,' he said. 'You and Mr Wharton must have been devastated.'

Mrs Wharton shrugged. 'We could see it was inevitable for a long time. We had a balance sheet like *Journey to the Centre of the Earth*. It looked as though we were tunnelling to Australia. You can only fall so far before you hit rock bottom.'

'But how did it happen?' asked Cooper.

'How? Well, it started with the crackdown on drinking and driving. Nobody gets up there any other way, do they? Then there was the smoking ban in 2007. We did our best, but who wants to sit outside in this environment? Customers were getting blown away by the wind in the winter, and eaten by midges off the moor in the summer. Then the recession came along. We actually thought that might help us for a while. People staying at home for their holidays instead of going abroad, you know. What do they call that?'

'A staycation?'

'Yeah. What a load of crap. Oh, more folk came to the Peak District, I suppose, but they weren't spending any money. Not in our pub.'

'The Light House used to have a very good reputation.'

'Oh yes. At one time Maurice Wharton was known far and wide. My husband was respected for the quality of the beer he served. Traditional ales, you know. We used to serve Hardy and Hanson, William Clarke, Marston's Pedigree. We had guest beers on draught, rotated on a monthly basis.'

'Greene King,' said Murfin.

'Timothy Taylor's Landlord,' said Cooper.

Nancy smiled again, just a little. 'All those. And we had a selection of over twenty malt whiskies. Irish and Welsh, as well as Scotch. Sales of beer declined by another ten per cent in our last year, in spite of a warm spring and a royal wedding, and all the things we thought might bring people out to the pub. The budget put duty up to nearly eight times what it is in France, and over twelve times the duty in Germany or Italy. And that's not to mention an escalator, so duty goes up two per cent more than inflation every year. It was crippling.'

For a moment Cooper had a sense of déjà vu, as if he was listening to the familiar litany of complaints from farmers like his brother. Things were always bad in the farming industry. Prices were never right, costs were always too high, the weather was either too dry or too wet. Small farmers were going bust for much the same reasons that Nancy Wharton was giving him. In a nutshell, they couldn't make their businesses pay any more.

'We're not alone,' said Nancy. 'Not by a long way. Jobs are being lost throughout the industry. The pub trade is being decimated.'

'My colleague Detective Sergeant Fry came to talk to you about Aidan Merritt,' said Cooper tentatively.

'I can't tell you any more than I told her.'

'I'd particularly like to know about any contact Mr Merritt had with other customers.'

'You know what? Aidan kept himself pretty much to himself.'

'Could there have been anyone who had a grudge against him?'

'A grudge? Like who?'

'Ian Gullick is a name that's been mentioned.'

Nancy looked away, no longer willing to meet Cooper's eye. It was a perfectly natural reticence, he supposed. Who would want to criticise their own customers? It was a kind of loyalty – and Cooper understood loyalty.

'I wouldn't know anything about it,' said Nancy finally.

'I'm sorry, really I am. It's horrible what happened to him, but what else can I say?'

Cooper nodded. A roadblock, then. Move on.

'I understand.'

She looked at him steadily. 'And I suppose you're going to ask me about those tourists, too – like the woman did?'

'Yes, I'm afraid so. The Pearsons. They were in the Light House the night before they disappeared.'

'Yes. We went through it all with the police when it happened. They spoke to everyone who might have had any contact with them, including me. It seems I served them at the bar.'

'Yes, I've seen your statement.'

'Well, then. I don't know what earthly use it could have been. Those two people were certainly alive and well when they left the pub. What good does it do going over every minute and every second of what they did in the days before they skipped off?'

'In case someone noticed anything about them, or the Pearsons gave away a clue of some kind about what they were going to do.'

Nancy picked up a woollen sweater and pulled it around her shoulders, as if she was cold.

'Well, there was nothing. Nothing at all. For heaven's sake, I didn't have a clue who they were. They came in the pub, and they were just some tourists, that's all. We used to get hundreds of them every week. Thousands in the summer. I had no idea they were going to be in the least bit different to any other tourists. When they came to the Light House, we didn't even know their names.'

'And then there was the previous night,' said Cooper.

'What do you mean?'

'The night no one ever talked about.'

'I'm sorry, I don't understand you.'

'The night before,' repeated Cooper. 'It was the night of the Young Farmers' Christmas party.'

'Party? Oh yes, that. Of course it was. But no one ever mentioned the Pearson people being there.'

'Did you not see them?'

'Why would I? The place was packed. It was just before we closed for Christmas. On a night like that, you never really noticed anybody. It was head down over the bar, trying to remember what drinks to ring up on the till.'

'You have two children, don't you?' said Cooper.

'Yes, Eliot and Kirsten. They're seventeen and fifteen. I don't know what I'd do without them. Kirsten is at Hope Valley College. She'll be doing her GCSEs this summer. She doesn't want to stay on after that, though. She's interested in becoming a beautician or a hairdresser.'

Cooper thought she sounded vaguely disappointed.

'Nothing wrong with that, Mrs Wharton.'

'No, no. Of course not, Well, Eliot is the clever one, anyway. He's in the sixth form at Lady Manners in Bakewell.'

'I wonder if we could speak to them?'

'They're not here.'

'Pity.'

Just then, they both heard a key turn in the front door, and a male voice calling through the house.

'Mum?'

Eliot Wharton was a tall young man, with short fair hair, flushed cheeks and large hands that dangled by his sides. Cooper wondered if he was a rugby player.

He looked at his mother, and then at Cooper and Murfin with the beginnings of hostility.

'Who's this?' he said.

'The police, love.'

'Oh. Again.'

'Is Kirsten with you?' asked Nancy.

'Yes, I'm here,' said Kirsten from the hall.

Cooper realised that there was hardly any room for anyone else in the lounge since Eliot had entered. They seemed to be uncomfortably close together, too close for anyone who might have problems over their personal space.

Nancy explained to her children what Cooper was asking. They both began shaking their heads simultaneously.

'That night, the night before the people went missing,' said Eliot. 'They were in the pub then, weren't they? The police asked us questions. But other than that . . .'

Cooper turned to Eliot's sister. 'Kirsten?

She shrugged. 'How would I know? I wasn't even old enough to be in the bar, was I?'

He wasn't sure about that. Too young to drink alcohol, or serve it to customers, yes. But not too young to be in the bar. Children under sixteen could go anywhere in a pub as long as they were supervised by an adult.

'I know your husband is very ill,' said Cooper. 'And there's nothing I can say that will help.'

'Maurice has good days and bad days,' said Nancy. 'Of course the bad days can be very bad indeed. The drugs control the pain, but they have a lot of side effects.'

'I understand.'

She studied Cooper closely for a few moments, pursing her lips and frowning, as if trying to make a difficult decision.

'Your colleague who came here asked if she could talk to Maurice,' she said at last.

'I'm sure she did, but if it's impossible . . .'

'I could ask him, if you like,' said Nancy. 'He might like to see someone who knew the Light House. It would only be for a few minutes. He gets terribly tired.'

Cooper realised that he must have achieved some kind of honorary status as a pub regular. He wasn't sure what

185

he'd done to earn that honour, whether it was his own infrequent visits to the Light House, his presence at the YFC booze-up with Matt, or maybe even the fact that he'd chosen Gavin Murfin to accompany him to the Whartons'.

Whichever it was, he felt grateful for the results.

'That would be very kind of you,' he said.

'I'll see.'

He looked round, and saw both Eliot and Kirsten watching disapprovingly. He wondered if there would be a family argument after he'd gone. They clearly didn't trust him the way their mother had decided to.

'The Light House was a good pub,' said Cooper. 'I remember when I was a teenager, the beer there was a revelation.'

'Greene King,' said Murfin.

Cooper looked at Eliot Wharton for confirmation, forgetting the young man's age because of the size and maturity of him.

'Eliot doesn't drink,' said Nancy.

'Because you're not old enough?' he asked in surprise.

'No, I'm just not interested,' said Eliot.

'It must have been tough growing up in a pub, then. Or perhaps that's *why* you don't drink?'

Eliot shrugged. 'I can do without it. I see plenty of people who drink a lot making idiots of themselves all the time. What's the point of it?'

Then Cooper remembered what Niall Maclennan had told him, and realised that this young man would have seen his own father deteriorating through alcohol consumption. It was a bit too close to home when it was within the family. He decided it was probably best not to ask any more questions on the subject.

'Still, you must all have found it very difficult moving from the Light House,' he said, as he got ready to leave.

Mrs Wharton winced, as if at a sudden pain. 'It was awful. We knew we'd never be able to find anywhere else that would suit us. And this is where we ended up. Look at it. I know the town isn't so bad, but this estate . . .'

'Not so bad?' said Eliot, a sudden anger in his voice. 'I never wanted to live in Edendale. It's a place where people come to die.'

Cooper looked up sharply at the expression. He'd heard it often before. He knew it as a reference to the number of retired people who moved into the area when they wanted a bit of peace and quiet in their declining years. But said out loud, it sounded odd, as if Eliot was referring to something else entirely.

Before he left the Whartons, Cooper paused in the doorway and turned.

'I was in the pub earlier that week, Mrs Wharton,' he said. 'The night the Young Farmers' party was held.'

'Oh, I know you were,' said Nancy. 'I remember you very well. I almost had to get Maurice to throw you out. You were, well . . . how should I put it?'

He held up a hand. 'Yes, I know. I'm sorry.'

She shrugged. 'Well, there's no point in apologising now, is there? It's all water under the bridge. All just history.'

'Was I . . .?'

'Yes?'

'Was I very obnoxious? When I had too much to drink, I mean.'

Nancy smiled sadly. 'Don't worry. You could never be as an obnoxious as some. There are people born into the world just to be a pain in the arse. You soon learn that in the pub trade.'

As he left the house and walked the short length of scrubby garden to the gate, Cooper looked at the street packed with old council houses. Both sides of the road were lined solidly with cars for which there were no garages or off-road parking spaces.

For a moment he was overwhelmed by the difference between this and the setting of the Light House – the wild open landscape, the sense of absolute isolation. Nature was right on the doorstep as you left the pub. All he saw here were clusters of wheelie bins, and motorbikes shrouded in multicoloured polyester covers.

From Oxlow Moor, the views stretched for miles in every direction, to the glowering presence of Kinder Scout in the distance. Here, he saw no further than an identical house twenty yards away across the street.

DI Hitchens tapped Cooper on the shoulder as he arrived back in the CID room at West Street.

'Ben, don't forget Henry Pearson is due to arrive with us this morning.'

'I hadn't forgotten,' said Cooper. 'Is Mrs Pearson coming too?'

'No, I understand it's just her husband. I'm sure he will have planned it that way.'

'To minimise the emotional complications, I suppose.'

'Yes.'

'What have we told Mr Pearson?'

'Just that some items have been found that we believe belonged to his son and daughter-in-law, which we'd like him to help us identify. He didn't question that; he hasn't even asked what items we found. But he seems to have dropped everything to come straight up from Surrey.'

'He'll want to know more when he arrives.'

'Yes, I'm sure he will. But we need to be a bit discreet, Ben.'

'Discreet? You mean we're going to hold back some information?'

'Yes. Until we're, you know . . . sure.'

'Sure about the identification of the items? Or sure that Mr Pearson hasn't been involved in some kind of conspiracy over these last couple of years?'

'It never does any harm to be certain,' said Hitchens.

Cooper felt a spasm of discomfort. That was going to be an awkward encounter. Relatives of victims often wanted to be told everything. It put a police officer in a difficult position to know far more than he was able to share.

17

Sometime during the past six months, Josh Lane had found himself a job at one of the biggest hotels in Edendale. Cooper had thought he might have moved on to a different industry altogether. Bar work wasn't the best-paid occupation in the world, after all. But he supposed some people enjoyed it. Lane had stayed on at the Light House right to the end, so why shouldn't he have looked for a similar job elsewhere?

But the hotel he was employed at now was rather more upmarket than the Light House had ever been, not to mention much easier to find. It stood on a rise overlooking Edendale town centre, with a view over Victoria Park towards the town hall and the market square. It was favoured by the more well-heeled tourists, and by production companies filming at locations in the area.

Lane was polishing glasses in a plush lounge bar behind the lobby. A few hotel guests sat around on sofas drinking coffee, rather than anything alcoholic. Cooper couldn't recall the Light House ever serving coffee. Anyone who asked for it would have been pressing one of Mad Maurice's red buttons.

It smelled very good, though, and Cooper was pleased when Lane offered him one.

'Latte?'

'Thank you.'

'A pleasure.'

Cooper sat on a high stool at the counter to drink his coffee. Lane was older than he'd expected. Another mistaken preconception perhaps. He'd imagined a young man in his twenties, maybe Australian, doing a bit of bar work before finding a real job in marine biology or whatever his degree had been in.

But Lane was probably in his late thirties, a little over-weight, a discreet piercing in one ear, his hair gelled into short blond spikes.

'Yes, I remember Merritt,' he said when Cooper opened the subject..

'Was there ever any trouble?'

'With Aidan Merritt? No.'

Cooper detected a subtle hint there. He felt he should take that reply as an invitation to ask a different question. There was a bit of information that Lane wasn't going to volunteer, but it was there to be obtained if he persisted.

'Who, then?' he asked.

'There were other customers who weren't so well behaved as Aidan Merritt.'

Okay, so that was the deal – Cooper needed to produce a name. He tried the first one that came to mind.

'Ian Gullick?'

'You're close,' said Lane.

'This isn't a guessing game,' snapped Cooper.

He immediately regretted losing his patience. Many individuals would clam up when they were spoken to the wrong way.

'No, I'm sorry,' said Lane. 'I'm just . . . well, I know we're not exactly doctors or priests, but if people thought we were gossiping about them, it wouldn't be good for business. I like to chat to my customers a bit – it makes them feel at ease. So they often end up telling me things they wouldn't want to be passed on.'

'Vince Naylor?' said Cooper.

Lane visibly relaxed.

'So there was trouble involving the two visitors, the Pearsons?' asked Cooper.

'A customer who'd had far too much to drink started trying to chat up . . . what's her name? Trisha. I'd rather not be too specific, but you've mentioned the name already, so you're halfway there.'

'Okay.'

'Anyway, he became a bit persistent, and it turned nasty very quickly. Her husband got into an argument with him. There would have been punches thrown, but Maurice stepped in.'

'What did he do?'

'He threw the drunk out, along with a couple of his friends who stuck up for him.'

'But not the Pearsons.'

'No, he let them stay. It wasn't their fault, what had happened. Not at all. Though I think her hubby had a bit of a temper on him, you know. He looked like a man who'd try to sort out a problem with his fists, even if he was likely to come off worst. You understand what I mean, don't you? You can see it in their eyes sometimes. You can tell someone who is a little bit too close to the edge, and won't take much pushing to go over.'

'Yes, I know what you mean. I've seen people like that, especially when they've got a bit of alcohol inside them. Do you think Maurice Wharton could see it too?'

Lane shrugged. 'He'd run pubs for a long time. He must have seen plenty of customers like that. You develop a nose for trouble after a while, I reckon. You learn to spot the type.'

'He had a pub over in Chesterfield for a while, didn't he?'

'Yes, and in a pretty rough area, not far from the football ground. Now that place was never known for its food and accommodation. It's a real drinker's pub.'

'So Maurice had enough experience to judge the situation and step in at exactly the right moment.'

'Yes, I reckon that would be a fair summary. His word was enough to sort it out at that point. He didn't need to call the dogs.'

'Dogs?'

'He had two Alsatians that lived out the back of the pub. He'd call them if there was real trouble. Not that it happened often at the Light House. They came with him from the Dragon.'

'From where?'

'The pub in Chesterfield. He needed them there.'

'I see.'

'I wasn't up there at the Light House when it all kicked off, of course,' said Lane. 'I mean, the fuss about that couple going missing in the snowstorm. When the police arrived, it was Christmas Eve, as I recall – a Thursday. I'd done my last shift on the Tuesday night.'

'Tuesday? Oh, and the pub wasn't open after that, am I right?'

'Yes. The Whartons liked to spend Christmas Day and Boxing Day on their own, as a family. So they always gave the staff a couple of days off. No one wants to work over that period anyway, if they can help it. And very few customers are interested in driving out on to the moors for their Christmas dinner, even when the weather isn't as bad as it was then.'

'So Maurice and Nancy would have been looking forward to a quiet time on their own with the kids.'

'Right. They certainly wouldn't have expected the police

and mountain rescue teams all over the place two days after the pub had closed for Christmas.'

'No, I suppose not.'

Lane laughed. 'I can just imagine what Mad Maurice must have said to them. In a way, I wish I'd been there to hear it. I bet it was priceless.'

'Yes, he's known as quite a character.'

'You can say that again. Everyone talks about Maurice Wharton. Even some of the staff here know of him.'

Lane arranged some glasses on the shelf above his head, and cast an eye around the lounge to see if there were any customers requiring attention. But all was quiet. It was a little too quiet for Cooper's liking, but that was probably why people came here.

'Have you seen the Whartons since they left the pub, Mr Lane?' he asked.

'A couple of times. It was sad to visit them in that little council house. Losing the pub hit Nancy hard. I think Kirsten and Eliot were the worst affected, though. It was their life, the place they'd grown up in. They used to love being able to walk out of the door and wander about on the moors. And both of them detested the idea of moving into town and living on that housing estate. They even had to get rid of the dogs. To be honest, I'm surprised Eliot's still there. But of course he was always devoted to his dad. He wouldn't leave Maurice.'

'I see. You must have got on all right with the Whartons. You worked at the Light House quite a while.'

'Yes, it was fine once you got used to Mad Maurice. Everyone liked Nancy, and Eliot and Kirsten are nice kids. People could take or leave Maurice, I suppose. But he was the one who got all the attention.'

'So what do *you* think went wrong at the Light House?' asked Cooper.

'Wrong? Oh, you mean the reason for it closing down?'

'Yes, of course.'

'Lots of things. I think it began when we had fewer pumps on the bar than there used to be. That's a bad sign.'

'Why?'

'The number of pumps reflects your throughputs. You've got to shift lager and keg ale within five days, and cask in three. Beer is a living product, you see. Overstocking leads to fobbing and deterioration in quality. If you're not going to sell the beer, you have to reduce the number of pumps. Maurice's throughputs had been going down for years.'

'Fobbing?' asked Cooper.

'Too much foaming when the beer is pulled through.'

'Is the quality of beer that important?'

'Of course. What do you think – that people just drink any old rubbish? Have you never heard of CAMRA?'

'I suppose so. It just never occurred to me that beer quality might have contributed to the failure of the business.'

'Well, there were other factors. All kinds of things might have affected the bottom line. Stock going out of date because of overordering, credit lost because goods were returned after their best before date. You can see there's a cumulative effect.'

'A slippery slope,' said Cooper.

'Exactly. I think it must have been difficult for the Whartons to get good staff, too. The students who worked there never had proper training. They were constantly spilling beer into the drip trays. Filling one tray a day with wasted beer is like losing fifteen thousand pounds' worth of sales over the course of a year for a pub that size.'

Cooper was impressed. 'You're very well clued up about the business.'

'I've got qualifications, my friend. NVQ Level Three and a National Certificate.'

Reluctantly Cooper put his empty cup down on the counter. 'Thanks for the coffee. It was very good. All we get at the station is something hot and wet from a machine.'

'No problem. Let me know if there's anything else I can do.'

'Can I contact you here?'

'I'll write my mobile number down for you.'

Lane scribbled the number on a sheet from an order pad and handed it to Cooper.

'Of course, you realise it was all show,' he said. 'I mean that "mad Maurice" business. Maurice Wharton was a top landlord in his time. Good at his job, loyal to his customers. They were like a big family to him. If you showed that you were willing to fit in at the Light House, he'd do anything for you.'

'Anything?' said Cooper.

Lane hesitated. 'Well, yes – I think so.'

At West Street, Luke Irvine had been busy tracking down the information that Cooper had asked him for.

'Ian Gullick is a market trader. Forty-five years old, married with one grown-up child, a son. They live close by, in Lowtown. Nothing on him in the way of a criminal record. Vince Naylor is a couple of years younger, and has a house right here in Edendale. He seems to be a jack-of-all-trades. He's had all kinds of work, mostly driving jobs. But he got a twelve-month ban for a drink-driving offence, so he had to take labouring jobs on local construction sites for a while. Now he's set up his own business doing small-scale property maintenance – kitchens, bathrooms, driveways, patios. You know the sort of thing.'

'What kind of vehicle does he drive?'

Irvine looked up from his notes. 'I don't know. But I'll find out.'

'Gullick, too.'

'I'm on it.'

There was no escaping the fact that the night after the argument with Naylor, the Pearsons had left the George and were never seen again. Their behaviour up to that point had seemed perfectly normal. The original inquiry team had traced their movements over the previous couple of days before their evening in Castleton, hadn't they?

'Where else had the Pearsons been in this area, apart from the Light House?' asked Cooper.

'Earlier on the day they went missing, they'd stopped for petrol at the Sickleholme service station near Bamford,' said Irvine. 'They'd bought a hundred litres of unleaded, which was close to a full tank on a Ranger Rover III series.'

'Sickleholme service station?' said Cooper.

'You know it?'

'Oh yes.'

Everyone who drove up the Hope Valley towards Castleton knew the service station. It was located at the bottom of the road up to Bamford, right by the traffic lights on the A6187. But the name was particularly familiar to Cooper at the moment. The garage at Sickleholme had a fleet of wedding cars, including classic Bentleys. They were on a list.

Irvine looked up, and Cooper nodded for him to continue.

'When the car was found at the cottage after the Pearsons were reported missing, it still had almost a full tank,' said Irvine. 'From the service station they visited the Riverside Herb Centre just across the road, where the credit card receipt showed they bought cheese, olives and some herbal tea. Only the tea was found in the cottage when it was entered two days later.'

He stopped speaking again, and Cooper realised that Irvine was looking at someone over his shoulder. There was only one person who could arrive so silently and immediately create such an air of tension around her.

Diane Fry stood in the doorway with her shoulders hunched as if she was cold.

'So where do you stand on this case, DS Cooper?' she said. 'What theory are you pursuing?'

Cooper could tell by her tone that she welcomed the opportunity to put him on the spot. And not just her tone either, but the use of his rank and surname. It was too formal, as if she was deferring to his position, respecting his opinion. But everyone in the room knew different.

'Would it surprise you if I said I was keeping an open mind?' he said mildly. 'We need more evidence one way or the other. At the moment, the bloodstained clothing is definitely leading towards the conclusion that foul play is involved in the disappearance of the Pearsons.' He saw Fry beginning to smile. 'But it's not enough without some confirmation.'

'You want a body?' she said.

'That would help.'

'What about these other visitors who spoke to the Pearsons the previous night?' asked Irvine tentatively. 'We haven't even made a start on trying to trace them.'

Fry shook her head. 'I think they're a red herring. Four red herrings, in fact. I mean, four unidentified strangers? It seems a bit like overkill to me.'

'You don't think they're important at all?'

'No, of course not. In my opinion, it's a deliberate effort to distract our attention. We could be chasing our tails for months trying to find those people.'

'But they could have information that would help,' said Irvine. 'One of the Pearsons might have let something slip about what they intended to do.'

198

'Seriously? If the Pearsons were plotting to do a bunk, I can't imagine they would have said anything to give the plan away. Especially not to complete strangers they met in the pub.'

'If they *were* strangers. We don't know that for sure. Whoever these people were, they might have been part of the plan.'

'How?'

'Well, I don't know. Their role could have been to pick David and Trisha up at a quiet spot where they wouldn't be seen, and whisk them away.'

But Fry was still shaking her head. 'It doesn't make any sense. Why let themselves be seen talking to the Pearsons at the Light House, then? If the plan was so good that two people were able to just vanish off the face of the earth without leaving a trace, that incident doesn't fit. It would be a major flaw in the planning.'

'Something could have gone wrong,' said Irvine uncertainly.

'I don't buy it.'

'Well that's a shame.'

Fry looked at him.

'So you're not even convinced by the bloodstains on the anorak found buried in the peat on Oxlow Moor?'

'It could be part of the plan.'

'Even if the blood is identified as David Pearson's?'

'It wouldn't be too difficult for Pearson to smear some of his own blood on his clothes and leave them for us to find.'

'But he didn't do that. They were buried.'

'Our hopes are resting on forensics, then,' put in Cooper. 'As always.'

'Not quite always. But still . . .'

'They ought to get something off the items dug out of the peat,' he said. 'I know there will have been some deterioration, but we'd be very unlucky to get nothing at all. Haven't we had any results back yet?'

'Still waiting.'

Cooper stared at Fry. He found he just didn't believe her. Forensic results could be slow, it was true. But he was sure that she was lying to him in this instance. Why would she do that?

Henry Pearson was almost exactly as Cooper had pictured him. He was a tall man, with grey hair and sharp, intelligent eyes that turned to deep pools of sadness when his face was at rest. Most of the time he was far from at rest. Pearson fixed his gaze on each of the officers in the room by turn, studying them as if he was trying to see right into their hearts. When he'd been round the room once, he started all over again, perhaps hoping he might see something different next time.

At the same time he was listening intently to everything that was said. He'd brought a briefcase with him, and opened it to pull out a leather-bound pad. Cooper watched him write a careful note of the date and time, and the place of the meeting. Underneath, he listed the names of the police officers present. He made notes as Superintendent Branagh spoke, but still looked up periodically to examine the reactions of the people round him.

'Naturally, Mr Pearson, in light of the new evidence, we're reopening the inquiry into the disappearance of your son and his wife,' said Branagh, seeming a little unsettled by Pearson's manner.

'Reopening?' said Pearson. 'I was under the impression that the case was never actually closed. Am I wrong in that?'

'No, sir. The inquiry is active, and always has been. But

the fact is, we exhausted all the avenues. It's only the new evidence we've turned up that has given us fresh leads to follow.'

'Is there a question of resources?'

'There's always a question of resources.'

'If money would help . . .' said Pearson.

As one, the officers in the room bristled, their faces a mixture of indignation and panic. The mere suggestion that someone had offered financial inducements was enough to cause consternation. Cooper imagined the investigations that might follow. A neighbouring force sent in to examine procedures and records, probing questions about bank balances . . . It was everyone's worst nightmare.

But that wasn't what Mr Pearson meant. He scanned the shocked faces, and almost smiled. It was no more than a twitch of the lips, which disappeared as quickly as it had come. But in that one second, Cooper saw that their visitor had a sense of humour, and he began to warm to him a little.

'I mean, in order to encourage witnesses to come forward, of course,' said Pearson. 'That's normal practice, isn't it? I've seen it done in other cases.'

'A reward?' asked Branagh, an audible hint of relief in her voice.

'If that's what you call it. If it might help to overcome the reluctance of certain individuals, I would be happy to put some cash up. If someone is still hesitating over what they should do, a reasonable amount of money could tip the balance in our favour, couldn't it?'

'It's true,' put in Hitchens, with a glance at Branagh. 'We've had results that way in the past.'

'Perhaps we can make a decision on that in a few days' time. Let's see what progress we can make in the meantime, shall we?'

'All right. I suppose I'll have to accept that.'

'Mr Pearson, can I ask you something? Do you remain convinced that your son and his wife have met with a violent end?'

'Yes, of course.' He hesitated. 'Obviously I'm very well aware of the stories that have been going round over the past couple of years. All that nonsense on the internet, all those wild theories. Every one of them is ludicrous. It's inconceivable that David and Patricia would have somehow managed to disappear and change their identities. If my son had known he was accused of doing something wrong, he would have stayed to face the music. He would have wanted to clear his name. He is not the type to run away.

'There's one more thing I want to say,' added Pearson.

'Sir?'

'Unlike most of you, I've spent every day and every week of the past two and a half years looking for my son and his wife. I've given every minute of my time to trying to locate David and Patricia, wherever they may be.'

Pearson looked around the room again, giving them the benefit of his steady gaze.

'And that,' he said, 'is despite the fact that I've never been entirely sure, deep in my own heart, that there was still someone alive to look for.'

18

The sense of isolation struck Cooper every time he got out of his car at the Light House. It wasn't just the feel of the wind on his face as it swept over the bare acres of moor. It wasn't the silence cither, which was almost unnatural given the attention the old pub was getting. The isolation seemed to be a quality in the character of the building itself.

It wouldn't always have been like this. The old roads had come this way, the packhorse ways and traders' routes – all the local foot and cart traffic that had followed the departure of the Romans from Britain. The Light House would have gradually grown up to service the passing trade, becoming a place to rest and change the horses before crossing the moor to markets in Chapel-en-le-Frith and Buxton.

But the people who'd come along later and built the modern road system had different ideas. They preferred to travel in the valleys, and take a more circuitous route to their destination. So the A625 and the A623 had developed, and taken all the traffic away to the north and south of Oxlow Moor, leaving the Light House isolated despite its prominent location.

From the first-floor windows the Whartons could have looked out and seen cars moving on both main roads in the distance, knowing that very few of those drivers would ever find their way to the pub.

Right now, a crime-scene tent stood incongruously in the middle of a vast expanse of blackened vegetation, like the aftermath of a nuclear blast. Black dust covered everything, and wisps of smoke and steam trailed into the air. The heat from the ground could still be felt, yet the peat squelched wetly underfoot.

There had been more than twenty pumps on site for over a week as the fire continued to burn. United Utilities staff were out in two Argocats with fire fogging units. Fogging had been developed to fight fires with low water volume, producing a high-density fog of water droplets that turned very quickly to steam and absorbed large amounts of heat.

Digging in the peat was going to be a long, laborious job. The smoke rolling across the moor made it look more dangerous than it probably was.

'If the wind changes and the fire begins to move this way, the fire service will have to abandon the moor and concentrate on protecting these buildings,' said Wayne Abbott, pulling off his face mask.

'Any more finds?' asked Cooper.

'Not so far.'

'I'm not sure if that's good news, or bad.'

Cooper gazed into the trench that was slowly being dug into the peat. He half expected to see a human hand or foot protruding from the ground, stained brown but perfectly preserved. If the Pearsons were buried here, theirs wouldn't be the first bodies to emerge from the peat bogs.

In the village of Hope, legend had it that the corpses of a grazier and his maidservant who had died from exposure on the moors thirty years previously were once put on public display. The two bodies had been so well preserved by the peaty soil that they were kept on show for twenty years before eventually being given a decent burial.

Inhabitants of the Peak District seemed to have had an

interest in preserving bodies. According to one old Peakland custom, the soul of a dead person could be purified by laying a heap of salt on the corpse's chest. A parson who called at a Calver farmhouse on the death of one of his parishioners was said to have been horrified when he found the whole body pickled in salt.

'Wear masks if you're going to be out here,' said Abbott. 'Don't take risks.'

Abbott was responsible for the meticulous art of crime-scene management – deciding where to search and what techniques to use, while taking care not to disturb potential evidence.

Cooper remembered Liz repeating a motto she'd learned in training as a crime-scene examiner.

'ABC. Nothing, nobody, everything.'

'Sorry?' he'd said.

'Remember your ABC. Assume nothing. Believe nobody. Check everything.'

'Okay, I get it.'

'It's worth remembering.'

During their training, student crime-scene examiners never knew quite what to expect at the end of an assignment. It could be a person hanging from a tree or slumped in a car dead from exhaust fumes. They had to feel that shock factor – they couldn't be sent off to their forces after training only to freeze when they saw a dead body. Part of the job was detaching yourself from emotion.

Cooper looked around for the presence of police vehicles. A liveried Honda CR-V four-wheel drive had left the pub car park and ventured out on to the edge of the moor. It was now sitting like a UFO on the black expanse of charred heather. He could see it a hundred yards away, with its red stripe and its light bar still flashing blue against a backdrop of smoke.

'It reminds me of a fire I attended once,' said Villiers. 'That was a grass fire, along about a mile of railway embankment.'

'You don't have experience of firefighting, surely?' said Cooper.

'Not really. But back in 2002 and 2003, our guys took part in Operation Fresco. If you remember, that was the operation to provide fire service cover during the strike by civilian firefighters. It went on for six or seven months.'

'The old Green Goddesses. Of course.'

Villiers laughed. 'They were what all the press wanted to take pictures of. But the armed forces have some modern equipment too, you know. In fact, there are professional firefighters in the RAF. They're needed at airfields. During the strike, they headed up specialist units, like breathing apparatus and rescue equipment support teams. Firefighting isn't such a mystery.'

Cooper shook his head. He found himself constantly amazed at the breadth of experience Carol Villiers had gathered during her career in the RAF Police. Just the number of countries she'd served in made his time with Derbyshire Constabulary seem incredibly parochial. He wasn't sure whether he envied her or not.

'Wayne, have they decided what sort of buildings have been uncovered?' asked Cooper.

'Just mine buildings,' said Abbott.

'Someone will be interested.'

At High Rake nearby, the Peak District Mines Historical Society had undertaken an eight-year excavation project, which had uncovered two steam-engine houses, a platform for a capstan and wooden gin engine, an ore crusher and an ore-dressing floor. The remains had mostly dated to the middle of the nineteenth century, when the mine was state-of-the-art. The highlight of the excavation was the discovery of the bottom third of a Cornish pumping-engine house, which had been set underground, a relatively rare and complex type of engine and thought to be the best surviving example in the world. Yes, there would be people interested.

'A lead miners' building?' said Villiers. 'They didn't have many structures on the surface.'

'Not so old as we first thought, then.'

'No. But see . . .'

Abbott directed Cooper a few feet away from the line of stones. He noticed a corroded iron plate lying in the burnt grass. He'd seen one of these before, only recently.

'A capped mine shaft?'

'Yes. I don't think this one was generally known about. It's not on any maps. We're checking with the Mines Historical Society to see if they have any information on, it, but I suspect it's one that got lost and forgotten.'

The plate was around three foot square and made of rusted iron on crude hinges. There was no lock or bolt on it of any kind, and it would be easy to raise, even using one hand. Another hole was covered by a larger buckled iron sheet, which hadn't been fixed down at all but simply rested on stone edgings. Cooper examined the hinges of the plate. They were caked in rust and covered in a layer of peat, with fragments of burnt vegetation fused to them as if stuck with glue.

Unlike the open-cast workings of Moss Rake and Shuttle Rake, these were vertical shafts dug deep into the ground by lead miners. Some of the local rakes were still in use for the quarrying of minerals like fluorspar and calcite. But the lead mines had fallen into disuse decades ago.

The two shafts had been fenced off at some time with a few posts and a bit of barbed wire. But the posts were gone, and the wire that had hung between them lay on the ground.

'Haven't you looked inside?' asked Cooper.

'No,' said Abbott.

'But there might be traces of the Pearsons down there.'

'No, no. That's not possible. These shafts haven't been opened for decades. Possibly for a hundred years or more.'

'I see.'

Abbott looked at him, as if sensing that he was disappointed.

'However,' he said, 'these old lead mines rarely had just one shaft. If there was a vein of ore running across this area, they would have dug several shafts to get access to it.'

'We'll find some more, then?' asked Cooper.

'If we look. Yes, I'm sure we will.'

When he lifted the plate, Cooper found he could look straight down into the hole, though without a torch he could see only a few feet into its depths. The shaft was simply hacked out of the rock and was barely wide enough to accommodate a fully grown man. The sides had been worn smooth in places by the shoulders of miners passing up and down. A single iron bolt had been hammered in as a makeshift foothold, but otherwise there seemed to be nothing to prevent a direct plunge into darkness.

Those old lead miners must have been small men. Poor people had been small anyway in those days, thanks to the general lack of nutrition. But perhaps miners had been chosen for their size, like jockeys. It would certainly be much easier to get access through the shafts if you were no more than five foot six and built on the skinny side.

There had been incidents recorded in the past of small children falling into mine shafts and being killed. But as Cooper looked at the width of the shaft in front of him, he found it difficult to imagine any adult being unable to prevent themselves from falling all the way in.

At least, he corrected himself, any conscious, living adult.

During their years at the Light House, the Whartons had tried to fight off the inevitable. Long ago, they'd moved away from the traditional hunting prints and picturesque Peak District scenes. The horse brasses and decorative plates had gone.

For a while, Cooper recalled, they'd opted for a cultural look – shelves of ancient hardback books bought in a job lot, modern abstract artworks, an occasional musical instrument hung near the ceiling. Then one day it had all vanished again, the pub closed for refurbishment, consultants swarming through the rooms, distressing the decor, jamming decrepit furniture into every corner – wooden benches and oak dressers, a reproduction writing desk. An antique look, he supposed. Nostalgic chic. It was an attempt to recapture some past that had never existed. Because the Light House as it appeared now had been a Victorian re-creation. Still a stop-off for travellers, yes. But it had been the height of modernity in its day. The facade hinted of aspirations to grandeur.

Well, the antiques were gone again, sold off to raise a bit of cash against the Whartons' debts perhaps. The main bar was left with a range of standard pub furniture, glass-topped tables and wooden chairs, scattered haphazardly, as if the clientele had abandoned the pub in a hurry.

'I want to take a look at the function room upstairs,' he said.

'Oh, the party?' said Villiers. 'Right, I see. Reliving the memories.'

They climbed the stairs to the first floor, where Cooper opened the door and examined the dusty floor and the little bar in the corner. The YFC party had taken place in this room, he was fairly sure. Even in his inebriated state, he remembered coming up and down those stairs. There seemed to have been a lot of people in the pub that night, though. Had someone else been holding a party here? Or was the function room spilling out revellers into the public bar from time to time?

Given the lack of records, it would require someone with a better memory than his to recall the facts. He could get Hurst or Irvine to trawl through the witness statements again, looking for someone who'd been attending a different party. Two days before Christmas, though? Whose memory wasn't hazy, especially if you were the kind to get caught up in the social whirl?

'Why not ask your brother?' suggested Villiers, as he was about to close the door again.

'Matt?'

'That's the only brother you've got, as far as I recall.'

'Yes, but . . .'

'He was there too, wasn't he? I mean, he was in the Light House that night. You came here with him. That's what you told us, Ben.'

Cooper said nothing, and found he was gripping the door handle a little too tightly. Villiers nodded, reading his silence as clearly as if he'd spoken everything that was in his mind.

'But you can't believe that your brother might be involved in a violent incident,' she said. And she paused. 'Oh, wait . . .'

He turned to look at her then, and watched the realisation dawn on her face, the memory of an incident, all too recent, when Matt Cooper had shot and injured an intruder at Bridge End Farm. Matt had been lucky to escape prosecution, a decision by the Crown Prosecution Service that had

210

reflected the public mood of the time. But despite the relief among the family at the outcome, everyone knew now. Everyone was aware that Matt Cooper had the potential for violence.

That knowledge, and that knowledge alone, changed everything.

Henry Pearson had been brought to the scene as a gesture towards good relations with the family. but who had tipped off the media, no one seemed to know. Photographers from two local newspapers snapped Mr Pearson as he got out of his car and spoke to DCI Mackenzie. A crew from a regional TV station had set up near the outer cordon, and a reporter was doing a piece to camera, with the moor and the crime-scene tent in the background.

Mackenzie didn't look happy about it, but he had to appear concerned and cooperative in front of the cameras. Possibly Mr Pearson had orchestrated all this himself. During the past two and a half years, he must have learned the best ways of handling the media. This was an opportunity for him to revitalise the interest in his campaign.

'No one has mentioned what forensic evidence you've obtained from the items that were dug out of the peat,' he said.

'Sir?'

Pearson looked at Mackenzie directly. 'For example, was there blood?'

It was impossible to refuse such a straightforward request for information from a member of the family.

'Yes, sir. There was.'

'And?'

Mackenzie held out his hands apologetically. 'I can't tell you any more at the moment.'

211

Diane Fry was waiting to speak to the DCI, holding back until he was free from the attention of the cameras.

'We've got some preliminary results back from forensics,' she told Cooper.

'Finally,' he said. 'And?'

'Those stains on David's anorak. Well, they're confirmed as human blood.'

'Pretty much as expected.'

'Yes.' She looked towards Henry Pearson, to make sure he was out of earshot. 'The trouble is, Ben – the blood isn't David Pearson's, or even Trisha's.'

Before he could digest the information, Cooper's phone rang. He looked at the display, but it was a mobile number he didn't recognise.

'Who is this?' he said.

'It's Nancy Wharton. I wanted to let you know that Maurice has agreed to talk to you.'

'When?'

'Now,' she said. 'It has to be this afternoon. Today is one of his good days.'

Maurice Wharton was a shadow of the man Cooper remembered. The meaty elbows that he used to rest on the bar at the Light House were bony now, and hung with pale, shrivelled flesh. There was a curious yellow tinge to his skin and in the whites of his eyes. His hands jerked spasmodically on the cover of his bed in the hospice room, and he lay back on the pillow as if already exhausted before the visit had even begun.

'Mr Wharton? Detective Sergeant Cooper, Edendale Police. Your wife said you'd agreed to talk to me.'

Cooper wondered if he was speaking too loudly. It was always a tendency when talking to the old and sick.

Wharton seemed to wink at him, one eye closing involuntarily.

'I know you, don't I?'

Cooper sighed. 'Probably.'

'You've been in the pub at some time. I remember faces. Even now, I still have my memory for faces.'

'Yes, you're right.'

'I don't get many visitors here. I don't want to, really. But Nancy says you're all right.'

'I hate to trouble you,' said Cooper. 'But we're conducting a murder investigation. Aidan Merritt. I expect you heard.'

'Yes, even in here.' Wharton nodded at the TV screen across the room. 'I keep up to date. I wouldn't want to die without knowing how Derby County were getting on.'

Cooper smiled, glad that Maurice Wharton still had his wits about him. Pancreatic cancer might not affect the brain, but he bet the drugs did. The chemotherapy, the increasingly powerful painkillers. What did that combination really do to the memory?

'I do get confused now and then,' said Wharton, as if reading his mind. 'There are bad dreams, and I'm not always sure when I wake up whether they're real or not.'

'Mr Merritt's murder is real. He was clubbed to death at the Light House earlier this week.'

'The pub is closed up,' said Wharton.

'Someone broke in.'

'Why would they do that?'

'We have no idea,' said Cooper. 'We don't know what Mr Merritt's reason was for being there. We don't know why the person who attacked him was there either. We're looking for any possibilities. So if you can help us at all . . .'

Wharton was quiet for a moment, breathing very shallowly, as if it used up a lot of his energy just to keep air moving in and out of his lungs.

213

'Aidan Merritt. He was one of my regulars. Funny, that.'

'What is?'

'That my regulars should die off before me. I didn't think it would be that way.'

'But Aidan in particular . . .?'

'The last person I would have expected to be getting himself into bother. He wasn't my type – too quiet, a bit studious. Not a big spender. But trouble? No, he was as quiet as a mouse. What was he doing at the pub?'

'That's what I'm trying to find out,' said Cooper.

'Beats me.'

Wharton began to cough, and Cooper waited while he cleared his chest and spat into a tissue. He wondered if he should offer to do anything, fetch a drink of water or what-ever. It was always difficult knowing how to behave when visiting the sickbed.

'You were asking Nancy about an incident with that couple, the Pearsons,' said Wharton when he'd recovered.

'Yes. It doesn't seem to have been followed up by the original inquiry when the Pearsons went missing.'

'Because it was all settled,' said Wharton.

'How was it settled?'

'I sweet-talked the visitors, made a fuss of them, did a bit of PR. Then I sorted the lads out. All over and done with, see?'

'The lads? Ian Gullick and Vince Naylor?'

'Ian and Vince. They're good lads really, you know. There's no harm in them.'

Cooper tried not to appear sceptical, but Wharton twisted his head on his pillow to look at him.

'You don't believe me.'

'I'd need more information,' said Cooper cautiously.

'Yes, that's right. Make your own mind up. Take people as you find them. But you don't know them like I do. I

214

saw the best and worst of people from behind a bar. You're on the wrong track with Gullick and Naylor. I might not get the chance to tell you anything else, so make a note of that.'

'Yes, sir.'

Wharton wheezed. 'I knew a lot of people at one time. Thousands. Now there's just the family. Family is very important, isn't it? Don't you agree?'

'Of course.'

'It's the kids I worry about most. Eliot and Kirsten. It's very bad for them. Their lives have been so disrupted, just when they're at an age when they should have some stability. And it's all my fault. I lost their home, brought them here into town, which they hate. And now I'm going to leave them in the lurch, thanks to this damn cancer. Even the life insurance won't pay out much. I'll be no more use to them dead than I have been while I was alive.'

'It's not your fault you got cancer,' said Cooper.

'It feels like it. It looks as though I did it to avoid having to put things right for my family, to avoid paying back what I owe them. And I owe them a lot.'

Wharton gazed out of the window again. A pair of gold-finches were fluttering around a bird feeder hung just outside his room.

'You know – the night they closed up the pub, I couldn't face being there,' he said. 'Not right *there*, on the premises. I ought to have been present, as the licensee. But I just couldn't do it.'

'I understand.'

'Do you? It was more than a pub to me, you know. It was my life, and my home.'

Cooper nodded. He thought he did understand, but if Mr Wharton preferred to think it was a unique feeling, it might be best to let him talk.

215

'So I sat in my car,' said Wharton. 'I parked up by the side of the road on Oxlow Moor, where I could see the pub in the distance, on the skyline. Do you know the spot I mean?'

'Yes.'

'I sat there for a long time, waiting for something to happen. And in the end, I saw the lights going out. It was dusk by then. I was sitting in my car, and I watched the windows of my pub going dark one by one, until . . . well, until the Light House ceased to exist.'

'It must have been very painful,' said Cooper.

Wharton smiled weakly. 'I thought so at the time. But the fact is, I didn't really know anything about pain until now.'

Wharton hardly ever met Cooper's eye during his visit. Occasionally he would glance quickly around the room, as if checking it was still there. But mostly, all he wanted to do was stare out of the window – not looking at the garden or the fish pond, but at something much further away, beyond the range of ordinary, physical vision.

To Cooper's mind, it looked like a long stare into the past. Wharton was a man drawn against his will to gaze at a vision of unhappy memories, a distant kaleidoscope of sadness and regrets. He hoped he would never see such a vision himself when he gazed out of the window in his old age.

'There was no way we could keep going,' said Wharton. 'But I didn't want to give up. I tried everything. In the end, I was so desperate that I trusted people I shouldn't have done. I signed an agreement. They were supposed to put capital into the business for a share of the pub. But they turned out to be liars and parasites. There was a bit of decorating, some old furniture got chucked out and some new stuff moved in. They called it a redesign.'

Cooper nodded. The nostalgic chic. He shouldn't have been surprised that it wasn't Maurice Wharton's idea of the perfect decor.

'And then when it didn't work out the way they'd told me it would, they pulled the plug. Just like that. They wanted their money back. Well, we'd already remortgaged, so the only thing we could do was sell up. I should have known, I should have been able to spot a wrong 'un a mile off after all these years. But I didn't.'

'Perhaps . . .' suggested Cooper hesitantly. 'Perhaps your judgement wasn't at its best.'

'What do you mean?'

'I've heard that when things went wrong, you began to drink too much.'

'I was bitter. I was angry. Yes, of course I turned to drink.'

'Alcohol never took away anger and bitterness.'

'No. But it numbs them for a while.' He turned away to the window. 'For some of us, that's the best we can hope for.'

He said it with such feeling that Cooper looked at him in surprise, studying him as if he was seeing him for the first time. Yes, there was more than a hint of bitterness in the eyes, a twitch of anger in the set of his jaw. A man who knew about alcohol, too. Not a good combination.

Wharton was silent for a while, lying back on his pillow as if he'd exhausted himself with the burst of emotion. Cooper sat quietly, waiting. He was reminded of the time he'd sat at his mother's bedside at Edendale General Hospital. He'd eventually fallen asleep in the chair, and had woken to find that she had died.

Now, he began to wonder whether Wharton was aware that his visitor was still there in the room.

'I was in the Job, you know,' said Wharton finally, addressing some spot near the ceiling.

'Were you?' Cooper had heard the capital J and knew what it meant. 'You served as a police officer?'

'You didn't know that, did you?' said Wharton. 'That's the trouble these days – too much information, all that data and intelligence flooding in. There's so much of it that it doesn't get through to the right people. Not the bits of information you need to know, anyway. Someone will have that fact on a computer back in your office. I suppose you'll ask them about it now.'

'Of course I will.'

'You know what they used to call me, don't you? Mad Maurice.'

Cooper nodded. Some people still called him that. He doubted whether Wharton would want to hear it, though.

'Well, that was me,' said Wharton. 'Mad Maurice. Not this pathetic thing that I am now. I'd like them to remember me as Mad Maurice, the terror of the Light House. Will you tell them that?'

'I'll be happy to, sir.'

'Right then.' He laughed weakly. 'So, if we're done here – why don't you bugger off? Haven't you got a home to go to?'

19

At Bridge End Farm, Matt Cooper looked round for Amy and Josie, then drew his brother across the yard towards the machinery shed, to be out of earshot.

The big shed where the tractor and equipment were kept had always been Matt's territory, and he treated it like a den, a place to go when he wanted to get away from the family for a while. Certainly, the girls had been well taught as children that they had to stay away from farm machinery.

'You know what it's like,' said Matt uneasily.

'No. Tell me.'

'The thing is,' said Matt, 'not everybody has much faith in your lot these days.'

'My lot?'

'Yes, your lot. You know what I mean.'

'The police.'

'Yes.'

'You can say it, Matt. It's not a dirty word.'

'Well, that's a matter of opinion.'

'Oh?'

Matt rubbed the sleeve of his shirt against the side of the big green John Deere, as if trying to wipe away a speck of dirt. It looked a bit futile given the amount of mud caking the wheel arches. The tractor was overdue for a wash.

'Some of the lads . . .' he said. 'Well, they don't have

anything good to say about the police these days. There have been far too many farms in this area targeted by thieves, and the cops have done nothing about it, except hand out crime numbers for insurance claims. It's no use when you've lost a vital bit of kit, or your best calves have vanished in the back of some toerag's trailer. People are finding that it's affecting their businesses, and their families are getting frightened, and there's no one they can turn to for protection.'

'I've heard all this before,' said Ben.

'Yes. Well you're going to hear it again, a lot more. And it won't just be from me. I'm warning you, that's all.'

Ben could see that Matt was nervous. The fact that his brother was a police officer had always been a bit of problem for him, constantly putting him in an awkward position where he was trapped between a rock and a hard place. The turning point had come last year, when Matt had taken the law into his own hands and shot a burglar in his yard. The moment he was handcuffed and arrested for attempted murder was the point when he decided whose side the police were on.

It was a common enough story. Ben himself felt uncomfortable sometimes when he heard about normally law-abiding citizens who found themselves on the wrong end of the criminal justice system for defending themselves and their property, or who got a speeding fine for doing forty-two miles an hour on an open road. These were the same people who saw burglaries and criminal damage being committed without any apparent effort by the police to investigate, and whose lives were made miserable by anti-social behaviour carried out with impunity.

For months now, he'd been hearing complaints that the Metropolitan Police had been happy to baton-charge peaceful pro-hunting marchers from the Countryside Alliance, but

220

had stood by and watched as rioters burned and looted half the city.

In this country, policing was supposed to be conducted by consent. But more and more often it seemed that the police were losing the support of the public. *Whose side are they on?* was a common cry.

'I'm sure you're able to talk sense into these lads, if they got the wrong idea,' said Ben.

'Well . . .'

'Aren't you, Matt?'

'I've tried. But it's a losing battle. I'm sorry, Ben, but that's just the way things are going.'

'So they won't talk to me.'

'They say they have nothing to tell.'

'Then the conversation won't take long.'

'There are two people still missing, Matt. And Aidan Merritt – did you know him? He got his head bashed in at the Light House the other day.'

'Yes, I know.'

Matt looked over his shoulder, fiddling with the tools on his workbench. Ben found himself beginning to get irritated by the pointless clatter. His brother had called him to the farm, so he must have something useful to say.

'Matt, you understand – it's either me or someone else they'll have to talk to.'

His brother sighed. 'Okay, I can set something up. They've said, as a last resort, that they'll meet you on neutral ground.'

'What is this? Neutral ground? Are we at war now?'

'That's what they said.'

'And these are people who were at the Light House the night the Pearsons were there?'

'At the Young Farmers' do, yes. They were down in the bar part of the time, playing pool. They know pretty much everyone. It's the best I can do.'

'All right, I suppose I'll have to take it. What neutral ground?'

'The old field barn on the Foolow road.'

'I know where that is. Tonight?'

Matt looked at his watch. 'Yes, if you can manage it. I just need to make one phone call.'

Ben nodded. So Matt's contacts were just waiting for the call to come out and meet him. It had all been a bit of play-acting really, that show of reluctance. They had both known the outcome.

Cooper was on a quiet stretch of road half a mile from Bridge End Farm. The road became very narrow and winding here, and the surface deteriorated, as if it was about to peter out into a farm track, the way some Peak District roads did. Only if you were familiar with the area did you know that you had to drive on for a few hundred yards to emerge on to a decent surface again, where the road crested the brow of the hill and began a descent into the valley.

The lights of the town would come into view by the time he reached that point. But here, with the trees overhanging the dry-stone walls, there was no light to speak of.

He glanced in his mirror.

'What the heck . . .?'

The car behind him was approaching too fast.

He felt a violent bump, and the Toyota slewed sideways, the nearside front wheel almost slipping into a shallow ditch just short of the stone wall.

Cooper fumbled to unfasten his seat belt. But by the time he'd opened his door and struggled out of the car, the vehicle that had bumped him was gone, disappearing into the darkness. He knew it was white, that was all. A white pickup. He couldn't be sure of the make, though he vaguely thought it looked Japanese. He had no clue about the number plate. It might have been obscured with mud. He might just not have been looking.

He cursed quietly. He'd be useless as a witness. With an hour or so, he'd be wondering whether the shunt had really been deliberate, or if it could just have been an unfortunate accident.

Still shaking slightly from the shock, he got back in his car, reversed it on to the road and carried on. What else was there to do?

The field barn hadn't been used for a while. Not for its proper purpose, anyway. At some time it had become surplus to requirements on whichever farm it belonged to. Too inconvenient for storing hay, too expensive to maintain, impossible to get planning permission for a conversion. So it had stood, damp and deteriorating, half of its roof fallen in, the ground around it scattered with sheep droppings.

Cooper steered the Toyota off the road and into the gateway. He killed the engine, but left the headlights on for a moment as he examined the building. It was big for a field barn, divided into two sections by a brick wall that was completely out of keeping with the pale limestone the building had originally been constructed from. The side nearest the road had been occupied by sheep in recent months. The other half had been used for housing farm equipment, and the doors were high and wide enough to get a tractor in. The roof was more intact too, with only the occasional missing tile that would show light through in the daytime.

Recent tyre tracks ran in from the road. The doors at the far end of the barn stood open, and he looked for the glint of a headlight or reflector that would indicate a vehicle parked partially out of sight. It was difficult to tell in the dark, with his headlights only just reaching, but he thought the barn was empty.

He got out of the car, locked it carefully and took a few paces into the field.

'Hello?' he called.

But there was no answer, except for a chattering of rooks in a copse of trees across the road. No traffic passed; there were no houses in sight. The field itself was empty too, the grass looking as if it might have been reseeded and left to establish itself. He turned and looked at the gate. An old chain hung from it, but it was broken off where it had been attached to an iron bolt in the stone wall.

'Hello?' he called again. 'Anyone there? It's Ben Cooper, Matt's brother.'

Still silence. He didn't know how many people were here to meet him. He couldn't even be sure of their intentions at second hand. In other circumstances he would never have come alone, without backup. He certainly would have made sure someone knew where he was going. But this was different. It was more personal.

And someone did know where he was, of course. Matt had arranged this meeting, or had at least passed the message on. His brother was complicit in whatever happened. That ought to be reassuring.

He moved forward a few more feet, smelled the odour of sheep from the open end of the barn. There were no sheep here now, but they'd left their mark in more ways than one. His boots squashed a carpet of black pellets underfoot as he moved.

'I arranged to meet someone here,' he called. 'Where are you? Come on out and let me see you.'

No answer. No sound of movement, no light of a torch to let him see where someone stood in the darkness. He took half a dozen more steps. The further he got from the road, the darker it seemed to become. That must be an illusion, because there were no street lights out here. The entire area was deep in that true darkness you only ever got in the countryside, when the sky was overcast with cloud as it was now. No stars, no moon, no glimmer of illumination from a nearby village or lights of traffic on a main road.

'Damn,' he muttered.

He was standing just short of the open doors now, so close that he would have been able to hear the tick of an engine as it cooled. He knew this must be a test. They wanted to see how he would react, what sort of person he was. It was a typical game to play. He ought to stop at this point, go back to his car, fetch the torch that lay on the back seat, switch the headlights on to light up the building again. But that would look as though he was scared. It would be a retreat. He knew that at least two pairs of eyes would be watching his every movement from somewhere in the blackness. He couldn't look weak, or they might just drive away and he would never get a chance to talk to them and hear what they had to say.

Cooper felt in his pocket for the reassurance of his ASP, the extendable baton carried by CID officers. Folded, it was small enough to be unobtrusive, but it extended to eighteen inches of steel with a flick of the wrist.

He took a deep breath and squared his shoulders, thinking, *Well, Matt, I hope you know what you're getting me into.*

When the two men appeared from the barn, they had balaclavas over their faces and carried weapons in their hands. Cooper was too busy trying to make out their eyes to take in the details of what they were threatening him with. So he missed seeing the first blow coming, and it caught him off guard. The impact in his side sent spurts of agony up his arm and down into his left leg.

'Stop. Back off. I'm a police officer.'

'We know that.'

The second blow came too quickly for him to react. It struck from behind, an impact with a heavy object on his back, throwing him forward. He stumbled as he tried to keep his balance. *Don't go down, you mustn't go down.*

A third swing from his assailant glanced off his shoulder and struck his temple. Cooper fumbled for his ASP, twisted his body, struck out at the dim shape looming out of the night. He heard a curse of surprise as the ASP hit home.

But then someone else grabbed him from behind. Cooper jabbed an elbow backwards and felt it sink into cushiony flesh. A whoosh of breath past his ear was followed by a relaxation of the grip on his neck. He twisted his hips and grabbed at an arm, forcing it back against the wall. He was vaguely aware of the size and weight of the body he was heaving against – a billowing torso and clumsy limbs, as if he was wrestling a king-size mattress.

He struggled to get a grip on something, but his fingers slid off the surface of a waxed coat. He could smell the wax itself, and deeper smells ingrained into the fabric. He saw the business end of a baseball bat swinging back for another strike.

Then lights came over the hill and swept across the field, briefly illuminating a corner of the barn.

'Shit,' muttered one of the men. 'Let's get out of here.'

The arms released him, and he dropped to the floor. He heard the confused sounds of running feet, an engine starting up, doors banging, someone shouting.

Groggily, Cooper picked himself up and felt the side of his head. There was no blood, but it was painful, and he could feel a lump developing where the the bat had hit him.

He lifted his eyes at the sound of a vehicle slowing, and

peered into the headlights to see a familiar face behind the wheel. The car stopped, a door opened and the driver jumped out.

'Matt? What are you doing here?'

'Thank God. Ben, are you all right? What happened?'

'What do you think? Somebody jumped me.'

'Why would they do that?'

'Because I was asking too many questions in the wrong place?'

'What questions? Who could be so worried about questions?'

'Actually, I thought you might know, Matt.'

His brother flinched away. 'What?'

'In case you hadn't put two and two together, I was attacked right after you talked to your mates who used to be in the Young Farmers Club.'

'No.'

'Oh yes. It's hardly open to debate.'

'They wouldn't do such a thing,' said Matt.

'I think so. But I'm just wondering whose side you're on.'

'I never wanted for this to happen.'

But Ben could hear the doubt in his voice, and see it in his eyes. He still knew his brother well enough for that. He'd retained some of the ability to read Matt's thoughts in an expression or a small gesture.

'If your friends had nothing to do with the Pearsons, what are they so sensitive about? Why do they object to people asking questions?'

Matt looked distressed.

'I was really hoping I wouldn't have to be the one who told you this, Ben,' he said.

'What? *What?*'

'There was something going on at the Light House,

something that had nothing to do with drinking beer. Maurice Wharton had lock-ins, you know.'

'Why? What was going on?'

'Drugs, they reckon.'

'I had no idea. You mean someone was dealing at the Light House?'

'Yep.'

'Did Wharton know about it?'

'I couldn't say. Though it's hard to imagine him not being aware of what went on at his pub.'

A blue Land Rover drove in to the gateway and stopped.

'Who's that?'

'The lads you were supposed to be meeting,' said Matt.

'What?'

'They phoned and said you weren't alone, that someone else was here.'

'So who were those guys?' said Cooper. 'I must have been followed. Was it a white pickup?'

'Ben, I have no idea.'

20

Ben Cooper woke up the next morning sore and angry. When he looked in the bathroom mirror, he could see a bruise developing rapidly on his temple. His hands were scratched and raw where he'd grappled with his assailants, trying to get a grip on a waxed jacket and a bloated body.

He'd reported the incident, without any expectations of a result. He was unable to identify the two men, and the farmers who'd turned up with Matt knew nothing about them, or what sort of vehicle might have been following him.

Turning his face from one side to the other in the mirror, Cooper hoped that nothing like this happened just before the wedding. He'd be in big trouble then. Very big trouble.

He had the impression that Gavin Murfin was whistling as he entered the CID room at West Street that morning. Murfin seemed to have perked up considerably since the arrival of Diane Fry. Everything he did was contrary to his previous behaviour. He'd disparaged Fry for years, referred to her in private as the Wicked Witch of the West. Now he seemed glad to see her.

It gave Cooper an uneasy feeling. In Murfin's present

end-of-term mood, he might be planning something drastic. A final farewell that would ensure he was remembered for ever, his name enshrined in station legend.

Murfin placed his bag carefully on the desk, looking thoughtful. Over the years, Cooper had learned that his colleague could occasionally produce a flash of insight from his long experience in CID. This might be one of those moments, if he was lucky.

'What are you thinking, Gavin?'

Murfin sniffed. 'I'm thinking about what's in this bag.'

'Which is?'

'A steak and kidney pie and a vanilla slice.'

'What else have you been buying?'

'Oh, nothing.'

Cooper peered into the bag.

'Blow-up Bonking Baa Baa? Seriously?'

'Stag night,' said Murfin, snatching the bag away.

'No need to be embarrassed, then.'

'I'm not.'

'That had better not be for me, Gavin,' said Cooper.

'Course not. I wouldn't dream of it.'

'Who else is getting married, then?'

'No one you know.'

'Really?'

'Yes, really. I do have a life outside the office.'

'A mate down your local pub, maybe?'

'Could be.'

'Well you don't have any other social life. Unless you're in the habit of making friends at the chippy.'

Becky Hurst was shaking her head in disbelief. 'Blow-up Bonking Baa Baa. Does that sort of thing still go on at stag nights? Incredible.'

Irvine laughed. 'What? Are you saying women don't get up to the same sort of stuff on hen nights? Have you seen

230

Edendale town centre in the early hours of a Sunday morning?'

Cooper leaned towards Murfin and spoke to him quietly.

'We need to talk, Gavin.'

'All right, I don't mind.'

'And I mean soon. When we go off shift today.'

'It's a date.'

Cooper straightened up again, turning back to face the room

'What's going on then? Anything?'

'You asked me to track down the vehicles owned by Ian Gullick and Vince Naylor,' said Irvine.

'Yes?'

'Gullick has a blue Ford Transit van. He's a market trader, so that makes sense.'

'And Naylor?' asked Cooper.

'A Toyota Hilux pickup.'

'A pickup? What colour?'

'White.'

'Of course it is.'

For a moment, Cooper forgot his bruises. Were things starting to come together at last? If so, it would be worth it.

'Did we know that Maurice Wharton was an ex-copper?' he asked.

Irvine nodded. 'Yes, it's in the files.'

'It's not unusual to find a retired police officer running a pub, is it?' said Villiers.

'He wasn't retired. He got kicked out. Gross misconduct.'

'Was he bent?'

'No. He put the boot into a suspect once too often. You wouldn't have heard about him because he wasn't serving in this region. He was down in London, in the Met. He was rooted out of the Territorial Support Group in one of the Met's regular clean-ups.'

231

'It's hard to imagine.'

'He went to seed a bit after they dumped him,' said Murfin.

'You can say that again.'

'He's a big guy, though. At one time, when he was younger and kept himself fit, he would have been pretty intimidating.'

Diane Fry entered the CID room, came to a halt in front of Cooper and tilted her head on one side to examine his bruises.

'I suppose you're going to ask what happened,' said Cooper.

'No, I heard.'

He wondered for a moment who would have rushed off to spread gossip to Diane Fry. She wasn't usually the sort to be whispering in a huddle over the coffee machine. But then he remembered her ability to enter a room unobtrusively, a trick that must allow her to overhear all kinds of things.

'I gather there's even a suggestion that it was some members of the local farming community who were responsible,' she said. 'I didn't know there was a provisional wing of the National Farmers Union.'

Cooper gave her a curt nod. It seemed the only suitable acknowledgement to the closest that Diane Fry had ever come to making a joke.

'Someone else's blood on David Pearson's anorak,' he said. 'So what happened, do we think?'

'The Pearsons did something bad, and realised they had to disappear?' suggested Irvine.

'They attacked or killed someone? But who?'

He shrugged. 'It's funny, isn't it? Apart from the timing being so far out, you'd think it might have been Aidan Merritt.'

Fry snorted. 'Oh yes. Out by around two and a half years, that's all.'

'It would be convenient, though. We'd solve two mysteries at one go.'

'Have we got any other theories, aside from these fantasies?'

Everyone was silent, until Hurst chimed in. 'We'll just have to hope for a DNA match from the blood.'

'Is that the best we can do?'

No one answered, and Fry sighed.

'It looks as though it is.'

'Otherwise, we're going to ask all the same questions that were asked before?'

'Yes, and as many more as we can think of,' said Fry.

'Why?'

'If you ask enough questions, the person who's lying will eventually change their story. Anyone who's telling the truth can't do that.'

'A small bunch of regulars were looked at closely by the original inquiry team. Vince Naylor, Ian Gullick.'

'Their stories tallied.'

'Everyone's stories tallied. At least anyone who was sober enough to remember what happened.'

'You left a name off the list,' said Hurst.

'I know. Aidan Merritt. It's too late to ask him any more questions.'

'It had to be someone local.'

'Why?'

'Well, who else was in the immediate area apart from locals?'

'Nobody that we know of, apart from the party of four tourists we can't identify.'

'What about guests staying at the Light House?'

233

'They'd already stopped taking bookings before Christmas, remember? There was no one staying at the Light House.'

'No one?'

'Well, no one who wasn't local. No one except the Whartons themselves.'

'Is that right?' Cooper turned suddenly to Murfin, who stopped chewing whatever it was he'd surreptitiously sneaked into his mouth. 'Gavin, when you finally got to the Light House that day, it must have been a few hours after the Pearsons had been reported missing?'

'Of course.'

'Who was there?'

'At the Light House? Just the Whartons, and a couple of regulars.'

'Which regulars?'

'Ian Gullick, Vince Naylor. They were always there. Practically lived in the place. They spent every hour they could in the games room.'

'It was the day before Christmas, though.'

'So?'

'Hasn't everyone been telling us that the Light House was always closed over Christmas? If the pub was shut, what were Naylor and Gullick doing there?'

'I don't know.'

'You didn't ask?'

'Ben, we were in the middle of a major search operation, not to mention the effects of a snowstorm. It never occurred to me to ask them what they were doing there. I suppose I just thought they were helping to clear the snow or something.'

'How had they come? In a four-wheel drive, or what?'

'I don't know. I can't remember seeing anything. When I think about it, I don't think even a four-wheel drive would have made it to the pub in those conditions. Our vehicles couldn't. We had to walk.'

'Yes,' said Cooper, picturing the depth of snow covering the access to the Light House from the road. 'There's only one way anyone could have got up there. It would have needed a farmer with a tractor.'

'I'm amazed this wasn't followed up at the time,' said Fry. 'Here are two individuals who might have had a grudge against the Pearsons. They were witnessed having an argument with them forty-eight hours previously, and they were on the scene not long after David and Trisha disappeared. What was the SIO thinking of?'

'There were multiple witness statements taken from customers and staff who were at the Light House on the night after the argument,' said Cooper. 'Gullick and Naylor had no contact with the Pearsons that night. Maurice Wharton said he would never have let the two of them back into the pub if they hadn't promised to behave themselves and stay away from the Pearsons. And by all accounts they did behave themselves. Apart from the angry words spoken the previous night, there was no suspicion against Naylor or Gullick, or any of their friends.'

'We need to ask them some more questions.'

'Of course. That's what we're here for.'

'One more thing,' said Fry. 'Samantha Merritt gave us the names of some teachers she said her husband used to have a drink with sometimes after school. We talked to those teachers. And guess what? They said that a group of them often used to go for a drink, but that Aidan Merritt hardly ever joined them. They couldn't explain why he would say that.'

'And what do you think, Diane?'

She shrugged. 'The usual reason would be an affair,

wouldn't it? You know, *I'm going to be a bit late, dear – I'm just going for a drink with a few people from school.'*

'The usual reason,' said Cooper. 'But . . . Aidan Merritt?'

'Why not Aidan Merritt?'

'I don't know. He just doesn't seem the type.'

'You never knew him. Or wait – did you? Maybe you had a private chat with him at the Light House some time? During the Young Farmers' soiree maybe? A drunken get-together over a pint of Old Moorland, was it?'

'No,' said Cooper calmly. 'I've just talked to a few people about him. That's what we do. We get an idea of what sort of person the victim was.'

'You don't need to to tell me how to do my job.'

'I'm not trying to, but—'

'So can you think of another reason why Merritt would consistently lie to his wife about what he was doing after work?'

'Well, no.'

'Okay. Then perhaps we could explore the possibility that he was having an affair.'

'Fine.'

'That wasn't too difficult in the end, was it?'

Cooper watched her leave. He wondered if Fry actually thought she'd won him over, convinced him with the force of her argument and brought him on to her side. Well, she might want to believe that. But all she'd done was convince him that he'd have to find a new approach to the problem.

'We could try asking the first Mrs Rochester.'

'Who?'

'Betty Wheatcroft,' said Cooper. 'Mrs Wheatcroft was very upset by the death of Aidan Merritt. She's a bit nervous about being on her own, I think. In fact, she seems to be developing irrational fears about someone coming to her house to attack her.'

236

'Violence like that can be very worrying to old people. They feel vulnerable, and they don't really know where the danger might come from.'

'Yes, you're right. But in my view she was a little too upset. It wasn't just a general fear. I'm sure Merritt meant something to her personally.'

That morning, Superintendent Branagh sat Cooper down in her office. DI Hitchens was already there, leaning against the window. His jaw was set in a stubborn line, like a man who'd decided on a course of action and was determined to go through with it.

'DS Cooper, how is your team settling down?' said Branagh.

To Cooper, it sounded very much like preparatory small talk. His team had been settling down for months already.

'Very well, ma'am. Thank you.'

'I'm delighted to hear it. We're in for rough times, you know.'

'We'll survive, ma'am,' said Cooper. 'We'll survive.'

Branagh nodded, but he had the impression she hadn't really been listening to the answer.

'I hate having to bring in outside help,' she said. 'I would prefer to feel that the division can do the job with its own resources. As you know, there's only one thing I detest more. And that's leaks to the press.'

'Yes, I'm aware of that.'

'But we had no choice in this case. The Major Crime Unit have taken responsibility for the Merritt murder inquiry.'

She put an unusual amount of emphasis on the last few words. Cooper glanced at Hitchens, who raised his eyebrows in acknowledgement of some unspoken message.

The superintendent frowned, noticing the bruise on Cooper's temple.

'Did something happen to you last night?'

Cooper automatically touched the sore place. 'No, it's nothing.'

'Not falling out with your fiancée over the wedding plans, are you?'

Cooper tried to laugh politely, but Branagh wasn't fooled.

'Oh well. None of my business, perhaps?'

'Thank you for asking, though,' said Cooper.

'No problem. The thing is, DS Cooper, we want you to understand that the presence of officers from the Major Crime Unit doesn't preclude us from taking appropriate action for ourselves when we think it's necessary. For example, if new information should come to light in our ongoing inquiries into the disappearance of David and Patricia Pearson.'

'Ah,' said Cooper, a light beginning to dawn.

'Which,' continued Branagh, 'I believe you've been working on.'

'I have, ma'am.'

'Well, I would be very happy to hear we'd made some progress in our part of this operation. A suspect or two brought in for interview, perhaps. That would be good news, wouldn't it? The sort of thing that would reflect well on E Division's capability. Do we understand each other?'

'Perfectly,' said Cooper.

He was sitting up straighter in his chair, feeling the adrenalin already surging through his veins at the prospect of action. Those bruises didn't hurt at all, now he thought about it.

Cooper stood up to leave the office. Branagh held him back by fixing him with her steady, piercing gaze.

'DS Cooper,' she said.

'Yes, ma'am?'

'Remember what I told you. Any problems or concerns

you have, feed them back to me via your DI here. You have our full backing.'

'I haven't forgotten,' said Cooper.

'In that case,' she said, 'I'll take it you don't have any problems.'

Cooper strode back into the CID room. Everyone looked up as he entered, as if sensing the new mood in the air already.

'Luke,' he said.

'Yes, boss?'

'Ian Gullick is running a greengrocer's business, you said.'

'He has a stall on the market in town twice a week,' said Irvine. 'The rest of the week he's probably setting up pitches on other markets around the county. Chesterfield, Buxton, I don't know where. But Edendale is his home ground.'

'And what day is it today?' said Cooper.

'Thursday. Why?'

'Because it's market day.'

'Are we going shopping?' asked Villiers.

'No,' said Cooper. 'We're going to make some arrests.'

21

Markets always seemed to be the coldest, windiest spots. He supposed it was in the nature of the layout – an open space with streets funnelling into it from every direction. In winter, stallholders often shivered in heavy overcoats and fur hats, as if they were trading on a street market in Moscow.

Shop windows all around the market square in Edendale were filled with posters advertising the town's campaign against the building of a new Tesco store. There was a Sainsbury's Local right here on the market square, but many of the other businesses were independents.

The register office was still located here in the town hall, but the magistrates' court and county court round the corner had a less than promising future. Court facilities were being closed and centralised in bigger population centres, just like police stations

Cooper had to admit that Edendale market wasn't the most exciting in Derbyshire. Chesterfield and Bakewell were both better. On this side of the market, the main attractions seemed to be a fish van, a plant stall, a hot-dog trailer, and a trader selling Union Jack rugs.

Ian Gullick was doing business today on his vegetable stall. Piles of potatoes and carrots failed to hide his beer gut, which stretched a T-shirt and a leather money belt to breaking point. Though his stall was right in front of Jack's Barbers, he clearly hadn't been inside recently for a wash and cut.

'Okay, we're going to go in nice and easy,' said Cooper into his radio. 'Gavin, can you see him from your position?'

'Yes, got him.'

Murfin was standing by the window of the tattoo parlour, just behind the artisan bakery, partially obscuring a poster advertising ear-lobe tattoos.

'Becky?'

'Right behind the stall.'

'Excellent. Let's hope the uniforms stay out of sight until we've got the cuffs on.'

Without showing any signs of hurry or drawing attention to themselves, they closed in towards Gullick's stall. A young assistant was weighing out onions for a customer, and Gullick himself moved down to the end of the stall to shift some empty boxes. When Cooper was within a few yards, the customer paid for her onions and the stall was clear.

'Right, move in.'

Cooper picked up speed as he moved towards the stall. But Gullick, seeming to sense that something was wrong, looked up and spotted him. Cooper saw the flash of recognition in his eyes. A pile of boxes went flying as Gullick barged his assistant out of the way and ran round the end of the stall, toppling a pile of Golden Delicious, which spilled into the aisle and rolled under the feet of passing shoppers.

'He's spotted us, Ben,' said Hurst. 'He's doing a runner.'

Cooper could see Hurst grabbing for Gullick, but missing.

'Police!' he called. 'Stay where you are!'

'Damn, I almost had him there,' called Hurst.

'Police! Stop!'

241

Gullick took no notice. It never did work anyway, unless you had a dog handler to enforce the command.

Cooper tried to dodge between the shoppers, who milled about in confusion, getting in his way. There was a crash, a splintering of wood, and someone screamed as if they'd fallen on to the stone paving.

'Gavin?' said Cooper.

'Yeah?'

'Where the hell are you?'

'Right here. Just waiting for you to join me, like.'

'What?'

Cooper pushed his way through the crowd, and Becky Hurst came panting up behind him. When the press of bodies cleared, he saw Gavin Murfin in his old anorak, standing there like someone's mildly confused uncle out doing his weekly shop.

At Murfin's feet lay a large shape in jeans and a white T-shirt, squirming desperately in his efforts to free himself from a heap of Union Jack rugs. Murfin bent, snapped on the handcuffs in two quick movements and straightened up again.

'You youngsters,' he said. 'All that running about, and it doesn't achieve a thing.'

Today was also Emergency Services Day in Edendale. Cooper had forgotten that. The whole of Victoria Park had been taken over to mount displays for the public. Crowds of civilians were passing through in their hundreds.

This park was also the site of the annual Christmas market. It was a popular attraction, bringing crowds of people into town. There was always a smell of roasting chestnuts in the air, and the sound of a fairground organ. In the evening, mime artists, stilt walkers and clowns would mingle with

242

the crowds in the lamplit streets, and Santa would turn up on his sleigh.

It was where David and Trisha Pearson should have been on their Peak District Christmas break, not trekking across Oxlow Moor.

A few uniformed officers and PCSOs from E Division had been allocated to Emergency Services Day. The mobile police office was here, with a PC inside demonstrating the old-style fingerprinting technique, which was always popular. A liveried Vauxhall Astra sat with its blue lights flashing and its doors open, so that children could sit in the driver's seat and tap the steering wheel to set off the siren.

'We've located Ian Gullick's vehicle,' said Becky Hurst's voice in his earpiece.

'A blue Transit?' asked Cooper.

'Yes, it was in the town hall car park, close to the market.'

'It's not a priority.'

'I thought not. Uniforms have picked up Gullick, and Gavin's processing him, since he made the arrest.'

'Okay.'

Cooper looked around the park. There was a dog handler too, with his modified Zafira and two dogs in cages at the back – a German Shepherd and a young Springer spaniel training for drug-sniffing work. There might only be two handlers on duty in Derbyshire at any one time, and they covered huge areas in those Zafiras. During the course of a shift they could do up to three hundred miles, a lot of that at night, and mostly on blue lights.

To complete the police presence, an off-duty officer dressed in a tracksuit had set up a couple of punchbags in front of the Ozbox van. Ozbox had been one of the big success stories for Derbyshire Constabulary since it was set up by Sergeant Steve Osbaldeston. It ran six mobile gyms, with two hundred officers volunteering their time to teach boxing skills to thousands of youngsters from problem areas. Old Ozbox himself had got the MBE a few years ago for his work. This was real community relations in action.

'Carol?' said Cooper. 'Are you still on Vince Naylor?'

'We're sitting behind him on Hulley Road.'

'What's he doing?'

'He's in his pickup making a phone call, as far I can tell from here.'

'Damn, that might mean he's already heard about Gullick.'

'Possibly. What do you want us to do?'

'Nothing hasty,' said Cooper. 'Just stay with him for now.'

'Fine.'

Cooper walked past the E Division Neighbourhood Watch tent. Buxton Mountain Rescue were performing an operation on a scaffolding tower using something called a Petzl nappy. Below the scaffolding stood the BMRT Ford Transit ambulance and Land Rover. Next to them, Derbyshire Cave Rescue Organisation had set up a plastic cave for kids to crawl through with lights strapped to their heads.

He stopped to pat the head of a SARDA rescue dog, a broken-coated collie with odd eyes. It was odd to find the rescue dog here in the park in the centre of Edendale, being fussed by the public. He'd just been thinking that the Pearsons ought to have been here enjoying the Christmas market instead of walking across the moors in the snow. And this dog might have been the very animal to locate them if they'd been lost or injured out there. Despite its appearance, he knew it had the ability to sniff out a human scent over a kilometre away in the right conditions.

'Hold on, it looks as though he's moving again,' said Villiers.

Cooper looked across the park in the direction of Hulley Road, which ran towards the bridge over the river and the traffic lights at Fargate. He couldn't see the white Toyota pickup from here, or the CID pool car behind it containing Carol Villiers and Luke Irvine. He pictured them moving off and passing the back of the Royal Theatre.

He began to head towards the corner of the park. A Fire and Rescue team were drawing a crowd by rescuing a mock casualty from an adjacent roof with the extending ladder and cage. He'd probably missed the chip-pan fire demonstration, which always attracted a lot of attention, especially when a firefighter threw water on to the burning pan to illustrate the wrong way to deal with it, sending a sheet of flame and smoke shooting up and over the demonstration vehicle.

He'd once seen a fireman playing up to the kids in the audience by wearing a wig that showed long hair peeping out from under his helmet. Then, after the blaze, he pretended his hair had been scorched, and removed his helmet to reveal a totally bald head. That was always good for a laugh.

Cooper looked for the Fire and Rescue Service's Argo Centaur 9500, the 8x8 ATV with fat tyres and a fire fogging system that was normally here for Emergency Services Day. But the Argo was missing today.

Of course, like every other bit of available specialist equipment, it was in demand. It would already be in use out on the moors – not battling a snowstorm like David and Trisha Pearson, but helping to fight those out-of-control moorland fires.

'He's stopping again,' said Villiers. 'Yes, he's getting out. Looks like he's working on a job here. Property on the corner of Hulley Road and Bargate.'

'I'm on my way,' said Cooper. 'Don't do anything until I

get there, and we have backup. We don't want another runner.'

'No,' said Villiers. 'Especially as we don't have Gavin here to make the arrest.'

The custody suite at Edendale wasn't one of the newest in the county. If the station ever closed in a further round of rationalisation, the cells might have a sustainable future as a museum of post-war policing. Basic wasn't the word for the facilities. But they weren't designed to encourage a long-term stay.

A few months ago, Cooper and some of his colleagues from E Division had travelled into Staffordshire to view a brand-new custody suite. A main desk like the Starship *Enterprise*, a phone connection from each cell to the desk, cells steam-cleaned every five weeks. Washbasins, no graffiti. It encouraged personal hygiene, reduced work and minimised risks for staff. They could put legal calls through to the cells.

'Gavin, we need to do the interview as soon as possible,' said Cooper.

Murfin nodded. 'Okay. I'll have a word with Custard.'

Villiers watched him go. 'I hesitate to ask, but . . . Custard?'

'The custody sergeant.'

'Oh, obviously.'

Vince Naylor had been drinking when he was pulled in. Stale beer seemed to leak out of his skin in place of sweat. He was a big man, bigger than Gullick, and it took three officers to escort him to the custody desk.

As soon as he was inside, he began to swear and shout. He became frustrated at the way the custody officers ignored him and went calmly about their job taking fingerprints and obtaining a DNA sample.

'What do I have to say to get a response out of you bastards?' he shouted.

'We're trained not to react to insulting or abusive words and behaviour,' said the custody sergeant calmly.

'Well fuck you then!'

'Cell Four.'

'I know you,' said Ian Gullick half an hour later, sitting across the table in Interview Room One. 'Cooper, right? I know you. And your brother.'

'That could be so.'

He laughed. 'Yes, I know you all right.'

Gullick's face was unnaturally flushed, and his eyes bulged slightly, as if he was permanently struggling under some intolerable pressure. He looked like a man unable to escape from the murderer's hands round his throat.

Cooper exchanged a glance with Carol Villiers, who was sitting alongside him with the tapes running. He tried to put some reassurance into the glance.

'We're here to talk about Aidan Merritt,' he said.

'Oh, Aidan.' Gullick sniffed. 'He was always a bit too clever for his own good, Aidan. Read books and things. He thought it made him better than the rest of us. Look how that turned out.'

'Mr Merritt is dead.'

'Exactly.'

'You knew him well, didn't you?'

'We were at school together. Didn't have many interests in common, though. Aidan carried on into the sixth form, did his A levels and all that stuff. He even went to college, I think.'

'So you went your separate ways.'

'Sort of. But, you know, he never moved out of the area.

247

We all thought he'd head off for London. Get away from the rest of us soon as he could. Lots of folk have done it before him, when they got a bit of an education.'

'But he didn't do that?'

'Not Aidan. I don't know why, but he stayed. Got himself a job in Edendale and stuck around. So we bumped into each other quite a lot. You know what it's like – you can't exactly avoid people for long in a place like this, can you?'

'He drank at the Light House, didn't he?' said Cooper.

'Yeah, that's right. Sometimes.'

'You must have talked to him when you saw him in there.'

'We passed the time of day. I mean, what do you think? We weren't exactly bosom buddies, though. To be honest, he came over as being a bit weird.'

'Because he read books?'

'That and other stuff.'

'He was a teacher, though. You might expect a teacher to be familiar with a few books. That's what he was inter-ested in, teaching English.'

'Yeah, right. They do say it was something else he was interested in.'

'What do you mean?'

'Well, what else do you get in schools other than books? Children.'

Cooper regarded him coolly. 'There have never been any allegations against Mr Merritt that I'm aware of.'

Gullick shrugged. 'I'm only telling you what people say.'

'That sort of thing is just pub gossip,' said Cooper. 'Because he didn't fit in with your group, he has to be some kind of pervert. What was the problem? He didn't like playing pool? He didn't want to get drunk like the rest of you?'

'He was odd. That's all I'm saying.'

Cooper took a breath, trying to resist the impulse to

248

defend someone he'd never even known. It would only take the interview in the wrong direction.

Villiers stepped in, picking up her cue from his pause.

'What sort of relationship did Mr Merritt have with Maurice Wharton?' she asked.

Gullick swivelled his eyes towards her. Cooper noted with interest that their suspect seemed much more wary of Carol Villiers than of Cooper himself. The threat of the unfamiliar?

'Maurice had a go at him a couple of times for not drinking enough beer. Said Aidan wasn't contributing to the profits.'

'What?'

'That was normal for Mad Maurice. But his heart wasn't in it with Aidan. He counted as a regular, you see. So he was accepted.'

'Why would Mr Merritt have been at the Light House on the day he was killed?'

'I don't know what Aidan was up to. He was a real dark horse, you know. A complete mystery to the rest of us. His brain worked differently somehow.'

'What do you think happened to the Pearsons?'

'Out on the moor, in the snow? Probably they just walked round in circles. That happens to people in bad weather. You can't get a proper sense of direction. I don't suppose they had a compass with them or anything like that. And don't forget, they were strangers to the area.' He shrugged. 'Hikers . . . Well, you know – they do all kinds of stupid things on the hills.'

'Yes, sometimes.'

'It's surprising no one heard them calling out for help. I mean, they must have shouted when they realised they were lost, mustn't they? Anyone would do that.'

Cooper thought Gullick was talking too much. He wasn't used to that in the interview room. Everyone had watched

TV and knew they were supposed to say 'no comment' all the time. But Gullick had even declined the presence of a duty solicitor. And now he seemed positively chatty. It didn't ring true.

'Mr Gullick, where were you at the time Aidan Merritt was killed?'

'Working, of course. Monday, was it?'

'Yes.'

'I was at Bakewell Market, then. It's Bakewell on Monday, Buxton on Tuesday, Derby Wednesday, Edendale Thursday, Matlock Friday and Chesterfield on Saturday. So I had the stall set up at Bakewell. I was there all day, from the crack of dawn to the bitter end. You can ask anyone – I'm not easy to miss.'

'Can I take you back a few years?' he said. 'There was an incident at the Light House.'

'What? Who . . .?'

Cooper glanced at his notes. Your friend Vince Naylor got into an argument with David Pearson.'

'Oh, that. Old Vince, he's a bit of a devil when he's had a few drinks. He started chatting up the woman, and the bloke took objection. He had a bit of a temper on him, if you ask me. I mean, it was all in fun. No harm in it. And it came to nothing anyway.'

'You left, didn't you?'

'Oh, yeah. Well, Maurice told us to. It was nearly closing time, so it was no hardship.'

'Were you driving?'

Gullick looked shifty for once. 'Er, well . . .'

'I'm not interested in drink-driving right now,' said Cooper.

'Well, yes – we were in my van. We sat outside the pub for a bit to get some fresh air and sober up, then we went home.'

'A bit of fresh air wouldn't sober you up enough to drive legally.'

'I thought you said—'

'Yes, all right. But I'm thinking that you must still have been outside when the Pearsons left.'

Gullick brooded for a while.

'I wouldn't know about that,' he said. 'I never saw them. It's not my concern what happened to them later. And it's years ago, surely? All water under the bridge by now.'

'Were you aware that Maurice Wharton was a former police officer?'

'Yes, I was. He didn't talk about himself, but it was fairly well known. Among the regulars anyway. He got shafted by the top brass. Took the blame for some incident down south.'

'Is that the way the story goes?'

'That's it.'

'He seemed to get a bit of respect in the pub, though. He sorted the lads out, when needed. He sorted you and Mr Naylor out, didn't he?'

Gullick held out his hands palm up, a gesture of innocence.

'Look, you had to keep on the right side of Maurice. If he gave you the hard word, you took notice. We didn't want to get ourselves banned. And, to be fair, we'd drunk quite a bit. Vince in particular. Oh, there was plenty of alcohol drunk.'

'I've heard that Maurice was drinking heavily himself by then,' said Cooper.

'Yes, that's true. And then there was Eliot.'

'Eliot Wharton doesn't drink. He told me so.'

Gullick laughed. 'Well, not any more. He was totally wasted that night in the Light House. Someone had been giving him spirits, I think.'

251

'He would only have been fourteen or so.'

'Kids start drinking early these days. You know that. But I reckon Eliot would have suffered for a few days. He wasn't used to that amount of alcohol.'

Cooper regarded Gullick thoughtfully. He couldn't make his mind up about him. Gullick was either very clever, or he'd failed to grasp the situation.

'What do you do now, since the Light House closed?' he asked.

'We drink at the Badger, near Bradwell. But it's not the same.'

'What do you think?' asked Villiers, when they'd let Gullick leave the interview room and go back to his cell.

'Well I wouldn't trust him. Would you?'

'Not even to sell me a bag of carrots.'

'We're no closer to knowing what Aidan Merritt was up to.'

'That only leaves one avenue then,' said Cooper. 'I'll have to ask the first Mrs Rochester.'

22

When Diane Fry heard about the arrests, she was furious. DCI Mackenzie didn't seem quite so perturbed by developments, which made her even more angry.

'Why does it bother you so much, Diane?' he said. 'I thought being back among your old colleagues wasn't a problem for you?'

That made her pause. 'No, it isn't.'

She could leave the self-analysis until later, but right now she felt as though somebody had got one up on her, and she knew who it was.

'Sir, what can we do to take control back in this inquiry?' she said.

Mackenzie smiled. 'That's better. Have you got any ideas?'

'We could interview Henry Pearson again. Make it more formal this time, rather than the kid-gloves approach he's been getting so far.'

'Yes, we could certainly do that.'

'We need to give forensics a kick up the backside to get some results from the Pearsons' clothing and possessions.'

'You've got it.'

'Also, I want a new search of those abandoned mine shafts.'

'It was done before,' said Mackenzie.

'I know.'

'So what's your reasoning, Diane?'

'My reasoning? Well, where's the best place to hide something so that it won't be found?'

'It depends on the circumstances, doesn't it?'

'In general terms.'

Mackenzie shook his head. 'I still don't know.'

'The best place to hide something,' said Fry, 'is where it's already been looked for.'

'Okay. But how does all this progress the Aidan Merritt murder inquiry? Isn't that what you're supposed to be concentrating your efforts on?'

Fry had to acknowledge that was true. It was the way she'd wanted it from the beginning, the fresh case coming to the Major Crime Unit, the rehashing of the older Pearson inquiry being left to local CID.

But she felt differently now. For reasons she couldn't quite articulate to herself, or would want to explain to Mackenzie, things had changed. She felt as though she'd been issued with a challenge, and she was going to meet it.

'If we can get to the bottom of the Pearsons' disappearance, then the reasons for the death of Aidan Merritt will resolve themselves,' she said.

'The two are so closely connected?' said Mackenzie. 'Is that what you believe?'

'Yes, I do.'

'You have my support, then. We'll get a new search started straight away.'

Fry nodded. Her brain was immediately ticking over, planning where to go to get the next bit of information that she needed – and wondering whether she could get there before anyone else did.

With exaggerated caution, Betty Wheatcroft looked right and left before letting Cooper in to her house.

'Is there a problem?' she whispered.

'Just something I didn't ask you before,' said Cooper.

'You'd better come in, then.'

She sat Cooper down in her sitting room and automatically began to make tea.

'Yes, Aidan did used to come and see me,' she said from the kitchen. 'He called in after school sometimes, particularly if he'd had a bad day. I think there were a lot of bad days recently.'

'Difficulties at home, in his private life?'

'I don't think so. At school, I'd say. Teachers get like that sometimes.'

'Why did he become a teacher in the first place, then?'

'Good question. Aidan once said to me that he couldn't think of any meaningful way to fill the terrible yawning void that stretched in front of him until the day of his death. So he became a teacher instead.' She looked at Cooper as she came back into the room. 'I *think* he was joking.'

'He had problems at work, then?'

She set a cup of tea in front of him. 'Aidan was soft. Too soft. Some of the older children must have made mincemeat of him in class. He was always worried about doing the right thing, you see.'

'There's nothing wrong with that,' said Cooper.

Mrs Wheatcroft narrowed her eyes as she looked at him. 'Oh, but it might not be the same as what you think of as the right thing. I'm not talking about automatically punishing people because they've broken some law. That isn't always what some of us would call justice. Not my version of justice, and not Aidan's either.'

Cooper nodded, though it wasn't in agreement, just an acknowledgement of what she'd said. He understood that position. Or at least he thought he did.

'Are you thinking I'm a daft old woman?' asked Mrs

Wheatcroft. 'I know I get confused, and my memory isn't as good as it used to be. But I know what I believe in.'

A light dawned on Cooper. 'Have you been in trouble with the police yourself at some time?'

'Yes, I was arrested once,' she said with a proud smile.

Looking at her now, it was difficult to imagine.

'What for?'

'I was at Greenham Common.'

'Ah.'

'I was part of the women's peace camp in the eighties. The cruise missile protest.'

'I remember. Well, I say "remember"; I was quite young then.'

'December 1983, it was. Difficult to think it's nearly thirty years ago. Fifty thousand of us joined hands and made a circle round the nuclear missile base. We cut through the fences, and some of us got arrested. I was at Yellow Gate.'

'Interesting times.'

'Interesting? You can't imagine the living conditions. We were outside in all kinds of weather. Cold, snow, rain, with no electricity and no running water. Frequent evictions, attacks by vigilantes. But we gave up comfort for commitment. We stopped nuclear convoys, disrupted their training exercises. Though it was non-violent direct action, a lot of women were arrested, taken to court and even sent to prison.'

'What about you? You didn't go to prison, did you?'

'No. I just got a fine and a ticking-off. I didn't take much notice. None of us did.'

Cooper drank some of his tea. It was horrible, and the milk tasted slightly off. But you had to be polite.

'We still haven't found any clue as to why Aidan Merritt was at the Light House on the day he was killed,' he said.

'I'm sorry. I wish I could help.'

'He talked to you about things, though, didn't he?' persisted Cooper.

'Yes, I did know there was something on his mind.'

'You did?'

'But he was all secretive about it. He said there was something he had to do. It was his moral duty.'

'But he didn't tell you what it was?'

'No, not him. He just sort of put his finger to his lips, and winked and nodded. If I'd been sitting next to him, I reckon he would have nudged me in the ribs. He gave the impression I ought to understand what he meant without him having to spell it out. I don't know what it was with Aidan. He'd read too many spy stories, perhaps. Thought he was George Smiley or something.'

Cooper thought it was interesting that Mrs Wheatcroft had referred to George Smiley when most people might have been expected to mention James Bond. It suggested she'd read a few Cold War spy novels himself. John le Carré, at least. If Diane Fry had been here, she wouldn't have noticed that. She wasn't much of a reader.

Mrs Wheatcroft eyed him curiously. He could practically see her mind working, trying to figure something out for herself.

'Didn't Aidan tell anyone else what he was doing?' she said.

Cooper decided to let her in on a bit of information. He felt sure it couldn't do any harm in this case.

'He phoned his wife, Samantha, and left a message. But she couldn't make any sense of what he was saying. It was something about the ninth circle of hell.'

'Ah,' she said. 'Dante's *Inferno*.'

'Of course. Dante's *Inferno*,' repeated Cooper. 'Yes, you're right. He was there while the moor was on fire, you see.'

'The fires, yes. I know about them. Was that it?'

Mrs Wheatcroft watched him silently for a while, until Cooper began to feel uncomfortable under her expectant gaze. There had been a teacher just like her years ago, when he was at school. She had never needed to shout or raise her voice to get his attention. All she had to do was look at him in that way, and it forced him to cudgel his brain for the correct answer, the one she was hoping for.

But this time he seemed to have failed. Mrs Wheatcroft's expression turned to disappointment. A moment later, she changed the subject.

'I heard they found some old mine buildings on the moor,' she said.

'You hear a lot of things,' said Cooper. 'But yes, you're right.'

'Aidan's father was interested in the old mines.'

'Was he?'

'He passed away recently, old Charlie Merritt. I suppose that might have been something else Aidan was depressed about. Charlie was a member of the local society.'

'You mean the Mines Historical Society?'

'That's it. He did some research for them, I think. Helped out with mapping the sites around the moors here. There were a lot of them at one time, you know.'

'Yes, I know.'

'Charlie Merritt always said there were some abandoned mines that no one had ever found. They just got lost, and then the heather and bracken grew over them.'

'Did he mention any locations in particular?'

Mrs Wheatcroft shook her head. 'Not to me. He was pretty vague. I suppose we just thought he liked telling stories.'

'What kind of stories?'

'Oh, about the superstitions the old lead miners had. And he liked to tell tales about children who fell down mine

258

shafts years ago and got killed. They *are* all superstitions, aren't they?'

Cooper put his cup down half finished, hoping Mrs Wheatcroft wouldn't notice until after he'd gone.

'I can't answer about the superstitions,' he said. 'But his stories about the children were probably true.'

When he got back into his car, Cooper sat for a few minutes before driving away, thinking about Mrs Wheatcroft's remarks on mining superstitions and Charlie Merritt's knowledge of the mines. Why had she mentioned that? Was there some connection that existed only in the old lady's mind?

He knew that a few mining enthusiasts still kept one peculiar Peak District practice alive. On Christmas Eve they went down into an old lead mine to light a candle as a tribute to T'owd Mon. It could be difficult to explain the concept to outsiders. It wasn't a specific old man, though it could sometimes refer to an unknown long-dead miner, or to entire previous generations of miners. In other cases, it was a reference to the actual mine workings.

Miners looked on T'owd Mon as a kind of collective spirit, an embodiment both of their predecessors and of the mines themselves. It had been their custom before finishing work on Christmas Eve to leave a burning candle on a good piece of ore as a tribute.

That ongoing connection with history was very strong in the Peak District. Cooper thought it was related to the fact that so much of the area's heritage was visible right there in the landscape, from the Neolithic stone circles and Iron Age hill forts to the mounds and shafts of the abandoned mines, all the way through to remnants of a more recent industrial past.

Cooper started the engine and put the car into gear.

Yes, when you could see it and touch it and smell, it

ceased to be history. You were part of it then. In many ways, it became your present.

Naylor and Gullick had been reinterviewed by Carol Villiers and Luke Irvine, and they were all getting exhausted.

'They're like the pair of figures in one of those little wooden weather houses,' said Villiers when they came out for a break.

'How do you mean?' asked Cooper.

'You know the kind of thing, where you get a sort of Jack and Jill in Bavarian costume, the woman coming out when it's sunny, the man only when it rains. They're always in and out, turn and turn about. But nothing really changes. It's too predictable.'

'Their stories tally?'

'In every respect,' said Villiers. 'They seem well rehearsed to me. Too confident.'

'Most people can't keep up a story for ever, if you keep asking them questions.'

'These two do.'

'Did you ask them what they were doing at the Light House the day after the Pearsons went missing, when the pub was closed for Christmas?' asked Cooper.

'Of course. They say they went up there out of curiosity. They saw all the activity and went to find out what was going on.'

'And that story was consistent too?'

'I'm afraid so, Ben.'

'That's a nuisance,' said Cooper with feeling.

'Sorry.'

'It's not your fault.'

Villiers glanced at her notebook. 'Gullick's alibi for the time of Merritt's death checks out. So does Naylor's. He was working on a job here in Edendale, laying a patio for someone who lives in Buxton Road. It took him and his mate all day.'

'And the pickup?'

'It was parked on the drive at the house, except for when Naylor's workmate went for their fish and chips at lunchtime. It's been examined. There's no sign of any recent damage, so it can't have been Naylor's vehicle that pushed you off the road.'

In the CID room, Cooper's desk was covered in files and reports. He pushed them to one side and surveyed his team. This was the way it always was in a complex inquiry – one step forward and two steps back.

'Anyway, it seems that Aidan Merritt was visiting Mrs Wheatcroft,' he said.

'The old biddy. What did you call her, Ben? The first Mrs Rochester?'

'That's her.'

'But surely they weren't . . .?'

'No. He visited her because she was lonely. Simple as that. Mrs Wheatcroft's husband died years ago, and her family rarely visit. That's why she used to spend time at the Light House. She'd worked there as a waitress or barmaid at one time. She felt she knew people, which she doesn't here in Edendale.'

'I always thought it must have taken a lot of effort for her to get up there and back for a drink when there are lots of pubs nearer to where she lives.'

'Yes. It was never about the drink; it was the place and the people. Since the Light House closed, Aidan has been visiting her once or twice a week, just to sit with her and have a cup of tea. He called in at her house on his way home from school.'

'Still, it's a bit odd.'

'Is it?'

'It's not as if she's related to him or anything.'

'True.'

'And you mean to say he never told his wife what he was up to? Why not, if he was just doing a good turn for an old lady?'

'Perhaps he was embarrassed about it. You just said yourself it seemed a bit odd. A lot of people thought Aidan Merritt was odd already. Ian Gullick and his pals would have laughed at him.'

'There's one other thing,' said Villiers.

'Yes?'

'I remember you saying that it all seemed planned, that the delay in a search getting under way for the Pearsons had been worked out, as if someone knew what the police response would be.'

'Yes.'

'Well, who would have been in a better position to know that than a police officer?' she said. She looked round the group, seeming to enjoy their shocked expressions for a moment. 'Or a former police officer.'

'Maurice Wharton?'

'Yes.'

'You think he masterminded the whole thing?'

'I think some of his regular customers looked up to him. I think they would have confided in Wharton, asked his advice, perhaps pleaded with him to help them cover up what they'd done.'

'It would explain why he began that spiral into depression and heavy drinking.'

'What? Do you think Mad Maurice had a guilty conscience?'

'Or he was afraid it would all come out. I bet he had nightmares about one of the people responsible making a mistake and letting something slip. They might have trusted Maurice. But did Maurice trust them?'

'So it's possible Maurice Wharton knew what had happened? Did he help Naylor and Gullick to conceal their crime?'

'Let's ask him.'

But Maurice Wharton was in no condition to answer questions. They found his wife and two children in the day room at the hospice, waiting in that tense, hushed atmosphere that fell in a hospital ward when the worst was expected.

'Can't you leave him alone?' said Nancy. 'What's the point of harassing the poor man now?'

'I'm sorry.'

'Oh, well. You can sit down for a minute, I suppose. Maurice was happy to talk to you the other day. Somebody different from the same old faces. He quite appreciated your visit.'

'I must tell you something,' said Cooper. 'Maurice told me he feels he's failed the children.'

'Failed? Tell me about it. As a mother, you feel as though you've failed your children every single day.'

Cooper asked about the incident with the Pearsons at the Light House, but Nancy Wharton shook her head firmly.

'It was all sorted out. Just heat-of-the-moment stuff, you know. Once everyone had sobered up, they would have forgotten all about it. No hard feelings.'

'You were closed over Christmas, weren't you?'

'Oh, we always were, every year. It was something Maurice insisted on. He's been a good dad to Kirsten and Eliot. His family is important to him.' She gave a short laugh. 'People were always trying to reserve a table for Christmas dinner, or book a room for a couple of nights.

They started phoning and emailing from about Easter onwards. Maurice took a lot of satisfaction in telling them to bugger off. He often said that if they were the sort of people who didn't want the company of their own family and friends at Christmas, he was damned if he was going to have them cluttering up the Light House.'

Eliot Wharton followed Cooper out of the hospice. Cooper stopped by the fish pond and waited for him to catch up, wondering whether the young man was upset and was going to accuse him of trying to harass his father. He remembered Josh Lane telling him how devoted Eliot was to his dad.

When Eliot stood close, Cooper was struck by his size. He must be as tall as Matt, not as broad, but getting that way. He was only seventeen, after all.

'You understand why we want to protect Dad, don't you?' said Eliot quietly.

It was almost an appeal, and it took Cooper by surprise. He experienced one of those moments when he was flung back into the past, to the shocking moment when he heard his own father had died. Those terrible memories still surfaced now and then, surging unexpectedly from the depths, vivid and painful.

'Yes, I understand,' he said.

Eliot nodded, turned and walked back inside. Cooper had to wait for a moment after he'd gone, letting the memory fade, for the pain to sink back into the depths it had come from. For that moment, he'd known exactly what it was like to be Eliot Wharton.

Cooper was bothered by the memories now. Talking to Josh Lane had brought some of it back: the vague awareness of an altercation, Mad Maurice stepping in and sorting it out – an angry mountain one second, a big jolly Santa the next as he placated the Pearsons. People around them laughing in amazement and slapping them on the back as if they'd been awarded a rare honour.

He shook his head as the scene disappeared. He remembered those shadows he'd seen in the smoke. They too had been like figures from the past, flickering through the present in desperate pursuit of some unfinished business. Or perhaps they were seeking something they'd long since lost. Life, love, innocence? Who could say?

But something, somewhere was evading him. He just couldn't see it for the smoke.

23

Cooper couldn't mistake Gavin Murfin's chestnut-brown Renault Megane hatchback as it arrived in Welbeck Street. Gavin never quite seemed to fit in his car properly, as if he had the driver's seat pushed too far forward towards the steering wheel. As a result, he drove with his fists moving up and down close to his chest, as if he was struggling with the buttons of a loosely fitting overcoat.

At that moment, Cooper was on the phone to Liz, trying to placate her.

'No, it's something I have to do. I've know Gavin for years. And he's leaving soon, retiring. You must understand that. It will only be one last time, honest.'

'Well I hope so,' she said. 'We have so much to do, Ben. So much to plan.'

'You can manage without me just this once, can't you?'

'I suppose so.'

'Thanks, love you.'

'Love you too.'

He could tell she wasn't pleased. There was an edge to her voice that he hated to be the cause of.

As he ended the call, he watched Murfin park at the kerb and struggle out of the car, waving cheerily at the window of the house next door. That would be Mrs Shelley, peering from behind her curtain to see who was visiting her tenant.

Cooper remembered Murfin's wife Jean making Gavin go on a diet once. He couldn't imagine how long it had taken her to get him to that stage. There must have been a phenomenal amount of nagging, nudging, hinting and downright bullying going on in the Murfin household. But the result had been a morose and dejected Gavin, who felt life had become pointless, and who could hardly bother coming into work.

'And how do you feel?' Cooper had asked him when he'd heard about the diet.

'I've got no energy. Nothing seems to matter any more. I really don't want to go into the office on a Monday.'

'I suppose you could phone in sick, Gavin.'

'I've used up all my sick days. I'd have to phone in dead.'

Now, Cooper sensed the same degree of dejection under Murfin's increasingly flippant exterior. He knew it was all a facade, a performance to avoid having to be reminded of the fact that his career was rapidly coming to an end.

'I thought we'd go for something to eat,' he said, when Murfin was in the hallway of his flat, making little kissing noises at the cat. 'Unless Jean is expecting you back?'

Murfin straightened up with an almost audible creak.

'No, I was hoping you'd say that. Jean's out at one of her meetings, so I'm left to my own devices, like.'

'The Gate is the nearest place. Is that okay?'

'Suits me. All this business with the Light House has made me hanker after a bit of pub grub. I don't mind what it is, as long as it comes with chips.'

'Let's go, then,' said Cooper.

'But are you sure you're off the leash?' asked Murfin with a sly glance. 'You're the one whose time is spoken for these days. Has Liz not got you booked for something tonight?'

'Don't,' said Cooper.

'You'll have to get used to it, young man. That's what marriage is all about, getting used to the ball and chain.'

'We love each other,' said Cooper. 'And we want to live together and do all those things together that other people do. That's why we're getting married.'

Murfin laughed. 'Of course it is.'

'This is it, Gavin. Being with Liz is my future, what I want for the rest of my life. And I'm very happy about it.'

'"Nuff said.'

Cooper led the way out of his flat. Fortunately, his own local was still open. The Hanging Gate was just a couple of streets away across the river. This pub still had the scenic Peak District views on the walls, as well as the same old CDs of sixties and seventies pop classics playing in the background. But it also still had Bank's Bitter and Mansfield Pedigree on draught.

The Gate was pretty much a town-centre pub, based on its location. But because it sat outside the main shopping area, it was left off the pub-crawl circuits – and it was certainly beyond the orbit of the Saturday-night clubbers, thank God.

Some of the bars a few hundred yards away in Clappergate and the high street were totally different in style and atmosphere. They were officially known as high-volume vertical drinking establishments. Hardly any chairs or tables were provided for customers, because it was accepted that everyone stood up, crammed shoulder to shoulder, clutching their drinks or resting their glasses on narrow shelves at chest height, sweating in the heat generated by the mass of bodies and shouting to each other over the music. Only young people enjoyed drinking in those conditions. The fact that he preferred a genuine local like the Gate sometimes made Cooper wonder whether he was getting middle-aged before his time.

But then he'd be married soon. Pubbing and clubbing would become a distant memory. The future for him held an endless vista of trips to IKEA, Saturdays spent putting up shelves, Sundays washing the car.

And children. Cooper took another swallow of his beer. He liked children. He was very fond of his two nieces, Amy and Josie. But having your own was surely quite a different matter. You couldn't just leave them for someone else to look after when you decided you'd had enough of them. Becoming a parent took a bit of thinking about. And a lot of planning. He supposed he should really start thinking about it now.

'Hey up, don't rush so much,' said Murfin as they entered the pub. 'You're going to get to the bar before me.'

'It's my round anyway.'

They found a table and ordered their food. Steak and kidney pie was on the menu at the Hanging Gate, and Murfin hadn't taken long over his choice.

'Just think, it'll be one long pub lunch for me in a few weeks' time,' said Murfin, relaxing with a sigh over his pint. 'I bet all you youngsters are getting jealous.'

'Gavin, what *are* you going to do with yourself when you've retired?' asked Cooper.

'I'm hoping someone will take pity on me. All I need is food, shelter and the basic Sky Sports package.'

He hoped Gavin really did have something lined up to occupy his time in retirement. Too many men went off the rails, gave up trying or died of a heart attack within the first couple of years of finding themselves adrift, without the anchor of a job. It was especially true where they'd done pretty much the same job all their lives.

It wasn't as if Murfin had a sideline or hobby. All he knew was police work, his experience was in his familiarity with the local villains, his conversation was about incidents from his past as a uniformed bobby or as a green young recruit to CID. And it would all be totally worthless once he walked out of that door for the last time.

His behaviour was becoming more and more odd lately, though. It was almost as if he wanted to get himself disciplined. That didn't make sense.

'Well, it's nice to have Diane Fry back with us for a while,' said Murfin cheerfully. 'It gives us another chance at sorting out the Wicked Witch of the West.'

'Just ignore her, Gavin. That's the best policy.'

Murfin smiled. 'Oh, I don't think so.'

Then Cooper realised what it was. Deep down, Murfin had become desperate to provoke a reaction, to make sure everyone was aware that he still existed. He wanted his name mentioned to the bosses at headquarters, even if it was for all the wrong reasons. Gavin was telling the truth when he said it didn't matter any more. Nothing mattered, really – except that the world should acknowledge his existence.

'Looking forward to the retirement party, Gavin?' he asked.

Murfin's expression changed.

'It'll be full of miserable, moaning old sods,' he said. 'I've worked with enough of them over the years. They'll be coming out of the woodwork in droves when they get a sniff of a free sausage roll.'

'Yes, I bet,' said Cooper.

He smiled at the irony of the complaint. The other day he'd come across Murfin reminiscing with a few of the other old stagers, remembering the golden age when PC stood for police constable, and not 'politically correct'. In fact Gavin would be one of the last to benefit from the old pension arrangements. Police officers were paying more into their pensions now, and senior officers were affected the most.

Cooper wondered how he would cope when his own retirement came round. His early days with Derbyshire Constabulary already felt as though they belonged to a different era. A Jurassic period, when dinosaurs ruled the earth. Dinosaurs not unlike Gavin Murfin, in fact.

He remembered a spell when he'd started working lates and found himself on drunk patrol. It was that time of the shift cycle that put him and a few colleagues on foot outside the pubs and clubs of Edendale town centre from ten at night until four in the morning. Each night it was a question of how many groups of young men would walk past and spot the police officers, with one lad grabbing his mate in a headlock and shouting, 'I've got him, I've got him.' How many times would he hear the words 'My mate is pregnant, can she wee in your hat?' or: 'You can smile, you know'? How many times would he hear his sergeant say, 'Just walk away, mate, and enjoy your night. You don't want to spend it in the cells.' Yet they didn't walk away, of course. There were always the ones who took it as a challenge, rather than good advice. Oh yes, he'd really enjoyed watching people get drunk as he stood in the rain.

He told Gavin this memory of his early career. In a way, it seemed to be the sort of thing they should be talking about in this manly heart-to-heart over a pint of beer.

'You're right,' said Murfin. 'Being the bloke who has to pick up the drunks every night after they've vomited on the pavement and urinated in shop doorways . . . well, it isn't as glamorous a job as it sounds.'

Cooper recalled that Murfin had been with Diane Fry at the Light House on Tuesday. Murfin was by far the most experienced of his team. Over the past few years he would have been the one to turn to for a bit of old-school wisdom. Down-to-earth, seat-of-the-pants, good old copper's instinct.

271

Not politically correct, of course. No, rarely that. But he was often right, all the same.

'Gavin, can I ask you something?' he said.

'Ask away.'

'What was your first thought when you arrived at the Light House on Monday, after Aidan's Merritt's body was found?'

Murfin scratched the back of his head.

'My first thought? To be honest, it was "Where the heck am I going to get a brew from in a place like this?"'

A little while later, Murfin set off to visit the gents, staggering slightly as he crossed the room. Cooper began to think about how he was going to get Gavin home.

'Now then, Ben. How's it going?'

He turned gratefully to the man who slid on to the stool next to him.

'Oh, fine. Thanks.'

He looked a bit closer, realising that he knew the face but for a moment was unable to place the name.

'As you can see, I'm on the other side of the bar tonight.'

'Ah, of course.'

Yes – Roddy, that was it. He had no idea of the surname. A genial, sandy-haired youth, he was a part-time barman right here at the Hanging Gate. Cooper didn't see him all that often. Perhaps his shifts were mostly during the day. But he knew the face well enough. Funny how difficult it was sometimes to recognise people when you saw them out of their usual context.

When a casual acquaintance wanted to start up a conversation with him, it was usually because they were angling for information. And Roddy was no exception.

'I was hearing about this business up at the Light House,' he said. 'That's a bit of a shocker.'

'Did you know the victim, Aidan Merritt?'

'Not him. But we all know the Whartons.' He laughed. 'Well, everyone knows Mad Maurice. It was sad that no one could help him save the pub from closing. A place like the Light House, too. Tragic.'

'I heard that the quality of his beer had been deteriorating for some time.'

'I think that's right. Hygiene problems, I would imagine. The boss here takes a lot of trouble over hygiene. Take line cleaning – it's always a chore, but it has to be done every week without fail. If you get dirty lines, you have yeast build-up. I wonder what Maurice's cellar temperature was like.'

Cooper looked at him, his mouth falling open slightly. Perhaps it was the effect of the beer on his brain, or the fact that he hadn't recognised Roddy straight away, but he was starting to feel particularly stupid tonight.

'His cellar?' he said.

'It has to be cool,' explained Roddy. 'Always between eleven and thirteen degrees Celsius, and constant. Sometimes people leave the cellar door open, or switch off the cooling at night, if they want to save money.' He shook his head. 'There are lots of nasties in a cellar that you don't want getting to your beer. Bacteria, oxygen, moulds, flies, wild yeast, dirt . . .'

'I get the picture,' said Cooper, though in fact his mind was flailing wildly in an attempt to form an image that just wasn't coming.

'I've worked in a few pubs,' said Roddy. 'And the cellar often becomes a dumping ground. You wouldn't believe the clutter in some places. The ice-maker, the chest freezer, the post-mix machine . . . People think they're out of the way yet still handy. I even saw a motorbike once. It was a lovely bike, but imagine the stink of petrol mixing with the smell of beer. That's a recipe for disaster all right.'

In the middle of the conversation Cooper became aware of a diesel engine outside, the sound of a large vehicle and the crashing of heavy items being delivered

When they left the Hanging Gate, the reason for the noise became evident. A brewery dray was drawn up in the street, and a wooden hatch set into the pavement was standing open for fresh kegs of beer to be lowered in.

'We must have drunk a lot if they needed to bring in new supplies at this time of the evening,' said Murfin.

'It's probably a regular delivery time.'

As he watched two draymen wearing leather gauntlets for roping kegs into the cellar, Cooper realised he'd always known at the back of his mind that the brewery dray delivered to the pub once a week. That must be true of all pubs, mustn't it?

He felt like smacking his forehead with his hand.

'How could I have forgotten that?' he said.

He fumbled for his phone as they walked down the street.

'Who are you calling?' asked Murfin. 'Not the fiancée? Are you having to report in?'

'Just something I have to do now before I forget.'

'You know your trouble, Ben?'

But Cooper had stopped listening to Murfin as he dialled a number and the phone was answered.

'Josh? It's Ben Cooper. Detective Sergeant Cooper, you remember? Good. I'm sorry to bother you, Josh, but I wonder if you'd have a bit of time to spare tomorrow? Are you working? If not, I'd like you to come up to the Light House for a while.'

Lane sounded reluctant, and even a little nervous.

'Yes, I could call in before I go to work. But . . . am I allowed? Isn't it a crime scene? *Police – do not cross* and all that?'

274

'You'll be fine with me. I can arrange it. Shall we say two o'clock?'

'Okay then. What do you want me to do?'

'It's simple,' said Cooper. 'I want you to show me the cellars.'

24

When Ben Cooper woke the next day, it was with the scent of smoke in his nostrils. He knew he must have been dreaming, imagining he was in the middle of a wildfire raging across the moors. He couldn't remember the nightmare, but he must have experienced it. It wasn't in his memory, but it lingered in his senses.

Gavin Murfin's brown Megane still stood outside in Welbeck Street. Cooper vaguely remembered Gavin heading off home in a taxi at the end of the evening. He hoped he'd arrived safely. There'd be hell to pay if he hadn't. Jean would certainly hold him responsible.

Cooper shook his head to try to clear it. He recalled making the appointment to meet Josh Lane at the Light House. And there was something else he ought to remember, too. But, like the dream, it was evading his grasp just now.

The news was bad this morning. The latest bulletins reported more wildfires. And this time they were on Kinder Scout. Cooper stared out of the window of his flat. The street outside looked the same as it always did. But the town wasn't affected by the fires, except when people complained about soot on their washing. The damage was happening out there, on the moors.

Cooper decided to skip breakfast, drank a quick coffee

and went out of the door. He wasn't due in the office for an hour or so.

This was Kinder Scout, after all. Kinder was the highest moorland plateau in the Peak District, part of a landscape almost unique to Britain, whose importance had only in recent years been fully appreciated. It was said that the expanses of peat on Kinder soaked up excess carbon from the atmosphere, and would continue to act as a carbon sink even if the climate became warmer and wetter, as the scientists predicted.

On the way, he called Liz, conscious that he ought to put things right if she was still unhappy about his night off from wedding planning. But for once she seemed to be the one who was preoccupied.

'Don't worry, I'll fill you in later when I see you,' she said.

'Is everything all right?'

'Of course. Tonight, then?'

'Absolutely. Or . . .'

'What?'

Cooper was thinking that tonight was too long to wait. He'd missed seeing her more than he could admit. Gavin Murfin just hadn't been a substitute.

'Well I'll try to see you for a few minutes during the day, if I can. You're on duty, aren't you?'

'Oh yes. Busy, busy. People keep finding crime scenes for us.'

'I suppose they do.'

Within a few minutes Cooper was driving through Bradwell into the Hope Valley, phoning in to get the latest update on the operation. He joined the A625 and turned on to a back road by the post office in Hope village. The road snaked its way between the River Noe and the Hope Valley railway line until it finally reached the assembly

277

point in a visitors' car park near the hamlet of Upper Booth.

As usual there was a problem with rubberneckers. Some members of the public liked nothing better than a good fire. They seemed to treat it as an alternative to daytime TV. As a result, cars were drawn on to the verge and into every gateway along the road. Nearer to the car park, they were lined up as if for a party, with a young man with long hair leaning on his car playing a guitar. Other people were using binoculars or taking photographs with their mobile phones. A middle-aged couple had set up a folding table and were drinking tea. Late arrivals were finding it difficult to get parking spaces.

On the narrowest bend, Cooper found cars projecting so far into the roadway that it would be impossible for anything as large as a fire appliance to get past. Someone ought to be here sorting this out, keeping the access clear. But it would mean taking resources away from where they were needed most. Not for the first time, the public weren't helping at all.

When he arrived at the assembly point, he was met by a national park ranger in his distinctive red jacket. The rangers were often the first line of defence against the spread of moorland fires. They were out there on the ground every day, and they didn't worry about working nine to five when there was an emergency situation.

'What I'm hoping for is that the wind will change direction,' said the ranger.

'To stop the fire spreading towards the villages?' asked Cooper.

The ranger shook his head, and jerked a thumb towards the road.

'No, so that all the gongoozlers get a face full of smoke. That might make them go home.'

Looking up the hill at the fire burning along the skyline, Cooper could see a helicopter hovering low over the moor, carrying a huge orange bucket full of water. It released its load to help douse the fire, and a moment later was heading back eastwards until it disappeared.

He glimpsed a farmstead sheltered by a belt of trees, reminding him too much of Bridge End. He imagined the farm where he'd grown up being threatened by a moorland fire. It didn't bear thinking about.

And this wasn't the first fire on Kinder. When he was younger, he'd walked across this moor while the peat below him was burning, warming the surface but not quite breaking through. It was a strange experience, like crossing a hotplate with clouds of richly scented smoke rising all around him.

'How did it happen?' he asked. 'Isn't the Fire Severity Index at its highest level already? The access land should be closed to the public.'

The ranger shrugged. 'We can close access land all right, but we don't have the power to shut public footpaths. Which is a nonsense, when you think about it – because a lot of those paths run right across access land anyway. People think they can hold barbecues in the middle of a tinder-dry moorland, as if they were in their back garden. Why don't they all go home and set fire to their own property?'

Cooper spotted the fire service's Argo making its way across the edge of the plateau, its fogging unit spraying water on to the advancing fire front. He remembered the whole of that part of Kinder being a bog at one time. You wouldn't have been able to walk across it, even in summer, without your boots sinking into water and evil-smelling mud soaking through your socks. He could still hear the squelch of his footsteps, and smell the fetid gas that was released from the sodden ground.

But he knew there would be no bog up there now. That stretch of moor had been dry for years.

'Which direction is it moving?'

'Westwards at the moment,' said the ranger. 'Towards Hayfield.'

'It won't get that far, surely?'

'No, we'll have it under control before then. But we're pretty overstretched. We're having to pull in all the resources we can. The trouble is, some of the other fires aren't completely damped down. They could flare up again.'

'Like Oxlow Moor?'

'Yes. Though there isn't much left to burn up there, to be honest.'

High above him, bright red embers were floating like fireflies against the bank of black smoke, and Cooper could see for himself that the fire was heading westwards.

Just away to the west was Kinder Downfall, a cascade of water falling vertically among shattered rocks. It was the highest waterfall in the county, where the River Kinder hit the edge of the plateau. On blustery days, the water seemed to flow upwards as the wind caught it in mid-air and hurled it back over the edge.

Below the downfall, the dark waters of Mermaid's Pool were reputed to be haunted by a spirit who could either grant eternal life or pull you under the surface and drown you. Myth said it was a site of ancient human sacrifices. He remembered looking down at the pool from the rocks and realising how obvious it was that it used to be much larger. You could make out the original shape from the slope of the ground, and from the beds of reeds standing where the shallower parts of the pool had been. It must have covered three or four times the area it did now, but its edges had retreated, the body of water shrunk to little more than a pond. It would be very difficult now to imagine anything living in there except a few small fish and the odd frog, let alone a water demon. Luckily the people of Hayfield didn't go in for human sacrifices as much as they used to.

He became aware that the ranger had finished conducting an agitated conversation on his radio and was cursing.

'What's the problem?' asked Cooper.

'Our temporary reservoir on the moor has been sabotaged.'

Cooper knew what he meant. He'd seen the big orange tank sitting in the middle of the moors. Because of the risk of fire, every year the national park rangers sited one of the water tanks out on Kinder. They held more than fifty thousand litres of water, and were large enough for a helicopter to lower its dipper bucket into, if necessary. Due to the remote nature of the moorland sites, tanks were often vital to prevent a fire from spreading. They usually stayed up there throughout the summer, and could be refilled from bowsers towed by rangers' Land Rovers.

'We had reports that the tank was empty, and when it was checked we found that somebody had cut the side of it with a knife,' said the ranger. 'The original cut was only about eighteen inches long, but the force of fifty-four thousand litres of water ripped a ten-foot hole. That's impossible to repair. We're just left with a big collapsed balloon.'

'What does that mean for Kinder?'

The ranger followed Cooper's gaze up the hill.

'The consequences of losing that tank could be devastating. They helicopter is using Ladybower Reservoir instead, but it takes a lot longer. We were hoping to stop the fire in its tracks, but that won't happen now.'

'A few more square miles destroyed, then.'

'You can bet on it.'

'And it's Kinder, too.'

'Yes, Kinder. What can I say?'

Kinder Scout had its own unique history. Britain's national park movement had started right here in the 1930s, when four hundred ramblers from Manchester staged a mass trespass on to grouse moors owned by the Duke of Devonshire.

The 1932 Kinder Trespass was the turning point in the campaign to open up access to the countryside. Five young ramblers had been jailed, and the resulting waves of support had ensured that Kinder was included when the first national park was created in the Peak District after the Second World War. Eventually, a later Duke of Devonshire had apologised for his ancestor's actions. How times changed.

It was an episode recorded in Derbyshire Constabulary history, too. About a third of the force had been deployed around Hayfield to intercept ramblers taking part in the trespass. One hiker convicted of assault on a gamekeeper had protested his innocence right into his eighties. It had taken an enlightened chief constable to make amends for that one.

Cooper went back to his Toyota. He had to accept that there wasn't much he could do, short of grabbing a beater and going up on the moor himself. Being here was just tormenting him, and he might even be getting in the way. He wished the ranger luck, and left.

Near Upper Booth, a couple of cars had been turning in a field entrance, and came slowly past him down the road. A silver Mercedes and a pale blue VW. As they passed, Cooper saw that their paintwork was covered in black specks, a shower of oily soot from the moorland fires they'd been watching with such enjoyment.

It looked as though the ranger's prayers had been answered. The wind had changed direction after all.

At West Street, Cooper sat down at his desk and tried to get his thoughts in order. It was taking a bit of an effort this morning.

He remembered first of all that he'd arranged to meet Josh Lane at the Light House later on. The cellars were one part of the pub he felt sure hadn't been looked at. Since nothing seemed to have been taken, a reason for the presence at the Light House of either Aidan Merritt or his killer still hadn't been established. But what might be in the cellars?

He was picturing a motorcycle now. That was Roddy who'd put the idea into his head. But Maurice Wharton hadn't been the type to ride a motorbike – or any of his family, except perhaps his son. Eliot was old enough to have a driving licence at seventeen, but he would have been too young when they lived at the pub.

Ah yes, Aidan Merritt – that was the second thing. According to Mrs Wheatcroft, Merritt's father had been interested in the abandoned mines, and knew the locations of all the old shafts, maybe some that had been lost for a while. Had Aidan picked up some of that knowledge from his father?

It was interesting to speculate, but Cooper wasn't sure how it fitted in with the inquiry. The mine shafts had been searched after the disappearance of David and Trisha Pearson, and there was nothing to suggest that Aidan Merritt had even had any contact with the Pearsons, let alone a reason to kill them.

So what else was there? Cooper tapped a pencil against his teeth as he gazed out of the window at the rooftops of

Edendale. There was something that still eluded him, a memory that he hadn't quite grasped at the time, and that was proving even more elusive now. He hoped it would come back to him at some point when he wasn't thinking about it.

DI Hitchens stuck his head round the door.

'Ben, have you got a minute?' he said.

Cooper went into the DI's office. Hitchens looked weary, drained of energy. He had a leaflet on his desk promoting a seminar for inspectors. *Meeting the challenges of the new performance landscape.*

'I wanted you to be the first to know, Ben,' he said. 'I'll be moving on soon.'

'Really?'

'Yes, one way or another.'

Cooper sat down. He didn't quite know how he felt about that. He was used to his DI, who had served in E Division for years. But everyone moved on eventually – especially if they were the least bit ambitious and wanted promotion. It always created a bit of uncertainty, though. Who would they get in his place? Hitchens might not have been the most dynamic DI, particularly in recent years. But sometimes it was better the devil you knew than the devil you didn't.

Automatically, Cooper's mind began to run through potential candidates for the job, those in other divisions rumoured to be tipped for promotion or transfer. On the other hand, might the DI's departure create a vacancy that would be filled internally?

'And you'll be losing DC Murfin soon,' said Hitchens. 'How do you feel about that?'

'Gavin has a lot of experience,' said Cooper, immediately conscious that he'd said it before, and not just once. Was it starting to sound as if he was damning Murfin with faint praise?

'Experience, yes. It's worth a lot. Or it used to be, anyway. Everything is different these days, as you know. We have to make cutbacks everywhere we can.'

'We're not likely to lose anyone else, are we?' said Cooper.

Hitchens shrugged. 'Who can say?'

Murfin himself looked surprisingly chipper this morning. His desk in the CID room was cleared of forms and was now uncharacteristically tidy.

'Diane Fry won't be here much longer, I suppose,' he said. 'She'll have her inquiry tied up in no time, and she'll be off back to EMSOU – MC.'

'Yes, I wouldn't be surprised,' said Cooper. 'Why, were you thinking of inviting her to your retirement party?'

'Maybe. It's been interesting.'

'Interesting? In the Chinese sense?'

Murfin gazed out of the window with a smile. 'Well, we might all have learned something from the visit,' he said.

Cooper followed his gaze. He could see Diane Fry's black Audi in the car park at the back of the building. She'd reversed it into a spot near the extension where the scenes-of-crime department was now located.

'What's that on her rear bumper?' said Cooper, his face crumpling into a puzzled frown.

'I can't imagine,' said Murfin.

'But it looks like . . .'

'Oh,' said Murfin overtheatrically. 'So it does.'

'Gavin?'

'Yes, Ben?'

'I suppose I shouldn't ask.'

'No, that's probably for the best.'

'It's going to be another mystery, then,' said Cooper.

'You mean, how . . .?'

'Yes. How Detective Sergeant Diane Fry, of the East Midlands Special Operations Unit – Major Crime, came to have an inflatable sheep tied to her rear bumper when she left West Street. And it seems to be wearing lipstick and eye make-up, too.'

'I suppose it's just a memento,' said Murfin. 'One last sheep to remember us by.'

Early that morning, a retired firefighter from Glossop called Roger Kitson arrived at Brecks Farm, near Peak Forest, along with hundreds of other people. He followed the directions of a steward as he drove his car through a gateway and into a field where vehicles were already lined up, many of them muddy Land Rovers and other four-wheel drives.

Roger was there for one of the biggest events of the year in the stretch of country around Oxlow Moor – the annual sheepdog trials. Every year, the trials were held in fields behind Brecks Farm, going on all day from seven thirty in the morning to around six in the evening. As well as the feats of the sheepdogs themselves, there was a children's play area, side stalls, and plenty of food and drink to make the day.

But one of the real highlights of the event was a four-and-a-half-mile fell race, and that was why Roger Kitson was at Brecks Farm.

Roger was sixty-two years old, but he was a runner – a member of a club based near Stockport. Fell running was a gruelling sport, but it was more about stamina than strength. Last year, a couple of members from Dark Peak Fell Runners had finished the Oxlow Moor course in less than thirty minutes, with the advantage of good conditions. They would face competition this year, though, as Roger saw there were teams entered from the Goyt Valley

Striders, the Hallamshire Harriers and even the Hathersage Fat Boys.

Before the start of the race, he strolled round the field to see what was going on. He could tell that the trials had already begun, from the distinctive whistles and shouts of the shepherd piercing the morning air. A collie would be hard at work already, chivvying a reluctant bunch of sheep into a pen.

On a table near the secretary's tent stood the gleaming NatWest Trophy, ready to be presented to the owner of the winning sheepdog, along with smaller trophies for Best Driving Dog and Best Young Handler. One local farmer was raising money for the Border Collie Trust by growing half a beard, and he was attracting a lot of interest from photographers.

Roger joined a mass of runners in shorts and colourful vests waiting to set off on the opening climb, all with their identifying bib numbers tied to their singlets. He recognised the DPFR in their brown vests with yellow and purple hoops, and knew he would probably be a long way behind them. As a spectator, he'd seen the leading runners coming in one by one, each checking a watch as they approached the finishing line. He didn't mind what time he clocked up, as long as he completed the course. There was a trophy for the first veteran to finish, but he didn't expect to come close to that.

Today, the runners seemed to be all ages, shapes and sizes, but Roger kept reminding himself that stamina was the key to fell running. He overheard runners discussing the relative merits of their Walshes, the performance of a pair of Racers against Elite Extremes. He was wearing Walsh running shoes himself – they were hard-wearing enough to cope with both rocks and the wet peat they would be running over when they were up on the moor.

And then the race got under way. Within minutes of the start, the back markers were already struggling on the steep, rocky ascent, and Roger was among them. He made slow progress in the first few hundred yards, manoeuvring for the best route over the uneven rocky ground, sometimes being obliged to use his hands to keep his balance.

Slowly he approached the top of the ascent. Up ahead, something seemed to be happening. The leading runners were on the moor and pounding over the heather. But just before the first descent, there was chaos, with runners milling around aimlessly as if they'd lost sight of the route.

'What's going on?' Roger asked the runner in front of him.

'I don't know,' he gasped.

They kept going, losing sight of the lead runners. As they crested the hill, Roger could see smoke in the distance, drifting towards the runners, a clump of dry heather bursting into flame.

'Oh God. It's another fire,' he said.

'No, they've found something.'

He heard exclamations, someone calling for a phone, another voice insisting they should call the emergency services.

'Is somebody hurt?' he said.

As a firefighter, Roger had first-aid training. He pushed his way through the cluster of runners to see what the problem was. When he got near, people automatically stood back to let him through, as if happy to let someone else take over.

Roger found himself teetering on the edge of a hole exposed in the earth. Breathing hard, he looked down, expecting to see someone lying injured. But at first he couldn't figure out what he was looking at. He wiped the sweat from his forehead as his eyes started to adjust to the darkness in the hole.

'Oh, shit.'

He took a step backwards and bumped into the runners crowding behind him. He panicked, terrified of losing his footing and stumbling into the hole to join whatever lay down there.

Because Roger had just seen . . . but what exactly *had* he seen?

Gingerly, he crouched and took a closer look. Yes, he'd been right the first time. It was a decomposed human hand, yellow and shrivelled, protruding from a bundle of black plastic, like a pale ghost rising out of Oxlow Moor.

25

Diane Fry knew that Henry Pearson was staying at a hotel in Edendale. Even if he hadn't left his contact details, she had seen him on the TV news – a shot of him getting into his BMW with an armful of files, looking serious and dignified, like a lawyer going into court to fight an important case.

Pearson had also done a few sound bites directly to camera, speaking about how determined he was to discover what had happened to his son and daughter-in-law. That clip would be used over and over in the news bulletins.

Fry could see clearly that the sequence had been filmed in the car park of the Holiday Inn on Meadow Road, with the spire of All Saints Church visible in the background at the bottom of Clappergate.

When she rang the hotel that morning, she was put straight through to Mr Pearson's room.

'Yes?' he said eagerly, when Fry announced who she was. 'Is there any news?'

'Not at the moment. But we'd like you to come into the station for a chat. If you could, sir.'

'I'll be right there,' he said.

Well, that was short and sweet. Eager wasn't the word for it. Mr Pearson sounded positively desperate.

While she waited, she checked in with DCI Mackenzie,

who was presiding over the incident room as SIO. Fry was grateful that he'd spared her this, the routine tasking and data analysis that went with a major inquiry. So far he'd given her a free hand, and she appreciated his faith in her.

Mackenzie confirmed that search teams were being assembled to begin operations on Oxlow Moor, focusing on the abandoned mine shafts.

'It's quite technical,' he said. 'The maps aren't as accurate as we'd like, and the extent of visible surface remains is unpredictable. So we need the specialists. But it will be done.'

'What about forensics?' asked Fry.

Mackenzie shook his head. 'Still no luck on the major blood source. We know it doesn't match the DNA profiles for the Pearsons. However, the lab say they've isolated another profile from the bloodstains. Small traces, but DNA from a separate individual.'

'A fourth person, then?'

'Yes, someone else who lost a small amount of blood. Also, there's a partial print recovered from David Pearson's mobile phone. Not David's or Trisha's. It should help.'

'If we can produce a suspect to compare it to,' said Fry.

'Exactly.' Mackenzie looked up. 'One thing we can be sure of, anyway.'

'What?'

'DS Cooper's two suspects aren't in the frame. These DNA profiles aren't a match to the samples Gullick and Naylor gave on arrest.'

When Cooper reached the weed-covered car park of the Light House, he could see only a few firefighters in the distance, still flailing with their beaters where hotspots were smouldering in the heather. Their activities had moved on and away from the pub. The nearest appliance was just visible on the edge of the moor, framed against the long ridge of Rushup Edge and the far-off Kinder Scout.

On the horizon, Kinder was also burning now, a double disaster. A brisk wind was whipping up flames twenty feet high across a front that must stretch more than a mile and a half. As the ranger had predicted, most of the firefighting equipment and resources had been drawn away from Oxlow to tackle the new wildfires spreading on the higher plateau.

If the fire was burning below ground level here, there was a danger it could burst up through the peat at any time. If that happened, the Light House could be at risk. There weren't enough men and equipment left on the moor to provide a spray curtain over the building and ensure those floating embers didn't land on the roof.

Again Cooper was overwhelmed by the impression of how isolated the Light House was. He and the empty pub were alone in the devastated landscape, like the last survivors of a nuclear holocaust. Despite the height and its commanding vantage point, he felt as though he was being observed. He imagined a movie camera in a helicopter, one of those dizzying overhead shots, pulling back to reveal that his tiny figure was the only movement in an expanse of desert.

'I don't know what film that would be from,' he said. Then he looked guiltily over his shoulder, in case he was caught talking to himself out loud.

Cooper shook himself and went to the back door of the pub, where a bored uniformed PC stood guard at the tape marking the cordon. The door was fixed permanently open now, and lights had been sent up inside the bar, where the body of Aidan Merritt had been found. How long ago had that been? Only a few days, surely? It seemed like a lifetime, though. Diane Fry had walked in here. And by that simple act, she had turned everything round.

Carol Villiers had already negotiated her way over the stepping plates to reach the main bar.

'So what are we looking for?' she asked.

'Cellars.'

She looked down at her feet, an automatic response.

'Access to the cellars,' said Cooper.

'I knew that.'

The furniture in the bar looked sad and rather seedy in the totally artificial illumination. From the ceiling hung horrible lights in fittings shaped like candles, but made out of some kind of rigid green plastic. Cooper could see the pictures on the walls more clearly, baffling images of steam trains and fly fishermen that bore no relationship to the history or location of the pub.

Somewhere there must be a trapdoor to provide access to the cellar from inside the pub. Cooper found it behind the bar counter, concealed by a pile of flattened cardboard boxes and old beer crates. He didn't think it had been hidden deliberately, just lost and forgotten under the general rubbish and disorder.

'We need to move all this stuff aside.'

Villiers helped him with the task. When the hatch was cleared, an iron handle became visible, set flush into the wood. Slowly Cooper eased the door up, and Villiers switched on her torch to locate a flight of stone steps. She recoiled at the aromas rising from the hatchway.

'Phew,' she said. 'There's nothing worse than the smell of stale beer.'

Cooper agreed. But there was more to the odour than that. A miasma rose around him, putting thoughts of ancient damp and mould into his mind. He felt as though he'd just opened Count Dracula's tomb, releasing centuries of decay.

He pulled out his own torch. 'Down we go, then.'

'You first,' said Villiers.

Cooper looked at her in surprise. 'What? Spiders?'

'Maybe,' she said dcfensively.

At the bottom of the steps, Cooper found a light switch. He was amazed when it worked, and the cellar sprang into view. Unlike the shuttered pub above, the cellar had always looked like this, bathed in artificial light. They were below ground, so there were no windows. And the air immediately felt cooler, with that hint of dampness.

Beer lines snaked up towards the bar, and a bewildering assortment of equipment lay around, some of it on shelves or left on empty kegs, or stored in the corner of the cellar. He saw a wooden mallet, stainless-steel buckets, disposable paper towels, a scrubbing brush, a pressure hosepipe, filter funnels and papers, a dip stick, beer taps and a gas bottle spanner.

A tiny space off the cellar had been turned into an office. Well, more of a storage room really, with a few dusty filing cabinets lined up against the wall, a desk covered in box files, and a pile of old magazines – *The Publican, Morning Advertiser*.

On a shelf, Cooper found a stack of old sepia and black-and-white photographs in their frames, which must once have hung on the walls upstairs. He picked up a particularly old photo in a gilt frame, and wiped the dust off the glass. It was a group shot, taken some time around the start of the twentieth century, he guessed. A formally arranged bunch of people was pictured outside the front entrance of a pub. A large man with enormous whiskers posed importantly in the middle of the group, with men in leather aprons and women in white smocks spread out on either side and behind him, some of them standing, others sitting awkwardly on wooden chairs brought outside from the bar.

The pub was recognisably the Light House, its windows almost unchanged to the present day, the shape of its chimneys visible along the top of the print. But the lettering painted over the door didn't say *The Light House*. The pub had gone by a different name a century ago. Cooper squinted a bit more closely, trying to make out the lettering. Surely it was . . .? Yes, he was sure. The pub had once been called the Burning Woman.

He put the photo down, and it slid off the pile with a scrape of glass. His automatic sense of disturbance at the name was probably a twenty-first-century response. No one would have thought anything of it back then. There were plenty of rural pubs whose names reflected gruesome episodes from history, or some lurid folk tale. The people of these parts seemed to have had particularly vivid and bloodthirsty imaginations.

He couldn't see the swinging wooden sign because of the angle the photograph had been taken from, but he guessed there would be a suitably graphic image to accompany the name. Someone would know the legend of the burning woman. Stories like that survived by word of mouth long after the signs had been taken down and the names sanitised.

'I can't help feeling the moulds are sending their spores directly towards me, even as I speak,' said Villiers.

'How did they get deliveries?' asked Cooper 'Can you see?'

'Over here.'

The double cellar doors to the outside were at the top of a narrow set of stone steps, with equally narrow ramps on either side. The hatches themselves were bolted on the inside. The bolts and hinges were old and starting to rust, reminding Cooper of the iron plate over the abandoned mine shaft.

He couldn't see even a crack of daylight round the edges of the doors. He tried to figure out where they emerged.

Why hadn't he noticed them from the outside? The only possible answer was that they too were covered by something. He remembered the pile of old furniture stacked against the back wall. Heavy tables with metal bases, wrought-iron chairs, a heap of torn parasols on steel posts. They had been chucked on a mound like so much rubbish. They must be lying right on top of the cellar doors. Maybe it had been for additional security. Or perhaps no one expected beer deliveries to be made at this pub for the foreseeable future.

'What was through there?' asked Villiers.

'A desk, a few filing cabinets. Loads of old paperwork just mouldering away. I suppose it's been left for the new owners, if anyone buys the pub at the auction.'

'What sort of paperwork?'

'Accounts, I suppose. Orders, deliveries, records of paying guests, VAT returns. Whatever. That would be part of the business history, wouldn't it? If you took the place on, you'd want to get an idea of how many bookings there were for the rooms. The time of year, where they came from and all that.'

'Yes, of course. But we're not thinking of buying the pub, are we? I mean – are we?'

'No. But it seems to me that the information we want might be down here anyway. We need to get scenes of crime here.'

Cooper inhaled deeply. He was trying to detect the presence of other smells in the cellar that shouldn't be there. No stink of petrol, thank goodness. So at least Maurice Wharton hadn't kept a motorbike down here. But his brain was running along another track. He was thinking of the temperature control. That cool twelve degrees Celsius.

'Carol, what is the temperature inside your fridge?'

Villiers looked startled. 'A fridge should be about three

degrees Celsius. Anything higher and you have the risk of bacteria. Anything lower and food starts to freeze.'

'I didn't know that,' said Cooper.

'Don't worry. Food probably doesn't stay long enough in your fridge for it to matter.'

Cooper nodded thoughtfully. Twelve degrees was too warm, then. Too high a temperature to preserve anything for very long. There would definitely be a smell by now.

'What are you thinking, Ben?' asked Villiers, watching the expression on his face.

'Oh, nothing important,' he said. 'I was just wondering about the deterioration in the quality of the beer down here.'

'Ben, that wasn't what you were thinking at all,' said Villiers.

He liked the way Carol understood him. She never seemed to read the wrong messages as Diane Fry so often used to do when they worked together.

'No,' said Cooper. 'You're right.'

In fact, the memory that had been eluding him had just come back exactly as he'd hoped, in a moment when he wasn't even trying to remember it. He'd recalled a look from Betty Wheatcroft, the slightly dotty old woman, the former teacher who'd been so disappointed at his lack of knowledge, the way teachers in his childhood always had been.

'No, actually,' he said, 'I wasn't thinking about that at all. I was thinking about the ninth circle of hell.'

Diane Fry took Henry Pearson into the little office she'd been given. She felt a bit embarrassed by it, because it was so clearly makeshift. None of the furniture even pretended to match, and the walls showed unfaded patches where the previous occupant had taken down his charts and year planners.

She promised herself she would have a better office one day. And it wouldn't be too long now, either.

But Pearson didn't seem to notice, or care, what sort of room he was in. He sat in the only available chair, declined tea or coffee, but accepted a glass of water.

He'd brought his briefcase with him, no doubt containing those files Fry had seen him carrying so importantly on the TV news. When he placed it on the desk, her heart sank. She hoped he wasn't about to whip out a file and start trying to win her over to his case. His obsessive earnestness reminded her of UFO nuts, conspiracy theorists and other cranks she'd encountered. Mostly harmless, but not the sort of person you'd want to get cornered by at a party.

Instead, he produced his leather-bound writing pad, opened it and placed a pen next to it before giving her his attention.

'First of all,' she said, 'I realise that some of my questions will have been asked before.'

'Many times, I'm sure,' said Pearson. 'The same questions have been asked over and over until I know them by heart. It was a surprise to me at first, the way the police work. But I'm accustomed to it now. Hardened would perhaps be a better word.'

'I understand.'

His grey hair was smoothed neatly back, and his eyes regarded her sharply. She remembered how, when he'd arrived in Edendale earlier in the week, he'd studied each officer he met, as if hoping to see something in them that he hadn't yet found.

'All that doubt and suspicion,' he said. 'All that cynicism. I've found it quite shocking. Why does no one want to accept the truth? David and Patricia haven't left the country

298

and changed their identities. They would never do that. A horrible crime has been committed, and my son and his wife are the victims. I really wish you and your colleagues would regard them that way.'

'You remain convinced of that?'

'I'm as convinced of that as I have been of anything in my life.'

Fry was pretty sure she'd heard him use those exact same words on TV, when facing the cameras.

'Despite the evidence?' she asked.

She was being provocative, of course – angling for a response beyond the practised phrases. But Pearson seemed to know that too. His answer came with a suggestion of weary resignation in his voice.

'Evidence? What evidence?' he said. 'Do you mean all those unconfirmed sightings, fake photos, forged emails, non-existent credit card purchases? Is that what passes for evidence these days? I think not.'

'But something we do possess,' said Fry, 'is compelling evidence of your son's illegal financial activities, prior to his disappearance.'

Pearson still regarded her calmly. 'I've never tried to make any secret of that, Detective Sergeant. In fact you might be aware that it was my cooperation with the authorities that led to the information coming to light.'

'Yes, you permitted the original inquiry team access to your son's private papers, and his computer records. It was very helpful of you.'

'I thought it would ultimately be in David's best interests.'

'Absolutely. Though it might be said that the embezzlement would have come to light anyway, in the course of inquiries. Then it might have cast a different light on subsequent events.'

'I'm not sure what you mean,' said Pearson.

'I mean that it's all about interpretation. Creating a consistent story.'

His jaw clenched then, his face set as if for an argument. She could see the amount of determination that was in him, the strength of purpose that had kept him going so long. For more than two years now, Mr Pearson had been campaigning to convince the world that his son and daughter-in-law were innocent victims who'd been caught up in some terrible fate.

Fry's phone rang then, breaking the tension.

'Excuse me,' she said. 'It might be important.'

'Certainly.'

She could feel his intense gaze fixed on her as she took the call. When she grasped the information she was being given, she wished she'd stepped outside the office to answer it. She couldn't help making eye contact with Pearson just once as she listened. Then she had to look away in embarrassment.

Fry ended the call and stared at her desk, knowing there was no way she could conceal her expression. The news had caught her off guard, with no opportunity to prepare for contact with the bereaved relative. This wasn't the way it should be.

But at least she was about to tell Henry Pearson that he'd been right along. That was some kind of consolation, perhaps.

It was Pearson himself who finally shattered the silence.

'What is it?' he said. 'There's something. I can tell.'

Fry took a breath and lifted her eyes to face him. 'Yes, that was my boss, DCI Mackenzie, in the incident room. We've had a call. It seems that some human remains have just been found in an old mine shaft on Oxlow Moor.'

'Human . . .?'

'I'm sorry,' said Fry helplessly.

'A body?' said Pearson. 'You mean a body. Just one? Well, it could be anybody.'

Fry shook her head. 'Two bodies. We can't be certain at this stage, but . . .'

She didn't need to say any more. She looked at Henry Pearson, saw the sudden draining of colour from his face. The attitude and expression were all gone, ripped from him like a worn-out coat. He'd turned instantly into an old, old man, exhausted and desolate.

But surely it couldn't have been such a shock? Hadn't he been expecting this discovery for more than two years?

As she watched Pearson disintegrate in front of her eyes, Fry was horrified at the realisation that crept into her mind, a certainty that she had been the victim of a huge scam, just like everyone else.

'You never thought they were dead at all,' she said. 'You've been playing your part all this time, waiting for the moment when they'd make contact again.'

Pearson hung his head and twisted his hands together. It was astonishing how a person could change so quickly. He looked smaller than he had a few minutes ago, more frail and crumpled, emptied of any strength or energy.

'There really was a plan for them to disappear, wasn't there?' said Fry. 'But it all went wrong.'

'Yes, it's true. I suppose there's no point in pretending any more.'

So it had all been a facade. Henry Pearson had been playing a role. The effort of putting on the performance must have been what kept him going. The necessity of maintaining appearances had been the only thing that drove him on.

But this . . . well, the person now sitting in front of Fry was a different man. He was the real Henry Pearson, the face behind the mask. And the face was a pitiful one, broken and wretched. This was a man who'd had to wait more than two years for the moment when he was allowed to grieve for his son.

'I didn't know whether they'd gone or not,' said Pearson. 'All this time, I thought they might actually have got away, that they'd just left the country a bit sooner than they originally planned. I assumed that David didn't get a chance to tell me or his mother what they were going to do. Or that . . . well, perhaps that he'd wanted to break all contact with us, too.'

'So you kept on with the pretence that your son and his wife must have been attacked and murdered here in Derbyshire. That was your agreed role, a way of distracting attention from the real story, from David and Trisha's actual whereabouts. The only trouble is, Mr Pearson – it wasn't a pretence.'

'In the end, we didn't know what to think. It was part of the plan that there would be no communication for a while, until we judged it to be safe. That time should have come over a year ago, when the police inquiry was shelved and the publicity had died down. Surely then, we thought, it would be safe? But no word came from David.'

'And you just kept on playing your part?' asked Fry. 'How could you do that?'

Pearson threw his hands out in a desperate appeal. 'What else was there for me to do? Please, can you tell me that? What else?'

26

The two bodies had been tightly rolled in heavy-duty black bin liners. The plastic wrapping meant that some areas of flesh had been protected from exposure to the air. If there was any good news, that was it. The uneven pattern of decomposition would increase the chances of a positive identification.

Fry shuddered as she joined the small group of people gathered on the edge of the hole. For her, the blackened heather further up the hill heightened the nightmarish nature of the location on the shoulder of Oxlow Moor.

The sight of the yokels playing open-air charades with their sheep down in the fields below didn't make things any better. It must be some kind of rural festival taking place. When she looked around, Fry felt as though she was trapped between two different kinds of hell.

'Wasn't this one of the mine shafts searched during the original missing persons inquiry?' asked DCI Mackenzie.

'It must have been. They all were.'

'So how is it we have this?'

'A secondary crime scene,' said Fry.

Wayne Abbott looked up from where he was crouching in the shaft.

'Well I can tell you one thing for certain,' he said. 'They haven't been here for two and a half years. The condition of the plastic is too good. In fact, the bodies look generally too well preserved. The pathologist will be able to tell you a lot more. She should get plenty of information from the post-mortem, given the state of the remains.'

Mackenzie looked at Fry, who allowed herself a smile. *Where's the best place to hide something so that it won't be found? Where it's already been looked for.* She wished she could remember who'd told her that, so she could thank them. It had been well worth repeating.

'So Henry Pearson wasn't expecting this outcome after all?' said Mackenzie.

'Not at all. It knocked the ground from under him completely. He won't be doing any more media interviews for a while.'

'Interesting.'

'More sad than interesting. He was still clinging to the belief that David and Trisha had managed to get out of the country and change their identities. Somehow he'd convinced himself that they'd covered their tracks so well that no one could make contact with them, not even him. So he just carried on playing his part regardless.'

'And yet his son and daughter-in-law have been dead for . . . well, how long would we say?'

'Shall we say about two years, four months, at a guess?' said Fry.

'From the moment they disappeared, then.'

'Yes.'

Mackenzie looked at the remains in their makeshift grave. The edges were crumbling, and the thick plastic was scattered with debris, stones and lumps of peat. The damage had been done by the fell runners. The impact of scores of feet pounding over the cover had shaken it loose and broken it into two pieces, which lay just inside the shaft. According to the initial reports from witnesses, one of the back markers had almost fallen right through.

'Is it possible,' said Mackenzie, 'that someone knew David Pearson was planning to do a bunk and followed him up here to stop him?'

'To make sure he didn't escape justice?'

'Yes.'

'Well, it's possible,' said Fry. 'We'd have to go through his business records again, follow up on everyone affected by his activities. But . . .'

'What?'

'Well, if the bodies haven't been buried here the whole time since the Pearsons disappeared, where were they until now?'

A short while later, Liz Petty arrived at the Light House with her crime-scene kit, looking a bit disgruntled at the call-out.

'There's a much better crime scene than this across the moor there,' she said. 'Two nice bodies, and all I get is a smelly cellar. I bet it's full of spiders, too.'

'Yes, it is,' said Villiers.

Cooper heard her voice from the bottom of the steps.

'Liz?' he called.

'Hello?'

'It's all right. It's me. Come on down.'

'Where are you?'

'In the cellar, of course.'

Liz's face lit up when she saw Cooper.

'Ah. Did you do this just so you could see me before tonight?'

'Obviously,' he said.

'I think I'd better get out of the way,' said Villiers. 'I'll be upstairs if you need me.'

As soon as she looked at Cooper properly, Liz drew in a

sharp breath at the sight of the bruise on his temple. He'd almost forgotten it himself, though his arm and shoulder were painful when he moved suddenly. But this was the first time Liz had seen him since it happened. He'd forgotten that, too.

'Oh, that looks sore,' she said.

'It's not too bad.'

She touched the side of his head gently with the tips of her fingers. Luckily she'd removed her latex gloves, and the touch was quite soothing.

'What on earth were you doing, going there on your own without backup?' she said.

'Oh, don't. It's just something that happens now and then.'

'Not to my husband.'

'Future husband.'

'Well, I want to make sure you're still around by then.'

She looked at the bruise again, and winced as if she felt his pain. But he wouldn't ever want her to do that.

Liz smiled and took Cooper's arm – a firm, affectionate touch that made him forget for a while that he was on duty and working.

'We shouldn't,' he said.

'I know. But it's a cellar, and no one else is around.'

'Even so.'

She squeezed his arm again. 'You're so well behaved. You could relax a bit more sometimes, you know.'

Cooper felt the temptation, but pulled himself together. It was a shame, but there were more urgent things to deal with.

'What was that you were saying to Carol just now about another crime scene?' he said.

'They've found two bodies. Haven't you heard?'

'Damn it. No, I hadn't.'

Cooper looked at his phone, and saw *Network lost*. They were below ground level, of course. Even if there was mobile phone reception on this part of the moor, the signal would be blocked by the cellar walls and the depth of peat lying around them.

He hated being out of touch. It was bad enough at the best of times, but now there seemed to be a major development, and he was unreachable. But someone could have called the officer outside on his radio. Airwave worked here, surely.

That led him inevitably to the suspicion that he was being deliberately kept out of the loop. The thought made him unreasonably angry.

'The bodies,' he said. 'Is it the Pearsons?'

Liz looked at him in concern at the change in his tone. 'Oh, I couldn't say. But that seems to be the assumption being made right now. Two bodies, dead for some time. They were found in an abandoned mine shaft up on the moor.'

Cooper gritted his teeth. 'A mine shaft? Really.'

'You don't sound too surprised.'

'No, I'm not,' he said. 'I suppose the bodies haven't been there for two and a half years, though. Not likely.'

'Again, I couldn't say. You'll have to ask someone else for information, Ben. I'm just a crime-scene examiner.'

He tried to calm himself. Of course it wasn't Liz's fault. Far from it. He shouldn't be speaking to her as though it was.

'I'm sorry.'

'It's okay.' She looked round the cellar. 'But we have our own scene, such as it is. So what's here?'

'It's more what's *not* here,' said Cooper.

'Such as?'

'Chest freezers.'

'What?'

'There are no chest freezers. They must have had big freezers here. They left all this equipment in the pub when they went – the kitchens are full of stuff. But no freezers.'

'Okay.'

'Look,' he said, 'there's a space against this wall where something of that size has been standing. You can see still the shape of it on the floor.'

'Stay back,' said Liz. 'There are shoe marks in the dust right in front of you. And if someone carried a freezer out, there might be prints on the wall.'

Cooper took a step backwards. 'And I think we should check the whole cellar for traces of blood.'

'Oh Lord, that means turning the lights out.' She sighed. 'Your theory being that this might be a primary crime scene?'

'Yes, possibly.'

'In that case, I'll need to call in and get a full team,' she said.

'But I'm guessing everyone is fully committed already.'

'Yes, we'd have to wait some time.'

'Come on, Liz . . .'

'Oh, now you're turning on the charm. You know I can't resist. Okay, you can leave me to it.'

'Thanks. I owe you a favour.'

'I'll think of something, don't worry.'

Cooper ran up the steps, and Villiers met him at the top.

'Have you heard, Ben?' she said.

'Yes, just now. Two bodies.'

'That stinks, doesn't it?'

'To high heaven.'

Villiers gave him a hand up out of the hatch. The space behind the bar counter was awkward and narrow. It couldn't have been easy for a man of Maurice Wharton's size to get through.

'If it is the Pearsons,' said Villiers, 'they should be able to ID them pretty quickly. There are DNA profiles on record. And of course there's a family member on hand. It depends what condition the bodies are in, I suppose.'

'It would be very useful to know that. I mean, what stage the decomposition is at. I wonder when anyone will bother to tell us.'

'Briefing tomorrow, at a guess?'

'That's no good.'

Villiers looked thoughtful as they walked out of the pub, past the rattling tape.

'Ben, what was that stuff you were saying earlier about the circles of hell?'

'The ninth circle, to be exact.'

'Isn't that what Aidan Merritt was rambling about when he called his wife, just before he was killed?'

'That's right. Everyone thought it was to do with the fires on the moor. He must have gone right through the smoke to get to the Light House. But there was something Betty Wheatcroft said to me. She pointed out that it was from Dante's *Inferno*.'

'The old biddy's not as daft as she looks, then?'

'No, not at all. I don't know where she gets her information from, but she knows more than she lets on. She's stubborn, though. Likes to play her own game. There was some detail she would have given me, if I'd asked the right question. I just didn't know what the question was.'

'Perhaps she just needs you to show a bit more interest,' said Villiers.

Cooper stopped by his car. 'You think so, Carol?'

'A lonely old lady, isn't she? I bet she really took to you, and enjoyed having a chat. So instead of telling you everything, she thought of a way of making you come back to see her again.'

He stared at her, astonished by the clarity of the insight. To him, it seemed a devious way of thinking. But in Mrs Wheatcroft's case, it rang so true.

They got in the car, and Cooper started the engine. He had Betty Wheatcroft's phone number in his notebook, but he had to wait until they were well down the road and on to Batham Gate before he could get a signal. The old lady's phone rang and rang, without even an answering machine or call minder cutting in.

'No answer,' he said. 'She must be out.'

'Where does Mrs Wheatcroft go now?' asked Villiers, as they approached the sharp bend on Batham Gate.

'What do you mean?'

'What pub does she go to? She can't have stopped going for a drink just because the Light House closed.'

'Well, as I said before, she went to the Light House for the company, because she knew people there.'

'Okay, so where did the people that she knew start going when it closed?'

'I don't know.' But then Cooper stopped, and corrected himself. 'Yes I do. Ian Gullick told me. He said they drink at the Badger, near Bradwell.'

'Could Mrs Wheatcroft get there easily?'

'It's on the same bus route as the Light House, and a good bit closer to where she lives.'

'It's worth a try, if we have time.'

'We're almost there,' said Cooper. 'Another two minutes, and we'll pass it.'

Betty Wheatcroft had found a corner for herself in the bar of the Badger, and was sitting with her glass and her plastic carrier bag, trying to ignore the loud background music and the beeps and buzzes of the fruit machines. This was a different kind of place, not what she'd been used to at the Light House.

Cooper saw her as soon as he came through the door. He noticed that her glass was almost empty, so he went first to the bar and bought her a half-pint of Guinness. She smiled when she spotted him, losing for a moment that slightly mad, desperate look. There was no surprise on her face. She gave the impression that she'd been expecting him, that he could even be slightly late. She might be putting a black mark next to his name in an imaginary attendance register.

'How nice,' she said. 'And what a good idea not to come to my house. People would start to talk.'

'I'm very glad I caught you, Mrs Wheatcroft,' said Cooper. 'There's something I need to ask you.'

She looked anxiously round the bar, then buried her face in her glass. She seemed somehow reassured by the slosh of the black liquid.

'What is it?'

'Last time I visited you, I mentioned the ninth circle of hell, and you said it was—'

'The *Inferno*. It's by the great Italian poet Dante Alighieri. The first part of his *Divine Comedy*. All about the medieval concept of hell. Lovely, isn't it?'

Cooper wasn't quite sure what she was referring to. At first he thought it might be the Guinness, or the music now playing in the background. Lynyrd Skynyrd's 'Free Bird', if he wasn't mistaken. Not really Mrs Wheatcroft's cup of tea, he imagined. So she must be referring to Dante's vision of hell.

'There's something particular about the ninth circle,' he said.

'Judas, Brutus and Cassius.'

'Sorry?'

'Judas, Brutus and Cassius,' she repeated more slowly, as

311

if remembering that he was one of her slower pupils. 'The ninth circle of hell. It's all about treachery.'

'Yes, that's what I was thinking.'

She took another gulp of her drink. 'In Dante's *Inferno*, each of the nine circles is reserved for a particular sin. They get more and more wicked as they move towards the middle. The ninth circle was reserved for the very worst sinners – the traitors. Judas, who betrayed Jesus. And Brutus and Cassius who stabbed Julius Caesar in the back. Do you remember this at all?'

Cooper nodded, hoping not to have to reveal the true depths of his ignorance.

'Is that what Aidan Merritt was talking about?'

'Yes, I think it must have been.'

She seemed to lose track of the conversation, gazing across the bar at no one in particular, then poking in her carrier bag as if she'd lost something.

Cooper tried to curb his impatience. He had faith in Carol's assessment. He had to let Betty Wheatcroft play her own game, at her own pace, if he wanted to get everything she knew out of her.

'The traitors,' he said slowly.

'Oh.' She licked her lips thoughtfully. 'Thank you. Well, in the ninth circle there were three different grades of treachery. Betrayal of family, betrayal of community, betrayal of . . . guests.'

'Guests?'

'Yes. A breach of the unwritten laws. The ancient code of hospitality.'

Cooper sat back in his chair, and looked at the old lady, with her wild hair and her plastic carrier bag. Many people would pass her by without a second glance.

'Mrs Wheatcroft, where do you get your information from?' he asked.

'Oh, I know it all,' she said.

'People tell you what they're doing?'

'No, not them,' she said, with a flash of contempt. 'Nobody ever spoke to me at the Light House, except for Aidan. As far as they were concerned, I was just the daft old trout in the corner. It's the same here at the Badger. And because they don't talk to me, they think I don't hear anything. I suppose they reckon I must be deaf. But I do hear. I hear everything.'

'And what did you hear in this case, Mrs Wheatcroft?'

She put a finger to the side of her nose. '*They* thought Aidan was going to betray them. But he was a decent man. Weak, but decent.'

Betty Wheatcroft suddenly looked very sad. Cooper knew she'd liked Aidan Merritt, and he'd wondered how long she could hold that back and pretend she wasn't too disturbed by his death. Her charade of secrecy was just part of the game. Underneath, she was a frightened woman.

'Who are *they*? Who thought he was going to betray them?' he asked.

'I can't tell you,' she said.

'Mrs Wheatcroft . . .'

'No,' she snapped firmly. 'Be told.'

He shut up immediately, hearing the exact same words and tone of voice that his grandmother had used to him when he was a child, pestering for an ice cream.

In another moment, she'd changed the subject back to safer ground. The past, the theoretical – so much less dangerous than the real, physical present. He wondered if she was scared by a genuine threat from some specific source, or whether she feared to make herself one more soul who was guilty of the sin of betrayal.

'Do you happen to have a copy of this book, Mrs Wheatcroft?' asked Cooper.

'The *Inferno*? No, why would I? Look it up, if you want.'

'I'll google it,' he said.

'Yes, you do that.'

She laughed then. It wasn't quite a cackle, but a chortle with an edge of unhealthy glee. Cooper thought perhaps he shouldn't have bought her that extra Guinness.

'Would you like me to give you a lift home, Mrs Wheatcroft?'

'That would be delightful,' she said.

Outside the pub, Mrs Wheatcroft greeted Carol Villiers like an old friend, though they'd never met.

'Hello, dear. Are we travelling together?'

'Give me your arm,' said Villiers. 'And let me take your bag.'

'No, no.'

Mrs Wheatcroft sounded suddenly distressed. She pulled her plastic bag out of reach, and clutched it to her bosom. Cooper heard the chink of glass. Full bottles, from the sound of it.

She settled in the back seat of his car. Villiers got in, looked at him, raised an eyebrow. Cooper shrugged. He fastened his seat belt, and they pulled out on to the road to head into Edendale.

'Yes, I remember it very well,' said Mrs Wheatcroft's voice drowsily from behind him. 'Right in the middle, hell wasn't fiery, you know – the sinners were frozen up to their necks in a lake of ice.'

'Ice?' said Villiers.

'Ice,' she repeated. 'And sometimes, they say, a soul falls into the ninth circle before the thread of life has been cut.'

'Before they've died, you mean?'

'Mmm. And the body left behind on earth is possessed by a demon, so what seems to be a living man is actually already dead, and has reached a stage beyond . . . repentance.'

On the last word, her voice faded away. Cooper looked in his rear-view mirror, and saw that the old lady was fast asleep.

An hour earlier, Diane Fry had taken a call from Nancy Wharton, the former landlady of the Light House.

Of course Mrs Wharton had really wanted to speak to Detective Sergeant Cooper, but he wasn't around. In fact no one seemed to know how to get hold of him, so the call had been put through to Fry as the next best thing. How nice to be a more or less acceptable substitute for Ben Cooper.

Fry could have phoned Cooper to pass on the message, she supposed. But why should she? All bets were off since Cooper had gone rogue and carried out those arrests, pulling in Ian Gullick and Vince Naylor for questioning. As far as she was concerned, there was no trust left to be broken.

When she'd parked her Audi in the street on the Devonshire Estate, Nancy Wharton met her at the door of her home, with Eliot and Kirsten standing close behind her, crowding the hallway with hostile expressions on their faces. Fry saw that she wasn't even going to get inside the house this time. Definitely second best, then.

'We heard the news just now,' said Mrs Wharton stiffly, speaking as though she'd rehearsed some lines to deliver.

'Oh? You've heard about the bodies that were found,' guessed Fry, though it didn't need much guessing. The media had arrived at Oxlow Moor before she'd got there herself.

'Yes, they're saying it's the Pearsons.'

'We can't be a hundred per cent sure at the moment, but . . .'

Even to Fry herself it no longer sounded convincing. Mrs

Wharton treated the stock phrase with the contempt it deserved.

'Well *I'm* sure,' she said.

'May I come in? And then we can talk about it properly, perhaps.'

Nancy shook her head. Instead she handed Fry an envelope. Then she began to back away into the hallway, as if she'd performed her role and was about to leave the stage.

'What's this?' asked Fry.

'It's for you. Or rather, for Detective Sergeant Cooper – but they told me he isn't available. So . . .'

'Yes, but what is it?'

'That,' said Mrs Wharton, before she closed the door, 'is my husband's confession.'

27

There was a welcome awaiting Cooper when he and Villiers returned to West Street. Diane Fry was pacing the corridor impatiently, and pounced on Cooper as soon as he appeared.

'We've been waiting for you,' she said. 'Where have you been? She'll only talk to you.'

'Who will?'

'Nancy Wharton, of course.'

'Where is she?'

'In an interview room.'

'Why?'

'She gave us her husband's statement, but obviously we have to question her. We need details, a full account of what happened.'

She was talking too fast, and Cooper wasn't able to take it in.

'Hold on,' he said. 'You'd better rewind a bit, Diane. You're losing me.'

Fry stopped, took a deep breath. 'Of course, you don't know about it. You're out of touch.'

'I wonder whose fault that is?'

'Okay, let's take a few minutes.'

Cooper sat down in her tiny office and read through the letter handed over by Mrs Wharton. It was signed by her husband in a slightly shaky hand, and dated Wednesday – the day that Cooper had talked to him in the hospice. He remembered listening to Wharton tell his story about the Light House closing, seeing the windows of the pub going dark one by one.

It was a very brief letter. More of a note, really. It merely stated that Maurice Wharton admitted full responsibility for the deaths of David and Patricia Pearson in December 2009, while they were guests on his licensed premises at the Light House, Oxlow Moor, Derbyshire. Wharton referred to himself as 'the undersigned', as if the formal language might give his statement some kind of legal authority.

'It's useless without evidence, of course,' said Fry, tapping her fingers impatiently as she watched Cooper read.

'Of course.'

'But there's one other thing you should know. David Pearson's financial activities were gone into at the time, during the original inquiry. But not thoroughly enough, it seems.'

'What do you mean?'

'Mr Mackenzie tasked one of the incident room teams to run a new analysis of Pearson's business dealings. And guess what popped up? Among the people who suffered serious losses when the embezzlement was discovered and the company went into receivership, we found M. and N. Wharton, owners of the Light House Hotel.'

Cooper shook his head in despair. 'You're right, it should have been picked up.'

'Well, I suppose it was just one of hundreds of cases in the files of Diamond Hybrid Securities. There was nothing actually fraudulent about their dealings with the Light House. The Whartons were just unfortunate victims. Collateral damage.'

'So you've brought Nancy in?' said Cooper.

'She didn't want to come. She seemed to think the letter would be enough – that we'd just accept it and go away, without asking any more questions. She's in for a surprise, though. We need to know exactly what happened. And we need some proof – witness statements, forensic evidence. Someone will have to interview the children. Eliot is seventeen. He's old enough to put in the witness box.'

'It won't ever come to court,' said Cooper.

'What? Why not?'

'Maurice Wharton is dying. He can't have more than a few days left to live, weeks at most. I bet Nancy would be at the hospice now, sitting at his bedside, if you hadn't pulled her in.'

'Well, yes – that *is* what she told me,' admitted Fry.

Cooper nodded. 'But you took no notice, did you, Diane?'

'Well what would *you* have done?' she snapped. 'I had to bring her in. It's all very well this caring and sensitive stuff, but there comes a point where even you have to follow procedure and do your job properly, no matter how many sob stories people tell you.'

With an effort, Cooper tried not to smile too much. He felt unduly pleased with himself for having provoked a response from her. Despite the impression she tried to give, Fry was very much on edge. Something had unsettled her, and he was content to think that it might have been him.

He stood up, still holding on to the evidence bag containing Maurice Wharton's letter.

'I'll go and talk to her then, shall I?' he said.

'Obviously, I'll have to sit in,' said Fry.

'Fine. But try not to upset her too much.'

Nancy Wharton was huddled close to the table, hunched in an awkward position, as if cowering away from the walls of the room. The interview rooms at West Street weren't very attractive, but her reaction was extreme.

Cooper recalled the furniture crammed into the Whartons' council house on the Devonshire Estate. He wondered if she'd already become constrained by her new life there, and now no longer knew how to relax and stretch herself out into the available space.

'Maurice has always had his faults,' said Nancy, before Fry had even started the tapes. 'No one knows that better than me. But he's not really a murderer.'

Fry shrugged. 'Oh, no one's a murderer,' she said. 'Not until they kill someone.'

Nancy tried to ignore her, though Cooper could see she found it difficult. *So do we all,* he thought.

The tapes began to turn, and Mrs Wharton was advised of her rights by Fry in a practised monotone that the older woman seemed to take no notice of.

'The thing is, we thought the Pearsons had been forgotten,' she said. 'No one seemed to be asking questions about them any more. So we relaxed a bit. It was a mistake, I suppose.'

'Not your first mistake,' said Fry.

Nancy turned towards Cooper. Though she'd been reluctant to come in and answer questions, she began to talk almost without prompting.

'You have to understand the position we'd come to,' she said. 'Just that day, we'd told Eliot and Kirsten it might be the last Christmas we spent at the Light House. We had to explain to them why it had happened, about the people who said they'd invest money in the pub and be our business partners, about the big loan we'd taken out for the improvements they insisted on. And we told them that they'd pulled out, and left us with a pub that was losing money, with debts we couldn't pay back.'

Nancy ran her hands over her hair and clutched her head tightly, as if to hold in the thoughts that were trying to escape.

'The children needed to know that,' she said. 'They were old enough by then. Well, we thought they were.'

'This would have been your arrangement with Diamond Hybrid Securities,' said Cooper. 'The company David Pearson worked for.'

'Not just that. It was him we dealt with. Him who sweet-talked us into committing ourselves beyond our means. But we never met him. So of course we had no idea who he was when he came into the pub. Not a clue.'

'Go on, Mrs Wharton.'

She paused for a while to collect herself.

'Anyway, the children were very upset,' she said. 'Kirsten cried, and Eliot went really quiet, the way he does some-times. I think that's what hurt Maurice most. He loves his children. He'd do absolutely anything for them. And there he was, looking at the prospect of being unable to make a living and keep them in their home. It made him feel useless, a failure. Maurice was already a man on the brink. He'd tell you that himself, if he was able.'

'And you kept quiet about it all this time,' put in Fry.

Nancy looked up at her. 'You can't blame us for trying to protect our family. Anybody would have done it. Yes, we covered it up for nearly two years, never said a word. But then the bank called in our loan and the pub was closed. Even then, it was weeks afterwards before it occurred to us that there might be a problem. We imagined someone buying the pub and finding something we'd missed. And then . . .'

She shook her head. 'But it was too late. We'd given up the keys, and we couldn't get back in. We felt helpless. As the auction got nearer and nearer, we started to panic. We had crazy ideas about how to prevent anyone from wanting to buy the place.'

'Hence all the stories going round about junkies and squatters, and the dangers of subsidence?' asked Cooper.

'Yes,' she said.

But she said it so quietly that Cooper's ears pricked up. She had hung her head to avoid meeting his eye. She was ashamed, perhaps. That was understandable. But suddenly he realised that she was mostly ashamed of something she wasn't telling them.

'It's easy to spread rumours around here,' said Nancy. 'It only takes one person to start talking about it in a pub, and it goes round like wildfire. No one knew that better than us.'

It was true, but Cooper wasn't letting it distract from the sudden weight of certainty that had formed in his mind.

'It was you,' he said, with a growing feeling of shock and anger. 'It was you who started the moorland fires. You actually hoped the fire would reach the pub. You planned to damage it beyond repair, so that no one would buy it. You wanted to see the death of the Light House.'

'It seemed the only way left to us. We thought we'd run out of options, but when the wildfires started, it was like a sign. We heard someone on the news saying that the fires were threatening farm buildings and isolated properties. I remember it now. We looked at each other, and we didn't have to say a word.'

Cooper stared at her, horrified. It was almost beyond comprehension that the Whartons could have tried to destroy the place they'd worked so hard to save. But that was what they'd been brought to, in the end.

Fry glanced at him, but said nothing. He could sense her unspoken message. He was getting off topic. They had to focus Nancy Wharton on the central issue.

'We need to take you back to that night in December,' said Fry. 'Tell us exactly what happened.'

Cooper watched Nancy fold her arms and lean on them, rocking her body against the table as she relived the memories. How had she imagined she could escape this process? Did she really think she could just hand over a letter and it would all be done with? Wishful thinking? Or had she completely lost touch with reality? Living with such a huge secret for so long might warp your perspective, he supposed. The biggest challenge she'd faced was deciding when the moment had come to let that secret go.

'The Light House was shut,' she said. 'We always closed the pub for a few days over Christmas.'

'We know that. So how did the Pearsons come to be there?'

'They came banging on the door late that night, and we recognised them from the evening before. So we let them in. We didn't want to. Well, Maurice particularly – he hated the idea of strangers being there in the pub, when it was a family time. It was worse than that, though. Maurice had been looking at the business accounts. Like I said, we truly thought it was going to be the last Christmas we'd be able to spend at the Light House. The children knew it by then, too.'

'So if you and Mr Wharton really didn't want strangers in the pub over Christmas, then why . . .?'

'They were both exhausted when they arrived,' said Nancy. 'The woman was on her last legs. They must have been wandering around the moor for hours by then. They'd been to the George in Castleton, and tried to walk back. Over the moor in the snow? Stupid. They were stupid to do that.'

It was a tendency that so many people showed when they were interviewed, the attempt to blame everything on the victims. If they hadn't done this, if they hadn't behaved like that . . . The sound of self-justification was so familiar in these interview rooms that Cooper could probably have heard it echoing back to him if he put his ear to the wall.

'Did they say which way they'd come from Castleton?' he asked.

Nancy looked surprised. 'Yes, they said they'd walked up The Stones. They must have come out on the hill at the top there.'

'Hurd Low.'

'Yes. Why?'

Why? Cooper had retraced their exact steps himself earlier in the week. He'd pictured very clearly David and Trisha Pearson choosing to take a route back to their cottage via The Stones and Goose Hill, leaving the street lamps of Castleton behind and climbing Hurd Low, hoping to follow the path that linked up with the Limestone Way. He'd imagined the light flurries of sleet turning to snow by the time they left the town. He saw them, within minutes, struggling through a blizzard, their torches useless in zero visibility, their track disappearing under drifting snow. He'd almost been able to feel the cold, to hear that wind moaning and whining like an animal.

Zero visibility? When Cooper had been up on Oxlow Moor this week, the prominent landmark he'd once known had been missing. The Light House had been dark and abandoned, windowless and dead. Though its roof line was still there, its characteristic presence was missing from the skyline.

But when the Pearsons had set off to walk from the George to their cottage at Brecks Farm, the Light House had still been occupied. The Whartons were at home, getting ready to celebrate Christmas with their family. All the windows would have been lit up, the decorations glittering, the Christmas tree sparkling like a beacon in the darkness.

Freezing cold and disorientated, they must have seen those lights in the distance and decided to seek sanctuary.

'They were frozen stiff and white all over, like a couple of snowmen,' said Nancy. 'If they hadn't been wearing warm clothes, I don't think they would have made it. When you live up that way, you have more sense. The road was covered in no time, and the car park was drifting over. The wind drives the snow over the moor, you see, and the Light House is the first place it finds to dump it on. We were ready for it, though. We were well stocked up with food, and we'd got everything in for our own celebrations. Only fools or tourists would have been out on the moor in that weather.'

'But the Pearsons were never completely lost, were they?' said Cooper.

'I don't know what you mean. Why not?'

'Because,' said Cooper, 'they were never out sight of the Light House.'

Yes, it was true that no one lost on the moors would stand a chance unless they found shelter. But that was the point, wasn't it? *Unless they found shelter.*

'Well, there we were with these two people on the doorstep,' said Nancy. 'No one had a hope of getting through that night. There wasn't much point in calling a taxi. What else could we do? Besides, there was an obligation on us. It came with being licensees of a place like the Light House. Those hundreds of years serving as an inn for travellers. All that history.'

'The unwritten law,' said Cooper. 'The ancient code of hospitality.'

'Yes, if you like.'

And right in the middle, hell wasn't fiery. The sinners were frozen up to their necks in a lake of ice.

'Which room did the Pearsons stay in?' asked Fry.

'Room One. We called it the Bakewell Room. It was the only one we could get ready quickly for guests.'

'So what went wrong?'

'Maurice looked at the register after they'd signed in. Then he checked the credit card transaction. A few minutes later I heard him go down into the cellar, where we kept the old records. There are a couple of filing cabinets down there.'

'Yes, I've seen them.'

'I followed him down, but he was in a bit of a state by then. He couldn't believe what he was seeing. And I can't say I blamed him. You can imagine how Maurice felt about finding them under his roof as guests – even as paying guests. And he'd let them stay himself, gone out of his way to make a room available for them.'

'Well, how *did* he feel?'

'He thought he'd invited vampires in. He'd always called them "the bloodsuckers". And there they were, under his own roof.'

Cooper nodded. It was odd that he'd been thinking about Count Dracula earlier in the day, when he'd opened the hatch into the cellar at the Light House. According to vampire legends, undead creatures like Dracula could only enter your house if they were invited in. He recollected fanged actors in horror films trying all kinds of tricks to fool a victim into issuing an invitation. But the Pearsons hadn't needed to trick Maurice Wharton, had they? Maurice had met with disaster because of his own moment of weakness, his uncharacteristic gesture of generosity.

It had been Christmas, after all. In the end, not even Mad Maurice Wharton wanted to be the man who said 'no room at the inn'.

'He sat in his own bar, drinking whisky,' said Nancy. 'Poor Maurice. He was consumed by bitterness. The hunger for revenge. Eventually, it, and the whisky, got too strong for him. Maurice took the baseball bat that he kept behind the bar. And then he let the dogs in.'

28

Fry gave Cooper a meaningful look, and he nodded. She switched off the tapes, and they took a break. It was time to let Nancy Wharton think about things for a while.

In the corridor outside the interview room, Carol Villiers took the chance to catch Cooper with a message.

'Ben, there's been a call for you. You're expected up at the Light House. You arranged to meet someone there?'

'Oh damn, I'd forgotten that. It's Josh Lane.' He looked at Fry. 'I really ought to go. In the circumstances, I think this might be extremely useful to us.'

'You think you can produce some evidence that relates to Mrs Wharton's story?'

'One way or another, yes.'

'Then go for it. We'll manage here.'

She was too eager for him to leave, of course. But it couldn't be helped. Cooper felt he had to leave some reminders with her before he went.

'You'll have to question Mrs Wharton about who was involved with the cover-up, who moved the bodies, who broke into the Light House. The Whartons had accomplices who were responsible for all that. And Aidan Merritt . . .'

'Yes, I do realise,' said Fry.

'So . . . why do *you* think Aidan Merritt got himself killed?'

Fry shrugged. 'Maybe the Whartons thought he was going

to betray them. He must have realised the whole thing was going to come out. Perhaps he decided to get in first with his confession. But someone else had their own plan. It was pretty desperate, and they couldn't allow Merritt to throw a spanner in the works. They were never going to let him start talking, not to anyone.'

'He looked like a weak link, I suppose,' said Cooper.

'Yes. So they got him to the Light House on some pretext, and made sure he didn't talk. The question is, who betrayed whom?'

Cooper shook his head sadly. 'That's the wrong question. In the end, they all betrayed themselves.'

Fry looked at him. 'You were lucky,' she said. 'Lucky that you survived the attack on Wednesday night. Or perhaps they just wanted to put you in hospital and stop you asking the wrong questions.'

'You mean the right questions.'

'I suppose.'

Fry turned away.

'Feel like picking up Ian Gullick and Vince Naylor again?' called Cooper as she left, but she didn't respond.

Even as he said it, he wondered whether he was in danger of rubbing it in too much. His decision to arrest and question Gullick and Naylor had been correct, though not perhaps for the right reasons.

Cooper went to collect his jacket and car keys from his desk in the CID room. He found Gavin Murfin filling a waste-paper bin with the contents of his drawers, and Becky Hurst looking at him expectantly, waiting for news of progress.

'It seems you were wrong after all, Gavin,' said Cooper.

'There's a first time for everything,' said Murfin casually.

'So Maurice Wharton killed the Pearsons, is that right?' said Hurst. 'But he must have had some help afterwards.'

'Some of his regulars, we think.'

'They helped to cover up for him?'

'So it seems.'

'I don't understand it,' said Hurst. 'How did Wharton inspire such loyalty? I mean, by all accounts he was a complete pain in the backside, who liked nothing better than insulting and abusing his customers.'

'True. And anyone who didn't know him took offence and never came back. But those others, the regulars – they must have seen through all that nonsense and recognised a different Maurice.'

'If you ask me, they just didn't want to see the pub closed down,' said Murfin. 'One thing you have to say about Mad Maurice – he kept a very good cellar. His beer was always top-notch. You can't say that about any of these keg places you see all over the shop now. Besides, he wasn't averse to a good lock-in when he was in the mood.'

'Not that you ever went to one, Gavin, considering it's illegal.'

'Course not. I just heard.'

'Well, it's right that his regulars were the people who kept him in business all those years,' said Cooper. 'They were the ones who kept coming back month after month, who spread his reputation far and wide. He owed a lot to those customers. Without them, he was nothing. And I don't suppose he wanted to let them down by closing the pub.'

'Is this all a question of loyalty, then?' asked Hurst, still puzzled. 'Maurice Wharton being loyal to his customers, and his regulars being loyal to him?'

'Yes, but loyalty is where it went wrong,' said Cooper. 'It's always a mistake involving someone else in an act like that. Most people can't even rely on themselves to keep a secret. But the suspicion that you can't trust a person who shares your guilty knowledge will really eat away at you over time. These people had more than two years of it. Frankly, it's a wonder they didn't try to kill each other long before now.'

DI Hitchens strolled into the room and put his arm on Cooper's shoulder as he listened to the end of the conversation.

'And the fires?' he said. 'The same people are responsible for those, I gather.'

'There's been a coordinated campaign going on,' said Cooper. 'The fires on Kinder were started deliberately and the temporary reservoir was sabotaged, but only as part of a diversion – to draw away firefighting resources. The real target was always on Oxlow Moor. Specifically, the Light House.'

'The chief fire officer is happy anyway,' said Hitchens. 'They like to identify people who start wildfires on the moors. Normally it's far too difficult for them to prove a fire was started deliberately, even when there's no doubt in their own minds. Even if there's no prosecution, they're glad to get a confirmed arson.'

Cooper nodded. He wondered if he should mention the irony that it was the chief fire officer himself who'd given the Whartons the idea of starting the fires. His comments in that TV interview had been well intentioned, but had fallen on the wrong ears. He might have thought he was doing good PR for the fire service, but mentioning the threat to isolated buildings had been a fatal suggestion to insert into the minds of desperate people.

He rattled his car keys as he was about to leave the office with Villiers, but turned back for a moment.

'Gavin . . .' he said.

'What?'

'Why is it that you never mentioned the word "cellar" until now? It could have saved a lot of trouble.'

Murfin shook his head. 'It's funny how that goes, like. It only came into my memory just now, when I started thinking about beer. I mean, you don't have any other reason to think about the cellar in a pub, do you? Not when you're just a customer. It's there under your feet, but you don't need to know about it.'

'A wonderful thing, the memory,' said Villiers. 'It can trawl up the most unexpected things. Details you were convinced you'd forgotten just pop into your mind from somewhere. And no one really understands how it works.'

'Don't they?'

'Nope. It's one of the great mysteries of the human mind.'

'I can't even remember what I had for dinner last night,' said Murfin.

'That's old age, Gavin,' put in Hurst. 'I bet you remember every day of the Blitz, though.'

Still Cooper hesitated. He'd known Murfin for quite a few years now, and he thought he could read below the surface of his words.

'Gavin, you didn't really believe that the Pearsons had skipped the country, did you? Not as much as you made Diane Fry think you did.'

Murfin smiled. 'You can't let someone like that have it all her own way, Ben. She needs someone to take the opposite view. It focuses her mind, see. After I'd said all that, she was dead set on proving me wrong and showing everyone that the Pearsons were victims of a violent crime. And so she did.'

'I told her I thought you might be right,' said Cooper. 'I was standing up for you, Gavin.'

With his smile developing into a satisfied smirk, Murfin

leaned back in his chair. 'Well, like I said before, we've all learned something, then.'

'So – Mad Maurice,' said Villiers a little while later, as Cooper's Toyota headed out of Edendale. 'It seems he wasn't a lovable eccentric after all. He actually *was* a psychopath.'

'I'm not sure,' said Cooper.

'You're not sure? But he killed two perfectly innocent tourists.'

'It's a bit too convenient, Carol.'

'What is?'

'The fact that he's dying. It's too convenient that Maurice Wharton will soon be dead and buried himself. It seems to me that that's what everyone has wanted all along – to be able to sweep the whole thing under the carpet and forget about it. And it's not going to happen.'

Villiers gave him a quizzical look. 'What's made you take this attitude?'

'I was thinking about Maurice Wharton, when he talked about how painful it was watching his pub closed down for the last time. Seeing the windows go dark one by one.'

'Yes?'

'Well, it's no wonder he found it painful, knowing what he did, and what had been hidden there. He must have realised the truth would be uncovered eventually. And there was nothing he could do about it by then, when he was sitting in that car in the dusk. It must have been like watching his own future being slowly snuffed out.'

'I see. And is that all?'

Villiers knew him too well. But Cooper didn't want to share all his thoughts. As so often was the case, they didn't come anywhere near to amounting to evidence.

In fact, he'd also been thinking about what Fry had told

him of Henry Pearson's reaction to the discovery of the two bodies. The collapse of the pretence, the crumbling facade. Everyone had their public face, the image they presented to the world. Even Gavin Murfin had cultivated a persona, a role that he played up to, so that everyone would remember him, even if it was for all the wrong reasons. It didn't reflect the real Murfin, the one behind the facade. And wasn't that the same with Maurice Wharton? It was all about image.

In the CID room today, the comments had been all about the Wharton of legend. The notorious Mad Maurice, the man who was known for his short temper and angry outbursts. He had a reputation for miles around as being irascible and unpredictable. Anyone with that idea in mind would have no difficulty picturing Wharton losing control, flying into a rage, and killing two people.

A reputation, yes. But reputations were built up over time. And surely it had been mostly an act in Wharton's case? He'd known perfectly well the appeal his eccentricity had for visitors to his pub. Many of them were drawn in to watch his performance. Of course, he had played up to the nickname. And so had everyone else. Even now, the whole of Edendale still called him Mad Maurice. Yet it was the way he wanted to be remembered. He'd said so himself, right there in the hospice.

In a way, it was almost like the story of the Light House itself. A brightly lit exterior, distracting attention from the darker corners within.

Yes, a reputation was very useful. A nickname created expectations in the people who heard it. Cooper wondered about his own response to that name. Had he been guilty of forming preconceptions about the way Mad Maurice Wharton would have behaved? Was he, like everyone else, being manipulated through his prejudices?

'Still bothered by the memories?' asked Villiers.

Cooper laughed. 'They haven't done me much good so far. The general impressions are right, but the details always seem to be wrong.'

'It's not a joke,' said Villiers. 'No matter how good your memory is, you can't recall every detail. So your mind fills in the gaps by using bits of other memories. You ask your inner eye to create a picture for you, but it can't show you blanks where faces should be, so it uses whatever material it can find. If we could analyse the images in your brain, we'd find that the man at the bar looked a bit like the person you arrested yesterday, his clothes were those of someone you just passed in the street, and his face was reminiscent of Brad Pitt.'

'Robert Redford,' said Cooper.

'What?'

'Nothing.'

'You get my point, though. One person's memory is too unreliable as evidence. Recollections become polluted by imagination.'

'So instead of imagination, what we need is a bit of illumination, some light to shine into those dark corners where we can't see.'

'Absolutely,' she said.

But as they crested the rise on Bradwell Moor, Cooper saw the smoke on the skyline. He remembered the devastating moorland fires, their flames rising twenty feet into the air as they swept across the landscape, scorching the earth bare to reveal what lay underneath. Those flames were illuminating places where perhaps there should have been no light.

When Cooper had left with Villiers, Fry decided to let Nancy Wharton cool for a while. She was given a cup of tea, allowed to go to the bathroom, asked again if she wanted a solicitor to be present with her in the interview room.

Nancy hadn't been arrested, but she must realise there was a possibility she could be charged with perverting the course of justice, perhaps assisting an offender. It might even come to conspiracy to murder, which carried a potential life sentence. But that was all in the future.

'What actual forensic evidence do we have?' DCI Mackenzie asked when Fry briefed him.

'The blood on David Pearson's anorak isn't his.'

'Yes, I know that. But we don't have a match.'

'Could we get a DNA sample from Maurice Wharton?' asked Fry.

'A dying man? We'd need very good justification for a thing like that.'

'It's insensitive, I suppose.'

'I'll say.'

'But if there was compelling evidence against him, it might be a different matter?'

'It would never come to trial anyway. Not in his condition. Even if he survived long enough, the CPS wouldn't put a dying man in the dock.'

'No, I'm sure you're right.'

It pained Fry to say it, especially when she couldn't help feeling that she was telling Ben Cooper the same thing.

'What's next then, Diane?' asked Mackenzie.

She looked at her watch. 'I have to pay a visit to the mortuary.'

Forensic pathologist Juliana van Doon had a long relationship with Diane Fry. For some reason, they had never got on. Fry had found herself at a disadvantage many times, put down by the pathologist without being able to take any retaliatory action.

But today seemed to be different. Mrs van Doon was either too busy to bother patronising her, or she'd heard that Fry had transferred from E Division and was hoping it would be the last time they met. It wasn't exactly a friendly greetings card with *Sorry you're leaving*. But some of the tension had gone from their relationship.

'The bodies aren't decomposed enough,' said the pathologist, brushing a stray hair back from her forehead.

'The peat slowed decomposition?' asked Fry.

'Peat? No, these bodies weren't actually buried in peat. From the photographs of the scene, it's clear they were lying in a disused mine shaft. With a bog body, it's the absence of air and damp, acidic conditions that slow decomposition.'

'Okay.'

'In this case, the heavy plastic wrapping would have slowed the rate of decay on some areas of the bodies, but not others. Those parts were exposed to the air and moisture, as well as to insects and so forth. But they still don't show anything like the rate of decomposition we'd normally expect. Not a rate that corresponds with a time of death more than two years ago.'

'Only one possibility, then.'

'Yes, I think someone must have done what we do in the mortuary – lowered the temperature sufficiently to stop the process of decomposition altogether. The bodies were frozen.'

Fry wasn't surprised by the news. 'Would that have been at an early stage after they were killed?'

'If you were going to get a human body into a chest freezer, it would have to be flexible,' said Mrs van Doon. 'Rigor mortis starts between three and six hours after death. That would catch most people out. Once rigor has set in, it becomes much more difficult to transport and dispose of a body. So I'd say they were frozen when they were still at the fresh stage, before the onset of rigor mortis. When they were unfrozen, decomposition would have restarted. Some of the exposed areas are just entering the advanced decay stage.'

'Cause of death?' said Fry hopefully.

'Oh, the number one on the pathologist's hit parade. Blunt force trauma.'

'For both victims?'

'Yes. Both suffered head injuries. The male victim has a number of other contusions and abrasions on various parts of his upper body, and notably on his hands. He also has some internal injuries, including a couple of broken ribs.'

'Were there any signs of bite marks?'

'Oh yes,' said the pathologist. 'At first I assumed some scavenger had got access to the bodies. A fox or something of the kind. But I'm not sure about that. The disrupted pattern of decomposition makes an assessment more difficult, but I'd say the bite marks seem to have been ante mortem. Before death.'

'Thank you,' said Fry.

Mrs van Doon looked at her slightly askance, as if she wasn't accustomed to being thanked for information like that.

'As for the female,' she said, 'she shows fewer signs of injury, and those seem to be mostly post mortem, except for one major trauma at the base of the skull. It looks to me as though your male has been in a fight and come off worst. The female victim – well, from the nature and position of the fatal injury, it's consistent with a fall.'

'A fall?'

'Yes. A fall backwards, with the head striking a solid object.' The pathologist demonstrated with a slap of a hand to the back of her own neck. 'Not the floor – a piece of furniture, perhaps, or a window ledge.'

She paused, watching Fry's reaction for a moment.

'In fact, Sergeant, my opinion is that this woman might have survived the injury if she'd received prompt medical attention. Which, evidently, she didn't.'

29

When Cooper and Villiers returned to the Light House, the scene seemed almost deserted. Cooper looked around for a scene guard, but saw no one. A forensics van was in the car park, and a marked Corsa stood at the corner of the building, with no driver in sight. The only sound was the crack and rustle of crime-scene tape, like the bones of the dead pub rattling in the silence of the moor.

Cautiously he walked round the exterior of the building. Apart from the absence of a guard, something else felt wrong.

But then he came across the pile of old furniture stacked against the back wall of the pub. Heavy tables with metal bases, wrought-iron chairs, a heap of torn parasols on steel posts. It was obvious now that they covered the trap doors for beer deliveries into the cellar. In an open space nearby, someone had burned rubbish, but only a patch of charcoal and pale grey ashes remained.

Bending closer, Cooper pointed out one of the tables to Villiers.

'This furniture has been moved at some time,' he said. 'Look, there's thick mould on the bottom, while the upper surfaces are relatively clear. It must all have stood somewhere else, and it's been piled up on the hatch.'

'If they removed chest freezers from the cellar, they must have brought them out this way, rather than through the pub. Then they covered the hatch to keep it closed, or to prevent it from being seen.'

Cooper straightened up. 'Yes, that seems likely. A couple of men could have done it, with a suitable vehicle. If only we could find where they dumped the freezers.'

Inside the pub, Liz Petty was still on her own, though she'd brought her gear back up from the cellar.

'Liz, who's supposed to be on scene watch?' he said.

'I can't remember his name. He went off to have a brew with the firefighters. It's dry work being up here for hours on end. I said it would be okay, since you and Carol were coming.'

'All right, I suppose.'

'Is something wrong, Ben?'

'No, no. Everything's fine.'

'Sorry, this is a slow job on my own,' she said. 'I'm hoping to get some help later. I shouldn't be single-handed, but you know what it's like.'

'Any results?'

'Well, I can't find any traces of blood in the cellar, so that's not your primary crime scene, I'm afraid. Shoe marks and fingerprints all over the place. Sorry again. Unless you can turn up the actual freezers for me?'

'No, but we need you upstairs, Liz. I think you'll find your bloodstains up there, though there's probably been a thorough clean-up.'

'Not too thorough to beat me,' said Liz cheerfully. 'Not with my luminol and UV light. You'll see me all lit up in a blue glow shortly. Which room in particular?'

'One of the guest rooms on the first floor. Room One – they call it the Bakewell Room.'

'No problem.'

She hesitated before picking up her case, and looked round to see if Carol Villiers was within earshot.

'By the way, the venue is booked. I thought it was best to go ahead and confirm with them. Is that okay?'

'Oh, yes. Fine. It was the perfect place. I loved it.'

'I'm so glad.'

Her face lit up the way it always did when she was thinking about the wedding. The big day couldn't come quick enough for Liz. He wondered how often she thought about it when she was at work. Was she figuring out the seating plan for the reception in her mind while she sprayed luminol in the cellar, looking for blood residue? Did bridesmaids' dresses take priority in her consideration over the lives of the two murder victims?

It was an unworthy speculation, and Cooper suppressed it. Of the two of them, Liz was the one who had her priorities right. While he was obsessing about details, and looking at the marks in the dust where an old freezer had once stood, she was thinking about their future together. Of course he knew which of them was right. It was why he wanted to spend the rest of his life with her. Liz would keep him grounded and sane. Without her, he would be lost. His future would have no shape or meaning. It didn't bear thinking about.

'And I looked at some menus,' she said, speaking a little more quietly as she heard voices in the entrance. 'I've got some ideas. We can talk about them tonight.'

'All right. Over dinner somewhere?'

She laughed. 'Dinner? Are you trying to placate me for standing me up last night?'

'Of course not. But if we're going to be talking about food . . .'

Liz touched his arm as footsteps approached the bar. 'I'll see you tonight. Are you going to book a table?'

'I won't forget.'

Cooper thought he'd better make a note of it, before it

slipped his mind. But a voice called to him from the doorway, as someone stood back to let Liz get past on her way to the stairs.

'Hello!'

'Hi. Is that Josh?'

'Yes.'

'Come this way. Just stay clear of the taped-off areas.'

'Your colleague outside gave me instructions,' said Lane.

'That would be DC Villiers.'

Lane was casually dressed in denims and a grey sweatshirt. He must change into his working clothes when he got to the hotel. The casual gear didn't suit him actually – he was a little too middle-aged to carry off the jeans. But his hair was already groomed, the discreet piercing in place, his smile affable. Despite his clothes, he was ready to be of service. If only everyone was so cooperative.

It was odd seeing Josh here – it felt a bit like the way Cooper had failed to recognise Roddy when he was on the wrong side of the bar at the Hanging Gate.

'What do you want me to look at?' asked Lane.

Cooper pointed at the open hatchway behind the bar. 'I'd like you to show me around down here.'

'In the cellar?'

'You're not afraid of cellars, are you?' asked Cooper.

'No, why?'

'I thought you sounded a bit nervous.'

'I've spent half my life in cellars.'

A moment later, Lane stood with him at the bottom of the steps and looked around the cellar. He examined the tangle of beer lines, the equipment lying around, the row of empty kegs. He reached out a hand to pick up the wooden mallet, then changed his mind, perhaps remembering that it was a crime scene. He shook his head over the stainless-steel buckets, the hosepipe and the piles of filter funnels.

'Most of this will have to come out,' he said. 'It's been standing too long. The new owners will have to scrap it and do a major clear-out before they can reopen.'

'We'll need to spend quite a bit of time here before they can do anything with it, I'm afraid,' said Cooper.

Lane bent over a pile of beer taps, and made a disgusted expression at the smell.

'Why?' he said. 'What is going on exactly? You didn't explain anything to me before. I mean, I'm glad to help, if I can, but . . .?'

'I can't really tell you much at the moment,' said Cooper.

Lane shrugged. 'Story of my life.'

'I'm truly sorry. I know that sounds pompous, but we're right in the middle of a major inquiry here.'

'Is it about the tourist couple, the Pearsons? Can you tell me that, at least?'

'Yes, I don't suppose that's much of a secret.'

'Not around Edendale.'

The lighting in the cellar consisted of fluorescent tubes. They cast a harsh light, and Cooper could hear a faint whine as if one of them was wearing out and getting close to needing replacement. It was a high-pitched noise, like a mosquito, and it would start to bother him if he had to spend much time down here.

'Josh, can you remember what used to be down here?' he said. 'I mean, anything that isn't here now?'

'I don't know. There was an awful lot of junk,' said Lane. 'Old Maurice got a bit slack in his last couple of years.'

'Slack?'

'He used to run a tight ship at one time, but gradually standards slipped. The cellar is a place you put things so they're out of the way.'

'A dumping ground,' said Cooper, consciously echoing the phrase used by Roddy.

343

'Exactly. A dumping ground.'

Cooper indicated the clean area on the floor. It was surrounded now by Liz Petty's evidence markers, the wall scattered with white dust.

'For example, what used to stand here?' he said.

Lane stared at the markers, and seemed at a loss for an answer. Cooper was disappointed. But he couldn't complain, really – he knew how unreliable memory could be, especially when the context was wrong.

'A freezer, perhaps?' he suggested.

'A freezer? Yes – I think you're right. A freezer.'

'Just one?'

Lane hesitated, still reluctant to commit himself. 'Well, I think there *might* have been two. Old freezers. They weren't used for the kitchen. There's a full-sized commercial freezer upstairs.'

'Do you happen to know when they were taken out?'

'No idea.'

'That's all right.'

Perhaps Lane wasn't going to be as useful a witness as he'd hoped. Nevertheless, Cooper led him to the far end of the cellar.

'What about this area partitioned off?'

'Oh, that,' said Lane. 'Maurice and Nancy called it the office. Actually, it was more of a place for them to be on their own when they felt the need. And somewhere to put things so they were, well . . .'

'Out of the way?'

'Yes.'

'But there are filing cabinets in here.'

'Yes, old business records, I suppose. Nothing of any interest.'

'No?'

Lane was getting a bit fidgety now. He looked at his watch.

'I'm sorry to be awkward, but I really should be leaving soon if I'm going to get to work on time. They don't like you being late at the hotel.'

'Yes, of course.'

He smiled uncertainly. 'Have I helped at all?'

'Actually, I think you have, Josh,' said Cooper.

'Oh?'

Lane looked at him, hoping for more, but seemed to realise that he wasn't going to get any information. He went to the steps and climbed up through the hatch.

'Did I tell you that I used to come here sometimes?' called Cooper. 'I remember this pub when it was all lit up and you could see it for miles.'

There was no reply for a moment, and he wondered if Lane was still there. Then a voice came down to him through the hatch from the floor above. He almost didn't recognise it, the tone of the words was so different.

'Don't worry, Sergeant,' said Lane. 'The place will be lit up again soon.'

Cooper frowned. What did that mean? Lane must be referring to the prospect of the pub reopening under new owners. The date of the auction wasn't far off now. Thomas Pilkington and his son would be getting stressed about the possibility of the police refusing to release their crime scene because the investigation was still ongoing, or of a potential buyer being put off by the story of a double murder.

On second thoughts, that might be a pretty good marketing angle. There were plenty of ghoulish individuals who would flock to visit a pub with a reputation like that. They would probably fight each other to book an overnight stay in the Bakewell Room. In no time, business would be booming again, with locals telling gruesome stories of the murderous Mad Maurice.

Cooper went into the area where the filing cabinets had

been stored, and looked at the desk covered in box files and magazines. The office, Lane had called it. A place to be alone? Well it was certainly quiet enough down here. But also a place to put things out of the way.

He found that the cabinets were unlocked. He slid the drawers out one by one, their runners squealing in protest. The noise seemed unnaturally loud in the cellar, reverberating painfully against the stone walls in the narrow space.

He flipped through the tabs on a series of suspension files, discarding invoices for deliveries, electricity bills, insurance documents, copies of VAT returns. He finally found an entire drawer marked 'Guest Records'. They went back to a time almost five years before the closure of the Light House, but fortunately they were arranged in date order.

Cooper wondered who had been responsible for keeping the records up to date. Was that Mad Maurice in his saner moments? Or had Nancy been the one with the organising brain?

Whoever he had to thank, it was easy enough to locate the record of the Pearsons' overnight stay in the Light House. Thank goodness the Whartons had been old-fashioned enough not to store all their records on computer. A copy of the entry from the register slid into his hand, dated that night in December.

Holding the page carefully by the edges, Cooper read the names of David and Patricia Pearson, their address in Dorking, their home phone number and nationality. The space for their car registration was left blank. The Range Rover had been at the Old Dairy, of course. But, as Nancy had said, they were checked into Room One, the Bakewell Room.

His eyes scanned down to the bottom of the page, until he located the signature of the member of staff who'd checked them in and taken their payment. But surely that wasn't an 'M'? No, it was definitely an 'E'. The signature read 'E. Wharton'. The Pearsons had been signed in by Eliot.

'Do you know what?' said Cooper to himself, his voice echoing off the cellar walls. 'I think we might find it's Eliot's blood on David Pearson's clothes.'

30

Henry Pearson held himself stiffly as he peered through the plate-glass window. In the tiled room on the other side of the glass, the body of his son lay on a stainless-steel table. Fry watched him as a mortuary attendant drew back the cover slowly, careful not to expose parts of the neck and shoulder that had suffered more advanced decomposition.

'Yes, of course it's David,' he said.

'Thank you.'

His eyes remained fixed on the pale face, barely acknowledging Fry's presence. According to Ben Cooper, David Pearson had once resembled a well-known actor, some old Hollywood heart-throb. Fry hadn't been able to see the resemblance from the photographs. She certainly couldn't see it now.

'What about Patricia?' said Pearson, still without moving.

'We can do the identification from DNA,' said Fry.

Henry Pearson turned to look at her then. 'But why . . .?'

'I'm sorry, sir. Decomposition. They were wrapped differently. So her face . . .'

Pearson swallowed, and rested a hand lightly on the glass to support himself.

'If I could get hold of the person who did this, I'd kill him and bury him myself. Then I'd dig him up and kill him again.'

The attendant drew the cover back over David's head. When they'd gone, the body would be returned to the drawer where it was being stored. David Pearson would go back into the freezer.

When Fry had escorted Pearson from the mortuary and seen him leave, she knew it was time to talk to Nancy Wharton again.

It was only a short drive from the hospital to West Street. Fry spent the time working out what she needed from Mrs Wharton. Names, of course. She had to break down any sense of loyalty and solidarity with her accomplices. Loyalty had no place in the interview room.

To help her think, Fry turned on the CD player. Annie Lennox was still there, waiting for her, the one person she could trust in an unreliable world. Lennox's voice came in over the first chords to an acoustic version of 'Dark Road'. She was singing about emotions she wasn't feeling, a meaning she wasn't listening to. Fry nodded her head to the song. She knew that particular dark road.

Between the two distractions, she managed not to notice much of Edendale until she was turning off Greaves Road into West Street. She reported to DCI Mackenzie, then called in to the CID room and collected Becky Hurst to sit in with her when she reopened the interview with Nancy Wharton.

'Poor Maurice,' said Nancy, her arms still wrapped tightly round her body. 'It was horrible. But he was out of control. He wasn't responsible for his actions. That's what I'll say, you know. That's what we'll all say.'

'But it isn't as simple as that,' said Fry. 'There was only one person who was capable of organising the clean-up. It needed a level head, clear thinking. Only one person was in any condition. And you don't drink, do you, Nancy?'

'I did that night,' she said. 'But not until much later.'

Nancy continued to tell the story. She no longer needed much prompting. Now that she was halfway there, she wasn't going to stop.

'Afterwards . . . well, some of the lads rallied round, and we all agreed on a story.'

'The lads?'

Her jaw was set in a hard line. 'I wouldn't tell you their names. Not for anything.'

Fry recognised a dead end when she saw one. But there were ways round it. More routes than one to the truth.

'Go on, then,' she said.

'At one time, Maurice only really felt at home in one place. Where the heart of the Light House was – in the cellar. So that's where we chose. We knew we'd have to move them, but it was the best place for the time being. The mine shafts were searched at the time, but the pub wasn't.'

Nancy nodded slowly. 'Well, it was strange, but it was only when we saw the fires on the moor and started to worry about the pub getting damaged that it suddenly occurred to us that there would be new owners going in. They would be sorting everything out, looking through the records. We'd put the old filing cabinets down in the cellar and forgotten all about them. It was the place we always put things we didn't want.'

'And when the inquiry ground to a halt . . .?'

'We thought it was all dead and buried.'

'Dead and buried? Not really. It must always have been in your mind.'

She shrugged hopelessly. 'Well, you're right. It was always in *my* mind. I was always wondering when something might happen, whether someone would talk. I knew it would only take a slip of the tongue, a careless remark.'

Fry couldn't imagine what it must be like to live with that sort of fear, the terror of a secret slipping out. No matter what Nancy Wharton said, it must fill every minute of your day, until you suffered from an unremitting paranoia about every little thing.

'Later on, we moved everything,' said Nancy. 'They buried the anoraks and stuff, but the bodies . . . well, have you ever tried shifting a body? It took a couple of quad bikes to get them well away from the pub on to the moor. Then a few fires were started to draw attention away. That nearly went wrong. The wind changed direction, and the fires moved towards the pub instead of away. My God, watching that smoke coming nearer and nearer, we panicked. We had to get the freezers out of the cellar. We knew there'd be evidence – blood, and so on. We'd already cleaned up in the bedroom, scrubbed the floor with bleach, replaced the carpet and the bedding, even stripped off all the wall-paper and redecorated. It never came to an end, the clearing up and covering over. The blood always seemed to be there.'

'Talking to yourself again, Ben?'

Cooper turned and found Villiers watching him. He had been so absorbed that he hadn't heard her coming down the steps into the cellar.

'No one else will listen to me,' he said.

She laughed. 'Liz Petty is working in the Bakewell Room, where the Pearsons stayed. She says there's blood residue everywhere.'

'I'm not surprised.'

'It's going to keep her busy for a while. She ought to have some help, Ben.'

'I know. I'll call in and chase someone up. Well, I will when I can get a signal on my phone.'

351

'I'm off network too,' said Villiers.

'It's these cellars.'

'Don't you start to feel a bit uneasy when you're out of touch? Or is it just me?'

'It used to be like this all the time when I was in uniform. We didn't have mobile phones, and the old analogue radios were almost useless in parts of this division.'

Villiers stepped into the office area. 'What are you doing anyway?'

Cooper showed her the guest record. 'What do you think of that?'

'It's a turn-up. But it doesn't mean Mad Maurice wasn't responsible for the deaths.'

'It shows that Nancy wasn't telling the truth, about that part of the story at least. And what was it she said in the interview? *You can't blame us for trying to protect our family. Anyone would have done it.* That word "family" suggests more than just Maurice to me. It sounds like a mother talking about her children.'

As he spoke, Cooper moved back into the main part of the cellar and stood under the delivery hatchway that led outside. Stepping up on to the stone ledge, he heaved at the hatch. He managed to raise the edge of one door an inch or two before the weight of the furniture stacked on top prevented it moving any further. If he tilted his head at an angle, he found he could just see through the inch of space he'd created. He saw a rusty table leg in the foreground, a patch of burnt earth, and a length of concrete stretching away from the building.

Then he blinked in surprise. A white pickup stood by the garages, next to his own car. A Mitsubishi L200, if he wasn't mistaken. But before he could see any more, the weight of the door proved too much for his bruised shoulder, and he had to let it down.

'Whose is the pickup?' he said.

Villiers stared at him. 'Pickup? I've no idea.'

'Has Josh Lane left?'

'I think so. I saw him out of the building.'

'Well did someone else arrive, then?'

'I don't know, Ben. You can't hear anything from down here.'

'Yes, that's true.'

Worried now, Cooper checked his phone for a signal and saw that it still read *Network lost*. Blasted cellar walls.

But he saw from the display that he'd received a text message before the network dropped. He tapped the messages icon and found a text from Diane Fry. *You need to know this. DNA match confirmed from blood. Call asap.*

'Mmm. But who is it a match to?'

'Sorry, Ben?'

'It's okay. I'm talking to myself again.'

'Liz will have to cure you of that. We don't want you getting a reputation as an eccentric.'

Cooper turned slowly and took in the cellar – the empty kegs, the abandoned equipment, the beer lines snaking upwards. He gazed at the ceiling, where the lines disappeared into the bar to connect to the pumps.

'We've missed something, haven't we?' he said.

'Have we?' said Villiers. 'We've been through every room – the kitchens, the bedrooms, all the stores and outbuildings. And now the cellars.'

But there was something lodged in the back of Cooper's mind – the part of the brain that most resembled a landfill site, full of unwanted debris. If you poked around in the detritus long enough, you sometimes unearthed a valuable item you'd thought was lost.

'Of course we've missed something,' he said. 'We've missed who the Pearsons talked to that night at the Light House.'

'The night there was an argument with Gullick and Naylor?'

'No, no – the next night, when it was the Young Farmers' party.'

'But we have lots of witness statements to show that, apart from the other tourists, the Pearsons didn't speak to anyone in the bar that night. No one local.'

'Of course they did,' said Cooper.

'No.'

'Yes.'

She threw up her hands in exasperation. 'So you know better than all those witnesses?'

'No. But I think they just weren't asked the right questions. Of course there was someone they talked to.'

'How?'

Cooper had that picture in his mind again of the people in the bar – the three middle aged men sitting on a bench discussing the quality of their beer, two young couples laughing at a table full of vodka bottles, an elderly woman on her own in the corner with a glass of Guinness and a plastic carrier bag. They all had one thing in common, and it was maddening that he'd missed it.

'Well, David and Trisha Pearson didn't sit in the bar all night without ordering any drinks, did they?' he said.

Villiers looked at him open-mouthed. 'Well, no . . .'

'So they talked to . . .?'

'The barman.'

He nodded. 'Yes, a nice, friendly barman who liked to chat with his customers. A barman called Josh Lane.'

Because of his job, Josh Lane might have known most about the Pearsons. And without being asked, Lane had volunteered the information that he wasn't here at the Light House on the day the Pearsons disappeared. That was almost certainly true. But he must have been here later, helping to cover up what had happened, and moving the bodies.

Josh Lane. *Just like one of the family*. Who had said that? The chef, Maclennan. Had Maclennan been closer to the truth than he thought?

And maybe Lane had helped to remove those freezers he'd been reluctant to acknowledge the existence of. If that was his Mitsubishi pickup, it would have been the perfect vehicle for the task. It also answered the description from the firefighters.

So Gullick and Naylor might have been part of a smoke-screen after all. Their names had cropped up several times. But they had most cleverly been floated by Josh Lane, with that pretence of loyalty to customers that now, in hindsight, seemed artificial and coy. Cooper couldn't believe that he'd fallen for it. He'd turned into a sucker over a cup of espresso and steamed milk.

In retrospect, it should have been clear the exact moment when Lane changed from a friendly, helpful member of the public to the more cautious former employee who couldn't quite remember what had stood against the wall. It had surely been when Cooper brought him down to the cellar and mentioned the Pearsons. The combination of the two must have made him feel as though he'd been led into a trap. If only, Cooper thought, he'd been so clever.

'Damn it,' said Cooper. 'Why have I been so stupid?'

Then he sniffed. His sense of smell had been on the alert for days. Now his nostrils were sending an urgent message.

'Can you smell that?' he said.

Villiers looked up. 'Yes, it's smoke. You must have smelled it before, Ben. It's been burning all week out there.'

'No, this isn't burning heather. It's something different.'

Cooper went to the hatch and tried to push it open. It didn't budge.

'Stuck?'

'I don't know.'

He rattled the handle without success, tried putting his shoulder against the trapdoor, thumped it hard in growing frustration.

'I can't believe this.'

'What's the matter, Ben?'

Villiers came across the room to join him. She didn't sound worried yet, and he tried to keep his voice calm to hide his steadily increasing anxiety.

'Okay, it does seem to be jammed. Just a bit rusted up probably. I don't suppose it's been used much for a long while.'

'We had no trouble with it coming in,' said Villiers doubtfully.

Despite her apparent calm, he could hear the beginnings of anxiety in her voice. She tried so hard not to let it show when she was at work, but he knew her too well to be fooled. It was his job now to keep her calm and give her the reassurance that he didn't actually feel.

'It'll just take me a moment.'

'That smoke, Ben . . .'

'What?'

'It's coming through the trapdoor.'

Cooper looked up. She was right, of course. No wonder the smell was so strong. The fire was close. Very close. But there was no way the smoke from the blazing moorland could have reached this far and come right into the building, not through locked doors and boarded-up windows.

There was only one possibility. The pub itself was on fire.

31

Fry remained silent – the best approach when someone like Mrs Wharton had decided to talk. All she needed was someone to listen. Let her thoughts run, and see where they took her. 'So then we decided on a fire further off, to get the firemen out of the way,' she said. 'And we chose Kinder. To be honest, I can't understand now how everything happened. When I think about it, I feel as though it was part of a nightmare. It all just got out of hand.'

Again Fry waited. But Nancy seemed to have dried up. She rocked slowly in her chair, suddenly resembling someone much younger. She was no longer the pub landlady with blonde streaks in her hair and a hard look in her eyes, but a young girl troubled by the terrible dreams she was trying to explain.

'After the pub was closed,' said Fry, 'someone broke into the Light House to get at the records of the Pearsons' stay.'

'Yes.'

'But Aidan Merritt had gone to do the same thing.'

'Had he? That can't be true, can it?'

'Yes, we think so.'

'No, you're wrong. Aidan was eaten up with guilt and was going to betray us. He'd said something to his wife, Sam, which she passed on to us. She said he was rambling on the phone about betrayal and guilt.'

'You might have misunderstood.'

Nancy went white, and sat down, trembling. 'No, surely not.'

Fry leaned closer. 'Who killed Aidan Merritt, Nancy?'

'I can't tell you.'

Well, that would come later. There was plenty of time. When Nancy Wharton realised she wasn't going to be leaving here for another twenty-four hours at least, she might change her mind. Fry decided to backtrack a bit.

'You said earlier that you told the children everything,' she said. 'Did you mean everything?'

'You can't keep secrets from kids of that age,' said Nancy. 'They know something is wrong, and they can get hold of the wrong end of the stick and blow it out of proportion in their own minds. It's not fair to them, and it can cause a lot of problems. I know, because it happened to me when I was in my teens. My parents tried to keep me in the dark, never told me anything. They said they thought it was for my own good. But you know what? By the time they split up, I'd come to the conclusion it was all my fault. I worked out in my own mind that if they weren't talking *to* me, they must be talking *about* me. I know it doesn't make sense. But everything is so confusing and stressful at that age. Maurice and me, we agreed a long time ago that we wouldn't be like that with our two. So we were as open as we could be about the trouble that our business was in.'

'And about what happened that night?'

Nancy looked at her then, not understanding the question. Fry opened her mouth to ask it again, but changed her mind. Instead, she sat and gazed at Nancy Wharton, watching the expression on her face alter. It was as good as an admission. But it was one Fry hadn't been expecting.

'You didn't need to tell them,' said Fry. 'Because they

were right there, weren't they? They were there when the Pearsons were killed.'

Nancy's mouth was shut like a trap, as if she was determined to prevent any words spilling out. But she couldn't control her expression. She hadn't learned to do that, not even after those two years of keeping her secret.

'Your son, Eliot,' said Fry. 'He'd been drinking, like his father. But he wasn't used to the alcohol, not the way Maurice was. A big lad, Eliot. And angry, too. But his father would do anything for him – anything, right down to taking the blame for the murder of two guests.'

'You'll never get the evidence,' said Nancy, with a bitter smile.

Fry stared at her, trying to analyse the meaning of what she was saying.

'But Nancy – I think we'll find the blood on David Pearson's clothing is Eliot's, won't we?'

Nancy shook her head – not in denial, but in confusion. She no longer knew what to say, or how she could protect her family. Her entire rationale was falling apart right there and then, and she couldn't cope with it.

'And where is he?' asked Fry finally. 'Nancy – where exactly is Eliot now?'

'I'm saying no more.'

With Mrs Wharton safely housed in a cell in the custody suite, Fry and Hurst drove to the house on the Devonshire Estate

Despite them hammering on the door and peering through windows, there was no sign of anyone being home.

'Blast. Where could they have gone?'

Hurst took a call from Luke Irvine at the office. 'Forensics,' she said. 'They've processed the smaller blood trace on David

Pearson's clothing and got a DNA profile from it. There's a match on the database.'

'Eliot Wharton?'

'No. He doesn't have a record, so he's not on the database. This is a match to Josh Lane, the former barman at the Light House.'

'Lane has a record?'

'A couple of convictions under the Misuse of Drugs Act. Fined for possession of class B substances.'

'Cannabis, amphetamines?'

'Correct. According to Luke, intelligence shows that he's been investigated for supply, but never brought to court. He's lucky there. That's a maximum of fourteen years for dealing, even class B. There's also an indication he might have been involved in a trade in ecstasy at the Light House. Personal intelligence, never substantiated.'

So Lane had been the fourth individual. And Fry felt sure that Eliot Wharton would be a match to the other DNA profile.

She tried to call Ben Cooper and got an unavailable message, so she sent him a text. It was quicker, and at least she knew it had been done. He would get the message and could call her when he was free. Cooper been meeting Josh Lane at the Light House, hadn't he? So he might know where Lane was now.

'Diane,' said Hurst, 'if they were involved in the death of the Pearsons, and they know there's still some evidence at the pub, perhaps in the cellar . . .'

'. . . they'll be anxious to destroy it before anyone gets to it.'

'Yes, that's what I was thinking.'

Fry watched a response unit pull into the street. She could leave them at the Whartons' house in case anyone returned.

'Becky, who's up there at the moment?' she said.

'At the Light House? Scenes of crime. And Ben went there with Carol Villiers. I don't know if they're still there or not.'

Fry experienced one of those moments when her heart lurched and her mind was filled with an irrational dread. She tried to fight it, but her skin had turned cold, and terrible images began to surge through her brain unbidden.

'Why would DS Cooper's phone be off network?'

Hurst turned in astonishment at the urgency of her tone. 'I've no idea. He could be in a dead spot. He could still be . . .'

'. . . in the cellars?'

Fry didn't wait for the answer. She was already fumbling for her car keys, heading for the street. There was no reason or logic for the way she felt, but she couldn't deny the force of it. The appalling certainty in her heart drove her body automatically to jump behind the wheel and ram the Audi into gear.

Even worse than the fear was a fact banging insistently at the back of her head – the knowledge that she might have created this nightmare herself.

When Cooper finally broke open the hatch, he could see smoke high above him, swirling on the ceiling of the bar, already starting to fill the room.

Raising his head above floor level, he saw that the source of the smoke was a roaring blaze at the far end of the bar. The door they'd come in through was consumed by a sheet of flame, and the fire was spreading rapidly along the room. The curtains were blazing, little tongues of fire creeping up them. Wooden furniture was smouldering, the glass tops of the tables cracking like gunshots. A pile of cardboard boxes

361

burned like a bonfire, spirals of card peeling away like charred flesh from a corpse.

Cooper saw a patch clear of smoke. He drew Villiers up to the top of the steps after him and pointed the direction out to her.

'That way,' he said. 'When you get clear of the hatch, go left.'

Somewhere, the flames were roaring so loud that he could hardly hear his own voice.

'Keep low,' he said, close to her ear. 'And get out fast.'

She nodded, and began to move. Then she stopped, and turned back.

'What about you?'

'I'm going for Liz. She's upstairs.'

'Ben, be careful.'

On the first floor, Liz might not even be aware of the fire. The smell of the smoke had alerted him in the cellar, but if she was wearing her mask as she worked on the crime scene, she would smell nothing. In a room with the door closed, the flames could be raging in the corridor right outside before she noticed.

Cooper grabbed an old bar cloth and held it over his face. Paper and wood were already burning, because they caught fire at low temperatures. Plastics and polyurethane needed higher temperatures to ignite, but they burned rapidly and gave off toxic gases. In a modern hotel, built of concrete and steel, staying in a closed room could be the safest option in a fire. But in a building like this, no one upstairs would stand a chance. The whole place would burn down.

The stairs to the function room were here somewhere, and the access to the guest bedrooms. There had to be a fire escape.

Smoke was moving up the stairs and filling the corridor where the bedrooms were. But the fire itself hadn't reached here yet. The flames were still being held back from bursting through into the upper floors. He didn't have long before these wooden floorboards started burning, though, and then the stairs would be gone.

'Liz!'

He found Room One from the sign on the door – the Bakewell Room. Inside, Liz glanced up astonished as he burst in. He must look an appalling sight. She was in her scene suit with her hood up but the mask pulled down.

'What's that beeping?' she asked.

Cooper hadn't even noticed it. 'A smoke alarm.'

'There's a fire?'

'Yes, we've got to get out. Now. Leave your kit. This is an old building, with lots of timber in the structure. If the supports burn through, the whole thing could come down.'

'Here, take a mask,' she said.

Cooper pulled the mask on, and they headed back to the stairs. Even through the mask, he could smell the reek of petrol. The conflagration was fiercest around the door of the bar and in the main entrance, so that must be where the accelerant had been spread. Some of the floorboards were already reduced to ashes; others were no more than lumps of charcoal.

He heard glass shatter. That was bad. The windows wouldn't hold against the fire.

'The boards over the windows are keeping the air out for now. We have a chance to get out before it really goes up.'

'Which way, though?'

Black smoke rolled across the ceiling and hung like a curtain, sinking steadily towards him in dense folds. Within a few minutes, the smoke layer was only four feet from the floor. Carbon monoxide was a narcotic gas. Two or three lungfuls of that smoke would kill them.

But the smoke and toxic gases were being forced right

through the building. They needed a secondary escape route.

'Stay low. Stay low, where you can breathe.'

In the corridor, the floor was scorched where the carpet had singed through, but the passage itself was clear of fire. Cooper peered through the smoke, trying to remember the way out from the back of the pub.

Blazing curtains fell on to furniture as their rails burned through, glass shattered as picture cords snapped and frames crashed to the floor. When the flames reached the ceiling, they would get flashover. It could reach five hundred degrees Fahrenheit in here.

The boarded-up windows were alight now, reflecting the glow of the inferno inside the pub. The fire was mirrored on to itself, doubling the size of the blaze until it looked like a vast furnace every way he turned.

The heat was becoming too intense to bear. Cooper could feel the exposed skin of his hands roasting as if he was a joint of meat in an oven. The smoke was pungent and choking, full of lethal particles from burning plastic and fibres.

He looked round to make sure that Liz was still wearing her mask too. And with an awful lurch in his heart, he saw that she was gone.

Fry and Hurst were close to the Roman road when they saw the smoke rising from Oxlow Moor. Hurst spotted it first, pointing it out with a cry of surprise.

'Another?' said Fry. 'It's not possible.'

'No, it isn't possible. Not like that.'

'Call in and find out, will you?'

Fry put her foot down harder on the accelerator, forgetting for a moment her nervousness of the narrow lanes and the stone walls that always seemed to crowd in and try to trap her car. A bit of music began to play over and over in her mind. It was if Annie Lennox was still there, inside her head, though the CD player was turned off. She was still singing that acoustic version of 'Dark Road'. Something about all the fires of destruction. *All the fires of destruction.*

'No, they say it's the Light House,' said Hurst in an odd, strained voice.

Fry stared straight ahead at the road as they drove towards the first tendrils of smoke drifting overhead.

'And?' she said.

'Persons reported.'

Swerving to avoid a car coming the other way on a bend, Fry cursed under her breath. *Persons reported.* It was a bit of fire-service jargon, but she recognised its meaning. There were people trapped in the fire.

Cooper flinched in pain as something dripped on to his face. It was hot and scalding, like melted wax. He brushed the blob from his cheek and saw a smear of molten green plastic on his fingers.

Shielding his eyes, he looked up at the ceiling. The light fittings were melting. They had once been shaped like candles, but now they were drooping, slowly dissolving into liquid that spattered his scene suit and landed in his hair.

He pulled his jacket over his head, conscious as he did it how futile a gesture it was. The protection wouldn't last long once the flames touched him. He had to keep moving.

He turned back towards the bar. Glowing embers faced him. Before he could move, a shelf bearing a line of optics tore away from the ceiling with a shriek and crashed to the floor. Glass flew in all directions, shattering into fragments, glittering in the flames like a shower of meteorites.

He pulled open the blackened door, keeping his body behind it in case of a back blast caused by a rush of air. The door handle was almost too hot to touch. Cooper looked at his hands, and saw that his fingers were red and blistering. The pain hadn't hit him yet, but it would.

He glimpsed something red on the wall by the door. A fire extinguisher. He grabbed it from its bracket, thumped the handle and sprayed foam towards the heart of the blaze. It subsided a little, and he kept spraying until the extinguisher was empty. Immediately, the fire flickered and sprang back to life.

'Liz! Where are you?' he called desperately.

But his voice was hoarse, and he burst into a spasm of painful coughing.

In the bar, smoke travelling across the ceiling hit a wall and rolled down to floor level. His mouth was parched, his throat sore from the smoke penetrating his mask. His eyes streamed with tears so that he could barely see, even if the smoke hadn't plunged the pub into unfathomable darkness.

He fumbled blindly along the wall, found a steel bar under his fingers and a door behind it. The fire exit. At first the bar wouldn't move. Crying out in frustration, he banged at it with his fists, kicked out at it, thumped it again. Finally, he spun round and grabbed the empty fire extinguisher, swung it hard against the bar and felt it give way.

But he must have inhaled too much smoke. He was getting confused. He didn't know where right or left was, didn't know where the doors were, felt as though he couldn't breathe at all.

Irritants hit his eyes and the back of his throat. He could barely open his eyelids. He retched and took a deep breath, in involuntary reaction. The smoke he inhaled was disorientating, dizzying. He went down on his knees. He knew he was giving way to the carbon monoxide, but he was unable to fight.

Now he saw shadows in the smoke, flickering and shimmering, dancing and shuddering, fading in and out. Was that a figure outlined against the flames? The smoke was black and thick and choking. Boards over the windows were burning.

Glass shattered, and a blast of air exploded the flames into a great roaring blaze, a wild beast devouring the furniture, ripping up the floor, stripping paper from the walls. A sheet of fire rolled across the ceiling and engulfed the room.

'Liz!'

His voice came as a feeble croak, and there was no answer.

Cooper thought he glimpsed a movement near him in the smoke. He reached out for an indistinct shape like a hand, but grasped at empty space and found himself falling forwards into darkness, until his face hit the floor and his mind swam into swirling oblivion as he lost those last shreds of consciousness.

All around him was shouting and screaming, a muffled roaring noise. The crash of falling stone. And the screaming.

Then silence.

Arriving at the Light House, Fry and Hurst jumped out of the car, but within a few yards they were driven back by the smoke and heat.

Almost choking, her eyes running with tears, Fry saw that two fire appliances were already on the scene and were tackling the fire at the back of the pub. Clouds of steam rose from the jets of water they were directing on to the ground floor, trying to suppress the flames for a team in breathing apparatus who were entering through the rear door.

The lights of the two appliances and the arriving ambulances bounced off the columns of black smoke pouring from the building. Flames erupted from another window higher up. The first floor was well alight by now, and smoke was beginning to trickle from between the tiles of the roof.

At last Fry saw two figures stumble out of the smoke. Firefighters ran towards them to support them, and she couldn't see who it was from the bodies in the way.

'Becky, who . . .?'

'I don't know. No, wait a minute – Diane, one of them is a woman. And the other is Eliot Wharton.'

'Oh God.'

A fireman in a respirator emerged from the building, stepped over the hoses and pulled off his mask. He shook his head wearily at the incident commander and mouthed something. Fry couldn't hear what he was saying. She strained her eyes, wishing she could lip-read.

It wasn't until the commander turned to look at her, and she saw his despairing expression, that hope began to die.

32

Ben Cooper came round slowly, becoming gradually aware of a buzzing in his ears, a scorched smell in his nostrils, a strange light stinging his eyes. He was being bounced around violently, and his head swam with dizziness and a thumping pain. His stomach lurched, and he rolled over to vomit, vaguely conscious of someone there on the edge of the light, waiting for him to do exactly that.

Some time later, he became conscious again. He had no idea how much later it was. Only a few minutes might have passed, but it could have been days. He was in a different place now. It was completely still, no sense of movement except for the dizzy swirling in his head, the residue of some shadowy, distorted dreams.

He listened cautiously to the noises around him, all of them unfamiliar. The smells were sharp and antiseptic. He couldn't figure out the sensations all over his body. His limbs seemed to be either too numb or too painful, and sometimes both at once.

He opened his eyes, and saw a brightly lit ceiling. He turned his head a fraction and saw someone standing over him, a looming shape, a face frowning with anxiety. He expected to see Liz. She'd been so much in his head, walking through those murky, half-conscious dreams, that for a moment he thought he was actually seeing her by his bed, and she was smiling that familiar smile that told him how glad she was to see him.

But his eyes came more into focus, and he realised the shape was his brother. It seemed so odd to be looking up at Matt against a starkwhite ceiling that he almost laughed, but found that he couldn't.

When he spoke, Matt's voice came from an immense distance in space and time. It was so faint and remote that it seemed to echo from way, way back in his childhood. Ben was carried away to an age when he was too small to look after himself, when he looked up to his big brother with adoration as his guardian and protector. Yes, Matt's voice came from that past. Its distance in time was created by the tone of his words.

'You're going to be okay, Ben. Just relax. Don't try to talk or anything.'

'What is it? I don't . . . Matt?'

'Yes, I'm here. Take it easy.'

Ben felt his head hit the pillow, as if his neck muscles had given up the effort to hold it upright. He was completely exhausted, his body drained of energy, sucked of its contents like an empty plastic bag. His hands felt wrong, and his feet too. Most of all, his head wasn't as it should be. His skin was too tight to his skull, too untouched by the air to feel natural.

'I don't remember . . .' he said.

'No. Well, it's probably best if you don't.'

There was some kind of message in the words. No, not the words, but the significance behind them. An unspoken message, coming to him directly in the way that he and Matt had always communicated, the way they used to talk without the need for speech. A total understanding. He'd thought it was gone in these past few years, but in this moment it had all come back.

Then he was shocked to hear his own voice, changed to the faint, scared sound of a child.

'What's wrong, Matt? Matty?'

But his mind was filled with hazy memories – images of himself flickering and shimmering, dancing and shuddering, fading in and out as if he'd become just one more shadow in the smoke.

And then there was another image. A figure in front of him, outlined against the flames. The smoke between them black and thick and choking. Boards over the windows were burning. He heard glass shattering, a blast of air exploding the flames into a great roaring blaze, a wild beast devouring the furniture, ripping up the floor, stripping paper from the walls. A sheet of fire rolled across the ceiling, and engulfed the room.

And then the figure was gone. In Ben's memory, he could see nothing but the smoke, feel nothing but the crash of falling stone. He could hear only the screaming.

Then, incredibly, a deafening absence of sound. And that silence was the most frightening thing of all.

'Liz?' he said, his voice croaking with fear.

But there was no answer in the room now. Matt was utterly quiet. Ben listened to that hush, recognising what it meant, remembering all the times that he and his brother had used such silences to share the most difficult things, a thought or emotion impossible to put into words.

It was strange the way a silence could say so much. It could tell the truth far more effectively than any platitude or cliché, or the most eloquent of speeches. This was a silence that came straight from the heart, and Ben under-stood it perfectly.

'Liz,' he said. 'Is she . . . gone?'

Finally Matt spoke.

371

'I'm sorry, Ben,' he said. 'I'm really, really sorry.'

Among sharp antiseptic smells, in a brightly lit room with a white ceiling, that was the moment. The exact moment when Ben Cooper's world came to an end.